PETITION

BY DELILAH WAAN

RESONANCE CRYSTAL LEGACY

Petition

Supplicant

JOIN THE RESONANCE GUILD

Get access to the deleted prequel, *The Resonance Guild*, and other exclusives. No spam and no ads; just regular behind-the-scenes updates about what I'm working on and what I've been reading.

Sign up here: https://www.delilahwaan.com/jointheguild

PETITION

DELILAH WAAN

Petition is the first book in the *Resonance Crystal Legacy* series. It is a work of fiction intended for a new adult/adult audience.

Content advisory:
https://www.delilahwaan.com/books/petition/#content

Report errors and formatting issues:
https://www.delilahwaan.com/errata/

Copyright © 2022 by Delilah Waan.

Second edition published 2024 by Paper Tiger Productions (ABN 30 176 535 485) Mailing address: PO Box 175, Leichhardt NSW 2040, Australia.

ISBN (eBook) 978-0-6455100-0-3
ISBN (Hardcover) 978-0-6455100-2-7
ISBN (Paperback) 978-0-6455100-1-0

Cover design by Damonza.

Map illustrations © 2022 Delilah Waan.

Printed and bound by IngramSpark.
Australia: Ingram Content Group AU Pty Ltd, Melbourne, Victoria.
US: Lightning Source LLC, La Vergne, Tennessee / Allentown, Pennsylvania / Jackson, Tennessee, United States.
UK: Lightning Source UK Ltd, Milton Keynes, United Kingdom.
Europe: Lightning Source UK Ltd, with facilities in Germany, France, and Spain.

The authorized representative in the European Economic Area is Lightning Source France, 1 Av. Johannes Gutenberg, 78310 Maurepas, France. (email: compliance@lightningsource.fr)

*For the families
who left everything behind
to seek a better life*

Map of the Ngutoccai continent

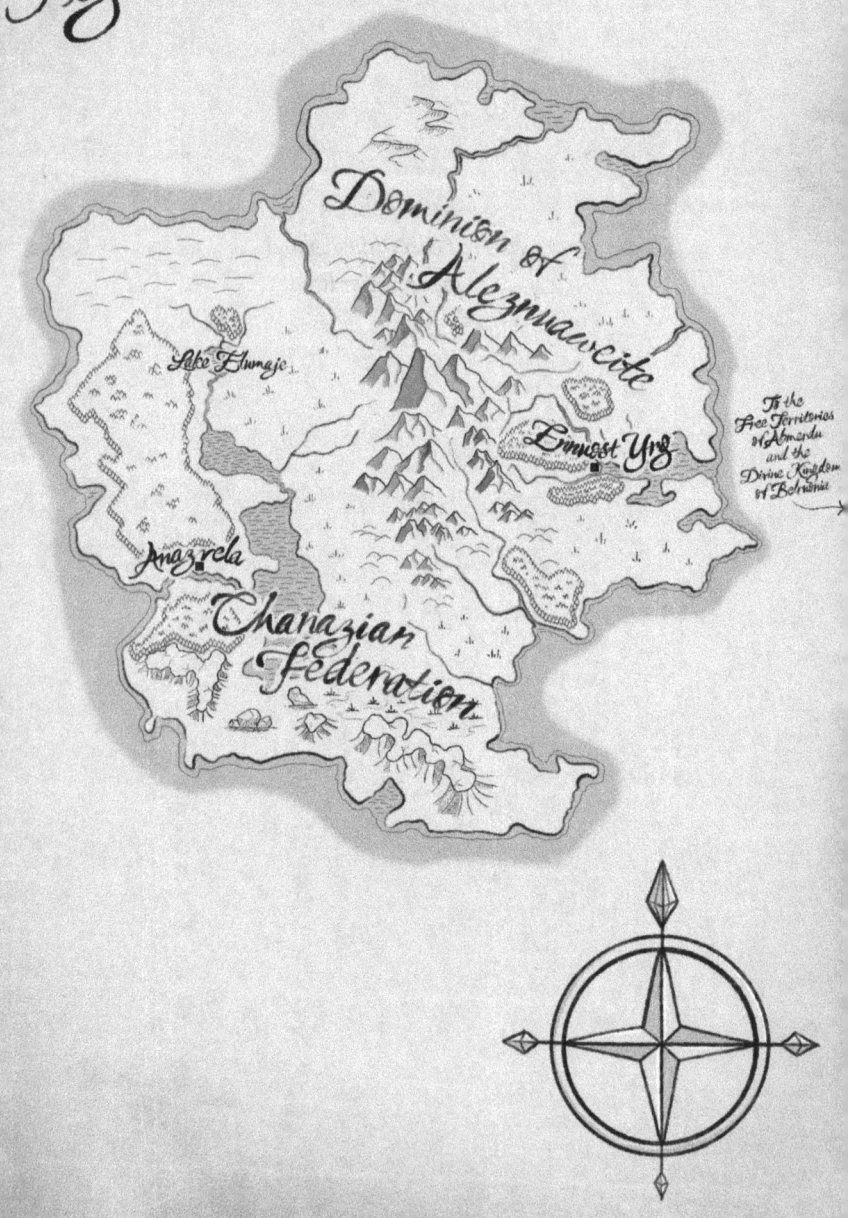

Dominion of Aleznuavcite

Lake Eluvaje

Ernoot Yrg

Anazrela

Chanazian Federation

To the Free Territories of Abmardu and the Divine Kingdom of Botrunii

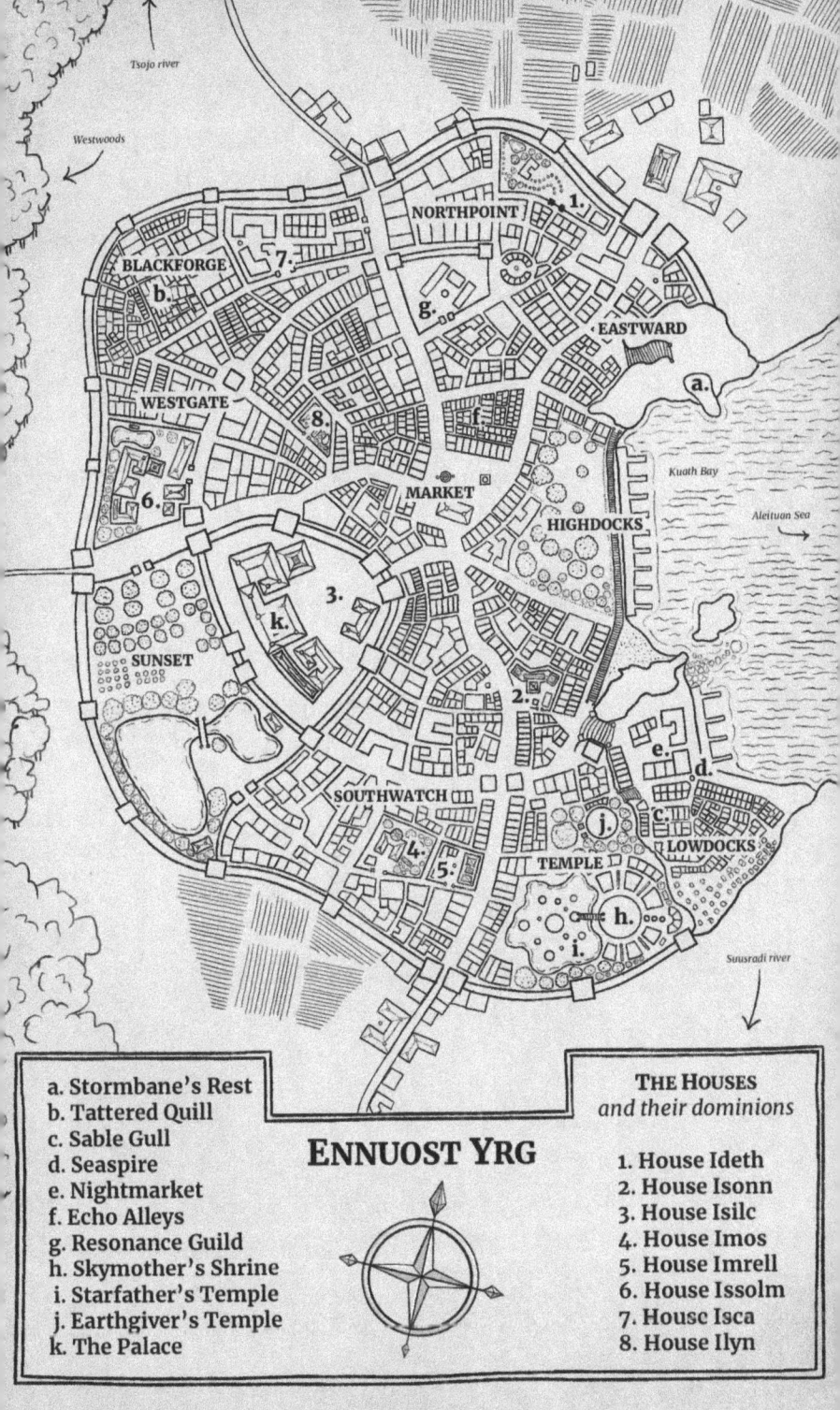

ENNUOST YRG

a. Stormbane's Rest
b. Tattered Quill
c. Sable Gull
d. Seaspire
e. Nightmarket
f. Echo Alleys
g. Resonance Guild
h. Skymother's Shrine
i. Starfather's Temple
j. Earthgiver's Temple
k. The Palace

THE HOUSES
and their dominions

1. House Ideth
2. House Isonn
3. House Isilc
4. House Imos
5. House Imrell
6. House Issolm
7. House Isca
8. House Ilyn

Tsojo river

Westwoods

NORTHPOINT

BLACKFORGE

EASTWARD

WESTGATE

MARKET

Kuath Bay

HIGHDOCKS

Aleituan Sea

SUNSET

SOUTHWATCH

TEMPLE

LOWDOCKS

Suusradi river

PROLOGUE: ANCHOR

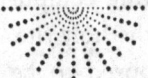

THE 19TH DAY OF EARLY SUMMER, 530 A.E./A.F.

AZOSH-EK TREMBLED AS THE FIRST SACRIFICE toppled over, face first, onto packed earth.

He tried not to breathe, but it did no good. The after-echoes of the heathen's death surrounded him like flames. Hundreds of tiny, purple-edged wisps of gold licked at his bloodied robe, squeezing through the needle holes and seams of the fabric to curl around his skin.

Bile burned in his throat at the sight. He ought to weep—no, he needed to flee! While this city of unbelievers did not keep a proper starwatch, there were regular patrols, and the next one was due to arrive any moment. But a wild laugh escaped his lips, one that made him want to embrace the night and dance.

Azosh-ek did none of those things.

He turned the body over instead and frantically hacked away at the corpse with the sacred blade Iweth-na had left behind—like some hog butcher using a common knife.

This…

This was all wrong.

Even reclaiming his anchor from the heathen's neck—

feeling the weight of its black chain settle across his collar-bones, its cool crystalline bite, and the familiar drain on his emotions—failed to comfort him. Iweth-na's absence from his mind was a yawning void. It gaped open like the dead man's chest, ragged edges alternating with neat incisions. Nothing like his usual delicate knifework; without Iweth-na to rule over his conflicting compulsions, his shaking hands had made a mockery of the holy rite.

Stars were not supposed to be alone. Not unless they were damned.

He carefully arranged the limbs, then opened a vein in his left arm to add an offering of his own. That was not part of his instructions, merely ritual tradition. Uvesht-mo said the forms did not matter, but the forms were all he had left.

May the Starfather look past his transgressions and judge him on faith alone.

His work complete, Azosh-ek stood stiffly, sacred blade in one hand, lumpy crystal in the other, and turned away from the mouth of the courtyard, towards the street. The moon was high now, a silver blaze that burned away the deepnight shadows in the courtyard, and he could hear the distant tread of booted feet.

Time to be gone.

1
PAYMENT

PETITION DAY
THE 22ND DAY OF EARLY SUMMER,
530 A.E./A.F.

PROPPING OPEN HER INK-SPLATTERED PARCHMENT with her elbows, Rahelu regarded her only means of getting her family out of their miserable existence in the Lowdocks and wished she could start over. Her cramped letters were barely visible—she had diluted her squid ink with so much water it left her brush pen as a faint gray trail.

If only she could afford proper resonance ink! Then she could attach her memories as proof of her abilities instead of relying on mere words.

It doesn't matter, she told herself as the dim light from the lamp flickered. By some miracle, the meager amount of fish oil had lasted all night. *The Houses will read every word of every Petition, no matter how unpolished, as long as I submit it on time.*

The very last essay question swam before her heavy eyes:

Enumerate the reasons why you would be an asset as a Suppliant. Provide specific examples of your mastery of the resonance disciplines.

Another one. Another question asking her to sell herself. The nonsense she'd written in response would make anyone laugh:

I am an experienced hunter (solo and group) with knife, spear, and rope-net, with over a thousand kills to my spear.

If fishing qualified. According to the Isonn trainees, it didn't—even if you needed quite a lot of skill to spear a moving target underwater—because fish weren't capable of spearing back.

I can hit a medium-sized target nine times in ten at a distance of twenty-five strides, or four times in five at thirty-five strides. My best verified throw is—

The lamp guttered out, plunging the interior of the hut into darkness. Thankfully, she could see just the faintest hint of the sky beginning to lighten, so she quietly gathered up her parchment, brush pen, the broken glass bottle that passed as her inkstand, and the half-splintered wooden stool she had been using as a desk.

She was not quiet enough and her mother stirred. "Nela?"

"Go back to sleep, anma," Rahelu said. "There is still another half-span before dawn."

Her mother sat up, and Rahelu braced herself for what was coming next.

"You did not sleep again." Disapproval emanated from her mother's figure in slow, rolling waves of resonance that filled their cramped living quarters like the rising tide.

Maybe she should ask her mother for help. Her mother could sell anything to anybody, even with only broken Aleznuaweithish and gestures.

But Petitioning was Rahelu's responsibility, not her mother's, so Rahelu only said, "It will be fine, anma. I am almost done," and ducked past the thin cotton sheet.

Rahelu walked several hundred strides down the rocky hillside until distance softened those waves of resonance to gentle lapping. There, submerged in the shallows of her mother's disapproval, she set up her makeshift study on a lonely patch of damp grass to review her Petition for the eighth time.

Was there anything, anything else she could possibly write, at all, to convince the Houses to accept her as a Petitioner?

Another quarter-span of hard thinking yielded no further ideas, though it did bring her father out, burdened with an assortment of nets, poles, traps, and her breakfast.

Rahelu leapt up to take the dented wooden bowl from him so he wouldn't have to bend down. As he released his grip, she clipped the side of the stool with her knee, sending her inkstand and parchment sliding.

Shit!

She lunged forward and saved her Petition—at the minor cost of several slices on three fingertips, one large ink stain, and her breakfast.

Her father kept his resonance aura muted, as always, but after her first year of Guild training, she'd gotten good enough to Seek out the emotions beneath his untrained Obfuscation. Right now, his aura was full of resignation, thoroughly tempered with love.

Her mother, however, her mother's exasperation—if she discovered this—was such a virtual certainty that an echo of that possible future manifested at Rahelu's mere thought:

'How can you be so clumsy? Look at all this wasted food!' Her mother waves the bowl in her face, with only a smattering of rice grains and

smaller flakes of boiled fish still stuck to the inside. 'Do you know how much this costs? A single grain of rice—'

Rahelu swiped her bleeding fingers through the ghostly vision and cut off the Augury. "Please don't tell anma."

Her father took out a bamboo-leaf-wrapped parcel of smoked fish from his tunic pocket and offered it to her; just as silently, she shook her head and sat back down, righting her fallen stool and parchment.

"See you at the pier at sundown," her father said.

He did not add *'with good news'*; he only ruffled her hair—like she was still a child—and trudged down the hill towards the Lowdocks proper, leaving her to salvage what she could.

The damage to her Petition was contained to one unsightly splotch that had obliterated the rubbish she'd written about the number of kills to her spear, but putting her food back in the bowl was a lost cause.

Tears prickled at the corners of her eyes as she chewed on handfuls of cold rice, boiled fish, and grass.

Stupid.

Food was food.

And the Houses would not judge her Petition on something as trivial as penmanship.

When it came to recruiting Petitioners, the Houses cast a wide net on purpose. They didn't want to miss *any* resonance talent. In the Dominion of Aleznuaweite, anyone could rise above their station if they worked hard and persevered.

That was the dream that had driven her parents to give up everything and move to the city of Ennuost Yrg. Rahelu shared that dream; she had sworn, with all the solemnity of a twelve-year-old child, to achieve it at all costs. It was the hope that sustained them through the bitter reality of scraping by in the Lowdocks.

And finally, after seven long years, that dream was within reach.

If Rahelu's Petition was good enough to be accepted.

Applicant Rahelu

Of no House and no family name.

And no sponsor.

Her Guild instructors had either given her blunt suggestions to invest in private tutoring (she'd nearly choked holding in her hysterical laughter at the notion) or had already reached their sponsorship limits.

Well, having a sponsor wasn't a mandatory requirement. No sense in worrying about something she couldn't control.

Guild rating: Graduate in good standing (accredited on the 15th day of early summer, 530 A.F.)

Rahelu's parents had not attended the grand ceremony last week. She had not expected them to; truthfully, she had not wanted to attend either.

Seeking: Beginner
Projection: Elementary
Obfuscation: Elementary
Evocation: Intermediate
Augury/Fortunement: Novice

The Guild's violet seal was stamped over the words; it shimmered faintly in the predawn light. She traced the lines with one nail, its edge catching on the tiny bumps of dried resonance crystal dust. Her fingertip tingled, and she was pulled back in time to the Guild Registrar's office two days ago:

The Guild Registrar wrinkles his nose at the unkempt girl before him. The odor of fish is overpowering the potted starbloom he keeps in his office for this very purpose and his resonance aura shifts into a queasy green-brown.

Her aura flares an indignant red in response—poor emotional control—as he authenticates her rating. Not the worst he's seen— actually a good deal better than some House-born—but not good enough for a sponsor.

No doubt he'd see her year after year, until she realizes her time would be better spent focusing on her family's trade.

Stormbringer. Whoever reviewed her Petition would see that too. She wanted to dismiss the Guild Registrar's opinions, just like he had dismissed her, but she couldn't argue with his points.

She didn't have any more time to agonize, though, because the sun was about to peek over the horizon.

Rahelu hurried back up the hill towards their cramped little hut, cursing. She'd idled for far too long, and now they would be late. There was still ink and blood to be washed off her hands and—

A hundred strides away, just outside their doorway, were two people wearing the forest-green-and-tan of House Isonn: a clerk brandishing a scroll and a heavily muscled bailiff who towered over her mother.

"Move!" Muscles said, her words carrying easily in the quiet of early dawn. "You had your final warning two days ago, and still you did not make your lease payment by sundown yesterday."

That money had gone to the Guild. To pay the processing fee for authenticating Rahelu's Petition.

Her mother bowed but stayed planted in their doorway. "We are sorry to be late," she said in broken, heavily accented

Aleznuaweithish. "We sell more fish today. Tomorrow. We pay tomorrow. Yes?"

Eighty strides to go.

Rahelu dropped the stool, her brush pen, and broken glass bottle and ran, rolling up her Petition and tucking it inside her tunic as her sandaled feet pounded up the rocky hillside.

"The House has given you lenient terms—well beyond the norm—and you have abused the House's generosity for far too long," the clerk said. "This is a lease with a defined schedule of installments, not an act of charity. Step aside so we can inventory and seize the assets you have in lieu of the overdue repayments."

Fifty strides.

"Yes, I understand we need to make the repayment." Her mother's resonance aura was full of swirling gray confusion; she spread empty hands. "We pay some later today, after we sell more fish. And we pay more money tomorrow. Please."

"Dumb Chanazian ghelik doesn't understand," Muscles said to the clerk and spat.

Rahelu's face flushed. Familiar old anger seethed; out past her resonance ward, turning her aura a glowing red.

"There'll be nothing inside worth hauling away. Just note that down so we can get out of this stinking slum. You can revoke the validity of the fishing license on that junk vessel back at headquarters, and I can go back to sleep. This is no decent span for respectable folks to be up."

Twenty strides. Muscles was twenty strides away.

"I can't do that without completing a physical inventory; it won't pass an audit from the House Seekers—"

Ten.

"—so just do what you need to do to move her out of the way."

"Hey!" Rahelu shouted, trying to bury her anger. Anger wasn't going to help; she needed something else. She drew on the swirling confusion around her mother, shaping the resonance into a fuzzy gray spear that vibrated with uncertainty.

The three figures at the top of the hill looked down in her direction. Pale gold relief broke through her mother's aura as Rahelu pulled every last bit of confusion into her Projection, but her arrival made no difference to the pair representing House Isonn.

"Wait!" Rahelu cried.

The bailiff strode forward with both hands out, reaching for Rahelu's mother, so Rahelu cast her Projection.

The spear of confusion shone a ghostly gray in her resonance sight—edges as clearly detailed as her real spear—and crashed into the Isonn bailiff's unguarded back.

Muscles stumbled, hands falling to her sides, then she turned around and around on the spot, her eyes darting from one figure to the next until her gaze landed on the clerk.

"You. You're…" The bailiff blinked. "I'm supposed to…" Blinked again. "I'm supposed to take you in, unless you can pay up." She took three uncertain steps towards the clerk before she stood still, eyes unfocused.

The clerk had backed away from his colleague, but his eyes stayed on Rahelu. "You attacked a legally appointed representative of House Isonn," he said. "You'll go straight to the Tidelocks for this as soon as I report you."

"You improperly authorized a physical assault on an unarmed citizen," Rahelu said, brushing past the clerk and the confused bailiff to stand in front of her mother.

"She was obstructing us from performing our duties!"

"Is that a formal accusation?" Rahelu asked. "Then, as a blood relative of a Resonance Guild member, she'll be exercising her rights to a public defense and an interpreter. I will register your accusation with the Hall of Judgment this eartharc, and then we'll see whose testimony stands up to a direct Seeking."

The clerk swallowed. "No need to complicate matters by involving the Adjudicators." He waved his scroll at her mother. "Just get her to move so I can do my inventory. Or better yet, pay the damned overdue installment, and we'll forget about this."

"The only assets we've got that are worth anything are three baskets of smoked fish." Rahelu stepped to one side, gently tugging on her mother's elbow and lifting the curtain so the clerk could crane his neck to see inside their hut. "The market value—which I'm willing to swear to before an independent Seeker—is eighty-six copper kez. You're welcome to take them with you and sell them yourself, or you can extend the payment deadline, as my mother requested, and we'll get you the coin tomorrow."

"What about that spear?" The clerk pointed at Rahelu's primary weapon, which was propped up against the far wall of their hut. "That's solid ash and quality steel." He eyed the ring on her left hand. "And you're wearing resonance crystal."

Rahelu laughed. "Get in line. Those belong to the Guild. Now, are you going to save us the trouble of hauling these baskets to Market Square or not?"

"Half the coin by sundown today and the other half by sundown tomorrow," the clerk said through gritted teeth. "And if you're a heartbeat late on either payment, the House will exercise its rights with respect to the termination clauses in the lease and revoke your fishing license as my colleague has suggested."

"Agreed," Rahelu said as the bailiff finally recovered her wits.

Muscles scowled, fists balled up and ready to swing. "You little shit."

Rahelu put her own fists up and smiled back as she

shifted into a defensive hand-to-hand combat stance. The older woman stood a hand-and-a-half taller, so she would have the advantage of height and reach. No doubt the bailiff knew how to fight, but the sloppiness of her stance suggested that she'd spent far more time lifting weights and intimidating ordinary citizens than exchanging blows with someone else trained in combat.

Rahelu, on the other hand, had spent the last five years sparring on a daily basis—and most of her opponents, including Nheras of Ilyn in particular, had the same advantages of height and reach, as well as a privileged Houseborn's access to private tutoring.

If it came down to a fair fight, Rahelu was reasonably certain she could hold her own.

She was reasonably certain the bailiff knew that too.

"Put your hackles down and let's go," the clerk said to the bailiff. "We've got another four visits to make before the first span."

Muscles glowered, then spat in Rahelu's face. The anger she'd suppressed so carefully boiled over, flooding the ambient resonance, and all she could see was red.

She was going to beat that muscle-bound bully until the bailiff was bruised and swollen beyond recognition and—

Her mother's voice—and her mother's vise-like grip on her elbow—cut through the bloody mists conjured by her anger.

"Thank you," her mother said, dragging Rahelu down into a low bow. "House Isonn is kind. We will not be late."

The two of them stayed like that, with their foreheads pressed to the ground, until the clerk and the bailiff were gone, and it was safe to get up.

Her mother immediately smacked Rahelu in the back of her head.

"Ow!"

"Idiot girl! What have I told you about showing respect?"

"Those two bullies don't deserve respect."

"They represent House Isonn, and so they are entitled to respect. It is not your place to judge whether they deserve it." Her mother shook her head. "Go wash your face and hands. If we hurry, we may still arrive before Hzin."

2
HOUSE-BORN

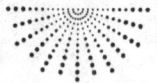

RAHELU AND HER MOTHER RACED THE LIGHT OF the rising sun westward through the terraced streets of Ennuost Yrg. By some miracle of the Starfather, they didn't slip once on the treacherous stair to the Temple district, and not a soul accosted them along the way to demand tribute.

Even so, they could not catch up to the leading edge of the eartharc rays sweeping across the city. By the time they staggered into Market Square on shaky legs, breath rasping in their lungs, the Isonn live fish haulers had already come and gone. They'd put the leaky barrel with her father's latest catch in a cursed inconvenient spot—between the southern entry to the pavilion and the east-west thoroughfare where there was no shade.

The barrel should have been waiting for them in their stall, next to a tank newly filled with seawater. Except Hzin and his son had got there first. Not only had they laid out reed mats and full baskets to claim the prime position, but they'd also parked their rickety handcart strategically to claim the second-best stall, bumping all five of the other seafood hawkers down one spot, leaving no room for Rahelu and her mother.

"Damn him to the seventh hell," her mother said, muttering Chanazian curses under her breath. "May the Stormbringer cut off that rapacious devil's grasping hands and shriveled testicles for bait and gulls peck out his covetous eyes."

Hzin didn't understand a word, but he and Rahelu's mother were practiced partners in this dance. The rotund little man looked up from counting his coins and smirked, sky-blue satisfaction pouring out of his resonance aura. "You are very late, Jenura. I hope there was no trouble."

"No trouble," her mother said. "Just other things to do." There was not the slightest hint of yellow in her mother's resonance aura to betray the truth. "Today a very important day."

"Ah, but of course." Hzin's eyes darted to Rahelu, and the ambient resonance in his double-sized stall was marred by a flicker of violet-green. "This year is a good year for Petitioning."

Rumor held that more Petitioners would be accepted than usual, and Rahelu believed it. Earlier in the spring, the Exalted Dominance had proclaimed that Aleznuaweite would be expanding its terms of trade with its trading partners, which meant the Houses needed to see to the details of that expansion—and they didn't have enough capable mages to fill all of those new posts. Some Houses had resorted to hiring mercenaries to cover their labor shortage.

"You are blessed by the Earthgiver to have such a clever daughter."

"Only in some things," her mother demurred, then looked at Hzin's son, who sat by the stall's saltwater tank with his legs crossed and eyes closed in meditation. "The Earthgiver has also favored you, Hzin, with such an obedient, hard-working son."

Fourteen years old and slight for his age, Bzel had tried to pass the Guild's entrance tests for three years running without success; today would be his fourth attempt. Rahelu felt the scratching of his untrained Seeking across her resonance aura like skittering cockroaches.

She poked his knee with the toe of her sandal, breaking his trance. "I told you not to practice today," she said. "You'll tire yourself out."

"Sorry." Bzel grimaced and rubbed both eyes. "I didn't forget; I just...I'm just making sure I'm ready."

He wasn't remotely ready. Rahelu had tried coaching him from time to time in exchange for Hzin ceding the better stall position to her mother, but he lacked a certain instinct for the resonance disciplines that she didn't know how to explain and the funds for a private tutor who was more qualified.

"Starfather bless you, Bzel," her mother continued. "Your parents must be proud. You have worked very hard."

But no matter how hard Hzin's son tried, Rahelu doubted he would ever pass the Guild entrance tests—she herself had only succeeded due to a combination of natural aptitude and sheer luck.

"And may the Starfather bless you too, Rahelu." The green in Hzin's aura deepened until it was the same hue as the Aleituan Sea. "You'll remember old Hzin, won't you, when you're a Dedicate?"

There was no sincerity behind those words, but it was nice to hear them anyway, so she responded in kind: "Yes."

"Please excuse us," her mother said. "We still have many things to do."

She turned south, away from the seafood stalls and their

saltwater tanks, back bent underneath the weight of a full basket.

Hzin resumed counting his coins.

"Wait for me by the north entrance," Rahelu said to Bzel. "And don't even think about trying more Seeking, unless you want to faint from resonance backlash again. I won't be there to carry you home this time."

"But I *will* pass this time, just like the Houses will accept your Petition." Bzel's wide-eyed stare was full of hope; how he managed to hang on to that while growing up in the Lowdocks was one of the Starfather's own mysteries. "Right?"

"Sure," Rahelu said and followed her mother, thankful that nobody present had the ability to see past her Obfuscation of the truth.

Eventually, they found an unoccupied spot in a barely trafficked corner, behind a spice merchant and a peddler hawking a dubious assortment of probably illegal potions, cures, and curios.

Rahelu helped her mother set out their baskets and drag their leaky barrel over. She couldn't tell if the fish inside were lethargic because they needed a change of seawater or because there was no room for them to swim around.

The spice merchant glared. "Can't you set up somewhere else? The stench of your rotten fish will scare away all of my customers!"

Rahelu opened her mouth to respond, but her mother smoothly elbowed her to one side and bowed.

"We are sorry to disturb you. Our usual place was not available. Perhaps you would like some fresh fish for your midday meal? We have many goldtrout, caught just three spans ago."

"Anma!" Rahelu hissed under her breath in Chanazian.

"He'll take all the fresh goldtrout, maybe even a whole basket! And he won't pay for it."

"Better than to lose it all," her mother muttered back.

"We don't have enough silverbream or sweetcod to make up the difference."

"Perhaps the Stormbringer will bless your aban today. And we still have tonight. I may be able to find some squid."

"Tonight, I will go too," Rahelu said.

"You will not," her mother said. "Today, the Houses will accept your Petition. Tonight, you must stay home and rest, so you may do your best in the challenges tomorrow."

Seeking or not, Rahelu couldn't tell whether her mother's statement was a vote of confidence in her capabilities or a command to do the impossible in spite of her deficiencies. "But—"

"Aban and I will take care of the repayment. We have sailed through more storms than you've baited hooks."

Talking to her mother was no use, so Rahelu gritted her teeth, wiped her hands, and checked that her Petition scroll was tucked securely into her waistband.

"I will come back as soon as I can," she said and went to collect Bzel, leaving her mother to haggle with the spice merchant.

———

THE CITY of Ennuost Yrg was always crowded on Petition Day, but this—this was something else.

Would-be Petitioners lined up on the left side of the Guild's great oaken gates. The queue stretched out into the street and wound past the Northroad, wrapping all the way around the city block until the end doubled back to meet its middle at the entrance to the Guild.

Rahelu's heart sank as she assessed her competition:

every single applicant in the line was common-born—those she knew on sight were outnumbered ten-to-one by unfamiliar faces. These strangers wore heavy travel packs and—as the line moved—shuffled with the weariness of people who had headed straight for the Guild as soon as the city gates had opened after a week of traveling from dawn to dusk. Most were already past their second decade, bearing well-worn weapons and resonance crystal pendants, and carried themselves with the confidence of independent mages.

She herded the gawking Bzel past the gates and inside the administrative building, where a much smaller line of applicants waited in front of the Guild Registrar's office.

"Luck, Rahelu," Bzel said, his voice tremulous as she deposited him at the end of his queue.

Rahelu tried not to notice how very ragged and small he looked in his rough homespun linen next to the others, who were all clad in the fine cotton dress tunics and trousers of House-born. Memory rose unbidden in her mind—*a shining silver coin, a storm of foreign words, bruises all over her skin*—and she pushed it away, before it could become an Evocation.

"Luck, Bzel." She squeezed his shoulder, then turned away, marching back through the doors and out the gate.

She was in such a hurry that she nearly collided with a tall, red-headed youth and a tanned girl with sun-bleached hair climbing out of an elaborately carved palanquin painted pale green with shimmering sky-blue curtains.

The Ideth boy's eyes widened as he started forward, reaching out a hand, and Rahelu immediately shied away.

"Sorry!" she said, raising both hands defensively and bowing as she backed away towards the line for common-born Petitions.

House-born, as a rule, were touchy about being disrespected.

She braced herself for pursuit—he looked determined to

come after her. Fortunately, his companion caught him by the arm and dragged him away into the courtyard, hissing furiously in his ear the whole time, allowing Rahelu to escape to join her own queue.

It would be at least two spans, perhaps longer, before it was her turn. She passed the time balancing on one sandaled foot, idly scratching incomplete resonance wards into the dusty ground with the toe of her other sandal as she watched more House-born applicants arrive. They breezed through the right side of the gate with their sponsored Petitions, emerging not even a quarter-span later to be carried off to one idle amusement or another.

"I've half a mind to *not* go to the Ilyn party tonight," said one applicant wearing the purple-and-black of House Isilc. "Not after I had to suffer through their pitiful excuse of a graduation banquet last month."

"The food was an embarrassment," said another. He wore a coiled whip on his belt. "Only a selection of fifty dishes and not a single one with crystal pear or even iced fruits. Hardly anybody ate anything—not even the dogs."

The dogs.

Instead of a faint scratch that barely disturbed the gravel, the next line Rahelu drew was a deep gouge in the road.

These spoiled brats were so fucking rich that their dogs ate better than she did.

"What could you possibly expect from a new House? Gilt paint won't change a sow into a mare. Be glad they're throwing their daughter at Ideth and not us," said the first House-born as she vanished inside an ebony palanquin covered in gold leaf.

"Small relief that." The Isilc House-born with the whip snorted. "House Ilyn is spending kez like a dreamleaf addict in an apothecary, and now I'm saddled with her and the rest of those climbers for the first challenge. If she didn't have the makings of a decent Harbinger..." He, too, disappeared behind the palanquin's lilac gauze curtains.

One of the House-born rapped out a coded sequence, and the four bearers hoisted the lacquered affair onto their shoulders in one smooth, coordinated motion, trotting off towards the Sunset district.

The line ahead of her shuffled, and Rahelu abandoned the current ward she was sketching to practice another design: one that deflected resonance instead of suppressing it. She visualized the impractical form—a rough square surrounding the Guild complex (inefficient, but she couldn't leave her place in line to make it circular), its uneven, jagged lines bristling outwards, like the spines on a sea urchin—and poured her concentration into reproducing the ward in rough gravel, a task complicated enough to force her to stop stewing over House-born privilege and focus.

She soon settled into a comfortable rhythm: move up the queue by two strides; extend the foundation line with her heel; carve out the ward's extensions with the outside of her sandal; repeat. A span-and-a-half later, her position in the queue had looped most of the way around the block. Another quarter-span and she'd finally make it around the corner, through the Guild gates and into the courtyard beyond, to submit her Petition.

"Let's get this farce over with," said a reedy, nasal voice Rahelu would rather not recognize at all.

Rahelu looked up to see Nheras of Ilyn and her cousins stepping out of a red-and-cream palanquin. All three scions of House Ilyn wore their focus stones—twice the size of Rahelu's Guild-issued training resonance crystal—on a silver chain around their necks.

"I've an appointment at Shuath's," Nheras said as she swaggered up the street, jeweled armbands and earrings jangling, with Bhemol and Kiran trailing in her wake like two starving alley mutts. Her disdainful eyes roved over the line of common-born applicants; she gave an audible sniff and a wrinkle of her nose when she saw Rahelu. "And I'd rather not arrive with my clothes stinking like this rabble."

Rahelu scowled back. Over the years, Nheras had made thousands of snide little remarks like that. Every time Rahelu had given in to her desire to pummel the Ilyn girl in the face, things had ended badly.

She was *not* going to let Nheras get to her. Not today. If Rahelu gave insult for insult, Nheras would take it as an act of provocation (never mind that she'd done the insulting first), and none of them would leave with their dignity intact. Besides, Nheras never took well to being ignored, so ignoring Nheras was the best way to piss her off.

Rahelu went back to drawing the final lines of her ward.

"I don't see why we need to show up and hand in these dumb Petitions personally," Kiran said, hands in his pockets. "Any messenger could have done the same."

"It's the principle of equality." Bhemol rolled his eyes. "As if anybody is stupid enough to believe in that."

Rahelu's foot jerked. One of her extension lines went too far, crossing past the ward's foundation lines and rendering the construction useless. A bright red flare surged past her personal ward before she could suppress it, lighting up her resonance aura.

Rahelu breathed, repeating her mantra over and over in her head. *I control my emotions; they do not control me*. Bhemol was an entitled ass whose opinion was about as informed as Lowdocks gossip. The ward she'd been tracing on the ground was just something to pass the time; it didn't matter.

She restrained herself, hurling one hard glare at the three House-born instead of a Projection.

Her eyes met Nheras's and the Ilyn girl sneered. "Clearly, many are, including some who should know better. The

Houses really ought to change this outdated practice of letting anybody submit a Petition. It's hardly fair to take their coin when most of them don't stand a chance."

Rahelu abandoned her incomplete ward and her earlier resolution to stay silent and scoffed. Loudly.

"What are you doing?" someone behind her in line hissed. "Let it go."

She ignored the admonition and the temptation to shape the anger rushing through her veins; kept her voice calm and steady as her eyes wandered over each of the Ilyn applicants. "Two in three House-born don't either."

"Nobody asked your opinion, fish guts," Bhemol said. "Why don't you crawl back to the Lowdocks instead of stinking up the place?"

"Nobody asked yours," Rahelu said, clasping her hands behind her back. "Yet here you are, inflicting our ears with your idiocy."

The girl ahead of her turned around and glared. "Will you shut up? Don't make things worse for the rest of us."

Kiran sauntered forward with one hand on his dueling cane. The other common-born applicants in the line melted away at his approach, leaving a space around Rahelu. "Bhemol asked you a question, fish guts. When a House speaks, you answer."

Rahelu shaded her eyes and made a show of looking left, then right and back, then shrugged. "Well, let me know when somebody sworn to a House shows up, and I'll answer to them. Last I checked, neither being spawned of your father's seed nor crawling out of your mother's womb guaranteed you a place in their Houses."

Bhemol growled and stepped up beside Kiran. "You don't belong here. Go back to the gutters, or better yet, to Chanaz. Don't shame the Guild; no House will take someone like you."

"House Isca took Tsenjhe. She's a Dedicate now."

Nheras arched one elegantly plucked brow. "Ideth's harlot is your shining example?" Her resonance aura rippled, shimmering with orange-amusement as her two followers snorted and laughed.

"If that's so, then you've been focusing on the wrong kind of petition," Kiran said, strolling around Rahelu, so she had to choose between turning to keep him in view and exposing her back to Bhemol and Nheras, letting him get behind her, or stepping out of line altogether.

The last one wasn't an option; not that the first two were real options either. Rahelu hedged and turned sideways so she could stay in line as Kiran circled her, keeping him to her left and the other two Ilyn applicants to her right.

But Nheras and Bhemol had also closed in, giving the rest of the common-born applicants other ideas: they reformed the line around her confrontation with Ilyn, cutting her out of the queue entirely.

Fuck! She should have kept her mouth shut.

Rahelu backed away slowly towards the opening of the next alley, keeping all three Ilyn applicants in front of her. Allowing them to chase her away would satisfy their pride; she could lose them in the back streets, hide for a quarter-span, then rejoin the back of the line after Nheras and her cousins were long gone.

They passed the northwest corner of the Guild's outer wall. Rahelu spun around to duck into the alley, but Kiran had anticipated her. Before she could run, he grabbed her with both hands and shoved her into the wall. Rahelu cried out as she slammed into rough brick, though she managed to turn her head in time to take the impact on the right side of her face.

"If you're so keen to follow in her footsteps, why don't you get on your knees?" He had her pinned with a forearm across her shoulders. "I confess I don't understand the Ideth obsession with Chanaz, but I'm an open-minded man."

His resonance aura surged, suffocating her with its deep purple-red thirst. He *liked* how she squirmed, caught between him and the wall; *liked* the brittle feel of the ivory shards in her aura as it resisted his; *liked* how she clenched her free hands into fists and stopped short of beating them against his thighs because striking a House-born meant certain retribution.

"Petition *me*," he said, his breath hot against her neck as he pressed his stiffened cock against her, his other hand fumbling at his belt buckle. "And if you are *very* skilled with your tongue, I might—"

Rahelu reached back, dug her nails into his crotch, then twisted viciously. Kiran screamed and collapsed to the ground behind her. She tried to run again, only to find her escape barred by the other two Ilyn applicants.

Nheras Projected a sorrowful air while Bhemol looked ready to tear Rahelu limb from limb.

"All these years, and you've never learned any better." Gold-and-amethyst earrings, wrought in the sign of House Ilyn, chimed as Nheras shook her head. "If you'd simply apologized for your disrespect, I would have let it go. I have better things to do than to waste my time on you—you would never have made it to the challenges anyway. But I can't allow a physical assault on a scion of House Ilyn to go unanswered."

"Assault?" Rahelu quashed the dull red anger-spear before it could burst through her aura. "*He* assaulted *me*."

Nheras waved off the truth as irrelevant. "Surrender your Petition," she said, holding out her right hand and wiggling a set of perfectly painted nails in demand. "Before this gets ugly."

A wall to her left.

A recovering Kiran in front, blocking the alley.

Bhemol to her right, with Nheras cutting off the way back to the main street.

Rahelu had no choice.

She sent Kiran to the ground with another kick between his legs, dashed past down the alleyway, and nearly strangled herself on a clothesline. Behind her, three pairs of booted feet tromped over cobblestone, and she cursed her flimsy sandals, which were a hazard all on their own.

She had to stay ahead, had to make it through to the East-ward, double back along Dedicate's Way, lose Ilyn some-where in Blackforge, before looping around to the Guild. She would be safe there, inside the courtyard: Nheras wouldn't dare try anything under the watchful eyes of the Dedicates supervising the Petitions.

Rahelu ducked around another corner, then leapt, cat-footed, up a stack of empty crates, swinging herself over the gutter and onto the rooftops. Shucking her sandals for better grip, she crouched down close to the roof tiles to keep her profile low and squat-crawled to the next house over.

She paused in the shelter of a chimney that belched out the scent of roasting pork and closed her eyes for a quick Seeking:

A tall figure, haloed in lines of gold over a darker green, stalks away towards the Guild gate, two streets over.

Nheras.

Two figures mill around the streets below. They wear shrouds of swirling gray confusion, leaving wispy trails of resonance behind as they search the east side of the Blackforge.

Stormbringer be thanked. Bhemol and Kiran wouldn't be catching up to her any time soon.

Rahelu clung to her Seeking and opened watering eyes.

Any Guild-trained mage could, of course, maintain a visualization of their resonance sense over the material world.

Usually though, they were doing so in the controlled environs of a dedicated meditation chamber, not while they were scrambling over five more rooftops and dropping down two stories.

She landed heavily, rolling to take the brunt of her fall on one shoulder. Bits of roof tiles cascaded to the ground around her; she groaned, winded, and didn't bother with shielding her face.

Right on cue, Nheras swanned around the corner to stand over her. Rahelu tried to get up, but Nheras *tsked* and planted a booted foot in her stomach.

The trademark Ilyn smirk flashed across the taller girl's face as she shook her head again. "Predictable." She extended her right hand once more. "I'm asking nicely, one last time. Give me your Petition. Now."

Rahelu coughed and prepared to spit out a mouthful of bile onto the expensive lambskin boot digging into her midsection. As she did, Nheras casually ground her toe into Rahelu's belly. She wheezed; the whole mess dribbled down her own chin instead.

The other girl followed up with another stomp. Rahelu screamed and curled up on her right side in pain. She scrabbled around for something—anything!—but her left hand came up empty.

Her right hand, though. Her right hand dug around in the open sewer and came up with gold.

Of a sort.

Nheras leaned down close, red-painted lips parted and readied with a victory taunt—and Rahelu lobbed her handful of squelchy, stinking sewer dung straight into Ilyn's open mouth.

Between the shrill screams of outrage, spluttered death threats, and wails of distress, Nheras sounded like three revenant shades from the sixth hell.

It was the sweetest music Rahelu had ever heard.

And the gate—oh, the gate!—it was only twenty strides away. She staggered to her feet and stumbled out of the alleyway. Her body nearly revolted; her intestines felt like Nheras had taken a warhammer to them instead of her boots.

"Hey! Watch where you're going!" someone shouted as she cut through in the wake of an orange-and-white palanquin. (She wasn't so far gone as to dare cut in *front*.) "What do you—"

The rest of the words were lost to the roar of blood in her ears and the more ominous sounds of close pursuit.

She tore down the road, thigh muscles burning, dodging a kitchen hand loaded down with two full pails of water, knocking a chandler onto his rear, bowing every which way in apology. She ran to the gate as if her life depended on it.

One glance back at Nheras's rage-filled eyes, and Rahelu decided her life probably did depend on it. She stretched her legs, tried to force her lungs into the measured breathing of Onneja's eartharc meditation, and swung her arms more quickly, as if that would help her flee more swiftly.

"Excuse me!" she yelled at the startled would-be Petitioners clustered around the entrance. "Please, excuse me! Coming through!"

"A bounty!" Nheras shrieked from behind. "A bounty! House Ilyn will pay a bounty of fifty silver kez to anyone who apprehends this ghelik. I will have her head to satisfy my honor!"

Oh no. No.

Nonononono. She was *so close*. The gate was *right there*!

But Nheras's words had sparked a purple-greed conflagration that rippled through the crowd's comingled aura.

The other common-born applicants closed ranks against her.

Before she could even think of another place to run to, another escape route, Nheras caught up. All pretense of House loftiness had vanished; the taller girl tackled her to the ground. Bits of gravel cut into her cheek as sharp nails dug into her back to snatch away her Petition.

Her Petition. Her family's only way out.

She kept her forehead on the ground as she shuffled around, smearing road dust and gravel into the cuts on her face, and abased herself in front of Nheras's lambskin boots. One, she noted with dim satisfaction (*don't think it don't feel it or Nheras will see it*), was caked with filth.

"Give it back, Nheras," she whimpered. "Please. I beg of you."

There was a *crackle* of parchment unrolling.

"Please, Nheras," she said again. "I will owe you a favor. One favor, with no conditions. Just give me back my Petition."

"I need no favors from a fish," came the derisive retort.

Rahelu cringed as those lambskin boots walked around her in a deliberate circle until they stopped beside her left ear.

Nheras crouched down. "I tried to resolve this as pleasantly as I could, but you just couldn't stay in your place, could you?" Her voice shook with fury. "No matter what I do or what I try, you always have to come along and ruin everything, and I am *done* with letting you get away with it."

The Ilyn girl stood up and raised her voice, so everyone within a thirty-stride radius could hear her. "I can't believe you wasted ink on this Petition. I knew you were a terrible mage, but this? This is just *embarrassing*."

Rahelu's hopes shriveled up and died, as Nheras read out her entire Petition to peals of laughter from the watching crowd. She remained face down in her obeisance, willing herself not to cry, knowing it was bad enough that everyone could see that she desperately wanted to anyway, just by looking at her aura.

"You don't belong here," Nheras said as she finished her mocking recitation.

The sound of valuable parchment tearing.

Again.

And again.

And again, until the small ivory pieces of Rahelu's dreams fluttered down around her head, and she was five years old all over again, lost in the first snows of winter.

"Go back to Chanaz, fish guts." Nheras wiped her filthy boot on Rahelu's only tunic. "And stay out of my life."

The Ilyn girl stalked away, shouting for someone to fetch her a washbasin with scented water, fresh towels, and a change of clothes, leaving Rahelu to painstakingly dig through the gravel and gather the scattered pieces of parchment.

She thanked the Starfather that Nheras had chosen to tear up her Petition instead of burning it.

As long as she could find every single scrap, she still had a chance.

3
HELP

Rahelu limped into the unnamed laneway between the Smoking Phial and Gherorg's Elixirs and stopped to catch her breath. Dragging her beaten-up, filth-splattered, bleeding carcass five hundred strides over to Blackforge had been agony, but the humiliation she'd suffered was worse.

Being scorned by House-born was one thing, but being scorned by the other common-born applicants?

That *burned*.

How could they side with the House-born over her?

It took her the better part of a span to find the entrance to the Tattered Quill. Like everything else in this part of the city, it was a third-rate establishment exactly as ramshackle as its name suggested. According to the scriveners guild, its proprietor, Xyuth, had barely met the requirements for a journeyman scrivener and was regularly late on his tithes. It was more surprising that he was able to pay his tithes at all—there was very little foot traffic in this part of the city.

Rahelu entered to the muffled chime of a small bell, whose tongue had gathered a mouthful of dust, accompanied

by the eerie creak of rusty hinges. It took a moment for her
eyes to adjust—the shop's shutterless windows were so
grubby that hardly any light passed through and the few
lamps scattered about did little to illuminate the interior. She
followed a single set of half-footprints—the tracks had been
partially swept away, probably by a hem of a long robe—from
the creaky door towards the counter.

Instead of the Copper Nib's neat stores, the shelves here
were organized haphazardly: sheaves of blank, low-grade
parchment weighted down with a jumble of mundane ink
sticks inside flimsy bamboo cases (odd); books on the more
esoteric applications of the resonance disciplines were
crammed in next to maps and Chanazian histories (even
odder).

All of it—including the jars of brush pens and yes,
tattered quills—was coated with a fine layer of dust that
stirred from the breeze of her passage, and she sneezed.

The only thing that seemed cared for was the heavy
bronze figure of the Earthgiver tucked away in the small,
candlelit wall niche beside the counter. The statuette's
rounded curves gleamed, casting faint reflections on the
rough wooden floors.

Did Xyuth get any customers?

A small sign on top of the counter (its precise letters read
'BACK IN ONE QUARTER-SPAN') suggested he did, though
he'd not been considerate enough to indicate when he had
departed. She duly waited, drumming her fingers on the ink-
stained countertop for at least a few hundred heartbeats, but
the small wooden door behind the counter remained firmly
shut.

A glance outside through the grimy windows told Rahelu
it was nearly a span past high sun. For all she knew, the sign
could have been sitting there since last week; its top edge

was just as dusty as the shelves, even if its face was relatively clean.

She should leave. Limp back to the Lowdocks and wash off what she could of her blood and the sewer muck. If she begged, Tlareth would relent and loan her a clean tunic that might let her step inside the Silver Seal without being thrown out immediately.

Or...

Rahelu's eyes drifted past the counter and over to the rosewood cabinets lined up against the back wall, as incongruous as a squad of city guards on patrol in the Lowdocks. None of the drawers were labeled, and there were no locks on them, either.

She slipped behind the counter and tugged on the knob of one of the smaller, flatter drawers. It opened without the least resistance, revealing an assortment of resonance crystal lenses resting on a velvet-lined tray.

Not helpful.

The next drawer contained a complicated-looking disassembly of metal parts and more resonance crystal lenses; the sixteen drawers after that contained tiny lead plates embossed with the letters of the Aleznuaweithish alphabet. Based on the rest of the shop's wares, she had expected the letters to be all mixed together, but Xyuth had surprised her —each drawer only contained plates of a single letter.

Rahelu rummaged her way through all forty drawers and found tweezers, penknives, more metal plates, thin steel wire, even more crystal lenses—everything except for violet resonance crystal dust.

She tried to ram the last drawer back into its place, but she'd misaligned the trajectory of her motion, so instead of getting a satisfying *clack*, she added a sore wrist to her tally of injuries.

Her aura trembled—ambient resonance warping around

her as the urge to topple every one of the useless cabinets consumed her thoughts.

Idiot! The throbbing pain in her stomach made it hard to think straight. *I rule my emotions*, she repeated to herself mentally. *My emotions do not rule me.* She was not going to make a fool of herself by struggling against a piece of furniture.

Instead, she leaned against the shabby wooden door and closed her eyes, breathing deeply in the seven-count pattern for Seeking. It took an embarrassingly long time, more than thirty heartbeats, before she managed to focus:

Two people in the workshop behind the door.

Their distinct resonance signatures pulsed in her mind— an insistent tapping that she felt, rather than heard, as vibrations in her skull.

One is a thin little man wearing a heavy smock. He wrings his hands as he paces from one side of the workshop to the other with short, hurried steps. Yellow spikes flicker over the churning purple-white mist in his aura and he keeps glancing at his companion.

No, that wasn't right. Xyuth's attention was on the empty space in the middle of the workshop, as if it held the answers to all the questions in the world.

His companion kneels on the floor in a rigid pose: veiled face lifted towards the ceiling and both hands outstretched to embrace the air. Her aura is the dim orange glow of a dying fire.

That aura carried an unsettling buzz that made Rahelu's teeth rattle.

The woman's low-pitched voice has the same sonorous tone as one of the Skymother's chosen and the detached quality of someone deeply immersed in Seeking or Evocation, though she wears no leather armband to mark her as a Guild-trained mage. Her muffled chanting reverberates through the wooden door like a temple bell rung underwater; the words are a stream running over jagged rocks—smooth vowels, chopped consonants, and guttural gurgles.

Xyuth freezes, his aura paling. His lips move as he advances on the woman—

Rahelu couldn't make out his words through the door. (Not that it mattered. While she could swear in the Free Territories speech with impressive fluency, sensible conversation was beyond her.)

The mage does not answer. He cries out; grabs the mage by her shoulders and shakes her furiously.

What did that idiot think he was doing? Everyone knew not to disrupt a mage in the midst of a working! The best you could hope for was resonance backlash.

And the worst?

Rahelu dropped her Seeking and slammed her shoulder against the door before Xyuth could do permanent damage. Something rattled on the other side—Stormbringer, it was barred!—so she kicked it repeatedly instead.

Fuck! That hurt.

Tendrils of bone-white mist seeped through the gaps around the doorframe; Xyuth's shouts piled one guttural phrase after another on top of the unknown mage's screaming. The ambient resonance bled crimson, but Rahelu couldn't tell whose pain it was.

If only she had—no, her spear would be no use either; an ax would be ideal, but a mace would suffice. A mace, or—

Rahelu hobbled over to the small shrine, her ears full of Xyuth's frantic pleas warring with the unknown mage's panicked cries. *Earthgiver, forgive this sacrilege,* she prayed as she heaved the statuette out of the wall niche. It proved too heavy to grasp securely in her hands; she had to wrap both arms around the statue's head and torso, lest she drop it and break her own toes. She swung, aiming for the join where the door's edge met its jamb.

WHAM!

The door shuddered; she was rewarded with a fist-sized, splintered dent and a ringing ache that shot through her palms all the way up to her shoulders. Rahelu ignored the pain; backed up ten strides, adjusted her hold on the bronze figure, and charged.

She crashed through into the cluttered workshop and immediately tripped on the threshold. The statuette slipped from her grasp to land on the floor with a hollow *thunk*, and only a quick twist saved her from being impaled upon the Earthgiver's horns. More pain lanced through her right side as she rolled to her feet, head whipping around to catch her bearings.

A solid brick wall to her right. Xyuth, cowering behind the worktable, his eyes screwed shut with a penknife in one shaking hand, to her left. Before her, ghostly overlapping echoes—

Xyuth, a woman, and a little girl stand before a small cottage in a wood, covered with leaves the color of burnished copper.

He carries the girl with a ragdoll clutched tight to her chest, away from the woman's dead body and the city gates.

The little girl sits frozen in a small wall niche, a glittering black rock in her hands. The edge of the crimson pool rushes from his opened throat across the splintered floor until it laps at her bare toes.

—and through those echoes, an open door.

The unknown mage was gone.

Rahelu stalked over to the workbench and glared down at Xyuth, who tried to disappear into his robes. "What in the Stormbringer's name were you thinking?"

The scrivener flinched and jabbed his penknife out in her general direction—a ridiculously ineffective gesture.

"Stop that!" Rahelu snatched the penknife from his fingers and hurled it through the fading Augury; its point stuck in a gap between two wooden planks on the far wall. "I ought to report you to my Guild."

"G-guild?" Xyuth's eyelids flickered as he glanced at her plain leather armband and the training resonance crystal on her left hand. "H-hello, hello!" He sagged in relief, his friendly tone not quite the right match for the pale gold suffusing his resonance aura.

"Who was that?"

He unfolded himself with the caution of a truewinter bloom unfurling its petals as he took in her battered condition. "I-I don't know. A stranger. She came to me for a f—" He coughed. Faint strands of yellow-green threaded through his aura. "A favor."

Some favor, to be repaid with such a powerful Augury, even if it was only a small glimpse of his futures. The possible echoes felt like close probabilities, perhaps a few days or a few weeks away, though she wouldn't swear to it under Seeking. Most mages, including herself, had little talent for true Augury.

"What favor?"

"Ah, ah, one of a...personal nature." He didn't meet her eyes.

That was a lie; she could feel the tension in his resonance aura. She widened her eyes, straining to hold them open and unblinking, until her vision was a wash of pearlescent colors. The scrivener's aura was a pulsing blue-green, laced through with nervous-yellow, but it shone bright and clear to her Seeking.

No lie?

Rahelu blinked and her vision returned to normal.

"If the honorable Guild member would forgive this humble scrivener his unfortunate circumstances…" Xyuth crept out from behind the worktable and sidled towards the door she had broken. "I-I am closed for the day. Please, this way, this way." He scuttled past her sideways, like a crabling fleeing from one rock pool to another.

Rahelu followed.

She could force the truth out of him—either by using a direct Seeking or by compelling him with Projection—but she didn't have the legal grounds, the House backing, or the Guild rank to do that. He was clearly rattled by the Augury (she didn't blame him; his futures did not look pleasant), the unknown mage was long gone, and she didn't exactly have the time to investigate further.

Best to drop the matter.

He came to a dead stop at the sight of his ransacked cabinets, then rushed over to pull open the drawers with his resonance lenses. "Wh-what—"

"Uh." Her cheeks were warm. "I'm sorry. That was me."

"*You?* Why?"

"I was in need of urgent assistance and you were…otherwise preoccupied."

"You had no right!" He selected a lens, dropped it inside a velvet pouch, and closed it with a sharp tug on the drawstrings. "You—" The red tinges in his aura trembled then faded as he recalled himself with a deep breath. "What did you require?"

Rahelu drew the scraps of her Petition out of her pocket and placed them on the ink-stained counter. "I need this document reconstructed."

"No."

Her heart skipped a beat. "What?"

"I am sorry, but I cannot help you."

"Cannot or will not?"

"Why did you come, thieving through my shop, instead of putting your demands to the Silver Seal?" His quick fingers rifled through the square drawers with the tiny plates and sprinkled a handful of letters from each into another velvet pouch.

Her earlier anger returned in full force. She was *not* a thief; had she found what she needed, she would have left...

Not coin, because she didn't have a single copper kez left in her purse, but she would have left a signed note. And come back later to pay her debt. Including the cost of the parchment she would have used for the note.

Also, how dare he pretend to be the victim when he was a traitor? Xyuth had to be either smuggling goods, or information, or both, on top of providing forgeries—he had no other way of paying his guild tithes when his wares were coated with years' worth of dust.

"Why did you assault a mage in resonance trance? You could have crippled her!" She slammed her fist on the counter, wincing internally as she scattered her precious scraps. "Give me one good reason why I shouldn't bring the Guild's Harbingers down on you."

Xyuth stooped to pick up a fragment that had fallen off the counter and landed at his feet; a few of the lines scribed glittered faintly in the dim light of the shop lamps. He fitted a resonance crystal lens to the socket of his left eye, squinting as he examined the scrap. "Violet resonance ink—of the restricted hue reserved for the Resonance Guild's exclusive use—on calfskin parchment. Made perhaps only three weeks ago: from the hands of Anest; her work is unmistakable."

He deliberately placed the fragment on top of the counter. This time, he met her eyes. "Give me one good reason why I shouldn't report you to the city guard for reckless destruction of property—and to your Guild for attempted forgery."

Rahelu ground her teeth and started reaching for Projection. She'd already wasted far too much time. It would only take a few heartbeats to overwhelm him with her desperate need to reconstruct her Petition. After she got what she wanted, she would also need to ensure that he would not report her—not a difficult undertaking as she could simply heighten his natural aversion to approaching the city guard or the Guild.

It was an elegant, brutally efficient solution.

And exactly the kind of thing Nheras would do.

Rahelu took a deep breath, relaxed her fist, and tried to summon the familiar mental image of a small lake beneath clear skies on a windless day. As she exhaled, she pushed that sense of gray-blue calm outwards into the ambient resonance until it solidified into a basic Obfuscation barrier.

"Honored scrivener, I apologize for the grievous insult I have given," she said and bowed. "I beg your forgiveness. Please." She bowed again, even lower, then slid the pile of fragments towards him. "You will be well compensated."

Eventually. Once—*if*—her Petition was accepted. That was the first test on the path to becoming an acknowledged Petitioner. Supposing that she survived Petitioning, she was guaranteed a place with one of the eight Houses—and she'd have coin enough to repay her family's debts and still have a fortune to spare.

Xyuth paused in the middle of packing the complicated metal disassembly into a bamboo case to scrutinize her with his left eye. It looked unnaturally large through the resonance crystal lens.

His Seeking was practiced—she could barely feel his perception at the boundary where her Obfuscation barrier ended and the ambient resonance began—but she could outlast him. He wouldn't have the training or stamina required to hold a sustained Seeking; he certainly didn't have the discipline to maintain control over his own emotions at the same time. Yellow-green anxiety was already worming its way through his resonance aura again.

Rahelu dropped her barrier and her attempt to pretend she was anything other than what she was.

"I don't have any coin right now," she said and resisted his Seeking no longer. "I will swear any oath you like, owe you any favor you desire, if you would help me put my Petition back together. Please."

He sighed. "I am sorry, my dear," he repeated. "But I cannot help you. Document reconstruction is chancy at best. You should return to your Guild and have a new copy made." He abandoned the half-packed bamboo case on the counter to grab a different sack and hurried towards his workroom.

She scooped up her fragments and followed, feeling light-headed at his words. "Are you saying it cannot be done?"

Inside, Xyuth's bloody futures still flickered; he gave them a wide berth and averted his eyes as he ducked behind his workbench.

That mage was *powerful*.

"It is possible, but such a delicate, complex undertaking..." Xyuth shook his head. "It would take far too long and far too much power. And I—" He drew his eyebrows together, doubling the number of wrinkles on his brow. "I must be gone."

Xyuth opened the iron door to his safe, which contained far more gold and silver kez than Rahelu had expected, and began emptying handfuls of coin into a small sack.

He thought that preventing a particular future from coming to pass was as simple as removing the people involved in the events from the physical location shown in the Augury.

He was a fool.

"No Augury is certain," she said. "I know it is difficult"—she winced at the platitude even as Xyuth paused long enough to throw her a glance of pure disbelief through the jumbled, translucent images of the cottage, his consort's butchered corpse, and his daughter's bloodied feet—"but you must not act as if it were."

"I cannot risk it; it would be like holding the knife myself."

"To act blindly is to hold the knife yourself. You do not know what events you may set into motion by acting other than you ordinarily would. You cannot know all the threads of possibility the Augury failed to investigate, ones that would work against your intentions."

The *plink, plink-plink, plinking* of coins being swept out of the safe into his sack did not cease. He hadn't been listening; he wasn't going to listen to her. Not unless she offered him something else.

The next words sat heavy on her lips.

Did she dare say them?

Xyuth's daughter looked small for her age; no older than four summers. The way she curled her tiny, bare toes away from the crimson pool...the dead-eyed stare she wore as her father carried her out of the city...

Rahelu walked through the live Augury, around the workbench, and crouched down beside Xyuth to hold her cupped hands out before him. One of the larger pieces of her Petition lay face-up on top of the pile; the letters *'ortunement'* were still intact.

Xyuth's eyes locked onto the parchment and he stilled.

"Help me," she said. "And I will do what I can to help you."

He took the fragments of her future.

She straightened up, steeled her nerves, and stepped inside his:

Xyuth trudges westward on foot, his daughter in his arms; a serpentine knife descends in a relentless black arc to plunge into his consort's back; the same woman flees through Southwatch from one door to the next as the sun bleeds across the sky; Xyuth takes his consort's shaking hands, his lips moving in wordless warning; Xyuth rushes home from the Tattered Quill, a heavy sack of coin in his arms—

Xyuth and his family in a small cottage; the three of them at the rail of a ship; Xyuth at the portmaster's office, face alight with hope; gold and silver coins spill across his ink-stained counter from a pair of scarred hands; the merry chime of Tattered Quill's doorbell as early summer warmth yields to truesummer heat; Xyuth leaves the High-docks, downcast; Xyuth rushes to the portmaster's office, a heavy sack of coin in his arms—

Xyuth's little girl, numb, mute with blood-stained feet; Xyuth rushes home from the Tattered Quill, a heavy sack of coin in his arms—

There.

The Augury fuzzed as she seized control of it, tracing the three branched possibilities to their shared root: a moment one quarter-span removed from the present.

Rahelu bore down on the point of divergence, reaching out to Xyuth's ghostly double with her resonance senses and both hands. She resummoned her earlier illusion of calm.

Blue-gray waves flooded the Augury.

Was she doing the right thing?

Too late to wonder now.

The Augury cut off abruptly—it had run out of power at last.

"Did it work?" Xyuth's voice came out as a barely audible croak. "Will they be safe?"

"I think so." Rahelu pressed her fingertips to her temples and frowned. "What is that?"

A glittering black gem lay in the middle of the workshop floor. A pretty thing that fit easily in the palm of her hand, with cut faces like a crystal. Its smooth surface was warm—cold—and dusted with golden flecks that felt like tiny, raised bumps.

A new kind of resonance crystal?

Xyuth shied away from it immediately. "Throw the cursed thing into the Aleituan Sea!"

No doubt that would be the wise thing to do. But...

"It looks rare. Valuable." An anchor of some sort?

She prodded at the gem with a tentative pulse of curiosity —and her Projection flowed *around* it without any reflections.

As if it wasn't there at all.

"Then it is yours." The scrivener got to his feet with a creaky groan. "Now come. Let us see what can be done about this Petition of yours."

4

SPONSOR

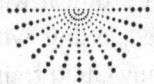

RAHELU CLUTCHED THE PRECIOUS BUNDLE XYUTH had given her with both hands as she zigzagged her way up the face of the Eastcliffs. By the time she reached the top, puffing heavily, she had to shield her eyes from the sun's glare to look up at the tall boulder that sat on the clifftop like some sentinel's watchtower. Its base was twice as large as her parents' hut and two of its sides sloped outwards as it rose from the large plateau above the Eastward—the seaward side extending precariously far beyond the clifftop over the foaming surf at least two hundred strides below.

Hardly anybody came up here (why would they? The Highdocks boasted an equally fine view) which was why Rahelu came so often. She circled around to the south side of the monolith and climbed, muscles and right side aching, until she collapsed in her usual spot, one stride from the very edge, facing east into the past.

Could she stretch out for a quarter-span and rest her eyes? Just a quarter-span basking in the early summer rays would almost be as good as a bath. (Gods, she would kill for a bath, though her nose had grown used to her stench, so a bath could wait.)

But no, the sun was already more than three-quarters of the way through skyarc, and it would take at least a half-span to hobble back to the Guild from here.

She should have gone somewhere closer, but the ignominy of the eartharc's ordeal was a fresh wound in her resonance aura. Anyone passing within ten strides of her would sense it without any Guild training, and she had borne all the ridicule she was capable of enduring for the year.

Actually, if she lived the rest of her natural lifespan held in utmost esteem, that would probably not be enough to erase the steaming pile of pig manure that currently passed as her reputation. Nheras would see to that.

Ignoring the protestation of her stomach muscles, she got up and stripped off her clothes to find that the resonance ward over her heart was almost broken. Most of its lines had rubbed off on the inside of her tunic; what remained was smudged and half-melted from perspiration.

Nothing she could do about that right now. Rahelu bundled her filthy tunic and her somewhat less filthy trousers into a vague approximation of a square pad, then gingerly sat again: cross-legged, on top of her makeshift, stinking cushion, clad only in her breastband and loincloth.

She laid out Xyuth's gifts upon the bare stone with far more care, weighing down three sheets of his best quality parchment with the glittering black gem and setting out her writing implements. Each heartbeat it took to properly grind the stick of violet resonance dust into a fine powder chafed her like coarse sand.

It took even longer to work up enough spit to mix the powder into ink—her mouth was as dry as stone—but she persisted until she was as ready as she would ever be.

Carefully, Rahelu cupped the fragments of her Petition in

both hands and mentally reviewed Xyuth's instructions. Dredging up all the patience she couldn't muster earlier in the day, she closed her eyes, breathed in and out with the waves, and *listened*.

First, she heard the wind. The port city of Ennuost Yrg was sheltered inside the Kuath Bay, nestled between the Tsojo river to the north and the Suusradi river to the south, and its wide, shallow harbor was one of the best on the entire Ngutoccai continent. Here, above the Eastward, facing out towards the open Aleituan Sea, the salty breezes carried the creak of tensioned ropes, the flapping of a hundred taut canvas sails, and the syncopated tread of bare feet scurrying about wooden decks punctuated with the occasional sailors' cries as trading vessels made ready to dock.

Next, the sun. Golden rays tingled against her bare skin and she heard—felt?—them as pure vibrations in the ambient resonance of the world. She visualized the individual rays as strings of a great celestial harp, stretching across the arc of the heavens, and the vibrations as individual notes of the Starfather's unending symphony.

Finally, she pulled her focus in close and tapped into the resonance crystal on her left hand. Normally, she wouldn't need its power—most first-year Guild trainees could Evoke the resonance of a memory going back a few years if they were trying it on an object they were holding and had a personal history with—but she wasn't attempting a straightforward Evocation. No, she was trying to reconstruct a document (immediately after a Fortunement she probably wasn't qualified to attempt) that she should have been able to submit without delay and interference *spans* ago.

Thanks to Nheras, she was here instead of selling fish with her mother back at Market Square or catching and gutting fish on the sloop with her father, so they could stay ahead of House Isonn's payment deadlines; deadlines that hung as heavy as any chain around their collective necks—

Rahelu's focus wavered as her anger surged. This wouldn't have been a problem if she could go about the city armed. Forget niceties and House-born privilege; Rahelu would have stabbed the point of her spear right in Nheras's uppity Ilyn face, then smashed those jeering white teeth into pieces and then—

Her breathing fell out of sequence with the rolling waves and her resonance vision collapsed. *Stupid, idiotic, fish-brained excuse for a mage!* she raged inwardly. The sun had shifted closer to the horizon while she distracted herself with pointless revenge fantasies, and now only three spans remained before day's end.

She reluctantly wrested her mind away from thoughts of mincing Nheras into fish food and painstakingly regained her rhythm.

Wind.

Sun.

Crystal.

Complete, utter abasement.

Jumbled parchment scraps rise from a pitiful figure groveling on a dusty gravel road. Large and small fragments dance, torn edge reuniting with torn edge, until her Petition reforms in Nheras's hands.

It was working! She could have cried, she could have screamed, she could have leapt off the edge and soared on the thermals with the gulls—she was so exultant she barely hung onto her Evocation.

Rahelu anchored the past she had summoned to her resonance crystal, tasted blood as it trickled from her nose, and shifted her focus from her own debased figure to Nheras. Her

Evocation blurred and she cried out in alarm, but the crystal on her finger was only warm, not hot, so she pressed on and drew more power.

The vision stabilized against the back of her eyelids; cradling the fragments in her left hand, she reached out blindly for her writing implements and copied what she saw:

Applicant Rahelu
Guild rating: Graduate in good standing (accredited on the
15th day of early summer, 530 A.F.)
Seeking: Beginner
Projection: Elementary
Obfuscation: Elementary
Evocation: Intermediate
Augury/Fortunement: Novice

By the time she inked the final lines of the Guild seal and opened her gummed-up eyes, the air had turned cool. She came to, shivering, and twisted around to look behind her.

The sun was a dim red and half-sunk into the horizon.

Shit!

She nearly spilled her handful of parchment fragments (which would have been an unmitigated disaster) as she tried to dress one-handed and gather her things at the same time. The trousers she managed after some painful contortions, but she forewent the tunic, wrapping it around her possessions: original fragments, new Petition, Xyuth's gifts, and strange gem. It would be better utilized that way.

Her descent was an ill-executed slide down the north side of the boulder; her barefoot flight down the narrow, winding steps cut into the Eastcliffs was hardly better. She took entire sections in twisting leaps, trusting to her memory of which remained firm and which had become unmortared over years of neglect—and she only avoided further injuries by the Star-father's own luck.

No crowds impeded her mad dash through the city streets; most folk from the surrounding countryside would have started homewards spans ago. Still, Rahelu stayed away from the main thoroughfares—they would be full of palan-quins as House-born flitted from one society engagement to another—and stuck to a familiar path through the back streets and alleyways north of Market.

She was two blocks away from the Guild when someone grabbed her by the elbow.

"Nela! What have you been doing?"

Gods, she should have paid attention to the growing chill of disapproval, but she'd tamped down her resonance sense as much as possible to avoid risking resonance backlash, so she had dismissed the sensation as part of nightfall.

"Not now, anma!"

She tried yanking her elbow back, but her mother had the vise-like grip of a fisherwoman born and raised in Anuvelomaz and shook her like one of their fishing nets.

"Running around the city half-naked like a Free Territories savage! Where are your sandals? And your face—"

"Anma, later!" she said, her fingers digging painfully into her own flesh as she tried to break her mother's grip. "I promise, everything later. But if you don't let me go *right now*, there won't *be* a later."

Rahelu struggled beneath her mother's searching gaze. Saw the calculation in her mother's eyes as she inventoried and weighed every aspect of her daughter's current condition —one filthy tunic, probably torn beyond repair (why else would she be clutching the stinking thing to her chest instead of wearing it?); sandals, missing, presumably broken or lost (nela was always so careless); and the face, a score of scabbed-over scratches on the left cheek, dried blood under both nostrils, a mottled bruise covering half her torso that would be difficult to see in the fading light, but not difficult enough for a fisher—and the final sum tallied.

Her mother wasn't wrong; Rahelu *had* been rolling around in the sewers, fighting, but this time, it really wasn't her fault.

She hated dropping her resonance ward; hated how it peeled back the layers of her outer being until her inner inadequacies were exposed. As soon as she had mastered a passable ward, she had never gone without one. (Especially not at home. Her mother didn't need resonance skills; she simply *knew* how Rahelu thought and felt about *everything* and unerringly picked the most devastating way to dismantle her daughter.)

Rahelu drew her palm across the gritty lines of ash-and-oil over her heart, collapsing her resonance ward. She felt her mother's mental presence through their contact point of wrinkled hand to elbow, and she allowed it.

No, not just allowed it. *Encouraged* it. She summoned every single moment of hope and anger and frustration that she had kept dammed up inside since they had arrived in this stupid, stinking, House-born-infested city; she let all those roiling emotions flood out of her body and into the world.

Let them all know.

Nheras was probably off regaling her equally odious friends at some pretentious House dinner party with the story of how she'd finally put the Lowdocks brat from Chanaz back in her place in the gutters; more to the point, so was every other would-be Petitioner who had witnessed their brawl, so it wasn't even like this was new news. Anyone who was anyone in Ennuost Yrg was already laughing at her comeuppance. How could she possibly think *any* House would accept her?

It took a moment for Rahelu to realize that she was free.

"Hurry!" her mother urged in a shaky voice. "It's not quite full-dark yet; you might still make it."

She ran.

RAHELU THRUST her Petition through the gap between the closing Guild gates. Heavy oaken doors clamped down on her left forearm; she screamed, swore up a storm in Aleznuawei-thish and Chanazian, then threw in a few of the more unsavory expressions she'd picked up from the Free Territory sailors who caroused—often—in the Lowdocks for good measure.

Somebody on the other side swore back. Their vocabulary might have been limited to Aleznuaweithish, but their imagination was no less impressive.

"We're closed," said a different voice. It was low-pitched, female, and sounded familiar, though Rahelu couldn't be sure.

"I don't need to come in," she called through the gap, waggling the scroll she clutched in her left hand. "I just need to submit my Petition." Her arm hurt like it had been run over by a fully loaded wagon, but it didn't seem to be broken.

"Are you deaf? We're closed!" growled the first voice. "Come back tomorrow."

"She can't do that, if that's really her Petition," said the second voice. "The Houses won't recruit again until next year."

"Then she can fuck off and try her luck then. Our instructions were clear: we sit on our asses, collect the scrolls, put up with the mewling kits until the sun goes down, and *read* these damned things. I've sat on my ass until I couldn't feel my buttocks; there were scrolls enough to weigh down this stupid crate enough to give *you* trouble so that *I* can't go and take the piss I've needed to for the last two spans. And we're still supposed to read and sort through these bonfire starters—"

Rahelu guessed Guttermouth (unfair, considering what had come out of her mouth and what she had rolled around in, but she wasn't feeling all that charitable at the moment) was quite capable of continuing his verbal diarrhea until starrise, but she wasn't going to stand around with her arm stuck in the gate and subject herself to that torture.

"For the love of the four heavens, just take my Petition. I got here before you closed the gate, didn't I?"

"She has a point," Patience said, raising her voice to be heard over Guttermouth's ranting. "We were supposed to close the gate *after* sunset, not *by* sunset." Something tapped her arm. Another scroll? "And her Petition did technically arrive in time, even if the rest of her didn't."

Guttermouth cut off his harangue and muttered something Rahelu couldn't make out through the mostly closed gates.

"I'll concede that," Patience said. "But—" and Patience dropped her own voice so she couldn't be heard through the gates either.

Rahelu shifted from one foot to another impatiently, then bent and twisted her shoulders one way, then the other. The bones of her spine cracked as she arched her back, wincing as the motion pulled at her abused stomach muscles.

"If you're going to stand there and debate procedure, could you at least release my arm and let me in while you do that?" she asked. "I'll be a good little kit and sit in the corner until you decide. Or I can help carry the crate so you can go take your piss."

"I'll piss on you, you little wiseass," Guttermouth said,

but the gate opened all the same and Rahelu stumbled inside gratefully, rubbing at her arm.

The two mages on the other side of the gate wore the leather armbands of Dedicates; Guttermouth was an unfamiliar face, but she recognized Patience on sight.

"Anenje!" she blurted out, before she remembered that Anenje had long abandoned her Chanazian name for one that was a close Aleznuaweithish approximation. "Sorry"—she bowed twice and corrected herself—"I mean, Dedicate Tsenjhe. I apologize for my presumption."

"Look at you." Tsenjhe smiled at Rahelu. "You're all grown up. I didn't know you were here! Why didn't you look me up? Are your parents well?"

"They are," Rahelu said, feeling warm.

Tsenjhe recognized her! The Dedicate had asked after her parents! That was something Rahelu had not expected. The older girl—woman now, she amended—looked very different to the Anenje she remembered, the very polished picture of a Dedicate: clad in immaculate pressed dark trousers and navy tunic with the sigil of House Isca emblazoned on her right breast in copper thread and the fine longsword on her hip; with freshly washed hair that had been combed smooth and fashionably braided instead of lank, greasy locks hanging loose about her shoulders.

Every inch of her was as well-groomed as Guttermouth —*more* well-groomed, since he wore his expensive shirt of sky-blue (woven from the finest wool, its buttons carved from mother-of-pearl) in a careless rumple.

Tsenjhe looked as if she had always belonged; had never spent a day—let alone the better part of five years—diving for Elumaje lakegrass and shellfish, caked in mud and covered in insect bites. Even if her smile was the same, the two of them stood so far apart now that Rahelu didn't know how to bridge the distance.

Perhaps if her Petition was approved and she passed the challenges that followed...

But even then, as a Dedicate, Tsenjhe would outrank her for many years.

No, things were not the same.

Could not be the same.

She left Tsenjhe's first question alone. "Thank you for asking. They'll be so pleased when I tell them you did. I..."

Guttermouth glared.

Rahelu dropped to the ground with alacrity as she remembered her place. "Honored Dedicate, I am shamed. Please, forgive me, I beg you."

She prayed—she hoped—that she wouldn't get her second beating of the day, but she braced herself anyway for the inevitable kick in her ribs (*the left side, please let it be my left side*) or her head if Guttermouth felt like he had been sufficiently disrespected. A certain amount of initiative was tolerated in Aleznuaweite—admired even; if it led to healthy profits—but disrespect was not.

The kick she expected never came. She dared lift her head a fraction off the ground to peek through her hair: instead of looming over her, Guttermouth had stalked off to one corner of the courtyard to...

Oh.

Guttermouth might dress like a House-born, but he certainly didn't act like one. Rahelu got up and dusted herself off, straightening out the slight crumples in her rolled-up scroll. "He really is very nice, isn't he?"

"His bark is a lot worse than his bite."

"Can he do that? In the Guild courtyard, no less?"

"Keshwar can pretty much do whatever he likes."

She glanced at the crate resting on the flagstones beside Tsenjhe. It was packed so full of Petitions the lid couldn't be jammed shut. "You really have to sort through all these tonight?"

Tsenjhe shrugged. "It's not as hard as you think. The sponsored Petitions, those that we can verify are genuine, go in one pile; the rest—"

"—go into the bonfire," Guttermouth said, jerking one thumb in the direction of the firepit at the center of the courtyard as he adjusted his trousers. "Don't be so shocked, kit. There're at least five hundred Petitions and limited places for Petitioners. No House will waste time and resources on an unsponsored Petition; it's a poor return on investment."

Rahelu's heart stopped for a beat.

It had all been for nothing then. Leaving Chanaz, five years struggling through her Guild training—all pointless. Even if Tsenjhe and Guttermouth were willing to accept her Petition on a technicality, they would have burned it straight away.

Nheras was right. She didn't belong here.

"I...I'm sorry for disturbing you, Dedicates," she said. Her voice sounded strange to her ears; it seemed to come from so far away that it was like someone else's voice altogether. "I... thank you for your kindness."

Rahelu looked at the Petition in her hand, unsure of what to do with it. She didn't want to take it home; the instant her mother saw it, she would know Rahelu had failed.

She could leave it here to burn, she supposed.

That thought *hurt*, though. Nheras and the others had laughed at it, but she had paid in blood and sweat for her Petition. She doubted anyone else whose scroll sat piled in the crate before her—sponsors or not—could say the same.

She kept the scroll and faced the gate; it was all she could do to leave at a measured walk instead of breaking into a run. She caught another quick, murmured exchange between Tsenjhe and Guttermouth, a light *smack* as one of them cuffed the other, then footsteps sounded behind her, and somebody turned her around and took the scroll from her hands.

"Here," Tsenjhe said. She laid an arm around Rahelu's bare shoulders, as if they were children again, and walked her back towards Guttermouth and the crate. "Why don't you take a seat"—she nodded to the bursting crate—"while we take a quick look at your Petition?"

Numbed, Rahelu did as she was told and perched on top of the lid, holding her bundled tunic in her lap. Anenje, wonderful Anenje, was being kind, but Rahelu held no illusions about the outcome.

"Here," Guttermouth said with a frown in his voice. "What's this?" The tap of a blunt finger against unrolled parchment.

Rahelu looked up to see him grab another scroll—one that had fallen out of the crate—and rub its parchment suspiciously between his fingers.

"This isn't a genuine Petition," he said slowly, as he compared the feel of the two parchments. "The script is good, a perfect copy even, right down to the flaws in the imprint of the Guild seal."

He handed off the two scrolls to Tsenjhe, who stared down at her Petition, then switched his scrutiny to Rahelu herself, pinning her in place with his eyes. "Where did you get this forgery?"

"It's not a forgery!" she said. "It's—fine, it's sort of a forgery, but it's not what you think."

"You admit it then," he said. "I'm impressed; if I had been more distracted, I wouldn't have noticed. But how?" he asked. "How did you do this?"

"I had a Petition," Rahelu said, then continued in a rush before he could repeat all those accusations about forgery. "A *real* one. With a genuine Guild seal of authenticity." She fished the torn fragments out of her coarse bundle and held them out for him. "And *this* happened. I didn't have time to get another one."

Or the coin. Somehow, it always came back to having enough fucking coin.

"You were the commotion during eartharc?" Tsenjhe asked.

Rahelu nodded.

"Document reconstruction is advanced Evocation," Guttermouth said. "Even if we were to believe you—which I don't, by the way—your Guild rating says you don't have the ability to do it."

"Use a direct Seeking then," she challenged him. "Go ahead. You're about to turn me in as a criminal anyway."

"I'm not going to string a little kit like you up on charges of forgery for this," Guttermouth said. "What do you take me for?"

Rahelu blinked. "You aren't?"

"Gods, no. Do you have any idea how many idiots try to forge seals from sponsors? Some of them even manage to fake the proper resonances quite convincingly. If I had to arrest every one of those dimwits, I'd not have a moment to myself until the end of harvest."

"Enough, you two!" Tsenjhe reached around Guttermouth's shoulder and poked at the fragments in his hand. "Rahelu, if you really can do document reconstruction—"

"I can't!" Xyuth had been quite clear on that point.

"—or something like it, then I'll let you in on a little secret. The Guild seal is special; it remembers what it is, even if it's destroyed. Anyone skilled enough in Evocation to reconstruct a document can reconstruct a genuine Guild seal."

Guttermouth nodded. "You reconstruct that seal properly, I'll sponsor you myself."

Rahelu stared, open-mouthed, and glanced at his

armband. "But I'm a nobody and you're, you're—" She swallowed, hard. "You're House Ideth."

One of the four major Houses. First and foremost among them, depending on who you asked. Based on the economic fundamentals alone, Atriarch Ideth should reign over Aleznuaweite as the Exalted Dominance, even if Atriarch Isilc surpassed her in wealth.

He shrugged. "What of it? House Ideth values talent over bloodlines."

The Ideth trainees had stood out to Rahelu because they were the only House-born who acknowledged their common-born counterparts with polite nods, but she'd never noticed them going out of their way to befriend anyone outside the Houses. Guttermouth had to be joking.

"Keshwar's mother has a long-standing policy of offering recruitment bonuses to anyone who discovers new talent."

His mother? What did his mother have to do with anything?

"And," Tsenjhe continued, "Atriarch Ideth places a high value on her son's advice."

Rahelu's head spun. *Guttermouth* was the son of Atriarch Ideth?

"You pissed in a corner of the courtyard. You said—" She racked her brains, then repeated his Aleznuaweithish curses back, word for word, complete with his exact inflection and tone of voice. "I've been calling you 'Guttermouth' in my head the whole time."

Tsenjhe guffawed and slapped her thigh. "That's you alright." She held out Rahelu's rewritten Petition to him as she turned to throw the other scroll. It flipped over end to end as it sailed through the air and landed inside the firepit with a resounding *clang*.

Rahelu winced.

"Thanks, Tsen." Keshwar put on a wounded look as he

took the rerolled parchment back from Tsenjhe. "See if I buy you dinner again."

Rahelu blinked and looked again: how had she missed the way the two of them stood, bodies angled towards each other, the way Keshwar's eyes lingered on Tsenjhe's face?

Suddenly, Kiran and Nheras's earlier comments made a lot more sense.

A roll of parchment tapped her impatiently on one shoulder. "Well, kit? Can you do it or not?"

Rahelu scooped up the fragments of her old Petition and breathed deeply. It was harder to focus without the rhythmic song of the waves, harder to willingly conjure her memory of the eartharc's fiasco. She sweated, struggling to pull the whole vision together again in her mind's eye, before she realized she was doing this the stupid way.

She didn't need all of the Petition this time, just the seal. And Tsenjhe had said the Guild seal remembered itself.

Focusing her mind through her small training crystal (warm against her chilled fingers), she called to the torn remnants—unbroken crystal to crystal dust mixed with fine violet resonance ink—and rode the resonance echoes back in time to the last moment the seal was whole.

Her resonance crystal grew unbearably hot as the fragmented pieces of the Guild seal in her hand flew up and out of her hand, then melded themselves back into a seamless bit of parchment.

A heartbeat later, she cried out as the training crystal on her hand exploded, leaving a ring of scorched skin around her finger. (The finger itself, thank gods, was still attached to her hand.)

"Great gods of Heaven, Fortune, and Judgment." Keshwar kept swearing as he took the circle of reconstructed parchment from her hand. When he touched the repaired Guild seal, it shimmered under his finger, proof of its authenticity.

Tsenjhe smiled and patted Rahelu's sore arm. "You may have grown but you haven't changed one bit."

"If...if that's all you require of me—" Rahelu swayed. The ground was spinning. "My parents...they'll be worried. Please...may I be excused?"

Tsenjhe caught her just as resonance backlash set in.

"No," Keshwar said. "You're coming with us."

5

LOWDOCKS

RIDING ON THE INSIDE OF THE PALANQUIN WAS not the comfortable experience Rahelu had expected.

At least she wasn't alone. Tsenjhe, Keshwar, the greatly depleted crate of Petitions, and three meals in lacquered wooden boxes were also crammed inside—and the two Dedicates were intent on cramming *her* full of advice for the challenges tomorrow whilst they continued reviewing Petitions. How they managed to look at anything was a puzzle: the floating cage Keshwar had ordered—through a personal relay crystal no less!—lurched with every step of the bearers, causing the oil lamp that hung from the overhead hook inside to cast wild, swinging shadows, making her as queasy as some land-bound farmer who had never sailed before. Gauzy curtains gave her the eerie sensation of floating in a void that was only broken by the occasional, formless glow of a streetlamp.

"You're not eating," Tsenjhe said as she scooped a handful of fluffy white rice into her mouth, then wiped her hand on a small square of damp cloth that had been conveniently provided in one of the many tiny compartments inside the meal box. "You need to eat, or you'll collapse before you even make it out of the Guild's training yard tomorrow."

Rahelu looked around at Keshwar's palanquin, at the cool herbal salve that Tsenjhe had helped her apply to her bruises and the burn on her finger, at the warm, beautifully painted meal box in her lap. It had to have cost more than all of her family's worldly possessions: the delicate brushwork depicting swallows shimmered with resonance crystal dust, and the whole thing radiated a soft, enticing warm orange glow that made her mouth water. "I—"

"Swallow every last morsel in there, kit," Keshwar said, breaking open another scroll and touching his fingertip to the shimmering orange seal stamped on it. "That's an order. If I see a single grain of rice left, I will rip up your Petition and use the pieces to wipe my ass the next time I need to take a shit."

Rahelu lifted the lid on her meal box and stuck her hand into the warm (warm!) rice. The fragrant round grains were slightly sticky with a faint sheen of oil, and it tasted sweet on her tongue. Following Tsenjhe's lead, she wiped her hand on her square of damp cloth and then picked up a bite-sized piece of grilled meat. It, too, was sticky sweet, reminding her of the half-eaten stick of candied fruit she had had—once— when she'd picked it up after some wailing House bratling had dropped it in the dirt of the Temple district, but the meat underneath the tantalizing glaze was succulent and nicely salted.

"What're you planning to use for weapons?" Tsenjhe asked. "Spear and knife, I assume?"

Rahelu nodded. "And net," she said. "I might not have the chance to use it in the combat challenge, but it's good to have a backup. Not many will expect it."

"Good. Keep it simple," Tsenjhe said. "The Elders won't be looking for style, just results. Tomorrow is no exhibition match; the purpose is to see whether or not you can live up to the claims you've made in your Petition. No one cares how you win, so long as you do."

"Yes, yes, that's all fine." Keshwar waved one hand impatiently. "But that alone won't be enough. You need a plan. What've you got?"

"Won't know until I find out what challenges the Elders have set." She shrugged. "Unless you can tell me?"

The two Dedicates shook their heads.

"I'll try not to attract attention, I guess." She glanced over at the sack of approved Petitions beside the Ideth heir; one end of her Petition peeked out of its mouth. On the inside of the scroll, next to the Guild seal she had reconstructed, was Keshwar's personal seal, its elaborate lines stamped in green-and-blue resonance ink.

"No one expects me to be there. I'll stay quiet, look sharp, and try to be quicker off the mark than anybody else."

She looked around the palanquin again, trying to estimate the number of scrolls left. The Houses usually limited their annual intakes to some ten or twenty Supplicants in total, but surely there would be more places this year, given the Exalted Dominance's proclamation.

"One in four odds aren't bad; I've faced worse." Better odds than the ones she had beaten today.

Tsenjhe turned to Keshwar, one eyebrow raised in query. He took her hand in his own, palm to palm, in a very familiar gesture.

Neither Dedicate spoke aloud: they were clearly holding some sort of Projected conversation. The exclusion grated on Rahelu, but she bit down on her tongue and concentrated on mopping up the remains of her meal with the stalk of a steamed leafy vegetable that tasted like sweet grass.

She was letting herself get too comfortable. Whatever affections Keshwar held for Tsenjhe, Rahelu herself wouldn't be included—she was lucky that he'd even listened to Tsen-jhe. By all rights, she should be hobbling back to the Lowdocks on her own two feet, not being carried around in a palanquin like some pampered House-born, her Petition a smoking pile of ash back in the Guild's courtyard with the other common-born discards and she none the wiser.

Even if he actually was as impressed with her little Evocation trick as he pretended to be, it wasn't truly that impressive. Evocation was her best discipline, but her performance on Guild tests had been rather average. She couldn't match Ghardon of Issolm for speed or power, for instance: he had consistently been the first-ranked Guild trainee since they started, his Evocations so intense that they often seemed more substantial than reality.

And Ghardon was just a newly graduated mage. House Ideth was the largest of four major Houses; they had some of the most experienced, most highly skilled, most sought-after Evokers in the Dominion.

Who was Rahelu in comparison to that?

Nothing. Even as a Petitioner, she would be nothing, and she would continue to be nothing unless the Houses accepted her as a Supplicant, and maybe not even then. Only one in ten Supplicants would ever make it past their oaths of Supplication to swear their oaths of Dedication.

But that was getting ahead of herself. No sense in building a fire when she hadn't caught any fish.

The palanquin tilted and made a sharp left, which Rahelu recognized as the turn-off to the Lowdocks. She hastily wiped her hands, replaced the lacquered lid on her meal box and set it to one side, then tried to bow.

It didn't work so well inside a palanquin, but she wasn't about to try and stand up while it was moving. For a moment, she imagined the whole thing tipping over as she unbalanced it, crushing the bearers with its weight, and sending the three of them careening down the side of the Saltcliffs into the Aleituan Sea, Petitions and all. If the Ideth heir died in a freak accident due to her, it wouldn't matter *how* dead *she* was; Atriarch Ideth would probably Evoke her spirit back from the seventh hell and bind it to a crystal for all eternity.

"Honored Dedicates, I thank you for your kindness," she said. "I am well recovered now, and it is late. It is not far to my home from here, and I should not keep you from your duties." She hesitated, then went on to add: "Please, I beg to be excused."

That wasn't done. If a Dedicate of a House had business with you, you dropped everything you were doing and they let you go at their leisure. If Keshwar wanted to keep her here, or anywhere else, it was well within his right to do so for as long as he pleased and no one would question it.

Not even her parents.

They'd given up the right to live by Chanazian ideals when they'd made the decision to come to Aleznuaweite. That was part of the price they had paid for a chance at a better life.

Keshwar eyed her and frowned, reaching for the longsword he had unbuckled and set to one side when they'd gotten in.

Oh gods. She'd said the wrong thing. "Forgive—"

He rapped his knuckles firmly on one side of the palanquin in a coded sequence and the bearers halted immediately to lower it to the ground and open the curtains.

"...thank you," she said, scrambling out of the palanquin with Xyuth's bundle. She turned around to bow three times, properly. "I will not forget your kindness. It is more than I deserve and more than I can ever repay." She kept her forehead on the ground as Keshwar rapped out another coded sequence with his knuckles, waiting for the bearers to pick up the palanquin and depart.

The palanquin creaked and two pairs of booted feet landed on the bare rock next to her head. She looked up in surprise to see both Dedicates belting on their weapons.

"Hey Tsen, what do you say we go for a lovely stroll by the pier?" he asked as he held out the crook of his left arm to the other Dedicate. He breathed deeply, nose wrinkling at the stench of fish juices mixed in with half-dried dung (animal and human) carried up by the sea breeze.

"What a romantic idea," Tsenjhe said as she took his arm —she was grinning and looked as if she *meant* it. "Come on, Rahelu, you can show us the sights on the way home. I'd love to stop by and say hello to your parents."

The two Dedicates started down the winding path to the Lowdocks before Rahelu could protest. She trailed behind, worrying at her lower lip, trying to think of a way to dissuade them, but took care to stay within arm's length so anyone would see that the three of them were traveling together.

(An unnecessary precaution with her resonance crystal destroyed, her tunic a stinking, unsalvageable mess, and her sandals gone. Even the Breakers would let her pass with the barest of hassles.)

How would her parents react to two Dedicates showing up on their doorstep?

Rahelu pictured everyone crowded inside their squalid hovel: Tsenjhe and her father discussing the differences between lake fishing and open sea fishing (what else could they talk about?); Keshwar, presiding over the impromptu gathering from his splintered seat upon their only stool in frowning silence (what interest could fishing possibly hold for the son of an Atriarch?) as the rest of them squatted around the coals, chewing on slightly rancid, day-old smoked fish, until her mother noted how the two Dedicates cleaved to each other, forgot herself, and dared pry as to whether a consortship might be on the horizon.

Gods.

She needed to avoid the entire possibility.

They passed through Northend unaccosted, Free Territory mercenaries and street gangs alike keeping a wide berth from the two Dedicates who moved purposefully through the haphazard streets, with resonance crystal gleaming around their necks and on their armbands, their free hands resting on their weapons.

It had not even been a quarter-span by the time they reached the Nightmarket.

"Which way?" Tsenjhe asked.

Rahelu thought fast. "It is almost starrise, so my parents will be asleep already. I don't want to disturb them." She gestured at the inn twenty strides away on the next corner, its worn wooden sign just visible from where they stood. "Tlareth doesn't mind if I stay overnight from time to time, so long as I help recharge some of her resonance crystals."

All true words. She kept her breath even and thought of the warm hayloft at the Sable Gull (so much more comfortable than the patch of dirt in her parents' small hut); allowed her tiredness and her yearning to sink into the clean straw to wash through her resonance aura.

Keshwar studied her intently. She wondered at his thoughts as she wrestled with the dilemma of whether she ought to meet his eyes or not. Would he be able to tell she had omitted some details just by looking into hers? Would she be able to keep up the pretense while looking back?

Better not risk it.

"Thank you again for escorting me back," she said, bowing low once more, her gaze fixed on his boots. The polished leather was scuffed at the toes and now covered with slimy muck, even though they had taken only the main thoroughfares through the Lowdocks. "If you would like to see more of the sights, might I recommend the Seaspire?"

She named the only shrine to the Stormbringer in the Lowdocks. It was not a true shrine; just a giant cairn that sailors and fisherfolk had built with offerings of whatever they could spare from their pockets before they headed out to sea. No food and nothing too expensive—pebbles and rocks mostly; sometimes bits of smooth seaglass or whittled driftwood. Once, during a particularly bad fishing season, Hzin's consort had left a fine ceramic teacup—chipped around its edges and its painted design long faded—which had lasted all of a hundred heartbeats before a less devout scavenger replaced it with a lesser offering.

Rahelu's father usually left blood.

"It's a little further east, just south of the piers and unique to the Lowdocks." That was one way of putting it. "You can take the north stair back to the Highdocks, which has a beautiful view of the Kuath Bay on a clear night like this."

"Very romantic," Tsenjhe said, her voice full of good humor. "Stop fretting like a mother cat, Kesh. She'll be fine. The longer we linger, the longer it'll take to finish sorting those Petitions, and it might even be daybreak before we can deliver them to Maketh. And if that happens, you might wish that those poor buttocks of yours were still numb."

And then, while Rahelu was still looking at their feet, Tsenjhe did something that caused Keshwar's resonance aura to flare a very noticeable rose-red.

"Alright, kit," he said, lifting Rahelu's face up with one blunted finger under her chin so he could look into her eyes. His tone turned serious. "Listen."

Rahelu froze, transfixed by Keshwar's intense pale stare. Something—some *things*—flickered in the depths of his gaze as his perception grazed her resonance aura, light as a moth wing. The Seeking he had refrained from performing earlier?

No.

Something else.

"Kesh..." Tsenjhe's voice, too, held an undercurrent of warning. "Let's go."

He blinked once—eyes briefly unfocused, like someone who had fallen into mage trance—then released Rahelu's chin.

"May the Starfather's own luck be with you tomorrow," he said. "Don't let me down, kit. I've got a perfect betting record, and I'm betting on you."

Tsenjhe flicked the three fingers of her right hand at Rahelu—the Chanazian sign of well-wishing—then strolled off towards the Seaspire. Keshwar winked at Rahelu and followed, jogging a few strides so he could grab Tsenjhe by *her* buttocks.

Rahelu stared after the two of them, watching as their resonance auras melded together in a low amorous hum, until their figures receded into the distance.

That night, Rahelu dreamed of blades and blood.

6
CHALLENGES

RAHELU SQUIRMED AS HER MOTHER TUGGED AT THE hems of her borrowed tunic and attempted to smooth out the wrinkles. It was a poor fit; Rahelu was a head taller and broader around the shoulders and chest compared to her mother, so she had had to borrow her father's tunic. Yesterday's stains (sea salt, sweat and yes, some fish guts they had hastily tried scrubbing out in vain) were still visible. The thing billowed around her frame like it had a mind of its own, but at least it was serviceable.

Her own tunic had been cut up for rags; they couldn't afford to replace it.

"Do not fret, nela," her father had said, after he wished her the Starfather's blessing. "It will be a fine summer day; far too hot for me to wear my tunic. If the Stormbringer smiles, I will bring back goldtrout to celebrate your success in today's challenges." Then he had left for the sea earlier than usual, clad only in trousers and slathered in aloe and fish oil, whistling cheerfully.

"Stand still," her mother commanded. "Don't slouch;

shoulders back and chin up, like you have a spine. Do that enough and they won't notice anything else."

Rahelu seriously doubted that, but she straightened her spine and held her head high all the same. She shifted her weight from her right foot to her left again, closed her eyes, and ran through some of Onneja's breathing exercises. Her fingers itched to add a few more lines to the resonance ward over her heart, but she left it alone.

Doing anything out of the ordinary would only make her more vulnerable, not less.

"You look like—"

An imposter. An arrogant upstart. A waste of space.

"—Enjela, when she prepared to steal away the stars."

A compliment?

Rahelu's eyes snapped open to find her mother regarding her with a soft little smile. She didn't need Evocation to count the number of positive things her mother had ever said about her in all of her seventeen years; just four fingers.

Five, now.

Her mother passed Rahelu her spear; she took it and ran her fingers over the haft and blade, checking for rust and weak spots out of habit.

"Will you be alright, anma?" Rahelu asked.

Her mother moved behind her to belt her tunic with a rough length of spare cord they normally used to trim sails, tying the ends together in a quick-release fisher's knot.

"I don't have to be at the Guild until sunlight hits the upper terraces."

"Don't be stupid." Her mother tucked their best knife into the small of her back. "The early boat catches the tide."

She wanted to point out that the tide came and went on its own schedule, and all boats—early or late—were carried out to sea at the same time.

Instead, she cradled her spear in the crook of her elbow,

pulled their smallest net down from its hook, and said, "Yes, anma. I'll come by the market as soon as I'm done."

She hesitated by the doorway. Shouldn't there be something more for them to say to each other on a day like this? Aleznuaweites were fond of physical affection. Sometimes she thought that maybe she ought to greet and farewell her parents with a kiss.

"Don't dawdle," her mother said as she shoved her own sandals at Rahelu.

"Anma!" she said. "I can't take your sandals. How will you carry everything to market barefoot?"

Her mother's right hand (which still held one sandal) moved, but Rahelu was quicker: the light cuff meant for the side of her face sailed over her head.

"How else do you think? Does a person carry things with their sandals? Don't ask stupid questions," her mother said. "When I was a girl, we couldn't afford sandals. I walked a thousand strides through the mountains to forage before sunup. I've calluses on my fingers thicker than those on the soles of your feet…"

Rahelu hastily put on her mother's sandals, ducked out through their curtained doorway, and jogged down the rocky path towards the Lowdocks proper.

RAHELU LURKED at the very back of the one hundred eager-eyed applicants assembled inside the Guild's training yard. Nervous energy thrummed all around her in the ambient resonance as the eight robed House representatives inspected their tidy ranks with impassive expressions, and the way the yellow-green pulses prickled against her resonance aura made her want to hop from one foot to the other.

"Listen up, applicants!" barked the senior Dedicate in

charge. He wore the yellow-and-white robes of House Imos and the armband of a Guardian—a mage specializing in defensive applications of the resonance disciplines. "I will only say this once and I will take no questions. You miss something, you figure it out; either with your brains or with Evocation."

A hand shot up four columns to her right from the middle of the ranks.

The Guardian ignored the hand. "Each of you is standing here because you managed to convince someone of your potential to become a worthy member of a House on the basis of your abilities as an individual."

Hah. No one else here wore the plain, undyed tunic of a common-born applicant. Rahelu would bet all the sea salt she could harvest in a day that she had been the only one who had had to convince anybody. She almost snorted but turned it into a cough at the very last moment.

That earned her a glare from the Guardian and the applicants next to her.

She wasn't sorry.

This business of filtering applicants on the basis of sponsorship violated the principle of equality. If they were going to do that, then the Houses should have made it a mandatory requirement for Petitioning.

"There are two challenges before you, and your success in the first will determine the advantage you begin with in the second."

One would be a physical combat challenge; the other would test how well they could integrate their application of the resonance skills. Not real tasks—that would come later, for those who were invited to become true Petitioners—but something like the Guild's semi-annual examinations.

Since they had gathered in the training yard, Rahelu guessed the combat challenge would come first, using the tournament ruleset with victory determined by total points scored rather than eliminations based on standard or quick spar duels.

Made sense—it was a fair and efficient way to gauge the capabilities of a hundred applicants.

"Today, you need to convince us you can work effectively in a team."

What?

She must not have heard that right.

A team challenge? What was the point of a team challenge when offers would be made on an individual basis?

Though all of the applicants stood shoulder to shoulder in neat, uniform rows, squinting in the bright eartharc sun, the divisions along House lines were clear: the purple-and-black tunics of Isilc clustered together on the left side of the first three ranks; a solid wedge of Imrell's orange-and-white beside the yellow-and-white of Imos in the middle; pale-Ideth-green-and-sky-blue over to the right—

Everywhere Rahelu looked, she saw House colors and prearranged alliances, and that made her want to scream in frustration.

If Tsenjhe and Keshwar weren't allowed to tell her what the challenges were, how did the rest of the applicants already know? As if they hadn't already cheated from the very beginning, by having sponsors from the time they applied for entry to the Guild.

She just had to hope that being a team of one would still count.

"Our criteria are simple: demonstrate that you can lead and—"

The raised hand four columns over to Rahelu's right and —she angled her head slightly to peer around the head of a sturdy youth with shoulder-length red locks and counted—

six ranks forward waved more insistently and even bounced a little, like its owner was itching to stand up on tiptoes.

"—take *orders*," the Guardian said in a chill tone and paused.

The raised hand froze, drooped, then disappeared back into the ranks.

"You have full discretion over your methods so long as you obey the laws of this city and uphold the code of the Guild."

That ruled out lethal force but not serious injury. Rahelu tightened her fingers around her spear; her damp palm made the ash haft difficult to grip firmly.

"Those who perform satisfactorily will proceed to the next stage by invitation, issued on a House by House basis at the discretion of each representative. Only one in five of you will receive a formal offer to become a sworn Supplicant of a House. The rest of you may reapply next year."

One in five applicants.

The Houses were only taking twenty Supplicants, the same amount as any other year. A murmur ran through the ranks: clearly, Rahelu hadn't been alone in assuming the odds were better than they actually were.

It didn't add up. Why would the Houses hire mercenaries from the Free Territories instead? That was a lot of liquid assets to use up in plugging a temporary labor shortage. Wouldn't it be better to invest in more Guild trainees and Petitioners? That wouldn't require any outlay of coin, would give the Houses a more highly skilled population to recruit from, and by the time the new Supplicants earned out their training debts, new revenues from expansion initiatives would cover the increased payroll costs.

"For your first challenge: there are ten tokens in the city. Organize yourselves into teams. You have until high sun to find them all."

Orderly ranks broke apart into chaotic huddles as the Guardian marched back to his peers. All eight House representatives turned expectant eyes on the applicants and Ideth's representative, a Seeker by her armband, shook her head.

While the others were occupied, Rahelu snuck away. She was more than halfway to the gate when she heard footsteps behind her.

Rahelu spun around, spear forward, ready to fight Nheras and her cronies.

"Hey now, easy!" said the youth with the red hair, raising both of his empty hands. He looked familiar in his tunic of pale green and sky-blue, but she couldn't recall a name to match his face. "I'm on your team."

The pendant he wore around his neck had one of the largest focus stones she'd ever laid eyes on, with a swirling pale gray haze that moved around *inside* the stone. It had to be an attuned legacy resonance crystal—a priceless heirloom passed down through generations of mages in his family, all specializing in Obfuscation.

Was this some kind of joke?

"I'm fine on my own," Rahelu said. She kept her spear pointed at him as she continued retreating across the courtyard towards the gate.

He followed. "One person does not make a team."

"Please stop following me." She glanced over his shoulder at the far end of the training yard where the rest of the Ideth applicants paid rapt attention to their leader: a tanned girl with sun-bleached hair who stared in Rahelu's direction even as she issued commands to the others. "I think your actual team is looking for you."

"No, that's just Cseryl being Cseryl." He casually waved at the Ideth applicants without looking back. "She'll do her part and stall the other teams. Smart of you to strike out while everyone is still bickering over tactics. First mover advantage always wins, so I'm sticking with you." He grinned and something in his expression reminded her of Keshwar. "By the time they sort their noses out from their backsides, we'll have a long head start."

That was too many nice things about her in one statement and his resonance aura was a flickering yellow-green. What was he up to?

His grin faded. "Please stop looking at me like that. I'm on your side, Rahelu."

She almost tripped on one of the flagstones as her mother's sandals caught its raised edge. He knew her name?

Walking backward, keeping her spear aimed at him, and trying to sense his sincerity without a full Seeking was too much. She stopped doing the first, maintained the second, and asked him point-blank: "Why? I don't even know you."

As soon as she said the words, he blanked out his resonance aura with an Obfuscation barrier. Far quicker than she could have managed, but not before she got a brief glimpse of his aura dipping into black-blue.

What? What did a son of Ideth care if she knew him or not? She was nobody.

"Fair enough." He held out his right arm to her and smiled; there wasn't a hint of the hurt he'd felt in his expression. "I'm Lhorne. And when my cousin came to wish me luck, he asked if I would look out for the other applicant he was sponsoring."

Keshwar. Keshwar had set this up.

He hadn't simply sponsored her out of pity or consideration for Tsenjhe. When he said that he valued talent over bloodlines, that he was betting on her, he meant it—enough to make arrangements that would even out the odds against her.

Keshwar was the only reason she was standing in the

courtyard with Lhorne, instead of hawking spotted cod with her mother. If he had sent his own cousin to safeguard his investment, then she wasn't going to argue.

Rahelu relaxed her stance and then nodded. "Honored to meet you, Lhorne," she said as she clasped his arm. "Now let's move!"

He wasn't paying attention to her any longer—he was too busy looking back at the other House-born. And he hadn't let go of her arm.

"Come on." She tugged her arm back, hoping he would get the message, but his grip stayed firm.

"Not yet," Lhorne said, his eyes searching the training yard. "We should wait for—"

"Do as you like." She broke free of his grip with a twist. "But I'm going." Rahelu deliberately turned her back on him and started walking.

"Rahelu!" Lhorne called out after her. "This is not how a team works!"

Their Guild training had included mandatory group assignments. None of the House-born who had been stuck with her ever bothered to do their part. They didn't need to make up for poor grades, but they enjoyed taking credit for Rahelu's efforts all the same.

"If you agree with my strategy"—a strategy that had met with Keshwar's...she couldn't exactly call it approval since the Dedicate hadn't explicitly endorsed it, but he hadn't come outright and said it was stupid, so she was pretty sure he approved—"then you know that every moment we spend here is a moment we can't afford to lose."

Well, maybe *he* could.

"Yes, but—"

Rahelu kept walking towards the gate. Cousin to the Ideth heir or not, she'd be better off without his help if he wasn't going to listen to her.

Frustration bloomed behind her. Unformed, so not a true Projection, but strong enough that the leading edges of its resonance splattered against her back, as if Lhorne had flung a full bucket of warm water after her.

That was uncalled for.

Her left hand was already moving to make a rude hand sign, then she thought better of it. She straightened out crooked fingers and directed her own irritation through a sweeping, backward wave of her open palm.

A quick glance up at the sun told her a quarter-span had passed while he had distracted her. Rahelu swore, stopped trying for stealth and picked up her pace. Her brisk walk soon turned into a jog, and before long, she broke into a run, her mother's wooden sandals announcing her passage across the polished stones of the courtyard with a loud *clack-clack-clack-clack*.

The Starfather's grace was with her: she passed through the gate without incident. It was a relief to be out on the street, fading into near-obscurity once more as she joined the muted chorus of gravel crunching beneath sandaled feet and handcart wheels.

Heavier, booted footsteps echoed her footfalls, a matched set with the sense of heavy resignation gaining on her.

Lhorne had listened, after all. Should she wait for him?

Her instincts said no. He'd already cost them a precious quarter-span of lead time that she needed to make up for.

But another part of her rebelled, the part that was still chewing over his words about teamwork.

So she slowed down for a few heartbeats, just long enough for a quick Seeking back in the direction of the Guild:

Pale orange stars pour out of the training yard across the Guild court-yard in nine uneven swarms. They scatter—

Shit. She glanced left. Lhorne was right there, open grin and all, breathing easily as if he hadn't had to exert any effort to catch up. There was no trace of his earlier emotions— instead, his clear green eyes were bemused and seemed to dare her to do more.

Well then. Rahelu answered him with a challenge of her own: she sped up.

If he couldn't keep up with her, that was his problem.

7

CONCORDANCE

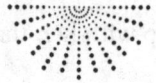

RAHELU SOON REGRETTED HER DECISION.

Lhorne *chattered*.

Constantly.

Even as they raced each other down the middle of the city streets of Northpoint, Lhorne kept talking at her the whole gods-cursed time. He had an opinion on the construction of every building on every street and relayed animated anecdotes about every person they passed on their way to the Eastward—from the shrouded figures inside the stately parade of palanquins to the gangs of street urchins who fled like rats into their boltholes at the sight of two applicants sprinting through the back alleys.

Only the Earthgiver knew how he managed to do all that without running out of breath in the slightest.

By the time they climbed up the Eastcliffs and sat cross-legged on the flat-topped boulder at its summit, her ears bled from the endless assault. Air rasped in and out of her throat until she felt like it was bleeding too, but she was not going to admit defeat by collapsing. Or by speaking and sounding as if she was winded, which she was not. She was just thirsty, that was all.

"Starfather, I'd forgotten what a view there is from here," he said, shading his eyes as he looked out towards the Aleituan Sea. Bright blue sparkles glittered in his aura. "It's been years since I've been up here to Stormbane's Rest."

Odd for an Aleznuaweithish landmark to have a Chanazian name. She closed her eyes and breathed with the ocean, irritated with herself for letting him distract her. Four spans was less time than she would like for this challenge, but she tried not to dwell on that as she fought to calm her racing pulse and regain her equilibrium.

"May I ask, oh wise leader of mine, what is your plan?" His voice had fallen into the rhythmic pattern of someone in light meditation.

"Oh, yes! Yes! Please, what's the plan?" piped up another voice from behind them.

Rahelu grabbed her spear and shot to her feet, switching to Seeking immediately.

She couldn't sense a soul besides herself, Lhorne, and the gulls.

"Who're you?" she asked, as she slowly turned on the balls of her feet. Lhorne had stayed seated, but he had to lean to one side to dodge her spear. *And why can't I Seek you?*

"Dharyas of Isca," came the reply. A moment later, a hand —waving in a very familiar manner—popped up from the south side of the boulder.

Isca.

Tsenjhe had made arrangements too.

Rahelu dropped her Seeking and the point of her spear, backing up to make space for her new teammate.

"Why did you two leave without me?" Dharyas asked. She had the delicate features of someone from western Aleznuaweite and sported long, spiraling lines of ritualistic scars on her arms. "We're meant to be a team!"

Rahelu looked away, out over the Kuath Bay, and braced herself for the inevitable: Lhorne would (rightly) put the blame on her, and Dharyas would expect some sort of recompense for the insult.

But Lhorne laughed and said, "I thought you might like to know how it feels to be abandoned for a change."

Rahelu jerked her gaze back to the Ideth boy.

He...he wasn't going to blame her?

One corner of his mouth quirked up when he caught her looking at him, then he turned back to Dharyas and put on an excessively sorrowful face. "I had no one fun to talk to last night."

"Liar," Dharyas said. "I know Nheras never left your side."

The corners of his eyes tightened briefly but all he said was, "Ilyn was very determined that no guest should want for company."

At that, Dharyas laughed too. "Then no doubt Bhemol was pleased by my absence. I feel sorry for you and Cseryl, Lhorne, but I can't say that I am sorry. Still, if I'd been a hair slower or"—she smirked—"less brilliant, I'd've had to waste another span to find you. Why, in the Starfather's name, are we all the way up here?"

Lhorne shrugged; clearly he wasn't going to save her this time.

"Uh," Rahelu said. "Sorry. That was my idea." Then honesty compelled her to add: "Actually, both of those things were my ideas. Sorry."

Should she bow? They were graduated mages now; the convention of treating all trainees the same no longer applied. But none of them were sworn to a House yet, either. Lhorne and Dharyas were mere ordinary citizens, like her.

Technically.

"You're forgiven," Dharyas said.

That…that was it?

"But you owe me," the Isca girl added.

Rahelu nodded, relieved. That was more like it.

"Hey," Lhorne protested. "Why does Dharyas get instant acceptance, even though she tracked and ambushed us, when I got the full interrogation?"

"You wouldn't have been 'ambushed' if you'd just waited for me like you were supposed to," Dharyas said. "Because then you'd have *these*."

She handed each of them a shimmering, thumb-sized brooch that matched the one pinned to her collar: a pretty spiral shell, decorated with a light coat of gold paint, with faint traces of resonance crystal dust mixed in for additional shine.

It looked like a cheap trinket, the kind sold by any number of enterprising dockside peddlers to visitors who had never seen the sea. But when Rahelu Projected a careful pulse of curiosity at the brooch, the embedded crystal dust glowed faintly and countered her Projection with a pulse of its own.

The strange glittering gem in her pocket hadn't done *that*.

"This is what you've been working on? I should have joined you instead of listening to Cseryl." Lhorne poked at his brooch, then lifted both eyebrows. "Very nice." He pinned it to the inside of his tunic pocket.

"You made these yourself?" Rahelu asked as she pinned hers to the waistband of her trousers.

Dharyas nodded. "I didn't even need Tsenjhe's help this time." Golden-pride positively oozed out of her aura. "These will block most Seekers unless they know exactly what to look for."

'Very nice' didn't even begin to describe the Isca girl's accomplishment. How had Dharyas managed to hide a fully self-sustaining Obfuscation barrier on such a small surface area? That was an advanced Imbuement.

"The effect is stronger if we stay within five strides of each other, though they're still useful if we're split up." Dharyas glanced at where they had put their brooches. "You may want to wear those someplace more convenient, or you'll have a hard time using the short-range message relay I built into them as well. And when I say short-range, I do mean short. Like within a hundred strides short."

A private message relay, integrated into a portable, self-sustaining Obfuscation barrier.

Both Rahelu and Lhorne stared at her.

Dharyas shrugged. "House Isca can't afford permanent cross-continental relay networks like House Ideth. We had to improvise."

"Aren't you afraid we'll steal the design?" Rahelu asked.

"You could try," Dharyas said. There was a mischievous sparkle in her eyes. "I doubt you'll have much luck though. Anyone who tinkers too much with the brooch will get an unpleasant little surprise."

"Forget the design," Lhorne said. "I've got to tell Aunt Mere we need to steal *you*."

"By all means—I'm open to considering any and all offers."

"Alright, alright," Rahelu said. "You're brilliant; we get it. Thank you for the miniature stealth relays. Can we please focus? None of us will get any invitations, let alone offers, if we place last in this challenge."

"We hear and obey!" Lhorne flashed that grin of his at her, all sincerity and goodwill, and it was unnerving. Now that she'd accepted they were a team, narrowing her eyes at him did nothing except to make his grin widen.

She shifted her gaze southwest instead, in the direction of

Market Square, as if two House-born waiting upon her words was a normal, everyday occurrence.

"The others are probably going to try brute-forcing their way through the challenge. They'll establish a Concordance to increase their range and power, then use a standard Seeking pattern to search for the tokens across whatever districts they've managed to claim."

While all Guild-trained mages had some degree of experience in combined workings, many preferred to work individually. Over time, they developed enough efficiency that they rarely needed more power than they could draw from ambient resonance or their personal focus crystals—particularly if they were sworn to a wealthy House or were born to a legacy family.

Unfortunately, the three of them didn't have decades of experience. Or time. Judging by the sun, a little less than three spans, perhaps, remained in the challenge.

Her teammates looked at each other, then back at her.

"Is that not how we're supposed to solve this challenge?" Lhorne asked.

Rahelu shook her head and plowed on, trying to articulate the thoughts that had been bothering her since she and Lhorne had left the Guild. "I have no doubt that—with a sufficiently large Concordance—some of the tokens can be found this way, but it's the obvious solution. Too obvious."

"Normally, I'm all for debating the alternatives, but I think you might be overcomplicating this," Dharyas said. "The simplest solutions are also usually the most elegant and effective; it's the complex ones that tend to blow up in your face."

"Are the Houses really going to go to all the trouble of organizing the Petitioning process just to see if we can perform the Guild's entrance test on a larger scale? It's a trick; the Houses have got to be looking for something more than that."

That gave Dharyas some pause.

Lhorne tapped his chin. "Let's say you're right. What would you have us do instead?"

They weren't dismissing her arguments just because she was the one making them. They were actually considering whether there was any merit to what she was saying.

It was a strange feeling, and she wasn't sure she could get used to it. Or that she even should get used to it. It would be better if she didn't; they were probably only listening because Tsenjhe and Keshwar had told them to listen to her.

But Rahelu would take what she could get.

"Well, from this vantage point, I can get a clear Seeking on an un-Obfuscated resonance signature anywhere between Northpoint to the Highdocks. A combined Seeking from the three of us should give us the range to cover all of the city comfortably."

"If that's different to what the others are doing, then I'm not following," Lhorne said. "We're still Seeking for tokens, with a Concordance."

"No, we're not." Rahelu smiled. "Everyone thinks this is a Seeking challenge—and it is, to an extent. But one resonance discipline, in particular, was mentioned specifically. And did you notice that we weren't given any instructions about what the tokens are?"

Lhorne looked blank, but Dharyas squealed and clapped her hands together. "I knew it! The moment Maketh said the whole thing about no questions, I knew. He ignored me deliberately."

Lhorne snickered. "And here I was thinking you were wanting to ask permission to—"

"What is with your family and piss?" Rahelu asked without thinking, then clapped both hands over her mouth and bowed deeply. "Gods, I'm sorry. I didn't mean to insult—"

Both of her teammates were laughing uproariously. Something inside Rahelu cracked open, and a breath later, she was laughing as well.

When they had all finally calmed down, Rahelu told them the real plan. "There's no point wasting our time sifting through every resonance signature in the city to determine if it's from a token or not. We'll Seek out the House representatives, then use Evocation to find out where they hid the tokens. And then"—she grinned and clapped Dharyas on the shoulder—"we'll test how well your invention works."

IT TOOK the better part of a quarter-span to establish Concordance, and it wouldn't have worked at all without Lhorne's pendant. (Rahelu had forgotten she had exploded her ring yesterday, and Dharyas's resonance crystal was too small to act as a focus for a Concordance of three.)

Tracking the House representatives, though, had been easy. Almost deliberately easy. By prior agreement, they focused their Seeking on the Guild training yard:

> *A single figure lounges against a stone column, its resonance signature an unmissable beacon.*

The signal was so strong it felt like a Projection-enhanced broadcast, the kind Imrell's Harbingers preferred. They followed its trail back in time, span by span:

> *A hundred and seven other, fainter points of resonance flow backward into the yard, then drift out again, until only the eight brightest signatures remain.*

"Ready?" asked Rahelu, her voice sounding slightly disembodied to her ears as she prepared to hone her resonance sense in on those eight signatures.

"Ready." Lhorne's mental presence was as solid and reassuring as an anchor, tethering her mind to the present.

"Ready," Dharyas confirmed.

The power of their Concordance diminished as the Isca girl pulled back, and Rahelu immediately struggled to hold all eight signatures in her mind at once.

Each one had to be kept distinct from the others, or their Evocation would look like a scrambled mess, but it was like trying to catch eight wriggling redfins bare-handed. As soon as she internalized one signature, the other seven would hammer against the inside of her skull, cutting through her concentration.

Their Evocation shivered until Lhorne dragged more power into their Concordance from his pendant. She felt him split his focus—constructing miniature Obfuscation barriers around each signature, tiny dampeners that made the clashing resonances more bearable. Enough for her to lock on to all eight signatures at last.

"Go," he said, his tone strained.

Rahelu slowly pushed the Evocation another span back in time:

> Eight stars wind their way across the city—alone, in pairs, and once, four of them spiral around the Temple district and meet in the Shrine to the Skymother—then reunite at their point of origin in the Guild's training yard.

"Got it!" Dharyas said. "You can stop now."

Their Concordance collapsed and Rahelu found herself lying face down on the rock, eyes watering.

"Ow."

Her nose was bleeding again, but it wasn't broken. She hoped.

"Ow," Lhorne agreed.

"Very ow," Dharyas wheezed.

Rahelu turned her head with an effort to look at her team-mates and her physical vision fuzzed between normality and the after-echoes of the Evocation:

A trail of phantom Lhornes wobble, fall over backward, and collide with the phantom Dharyases scribing frantic lines on a dozen sheets of parchment.

Past and present warred in Rahelu's vision until the present solidified into a heap of tangled figures—Lhorne's legs hung over the western edge of the boulder while Dharyas was half-crushed beneath his shoulders.

Lhorne rolled over so Dharyas could breathe. "What did you do to push yourself so close to resonance backlash?" He heaved himself back up onto the boulder with obvious effort and rested his forehead on rough granite. "Try to raise Dethi-ram's shade?"

Rahelu wanted to throw up. "Sorry," she croaked. "I didn't know it would be that...nauseating."

She forced herself vertical anyway (and only threw up a little in her mouth, which she spat out into the bay). They were losing time; Nheras and the others must be searching by now.

The three of them stared at the whorl of lines Dharyas had drawn. The precise lines crisscrossed the entire city and appeared almost random; there wasn't any obvious discern-able pattern to the paths that Rahelu could see.

But each of those signatures had stopped once—two of them twice—during the course of their journeys, and Dharyas had marked every stop in her careful hand. Four

were clustered together in a five-block radius inside the
Temple district; the rest were scattered throughout the city.

"Huh," Lhorne said, then his expression cleared and he
chuckled. "So Maketh does have a sense of humor!"

What?

"If he does, then I'm not seeing it," Dharyas said.

Rahelu agreed. "Do we go straight for the cluster?"

Lhorne shook his head. "You were right; the Houses
aren't looking for obvious solutions. This is a trap. Specifically, it's Csonnyrg's Trap—it's one of the lesser-known
Obfuscation formations, usually used for guarding treasuries,
that sort of thing—and the tokens are its connected anchors.
The first six are safe to touch; there's one key and five decoys
—and now that we know their approximate location, finding
them won't be a problem—but that cluster of four is the
lynchpin that locks the formation together. If we pull those
out of position in the wrong order, every single anchor will
start broadcasting, and this challenge will turn from a skilled
hunt into open chaos in a heartbeat."

"So it is." Dharyas closed her eyes briefly. Rahelu waited
for the telltale whisper of the Isca girl's Seeking brushing
over her aura but she felt nothing. Not even the slightest of
shivers.

Those brooches really were something.

"The only way to dismantle the barrier properly is to find
the key—and then follow the correct order of operations."
Lhorne's clear green eyes gleamed. "We get that right, we get
all of the tokens."

All of them?

Rahelu had been aiming to secure just one token. Perhaps
three—one for each of them—at the most. Going for all ten
seemed ridiculously ambitious and impossible, and yet...

"Who else might be able to figure this out?" Rahelu
asked.

"Isonn, of course," Lhorne said, then he reconsidered. "Perhaps not. They have numbers on their side and more combat experience. They'll prefer to shadow the other teams until someone with more strength than brains finds a token, then Isonn will bring their whole hunt-circle down on them without mercy. Isca's with us—"

"And you're so very blessed to have me," Dharyas said, without breaking her Seeking trance.

"—and the rest of the Houses don't have anyone with the necessary skill level in both Obfuscation and Evocation." He grinned at Rahelu. "And with these"—he tapped his brooch—"they can Seek all they like but they won't find us. This challenge is ours."

Typical House-born arrogance; he was counting his profits before he'd even realized them.

"You don't think Ghardon could do it?" Anything Rahelu could Evoke, Ghardon could Evoke. And he would do a better job of it too.

"Issolm might be able to find the tokens," Lhorne said, "but as to whether he can safely dismantle the barrier..." Lhorne's grin grew even wider. "He's been ranked behind Jhobon of Imrell for years."

"And us," Dharyas said. She opened her eyes to study the ten points connected by a mess of swirling lines.

"Imrell won't be able to find the tokens, except by conventional means, and then they'll have Cseryl to deal with."

Huh.

"We go in, get the key, disarm the barrier, then sweep up the rest." Dharyas gave a sharp, satisfied nod. "Simple as can be." Her finger tapped a spot on the parchment that corresponded to the fountain at the street that marked the border between Northpoint and the Eastward. "If this is the key, then we're in luck. The other teams have passed through already; only Imos and Isilc are still searching around Market and the Highdocks."

"Can't say for certain until we get closer. There are five variations of Csonnyrg's Trap"—Lhorne pointed out four other possibilities in Market, Sunset, Westgate, and South-watch—"and Maketh could have used any of them."

"That's a lot of ground to cover," Rahelu said.

All three of them glanced up at the sun. Nearly half of the allotted time for the challenge had lapsed. She mentally plotted and replotted routes in her head—from the looks on her teammates' faces, they were doing the same.

"We'll have to split up," Lhorne said. "Listen..." He launched into a hurried, highly technical lecture on how to identify a potential anchor and whether it was a key. Rahelu could barely follow half of it; she'd dropped Obfuscation studies after third-year in favor of Seeking.

The Houses had set this as a team assignment for a reason. She couldn't have pulled off that Evocation alone—and Ghardon couldn't have either, she was sure. And they couldn't risk leading the other teams to any tokens; they didn't have the numbers to hold off any attacks.

That left only one viable option. She turned the idea over and over in her mind—it was built on top of dubious assumptions and full of flaws—but she didn't have enough time to come up with something better.

"Dharyas?" Rahelu asked, cutting Lhorne off mid-sentence. "Can I borrow your clothes?"

8

BAIT

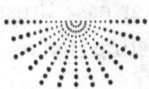

Second alleyway to your right, Dharyas sent through their relay. The Isca girl had stripped down to her shift, revealing a twisting network of ritualistic scars on all four of her bare limbs, and wore Rahelu's knife tucked in her boot. Covert stares followed her as she wandered through Market at the front of their group, one scarred hand idly flipping her own dagger. *There's something wedged between the walls.*

I see it, Rahelu sent back. She waddled over to the mouth of the alleyway—belly first, net tucked inside her own shift, and Dharyas's outer clothes clutched close to her chest—and made a show of leaning against the wall for support. And there, right at her eye level, was a small metal disc tucked into a gap between two bricks where the mortar had loosened and fallen out recently.

Putting one hand over the gap as if she were simply bracing herself, Rahelu reached out to the token with a light Seeking. It emitted the faintest of resonance signatures: a gradual ebb and flow so slight you would have thought it part of the normal fluctuations in the ambient resonance, except for its regularity.

She sent the signature to the others. *Fourth time lucky?*

No, Lhorne answered. *Add it to the pile.*

She drew the silver disc out of the wall and slipped it into his pocket with its fellows as he marched past. He wore her father's tunic well (even if it was a little too tight at shoulders and chest since he had pulled it on over his own tunic), and he looked far more at ease dressed in rough homespun linen with her spear resting against his shoulder than she had expected.

An image of a footbridge spanning the narrow mouth of an inlet to a fishpond in the Sunset gardens flashed through their relay. *See you at the next one,* he sent. He stopped to haggle with a vendor selling grilled rice dumplings.

Oooooh good idea, Dharyas sent as she sheathed her dagger and turned west towards the palace. *Get me the ones with salted cod, please. And no pickled plums.*

Sure. What about you, Rahelu?

He pulled out a silver coin and Rahelu felt an uncharitable stab of envy at the sight—that was more than enough to cover the overdue installment to Isonn.

No, thank you. Her stomach disagreed with her decision—thankfully Lhorne was too far away to hear its protest—and she scurried south through the alleyway before she could change her mind.

The connection between their relay brooches snapped as she left Market behind for the cramped streets of Southwatch. She hugged her 'laundry' close; kept her head down and eyes off anybody she passed, envying Dharyas and Lhorne their freedom to bear arms openly. Without her spear, her armband, her ring—not even her knife!—Rahelu felt naked, despite the fact that she was carrying more clothes than she had ever held in her life.

She flitted past at least three or four packs of scantily clad, ritualistically scarred crew members on her way to the common entrance to the Sunset gardens. Ennuost Yrg was full of new arrivals from the Free Territories. More and more of their ragged mercenary ships ported in every week, and their passengers lingered for longer and longer. Many sported resonance-crystal-studded leather bracers bearing the sigils of Houses Imrell or Imos. They wore House colors but behaved like brigands. One band eyed her hungrily as she scampered past, greed billowing off them to taint the ambient resonance like bitter smoke.

But this part of Southwatch was under Ilyn control (and heavily patrolled by the city guard besides), so they did nothing more than trail her at an uncomfortably close distance until she crossed over into Sunset, one nerve-wracking quarter-span later.

And...there! Something pulsed from the southwest. A scrap of an intricate beat, faintly sketched through the ambient resonance, the beginning and end of the signal abruptly truncated. Not enough for her to be absolutely sure, but it *was* coming from the right direction.

Rahelu ran towards the fishpond. She prowled its banks, searched through the reeds and underneath every ornamental rock, scoured every gap between the red-painted planks and joints of the narrow footbridge—once, twice, thrice to no avail. She combed through the pond's surroundings: the grass, the gravel, the trees—following the tantalizing, fragmentary signal that appeared and disappeared with irregularity in a different place. Every. Single. Time.

Stormwinds, earthquakes, and darkness! Rahelu threw her bundle of 'laundry' at the enormous willow tree next to the inlet and swore some more. Where was this fucking key? Where were the others? High sun was a little more than a span away, and they were no closer to finding the key than they had been at the beginning of the challenge.

She shouldn't have listened to Lhorne.

She should have insisted they grab the three closest tokens and run back to the Guild like rabid bharost slavered at their heels. And now she was alone, without a single token to show for her efforts.

Stupid, stupid, stupid!

Key or not, once she found *this* token, she was going straight to the Guild to hand it in for whatever partial credit it would get her. It had to be here—they had eliminated all four of the other possibilities—but the House representatives could have hidden it in a million different places in this small stretch of the Sunset gardens.

She kicked up clods of tufted grass—nothing—and shook the willow's branches—still nothing, except for bits of peeling bark and leaves that fell into her hair—so she yelled and followed up with several more well-placed kicks against the willow's trunk and lower branches.

The miserable overgrown plant swayed, then hit her back, right where Nheras had struck her yesterday.

Well, that had been utterly unproductive.

Seething with frustration, Rahelu pulled her net out from underneath her shift and plonked herself down in the middle of the patch of turf she had just destroyed. She sat on her hands (so she could not yank on the long, trailing strands that hid her from view) and closed her eyes, imagining the resonance of her beating heart as waves that swept through her body and flowed out into the world with each exhalation. As she drew in the next breath, she also drew on the ambient resonance all around her, pulling in the wash of resonance patterns emanating from the city's inhabitants with her resonance sense.

Blackforge, Northpoint, Eastward, most of Temple, and the Lowdocks were outside her unamplified range; but if she stretched, she could reach all of Sunset and half of the adjacent districts with the barest of Seekings. City block by city block, she sifted through tens of resonance auras at a time, looking for those that vibrated in sympathy with the mix of urgent purpose, ambition, and resolve in her own aura.

One was just a few strides away.

Rahelu's eyes snapped open. She lifted a half-numbed hand to peer through the silver-green leaf curtain and froze: a figure garbed in white-and-black crouched at the edge of the pond. The other applicant had rolled both shirt sleeves up, hands poised over the surface as though she were about to strangle her own reflection—but her head was turned towards the willow tree as if she had sensed Rahelu's Seeking.

Issolm. Issolm was here.

Rahelu didn't breathe—didn't blink, didn't so much as *think*—until the other applicant broke off her search in favor of focusing on the water.

Thank gods for Dharyas's brooch. Rahelu waited until the Issolm girl had removed her crossbow from her belt to place it on the grass beside her and plunged both arms into the water. Noisy splashes covered the rustle of willow fronds as Rahelu edged forward into the open, carefully gathered the edges of her net together, and readied herself to throw.

The net's stone weights clacked softly despite Rahelu's best efforts, but Issolm was far too preoccupied to notice. She swept hands through the water after an enormous carp, like a beggar digging through a tavern's refuse in search of a meal. Quick as any redfin, the carp darted away through the wind-rippled pond—a brilliant, marbled, silver-black, orange-edged flare—whipping its fellows into a frenzy.

"You stupid fish!" Issolm strode into the pond, trampling water lilies and lotuses. "Come back here!"

The carp obliged; it twisted abruptly and leapt out of the water, straight at Issolm's face. And Rahelu could suddenly sense two more overlapping resonance signatures.

One was the carp's—a blurry little cloud filled with sharp orange and green notes of pain and distress. It lobbed tiny, barely formed Projections in every direction as it arrowed through the air, bent on revenge against the horribly loud, giant monster invading its home.

The other came from the small silver disc stuck in the carp's mouth.

Issolm gave a little squeal and jerked back as she screwed up her eyes. To her credit, she didn't waver from her mission: she brought both hands up to catch the fish by its midsection.

Bad idea. The carp slipped straight through the Issolm girl's hands with a furious wriggle and gave her a parting smack in the nose with its tail for good measure. As Issolm cried out, the carp's resonance aura flared gold to match the sunlight on its scales—and it dove back into the water with a satisfied splash.

The Issolm girl sighed and shook her head as she regarded her slimy hands. "Bested by a fish."

It was so gratifying to see an uppity House-born make the kind of mistake Rahelu had known to avoid since she was a four-year-old child.

She couldn't help herself; she snickered.

Shit.

Rahelu burst into motion, holding her net to one side as she ran. The Issolm girl spun—saw Rahelu—and immediately sprinted for her loaded crossbow.

Shit, shit, *shit!*

Issolm scrambled out of the pond and snatched up her crossbow.

They were seven strides apart.

A fair, if less-than-ideal, range for a net.

Deadly, for a crossbow.

Rahelu had no choice.

She threw her net—it spread out as it flew, a circle four strides across—then she threw herself to the right as Issolm pulled the trigger.

CLICK!

A heartbeat later, a crossbow bolt slammed into the ground. It exploded one of the clods she'd kicked up earlier, sending grass and dirt flying, then—

Clack-clack-clack-CLACK!

—her net wrapped itself around the other girl and Issolm toppled over on the grass.

"Hey, fisher girl." Issolm's voice was cheerful, as if she hadn't just tried to kill Rahelu. "Nice throw!"

"What in the eight hells was that?" Rahelu got up and stomped past the other applicant—and was proud of herself for only thinking about kicking Issolm in the ribs. "What part of 'obey the laws of this city and uphold the code of the Guild' was unclear to you?"

"Nothing." The Issolm girl wriggled in a part-shrug, part attempt to free herself. "I was aiming for your shoulder."

"Who brings a crossbow to a non-lethal contest?"

"Someone who's interested in winning." Issolm flopped around on the ground again. "I'm lousy with melee weapons. Say, how about you let me out?"

"No." Rahelu circled the pond with slow, measured strides, following a silver-black ripple in the water.

"I'll give you my word that I won't shoot at you again today," Issolm said.

"That's a poor trade," Rahelu said. "You won't get a chance to shoot me, if I just leave you in there. Whoever taught you to bargain did a terrible job."

"If it's a matter of price..." More rustling, followed by another dull thump. "Ten silver kez."

Ten silver?

"Fifty, if you help me catch that fish and give me the token."

Her mother's sandal caught on one of the ornamental rocks, and she stumbled. Pain lanced up through her knees—she bit the inside of her cheek and thought a whole string of Aleznuaweithish curses—then she leaned forward over the water as if she had planned to do that all along.

"No? An invitation to the Isilc dinner party tomorrow night. They say the Exalted Dominance himself will be in attendance."

She'd rather shoot herself with Issolm's crossbow than go to one of those affairs. Rahelu took a deep breath and scooped up a handful of white pebbles, scattering them across the pond. As she exhaled, she extended her right hand out (palm down, hovering just above the surface, as far as she could without falling in) with the gentlest of Projections: a cool, soothing, blue-gray mist.

"A kiss from my brother?"

Focused as she was on controlling her Projection, Rahelu's violent reaction to that ridiculous proposal slipped past her resonance ward.

"Oh he'll be so pleased to hear about *that*." Issolm laughed. "What about a kiss from me, then?"

Rahelu didn't answer that either; she was too busy holding her breath. There had been the briefest of flickers in the ambient resonance, accompanied by a *splish* that might have come from a fin.

"Ah well, it was worth a try. You know, this discussion would go a lot more efficiently if you would stop blocking me or just tell me what you want."

A cold, scaled nose stung her palm; Rahelu gently dipped that hand into the water to cradle the carp's belly. She kept her Projection going, wrapping the carp inside layers of blue-gray mist until the orange and green thorns in its resonance aura disappeared and its tail and fins drooped.

Poor little thing. She pried the token free from its jaw, then released her Projection, expecting the carp to swim off.

It lipped her fingers instead.

"Don't be so greedy," she said to it, pulling her fingers away. "That's how you got into trouble."

The carp leapt, clearly hoping to repeat its previous trick, but Rahelu had already moved well back from the edge of the pond. It landed back in the water—splashing no one—and swam away with a miffed little flip of its tail.

"Oh, I know!" the Issolm girl said, and there was a soft *click*.

Rahelu stiffened, then turned her head very slightly. Enough to see the Issolm girl standing behind her, just out of grappling range, with her crossbow in her hands and a wide, cheerful smile.

"The token in exchange for your continued good health," Issolm said. "That's a worthy trade, isn't it?"

"Doesn't say much for your word. You promised to not shoot at me again."

"It was a time-limited offer, and you declined it. I don't see how that's my fault. You can have thirty heartbeats to decide." She eyed the slow currents of ambient resonance wrapping around Rahelu and added: "I'll take any attempts at Projection or sudden movements as a 'no.'"

Rahelu let go of the ambient resonance she had gathered immediately.

Uh, guys? Are you there?

No one answered.

A chill ran down her spine. How could she have been so stupid? The two House-born were obviously friends—they had every single token they'd gathered over the last span; her weapons; her father's tunic. She'd given it all to them, with nary a second thought. A little banter, brief pretense at including her in their friendship...and she'd taken the bait, too shortsighted to recognize the hook dangling in front of her.

"...eighteen. Nineteen..."

No spear, no net, and no knife.

And no backup.

The pond was too shallow; both the willow and the foot-bridge were too far, and there was no other cover—the orchards were at least two hundred strides north.

"Twenty-five—"

"Alright," Rahelu said, holding up the token. She looked her opponent straight in the eyes. "I need some assurances first."

"Wise decision." Issolm beamed. "Much nicer working together, don't you think?"

"Swear you won't shoot me from the moment I let go of this token until the end of this challenge."

Issolm shook her head. "I'll swear to not shoot you for the duration of this challenge so long as you hand me the token peacefully and make no attempt to recover it."

Damn.

"I'll relinquish the token if you drop your crossbow in the pond."

"I don't think so." But the Issolm girl did drop the crossbow to her side as she held out her hand.

The moment Rahelu stepped forward, the crossbow swung back up.

"Don't come any closer."

They stared at each other, at an impasse, both of them all too conscious of the sun climbing to its zenith overhead.

"Here," Rahelu said, moving her hands very, very slowly, towards the seashell brooch pinned to her shoulder. "Let's make a show of good faith." She undid the clasp with fingers that felt too stiff, curling the fourth and fifth fingers of her right hand over a clammy palm. "I will toss my Obfuscation barrier away"—she gestured over the other applicant's shoulder, in the direction of the orchards—"if you put your crossbow on the ground. Agreed?"

"On three," Issolm said. "One." She sank to the ground in a slow crouch.

"Two." Rahelu drew back her arm.

"Three."

As Issolm let go of her crossbow, Rahelu threw.

Her opponent's eyes tracked her hand, then widened as two glittering objects—one gold, one silver—arced through the air and towards the orchards. "You—"

Rahelu ran forward, kicked the crossbow into the pond and kept running as she heard the other girl curse and scramble to follow. They dashed across the wooden planks of the footbridge, the hollow footfalls of her mother's sandals and Issolm's boots reverberating as loud as thunderdrums, sending nesting jays shrieking into the air from the nearby willows.

Beside her, the Issolm applicant ran with one outstretched hand, already Seeking—somehow maintaining focus while skirting fallen branches and evading Rahelu's attempts to shoulder her aside.

Ahead of them, two people burst through the orchards.

One was bare-limbed and wore her dark locks pulled back in a single tail. She lifted a hand, and the only warning they got was a brief flash of sunlight before a steel dagger hurtled through the air.

It split their trajectory—Rahelu dodged left as Issolm veered right—and that was enough to let the second, spear-wielding newcomer dash forward and scoop up the token.

Issolm skidded to a stop in front of him, just outside spear range.

So did Rahelu.

"And that makes six." Lhorne grinned at Rahelu and winked. He flipped the silver disc in the air before tucking it away in his pocket. "Nice work, Rahelu." He strode over to her without hesitation and held out her spear, haft first.

"Thank you," she said, her voice shaking. She clutched her spear like a lifeline. *Never again*, she swore, she was never going without a weapon, ever again.

"Six?" Issolm whistled. "What did you do to my brother?" She closed her eyes in Seeking, seemingly unafraid of being attacked mid-trance, and added, with a slight wrinkle of her nose: "And what in the four heavens are you wearing?"

"I did nothing," Lhorne said blandly. "He did it all himself." His mouth twitched, but he said no more as he took off his borrowed tunic and returned it to Rahelu. There was a dark smear on the front, and as she pulled it over her head, she caught a whiff of dog piss and rotten eggs.

What had he been doing?

"Not all," Dharyas called out from behind Rahelu, reclaiming her dagger. The Isca girl continued searching through the grass, one hand on the brooch pinned to her collar. "I helped."

Issolm's eyes flew open. "You didn't!" she gasped, and then she broke out laughing. "Oh, he's in such a state. I ought to swear revenge, for the honor of House Issolm, or some such thing, but this is just too good. Next time, you should let me help. In fact..." She grinned as she looked from Lhorne to Rahelu. "I could be of help right now."

Dharyas's scoff was audible, even from fifty strides away. "Since when does Issolm volunteer to help anybody?"

"Why, all the time. It's better to work together when our interests align," Issolm said. "There's still four more tokens out there—and I know where they are."

"So do we." Rahelu leveled her spear at the Issolm girl. "I don't see why we need your help."

"Perhaps you don't. But I do think you'll be wanting my help for the next challenge. Even Ilyn has a bigger team than you do."

The next challenge? Rahelu found herself at a loss for words. She hadn't so much as thought about the next challenge; she'd been far too focused on not losing this one.

Lhorne studied the Issolm applicant intently. Without her brooch, Rahelu wasn't party to his silent conference with Dharyas, and she didn't know him well enough to read the expressions flitting over his face.

She did, however, feel him reaching out to Issolm with a Seeking of his own, so she did the same: the Issolm girl's aura was a confident, steady yellow, through and through.

"Elaram," he said. "If we let you join us, do you swear to join our team wholeheartedly, without any ulterior motives?"

"Yes." No hesitation whatsoever.

"Will you swear to follow my instructions?"

"Yes." Not a single flicker in her resonance aura.

"Even if those instructions require you to oppose others of Issolm?"

"Yes." Elaram pouted at him. "Really, Lhorne, what do you take me for?"

"No reflection on you," Lhorne said, his voice light. "Just doing my due diligence."

"And?"

He glanced at Rahelu, as if to ask permission.

If she said no, would he refuse Elaram, just on Rahelu's say so? She looked around for Dharyas, but the Isca girl was all the way back at the willow, getting dressed. She looked at Elaram. The Issolm girl gave Rahelu a dimpled smile and a friendly wave, her resonance aura shining as pure and clear as a mountain spring.

Rahelu settled on a noncommittal shrug.

"Alright then," Lhorne nodded to Elaram. "First instruction: Imos and Imrell are prowling around just south of Market. Go draw them off."

"Very well," Elaram said. "Can you loan me a weapon?" Then, with wide-eyed innocence: "I've misplaced mine."

Lhorne sighed, unclipped his dagger from his belt, and handed it over.

"Thanks!" Elaram flashed him a bright, sunny smile. "See you back at the Guild." She darted east without a backward glance.

"Was that wise?" Dharyas asked as she rejoined them, looking like an applicant of House Isca once more. She held out Rahelu's brooch and net (she, too, smelled faintly of sulfur and urine), and Rahelu took them gratefully. "Cseryl's not going to like this."

"She was sincere," Lhorne said. "Would you have us turn down an advantage?"

"Are you sure Elaram will be an advantage?" Dharyas retorted.

"She was sincere," Lhorne repeated. "Come on, let's hurry."

"Yes, let's," Rahelu said, striking northeast towards the Guild. She had gone ten strides before she realized the other two hadn't followed. "What are you waiting for? We've got to get back now; there's only half a span left."

"And four more tokens," Lhorne said. "Issolm were the only ones who were even close. Now that Elaram's on our side, they won't be getting anywhere. Ilyn have set up a cordon around the general area, but they can't pinpoint the exact location—the fact that there are four tokens is confusing them."

"If that's so, then we've already won," Rahelu said. "Six tokens recovered out of ten is a sound victory by any measure, even if Nheras and her pack get the last four. Assuming they can even find them by high sun."

"Sure success for uncertain gain is a poor trade," Dharyas quoted.

Gods be praised; at least one of her teammates was reasonable.

"A House that risks nothing is a House that will soon be surpassed," Lhorne countered.

"True," Dharyas conceded and identical, matching wicked expressions spread across the two House-born applicants' faces.

Oh no. She was not risking her family's future for the sake of his ego. She pointed her spear at Lhorne as she stalked over, opened her mouth to demand back the last token, and to tell him he could go straight to—

"Temple is just one district over," he said, green eyes alight and not fazed in the slightest, "and we have the key. Are you really going to give up when we're this close?"

———

RAHELU FLATTENED herself back to back against a statue, and peered through the gap underneath its left armpit at the perimeter Nheras had set up. Four applicants wearing the red-and-cream of House Ilyn, including Bhemol and Kiran, stood sentry just inside the main entrance to the Skymother's Shrine. Nheras herself was tapping her foot impatiently as she followed an Isilc applicant from one altar to another. She looked like she wanted to kick over the piled offerings she passed by out of frustration.

Why do I have to be bait? Rahelu sent, gripping her spear tightly in her right hand. Communication through a resonance crystal relay was akin to Projection and, right now, it was extremely unsatisfying—she wanted to vocalize those words with a hiss.

Because you've got the most experience with bait! Lhorne sent. She could picture the grin on his face.

A fisher joke? Really?

Just when she was starting to think he might not be like the other House-born too.

Oh, come on, where's your sense of humor?

You'll have to work a lot harder if you want it to show up. Why can't Dharyas be bait? Ilyn has no love for Isca either.

Everyone knows that Nheras's hatred for you has no bounds, Dharyas sent. *Besides, did you take fourth-year Obfuscation studies?*

She hadn't. She'd failed the Intermediate level examinations for Obfuscation twice and decided to focus on her private study of resonance wards instead, even if it wasn't something the Guild taught. Wards didn't blow up in her face if she got them wrong and add the replacement value of any destroyed resonance crystals to her Guild debt.

Now stop stalling, Lhorne sent. *The sooner you do this, the sooner we can return to the Guild.*

I should have stabbed you both when I had the chance.

And do without my brilliance?

Maybe not. They couldn't have secured any of the six tokens they had so far without Dharyas's invention.

I should have stabbed Lhorne when I had the chance, Rahelu amended. She resisted the urge to touch the throbbing bruise across her stomach, tried to stem the rising tide of panic at the thought of Kiran running her down and pinning her against the walls of the shrine's labyrinthine hallways. Every muscle in her body locked up. If she walked out there, alone…

Some of her emotions must have leaked through the relay because the other two dropped their banter and turned serious.

You can do this, Dharyas sent. *You just have to buy us enough time to dismantle the barrier. Four hundred heartbeats, no more.*

"Where is it?" Nheras demanded, as her aura bled from an impatient yellow-orange to a dangerous dark red. Her edged voice echoed oddly around the shrine. "I swear by the Skymother, if you've been wrong the whole time—"

Remember we're a team, Lhorne added. *We won't leave you to face them alone.*

"For the last time, I'm not wrong. Either shut up so I can work, or take a look yourself!" the Isilc applicant snapped back, his right hand going to the handle of the coiled whip on his belt. "The resonance signature is moving, alright?" He looked like he wanted to gouge his own eyes out. "Every time I think I've got a lock on it, I pick up a stronger resonance from another direction."

Rahelu took a deep breath and moved out from behind the cover of her statue. "Looking for this?"

She held up the first token they had found and tossed it casually in her left hand. It glinted softly as it caught the light from the many candles illuminating the shrine before she snatched it out of the air.

"Fish guts," Nheras said flatly. Her eyes slitted as she gestured, Projecting a wave of curiosity that swept out from her hand and flooded the shrine. "I told you to stay out of my life."

Belatedly, Rahelu tried to raise the most basic of Obfuscation barriers, but Nheras was leaving nothing to chance: the Ilyn girl drew as much power as she could from her focus stone. The tidal wave of resonance crashed into Rahelu, obliterated her pathetic attempt at a barrier, and overloaded the Obfuscation barrier in Dharyas's brooch instantly, leaving Rahelu defenseless against Nheras's emotional assault—her personal resonance ward was directional and designed to contain her emotions, not withstand external resonance.

Stupid! Stupid, stupid, *stupid*, to get so complacent just because Dharyas's brooches had worked so well all eartharc. Nheras was...Nheras was...

Nheras was a wonder. The gods' gift to the world. No other person in existence was so fascinating, so worthy of study, as Nheras Ilyn. Her face was utterly captivating; her...

"Give me that token," Nheras said, holding out a glorious hand. Slim fingers, every one beringed, beckoned her closer, and Rahelu was thrilled at the idea that she could make Nheras happy, that Nheras would allow her to approach and—

Lhorne and Dharyas slipped through the doorway behind Nheras. *We're in!* he sent, and the sudden mental intrusion shook her out of her trance four strides away from Nheras.

The distance was too far away for the Ilyn girl, who had drawn her baton as soon as her Projection was broken.

But Nheras was well within the range of Rahelu's spear.

And Rahelu did not hesitate. She shifted her spear in her grip, holding it two-handed in a basic staff fighting stance, both feet planted wide, and struck. The butt of her weapon cracked against Nheras's right temple, and Rahelu followed up with a quick Projection of her own—a diluted measure of her earlier nausea.

The combined attack should have stunned Nheras at the very least, yet the Ilyn girl only dropped to her knees, wobbling.

All of Rahelu's impotent rage from yesterday boiled in her veins and screamed for her to attack again. (*Stab her with the pointy end!* it shrieked, in complete disregard for the rule about not using lethal force.) Her muscles twitched, primed for the follow-through that would shatter Nheras's perfect, white teeth forever. She took another step, and another, lifted her spear and—

Something whistled through the air, arrested her spear mid-thrust, and ripped it out of her hands.

Rahelu had forgotten about the applicant from House Isilc. With a quick twist of his wrist, his whip tossed her spear to one side, where it clattered against a mural of a woman whose visage spanned the sky. Behind him, the other four applicants from Ilyn who had been guarding the main entrance arrived at a hard run.

They took in the situation at a glance—five-to-one odds (Nheras was still doubled over on the ground)—and charged.

Rahelu turned tail and bolted out of the atrium and down the east corridor, running for one of the side entrances.

Mission accomplished. Are you guys done?

Almost. Two down, two to go.

She reached an intersection, hesitated for a fraction of a heartbeat, then took the right-hand corridor.

Find them yet?

Another intersection. This time, she went left, trying to keep heading east.

Dual sensations came through the relay. Rahelu's vision temporarily tripled: a mirrored vision of two tokens resting on a bronze altar overlaid on top of the corridor she ran through.

Lhorne and Dharyas were arguing about which token needed to be removed first.

Her eyes blurred, and she slammed her left shoulder into the sharp corner of the corridor as she turned too early.

I'm a little busy! Rahelu sent back along with a healthy surge of panic as she recovered maladroitly. She started scanning the corridor through her tripled vision for some other avenue of retreat. *Fuck the order of operations; just grab them both at the same time and LET'S GET OUT OF HERE.*

Apprehensive resignation flashed through the relay, but the transmitted double vision disappeared as she skidded through to the end of the hallway and into a four-way inter-section where each arched opening was framed by a pair of graceful marble pillars. She grabbed the closest one to her right, using her momentum to swing abruptly around to hide behind it.

She tried to keep her breathing light as she listened for the sounds of pursuit.

Ten piercing bolts of alarm struck her—nine originating from somewhere to the northwest and one from her own fist. She dropped her token and gasped, clutching her head against the repetitive assault of the resonance beacons unleashed by Csonnyrg's Trap.

Oops, Dharyas sent. *Sorry.*

"Behind that pillar!" Isilc shouted, his voice reverberating through the corridor she had come from. There were three or four of them, and they were perhaps fifty strides away.

Can you make these things shut up?! She couldn't see straight, couldn't think—the alternating alarm Projections turned the hallways into an eye-watering nightmare that strobed between a darkened blood-washed world and one that blazed with white lightning.

Too late for that. Lhorne's sending was terse—a moment later, a heavy fatigue settled over the ambient resonance and the beacons were reduced to a muffled whine. *That's the best I can do. Meet you back at the main atrium.*

Rahelu's fingers trembled as she unhooked her net from her belt and readied herself to throw.

Three.

Two.

One.

Her net flew straight and true, and Bhemol and Kiran ran right into it. Its weighted ends clacked as they wrapped around the two Ilyn applicants and sent them crashing to the floor.

Rahelu didn't wait around to see who was coming next. She scooped up the fallen token (she yelped; it stung worse than a jellyfish), leapt over the struggling Ilyn forms, and darted through the open passage towards the atrium.

She was going to make it! She just had to weave through the double rows of altars, leap one half-flight of stairs from the dais, and the way to the main entrance would be…

…barred by Nheras. Who was armed with Rahelu's own spear and that eternal smirk.

"You," the Ilyn girl said, "are far too predictable."

"So are you," Rahelu said, the pain and panic in her aura masked with the barest veneer of unshakeable gray-blue calm. She smiled back and deliberately shifted her gaze to a point behind the Ilyn girl's shoulder.

Nheras's smirk faltered. Right on cue, Lhorne and Dharyas materialized behind her.

To give credit where credit was due: Nheras was fast; she'd begun turning the moment she sensed the confidence rolling off Rahelu.

But that wasn't fast enough, because Dharyas had already drawn her shortsword and clubbed the Ilyn girl over the head with her hilt.

"Come on," Lhorne said. "We need to run."

9

ALLEGIANCE

RAHELU AND HER TEAMMATES DASHED PAST THE Guild gates right at high sun with Ilyn on their heels. Isilc, Imos, and Imrell thundered across the open courtyard like a herd of stampeding bharost, while Isonn fanned out in all directions to cut off potential avenues of escape.

Lungs and leg muscles burning, Rahelu redoubled her efforts to reach the House representatives who waited in the training yard. It had been transformed—instead of an empty field, they had to skirt around Issolm applicants waiting in ambush behind rough-hewn, horse-sized, randomly arranged stone blocks.

Several three- and four-block piles looked like block fortresses assembled by a giant hand; the rest were scattered haphazardly in singles and pairs. Colored pennants—numbered one through ten—flapped in the breeze, tied to thin poles wedged between blocks. Each pennant pulsed bright red in Rahelu's resonance vision; the cloth must have been treated with resonance crystal dust to carry a Projection like that.

When they broke through to the clearing on the south

side of the yard, Rahelu discovered Ideth—and Elaram—had already returned. They cheered and clapped as Rahelu, Lhorne, and Dharyas sprinted over to the Guardian supervising the challenge and handed over ten tokens.

Safe! They were safe at last.

Rahelu turned and flinched. The ambient resonance was a simmering crimson; the training yard full of applicants aiming resentful glares. Glares that were filled not with daggers but a whole armory's worth of weapons.

Dharyas answered Ideth's cheers with a gleeful shout of her own, punching one scarred fist in the air. Lhorne was more restrained; he simply grinned and gave an exaggerated version of a street performer's bow.

Can you guys not make it worse? Rahelu sent.

The waves of anger billowing off Nheras had grown so intense that they bordered on Projections. And when the Isilc applicant with the whip stalked off to rejoin his fellows, he did so without a backward glance at Nheras—as if he had never been part of her team in the first place—and the ambient resonance in that section of the training yard rumbled.

They're going to hate you no matter what you do, Lhorne pointed out, *unless you plan on being less capable?*

Well, no. She couldn't do that and still get into a House.

So she straightened up, put her shoulders back, and lifted her chin in her best imitation of Nheras's arrogance as she followed Lhorne and Dharyas over to the disciplined ranks of Ideth applicants.

The rumbling in the ambient resonance spread. Seizing all ten tokens had seriously pissed off the other teams—to the extent that Isilc and Imos still scowled at Rahelu and her team instead of at each other. Whiplash, in particular, was grinding his teeth so hard that he could have chewed through stone, and when he caught her eyes, he jabbed the fingers of his left hand at her in a rude gesture.

Rahelu tucked her spear underneath her right arm and answered Whiplash with a two-handed gesture of her own that meant 'go fuck yourself' in the Lowdocks. Since it was a Free Territory hand sign, he didn't understand it, but the Imrell applicants who stood on the other side of Imos did, and they sniggered.

Don't let them get to you, Dharyas said as they settled in beside Ideth—Elaram immediately took the opportunity to sidle up next to Lhorne, heedless of Cseryl's displeasure. *Eventually, they'll have to accept reality.*

Rahelu doubted that, but she kept her thoughts to herself and her fingers gripping the haft of her spear as the Isonn representative stepped up on top of a stone block to announce the second task.

"For the next span, your objective is to work as a team to capture as many banners as you can. Your own banner is worth three points. Each banner you capture is worth one additional point."

Focus, idiot! Rahelu pulled her mind back from her daydreams of dropping Nheras and Bhemol and Kiran and Whiplash off the Eastcliffs into the Kuath Bay and did what she should have done the moment they'd completed the first task: assess the competition. She scanned the training yard and started counting teams.

All of Ideth (save Lhorne), she assumed by the united front they presented, would count as one team under Cseryl's leadership.

Five strides away, there were two hunt-circles of leanly muscled applicants from Isonn, perching patiently on top of stone blocks and chewing on wakeleaf with spears in hand, looking completely relaxed and unbothered by their failure in the first challenge.

On the other side of Isonn, the applicants from House Isilc had divided themselves into two smaller teams; whereas the Imos and Imrell applicants had opted for one larger team each. Then there was Nheras's team for House Ilyn plus their ragtag team of three (four, counting Elaram) that included House Isca, since Dharyas was their only applicant.

That was seven Houses and nine teams accounted for, but there were ten banners. Where was House Issolm?

And then she finally noticed that Elaram was not alone in choosing to ally with another team: all of the applicants in white-and-black had mixed themselves in with the teams from the four major Houses. No two Issolm applicants stood together, and there was always at least one standing at the elbow of the more commanding applicants from Houses Isilc, Isonn, Imos, or Ideth. If Rahelu hadn't been so preoccupied, she would have picked out Ghardon of Issolm at Whiplash's shoulder.

Rahelu poked Elaram in the back. "What is your House doing?"

"Hmmn?"

"How does the Issolm team work if you're all spread out like this?"

"What do you mean?" Elaram asked. "There's no rule requiring applicants to abide by birth allegiances when forming teams, just tradition. We're free to ally with whomever we please; choose whichever House we please." She beamed. "Of course, most of us do end up swearing to House Issolm. It's an easy choice to make once you see that none of the other Houses offer quite the same freedoms."

Does that satisfy you, Dharyas? Lhorne sent.

That is a very Issolm thing to do, Dharyas sent grudgingly.

But where's the tenth team? Rahelu sent, along with an image of the nine teams she had counted. *Successful as we were,*

I doubt it was enough to be awarded with a starting advantage of two banners instead of one.

Ah, Lhorne sent. *No. Here.* He returned her image—along with his sense of the Ideth applicants as two teams.

One banner per team and unequal teams. And suddenly, despite the presence of allies on either side, Rahelu felt alone all over again. Across the yard, House Imos huddled close with its vassal, Imrell, already planning.

"You may use any means at your disposal, other than lethal force."

Stormbringer. As a new House, Nheras was leading the smallest team (besides their own), and team Ilyn outnumbered them almost two to one. The rest of the applicants would surely want revenge for being outclassed in the first challenge; if she were them, the obvious course of action would be to eliminate the smallest teams, one by one. They would have to spend the whole span fleeing—if they even had a chance of outrunning the others—because there was no way they could match those odds.

Forget her tired legs; Rahelu's whole body—scratched face, sore shoulder, bruised forearm, abused stomach—ached at the very thought.

We're dead, Rahelu sent.

You and I are dead, Dharyas sent back.

Hey now, don't you think that's a little unfair? I'm on the team too!

At Lhorne's wounded puppy act, both Rahelu and Dharyas looked significantly at the rest of House Ideth, and Elaram narrowed her eyes at their synchronized movement.

Exactly, he sent. *We'll all be fine. You'll see.*

"While points will be tallied at the conclusion of the challenge based on your teams as you determine them at the end of the span, you will also be judged on your individual perfor-

"Good plan!" Elaram applauded enthusiastically. "You can count on me to do my utmost in keeping these banners close until the very end of the challenge."

"It's a terrible plan!" Rahelu said. "If team alliances are going to fall along House lines, then we've already won this challenge. Isilc has two banners; Isonn has two banners; Imos and Imrell have two banners together, which leaves Ilyn with one."

Lhorne shook his head again. "Not good enough. Ilyn might ally with one of the others, which would automatically put that alliance level with ours and give them the numbers to take on the others."

Dharyas snorted. "No one's going to ally with Ilyn. Isilc can't stand them, Isonn doesn't need them, and anything Ilyn could offer Imos, Imrell already has that covered."

"Are you saying that as an Augur?" he asked, green eyes sharp. "Because that changes things."

"No," Dharyas said. "There's no time to run a proper Augury. I'll concede that Ilyn striking an alliance is not out of the realms of possibility, but it's far from the most likely possibility."

"The most likely possibility," Rahelu said, "is the other teams will trade banners the way two drunkards trade cups and blows and wind up with black eyes and bruises for their efforts with neither the winner. It's better not to interfere and leave them to it. Sticking our noses in will just give them a reason to unite against us."

"Look." Lhorne gestured at the field below.

Rahelu, Dharyas, and Elaram looked as the final team (Imrell, by their orange-and-white tunics) took up defensive positions around the tenth banner, on the northern side of the training yard.

"Isonn's got the next best fortifications"—he pointed to a smaller formation just south of their fortress—"but their offensive combat style won't let them use it effectively. The rest of the teams"—Lhorne pointed again: they huddled around scattered stone blocks that offered no real cover for anyone defending the banners but plenty of cover for attackers to get close—"will need at least half their number focused on guarding their banners. When the rest of Ideth gets here, we can field an attacking force twice the size of any team's defense. Keeping everybody holed up in here would be a waste of resources and opportunity."

"Criminally inefficient," Elaram said.

When he put it that way...

"Once the challenge starts, I won't be able to keep an eye on everything from up here. That's why I need you two out there, scouting. Nobody else can do that a tenth as effectively." Lhorne winked at Dharyas.

"No arguments from me," Dharyas said.

There were no arguments from Rahelu either. Lhorne's plan did make an awful lot of sense.

She still didn't like it.

Specifically, she really didn't like the idea of venturing out, alone and unprotected, except for her spear and resonance ward, into the middle of a ten-way fight between House-born hurling Projections and swinging weapons, regardless of whatever the Isonn representative had said about non-lethal force.

There was a lot of room for interpreting what 'non-lethal' meant, exactly. Nobody had put any guards on their weapons, except for the archers. (She'd seen Ghardon of Issolm swapping out his normal quiver for one full of training arrows, tipped with blunted arrowheads wrapped in so much padded cloth that they resembled puffy balls of cotton.) And, if Rahelu hadn't dealt with it, Elaram would have had a cross-bow, of all things!

Her reluctance must have been far too obvious because

Lhorne turned his grin back on her and said, "Don't worry, Rahelu. I wouldn't send you out there without something to protect you."

And before she could say anything, he took off his heirloom pendant and hung it around her neck, right as the Isonn representative shouted, "Begin!"

THE TRAINING YARD exploded into motion.

"Go, go!" Lhorne yelled.

Dharyas vaulted over the northern rampart, landing on packed earth with a loud *thud*. She darted off, moving swiftly from cover to cover, shortsword at the ready.

"Set up a passive Seeking three strides deep around our perimeter," Lhorne said to Elaram. "I want to know the moment anyone not wearing Ideth colors approaches, excepting Rahelu, Dharyas, and yourself." He glanced over at Rahelu. "What are you still doing here? Go!"

"But—"

"Less talking, more scouting!" he said, hands on the western rampart, scrutinizing the way Imrell and Ilyn clashed in the northwest corner.

"You can't just...just *give* me something like this!"

Houses had warred within themselves, and with each other, over such resonance crystal legacies.

"It's mine, so I get to determine how it is best used, and right now, you need that pendant more than I do," Lhorne said, his attention already on a different part of the mock battle. "Now go!"

He was right.

It was his turn to lead, his strategy was sound, he was trusting her with a priceless focus stone, and he wasn't even yelling at her, even though she was standing around distracting him with irrelevant concerns, disobeying his orders after he'd spent all eartharc following hers when she hadn't explained herself half so well.

Rahelu stopped wasting time.

She hopped her way down five large steps to the ground level, pausing at the bottom to tuck the pendant inside her tunic and plan out her route: a straight run to the smaller, neighboring formation to the south before zigzagging between the standalone blocks surrounding the second-largest formation on the field—a long, shallow plateau with larger blocks jutting out at random. Two banners flew at either end of the plateau, and the two teams wearing the colors of House Isilc and House Imos were already facing off.

She waited until the first House Ideth team arrived with their banner and reinforcements for Lhorne. Once three Ideth applicants—two of whom wielded mage-staffs topped with resonance crystals the size of her fist (surely there was no way they could manage to use those as focus stones yet!) and the third held a wicked-looking greatsword—took up guard positions around the stairs, she dashed south.

As she ran, she spotted the second Ideth team stranded in the no-man's-land between their original formation (three blocks, arranged like a doorway) on the western side of the yard and their destination. The Ideth applicants drew together, back to back in two ranks, as both Isonn teams descended on them from opposite directions. Six Isonn applicants gripped the chains of their resonance necklaces: Rahelu could feel the paralyzing fear they manifested, even though their Projection wasn't directed at her.

Isonn have got the second team pinned, Rahelu sent. *Should I go in and help?*

No, Lhorne sent. *Find out what the Isilc teams are up to.*

She acknowledged his order and sprinted towards the smaller neighboring formation Isonn had abandoned. Odd, because it offered some decent cover (she duly tucked herself inside a niche) in an otherwise sparse area of the yard.

Taking out Lhorne's pendant, Rahelu closed her eyes and listened to the noises that reflected off the stone blocks all around her: sharp *clacks* as cudgels met staves, bright *clangs* of sharpened steel edge against sharpened steel, occasional *thunks* and *clatter* of blunted arrows on wood shields and sandstone.

Visualizing a blank stone surface in front of her, Rahelu breathed in and drew on the ambient resonance in the training yard: mixed ambition-determination from the applicants and calm-boredom from the House representatives. She sorted through them, discarded the eager pulses of ambition, blended the stately rhythm of calm, underscored it with the even slower beat of boredom, then overlaid that foundation with the restless drive of determination. After a whispered prayer, she pushed the Obfuscating resonance through her hand and into the pendant.

It took a slow count of eight for Lhorne's cloudy crystal to pulse in the sequence she set. Hopefully, it would mask her own resonance signature enough that nobody would detect her while she was occupied with her Seeking and vulnerable.

Imrell just crushed Nheras's team and took the Ilyn banner! Dharyas reported gleefully. *Looks like they're heading south to join up with House Imos. Team Ilyn looks a bit lost, like they don't know what to do.*

Nheras was having a bad day from the fifth hell; the Ilyn girl was used to having numbers on her side. Rahelu grinned to herself as she closed her eyes, Seeking:

Waves of Projection flare all over the training yard. Volleys of red-anger spears are followed by real, blunted arrows; black mists of despair bubble around hastily erected Obfuscation barriers; tides of

bone-white fear surge from one end of the field to the other. A hundred
figures attack, flee, give chase, exchange blows...

She focused on the two groups on the plateau. As Lhorne
predicted, both House Imos and House Isilc had split their
teams: one half to defend their banner and the other half to
launch an assault on the opposing team's banner. House
Imos had a slight advantage in numbers, but House Isilc was
better equipped, so neither side could gain the upper hand
over the other.

That might change soon, as the second Isilc team broke
through one of the Isonn hunt-circles and rushed towards the
plateau. Rahelu nudged her Seeking northward, found the
Imrell team barreling in her direction, and triangulated the
distances.

Nothing to worry about from this side, she reported through
the relay. *Isilc and Imos are at a stalemate right now, but I think
the second Isilc team will get here before Imrell does. If that's the
case, Imos will lose their banner, and they'll be at each other's
throats.*

Good, Lhorne sent. *Isonn are coming after our banners, but
they're carrying both of theirs with them.*

Sure enough, the Isonn hunt-circle that had been stalling
the Isilc reinforcements now swarmed around the structure
under Ideth control, bright green cloth flapping in their
midst.

*I want you and Dharyas to come back towards our base; see if you
can snatch theirs while they're preoccupied with breaking through our
defenses.*

Too late, Dharyas sent. *Someone else beat you to that idea.*

With most of the Isonn hunt-circle focused on attacking
the Ideth fortifications, Nheras and her pack had managed to
split off a smaller group of Isonn applicants—including their
banner bearer—from the larger hunt-circle.

Unable to rejoin their teammates, the Isonn splinter group fled westward, across the open yard.

Ilyn immediately gave chase, determined to recover a banner—any banner—since their own was lost.

The beleaguered Isonn applicants reached the doorway formation and closed in protectively around their banner bearer, forming a second, smaller hunt-circle. Individual applicants dashed in and out of position, fending off the flurry of weapon strikes and Projections from the Ilyn attackers.

House Isonn was holding up well against the onslaught until Bhemol tripped the Isonn defender leading the hunt-circle. It collapsed; Nheras shouted in triumph as she held the green banner aloft, then all of Ilyn pelted north, scrambling to put solid stone between their newly acquired banner and the Isonn team they had stolen it from.

Lhorne swore. *Ilyn is too far away now, I can't split our forces across that distance. We'll have to try for one of the Imos banners, perhaps, while they're working to reclaim the Imrell banner. Rahelu, go—*

Something didn't add up.

How many banners do you see on the field? Rahelu asked suddenly. *There are five over here: I count three in Isilc possession—both of their own plus the Imrell banner—and Imos and Imrell have two: the Imos banner and the Ilyn banner.*

Still three banners here, Lhorne replied. *Ours and both Ideth banners.*

Eight.

Nheras and her team are running around the northern end of the training yard with the banner they stole, playing hide-and-seek with Isonn, Dharyas reported. *I don't see any others.*

Nine.

What? Lhorne sent. *She should have two. You're sure?*

Yes. I've checked them all three times; they only have one.

Rahelu frowned. *Why did you think they were carrying two banners, Lhorne?*

I felt it, he sent. *Isonn had one person carrying both banners together, and they'd used a sloppy Obfuscation. I sensed two signatures through their barrier.*

Well, you're the expert, Dharyas sent. *If it's not here though...*

Rahelu's frown deepened and she dove back into Seeking. She pinpointed eight bright red pulses of alarm straight away, exactly where she expected. The Isonn beacons were more difficult to locate; she had to stretch her resonance senses further to pick up the diffused signals. But just as Lhorne said, there were two blurred signatures that pulsed on the north side of the training yard, where Dharyas had only seen one banner.

And next to her, pulsing so faintly she almost thought she imagined it, was an eleventh signal.

By the Earthgiver's own dark heart and the Skymother's harp, Rahelu swore through the relay. *Isonn set up a decoy; the real one is over here.*

What?! Where???

Rahelu sent back the barely perceptible eleventh signal she had picked up in her Seeking, then hung onto her visualization as she opened her eyes to inspect her hiding place.

And right there, wedged even further into the niche, was the second Isonn banner.

Found it!

Wait! Don't—

As soon as her hand touched the pole, House Isonn's Obfuscation barrier around the banner collapsed, triggering a hidden Projection that shattered the barrier Rahelu had anchored to Lhorne's pendant. The banner pulsed a blinding red, its original resonance signal enhanced by another Isonn Projection that simultaneously struck half-a-dozen purplish-black fear darts into her heart.

Fu—

She runs through the darkened alleyways of Ennuost Yrg in ill-fitting sandals, fleeing from the shadowy figures that hunted her. Disembodied ghouls hang in a row on garottes strung between buildings, flapping in an invisible wind. She tears through them, and they cling to her neck, her arms, her face, smothering her with their dread touch.

Behind her, the shadows grow wings and screech as alleyways transform into uneven rooftops that crumble beneath her feet. Chill sweat forms on her brow; her breath shudders in her chest. She flees, leaps, screams, as a short drop to safety becomes a fall into oblivion.

Her bones shatter beneath a giant foot that grinds her into the cobblestones, again and again, until there is nothing left of her body except for a reddish-brown paste. And still the foot lifts; this time, it will crush her skull and—

Rahelu screamed for real as she shot to her feet and struck out blindly in a spear-thrust with the banner. The end of the pole swung through empty air; she looked up to see the furious Isonn applicants—a hunt-circle twenty mages strong!—descending upon her hiding place.

You're dead, Dharyas sent. *But I'm coming to fetch your corpse.*

Thanks. Rahelu hurriedly backed into her now-exposed niche, shoved the banner behind her, and grabbed her spear.

You just need to hold out for another hundred heartbeats; I'm sending Cseryl with reinforcements, Lhorne sent.

Three Isonn applicants, wielding spears of their own, advanced on her. Designed for hunting elk, bears, and other large predators, their weapons were at least two-and-a-half hands longer than her own.

Now she knew how each and every one of the thousand or so fish she had stabbed felt, as they flopped around helplessly on the deck.

Rahelu backed further into her niche so they had to attack

her one at a time, then spun her spear in a basic defensive pattern. One took the bait and charged in, aiming for her left side. She twisted and blocked his strike with her haft, knocking his spearpoint to one side where it struck sparks as it scraped against the sandstone block.

Using the momentum of her parry, Rahelu followed through to pin her opponent's spear against the ground, but he had anticipated her; he moved with his spear and launched a kick at her head. She had to yank her own spear back to avoid being disarmed as she ducked, then jabbed the point of her spear at his foot. It skidded off his tough leather boots, but he still yelped in pain and toppled over mid-kick.

His spear landed on the ground with a clatter; Rahelu snatched it with her off-hand as the next Isonn applicant attacked. Rahelu cast her own spear, forcing the other girl to dive to one side. Somebody grabbed her by one ankle and heaved—her first opponent had recovered—so she took a page out of Nheras's playbook: she went with the motion, allowing her attacker to lift her foot off the ground, and then, as he was caught off guard by her lack of resistance, promptly stomped on him. He wheezed, winded from the blow, and she winced in sympathy.

"Sorry!" she said. He tried to get up, so she walloped him in the belly with the butt of his spear, hating herself for her actions, hating Nheras for giving her the idea, and hating the fact she couldn't justify hating Nheras for it because this was *an incredibly effective* way to disable an opponent without causing permanent damage.

"Come on!" Dharyas shouted as she clubbed a third Isonn applicant on his head with the hilt of her shortsword. "Grab the banner, and let's go!"

Rahelu didn't need further encouragement: she tore the banner off its pole, stuffed it inside her tunic, and sprinted after Dharyas. The Isca girl charged through the gap in the hunt-circle their Ideth reinforcements had won—Lhorne had had to send everyone except Elaram to match Isonn's numbers—and all of them beat a hasty retreat back towards the safety of their miniature fortress, a mere twenty strides away.

"Good work team!" Lhorne cheered from atop the fortifications where three Ideth banners flew, his figure backlit against the sun. "That's victory for House Ideth and—"

A shadow rose up beside him and pulled down the banners.

"Lhorne, watch out!" Rahelu yelled. "To your left!"

Elaram hefted the banner poles and swung. Lhorne turned—too slowly—and staggered backward as the blow crashed into his chest. He fell, cracking his head against one of the ledges.

He didn't get up.

"Lhorne!" Dharyas cried. "*Lhorne!*"

Loud cries of outrage rang out all around Rahelu, overlapping with the surge of white-hot anger, as House Ideth bellowed:

"Turncoat!"

"Sneak!"

"Dirty Issolm traitor!"

Elaram yelled back, "Don't take it so personally! We're just following the rules!" She slid off the edge and disappeared with their banners.

Abandoning their orderly ranks, the Ideth applicants overtook Rahelu and Dharyas, running past the entrance to their stone formation in pursuit of revenge.

"Go check on him!" Dharyas yelled over her shoulder as she followed. "I'm going to help get our banners back."

All around the training yard, Ideth's cries were joined by other shouts of fury:

"After her!"

"Give that back, you backstabbing bastard!"

"You lying scoundrels!"

"I told you, I *told* you: never, *never* trust Issolm!"

Chaos erupted as House Issolm revealed their true allegiance; every applicant in white-and-black had absconded with their team's banners. Boundaries between skirmishes dissolved as the betrayed Houses sought vengeance in the last few hundred heartbeats remaining.

Rahelu scraped her hands and knees on the oversized steps of their stone formation, pushing herself up by leaning on the stolen Isonn spear. Lhorne was at the top, slumped over but breathing steadily. She laid her spear to one side, put both arms around him, and heaved until she managed to ease him into a more comfortable position. She felt at the back of his skull with her fingertips; there was a slight swelling on one side, but her fingers came away without blood.

"Lhorne?" She shook his arm gently. "Can you hear me?"

He stirred, and the awful, tight feeling in her chest relaxed slightly.

Can you hear me? she repeated through their relay.

...hurts, his reply came back as his eyelids flickered. *Who...?*

Issolm.

Issolm, he repeated. *Should've known.*

The ambient resonance burned—so thick and hot was the collective rage against House Issolm's treachery that Rahelu felt it as iron bands squeezing her ribs, urging her to dive over the edge of their stone formation and sink feet first into the depths of the fray.

She would dismantle that traitorous bitch who had dared to lay hands on Lhorne. He had been her first ally—no, her first *friend*, since Tsenjhe—the first person in this gods-cursed city besides Keshwar who accepted her as she was. She would tear that filthy Issolm pretender limb from limb with her bare hands; rip her throat open with her teeth and—

...*Rahelu?* a large hand clasped her own, which was now clenched in a tight fist. *Where...?*

She was lost, floating in the ocean of uncontrolled resonance that crashed all around them. Weapons had been abandoned; the melee turned to savage brawling as Isilc tackled Imrell to the ground before they could snatch a banner from an Issolm applicant who rammed his way past an Isonn hunter to regroup with his fellows, only to be hauled up short by Imos, who was, in turn, mobbed by House Isilc.

The warm hand over hers tightened. *Rahelu*, Lhorne sent. This time, his call was a quiet Projection that bypassed her resonance wards through their clasped hands and reverberated through the resonance pendant he had loaned her; the pendant that rested beneath her tunic, against her skin and over her pounding heart. *Come back.*

Rahelu clung to his Projection, to the feel of his calloused fingers, and clawed her mind back from the brawling mass of applicants and the edge of sanity. Lhorne reeled her in, helping her force back the raging ambient resonance with a cool blue-gray calm that neither of them felt, carving out a bubble of serenity around the two of them.

She looked down and found Lhorne, lying on the sandstone just as she had left him, but he was looking straight back at her, with his clear green eyes.

"Thank you," she spoke out loud, raising her voice to be heard over the muffled blows from the brawl below, tugging her hand free from his.

She didn't trust herself to answer via Projection.

His eyes lingered on her face and she tried to suppress the sudden, unexpected rush of heat that flashed through her body.

Rahelu looked away and squinted up at the sun. "Time's

almost up," she said casually, as if they had been talking about simple logistics.

Too casually perhaps.

Lhorne's a bit dazed, but fine, she sent through Dharyas's relay.

He didn't look so dazed anymore, but he also didn't contradict her. *Any luck reclaiming our banners?* he asked.

It's madness down here, Dharyas sent. *Isilc and Imos almost teamed up for a heartbeat; you'd think those Issolm turncoats would be the ones taking a real beating, but they prepared for this. They had other teammates covering their retreats with Projection.*

She could still feel Lhorne's eyes on her, so she shuffled to the northern side of their fortification and used her spear to lever herself up enough to peer over the edge. Nheras's team had bunched together in the northwest corner, their backs to the fence with weapons readied and facing out, determined to have no part in the melee. They'd been fortunate; as a new House, no Issolm applicant had bothered infiltrating their group, so the Ilyn team was still in possession of the Isonn banner they had captured.

I think Isilc managed to steal two banners back, Dharyas continued. *So did Imos. Isonn seems to have given up; they've pulled out of the brawl and moved off to the south end. But near half of the applicants left in this mob have succumbed to the Projections and are just tearing into anyone, whether they're wearing Issolm colors or not.*

And there, thirty strides away, flitting from the cover of one sandstone block to another as she fled northwards, was Elaram. She'd lost all three poles and two of the banners in her flight—had probably thrown them away in order to escape the melee—but she still clutched the third and final banner in her left fist.

Banner one.

Rahelu touched the stolen Isonn banner inside her tunic. Ilyn had one banner (not their own); Isilc had recovered two banners (unclear whether one or both were their own); Imos had one (also unknown whether it was their own). If Rahelu could steal back her team's own banner, that was worth three points on its own—plus another point for the second Isonn banner inside her tunic. That was six, which left four banners unaccounted for (presumably in Issolm hands).

They might still be able to salvage this; it depended entirely on whether any of the other teams had recovered their own banners. If they had, then it was a clear win for House Isilc, but if they hadn't, then her team could still win.

Dharyas! she sent the image through the relay. *How close are you?*

Frustration came through the link, along with a sensation of strained muscles and the ring of steel-on-steel as Dharyas parried a wild stroke from someone's longsword. *Not close enough.*

Rahelu swore. She didn't want to leave Lhorne here, alone and undefended.

Go, go! Lhorne sent. *I'll be fine.*

She hesitated, then nodded, descending the large stone steps in hurried leaps, bracing herself against the renewed fury of the ambient resonance as she left the safety of Lhorne's bubble of calm and headed north, after Elaram.

She tried to run lightly, holding her weak attempt at Obfuscation for the handful of tensioned heartbeats it took to skirt around the melee. It was spiraling out of control rapidly as applicants lost themselves in the burning rage-haze churning around the press of bodies.

Fifteen strides ahead, Elaram broke out from the cover of one stone block and made a run for the next.

Rahelu reached behind her and found a strong source of pain: someone had forgotten about the rule regarding non-lethal force and stabbed someone else. She seized that pain, grabbed it like a fishing line and threw it in a focused Projection at the traitor.

She didn't wait for the Projection to land before she reversed her grip on the Isonn spear and closed the distance, swinging it in a two-handed overhead strike to smash the blunt end against Elaram's shoulder.

The Issolm applicant screamed as her collarbone cracked from the force of Rahelu's strike, her right arm falling limp at her side. Banner one drifted to the ground and Rahelu snatched it, tucking it inside her tunic with the other banner, then took off, back in the direction of the abandoned Ideth stronghold.

I've got it! she sent.

She was twenty or so strides from safety when the red haze puffed away before a powerful counter-Projection that had to be the work of the House representatives. Calm blanketed the field, and applicants dropped weapons, sagged to their knees, or lay flat on the ground, groaning at their wounds.

As the House representatives began walking the length and breadth of the field—taking stock of injuries, counting banners, handing out small fist-sized spheres—Rahelu struggled through the altered ambient resonance, dragging one leaden foot after another until she got back to the top of their fortress.

Breathing heavily and aching all over, Rahelu pulled out the two banners from inside her tunic and tied them to the Isonn spear. She jammed it into a crevice between two stone blocks with trembling arms, then allowed herself to collapse on the sandstone beside Lhorne.

10

PUZZLE

"I STILL THINK YOU SHOULD GET A HEALER TO TAKE a look at you," Dharyas said as they followed Lhorne out of the Guild, at the head of an entire train of Ideth applicants.

"Mother says I was born with an iron skull." Lhorne dismissed Dharyas's concerns with a wave. "But I will be in dire straits if I don't get something to eat in the next span, and then the two of you will need to carry me home."

He grinned at Rahelu, leaning on her still, as he led them down the wide, evenly constructed streets of Northpoint, past a crew of neatly uniformed street sweepers collecting the animal dung left behind by passing wagons and washing the cobblestones. The two of them must look ridiculous together: he in his House-born dress clothes of pale green and sky-blue, and she in her father's oversized fish-gut-stained tunic.

And there was still the matter of his heirloom resonance crystal around her neck. She should have returned it as soon as the challenge ended, but they'd been exhausted and preoccupied with getting down safely, and then Dharyas, Cseryl, and the rest of the Ideth applicants had swarmed around them and given them both long, considering looks and Rahelu was most definitely *not* going to fuel any speculation by returning Lhorne's pendant in front of them all.

Rahelu tried to ignore the warmth of his arm across her shoulders and concentrated on blocking out all of the chatter around them by visualizing the way the Elumaje's smooth glassy surface reflected the pale harvest sky on a windless day.

The inside of the Atriarch's Cup was well-lit, with lanterns (lanterns! *Not* candles) hanging at even intervals upon the walls. Its main dining room smelled of fresh wood shavings mixed in with the slight fragrance of pine and fir needles and the more mouth-watering scents of freshly baked loaves and roasting meat—about as far as you could get from the rancid stink of stale body odor, smoky incense, and week-old food of a Lowdocks tavern.

"Food!" Lhorne gestured frantically at one of the servers as he ushered Rahelu towards a large booth at the back of the tavern. "And a mug of your third-best ale for everyone."

"Except me," Rahelu said. "No food and just water, please." She would stay long enough to not offend her new friends, then go check in on her mother at Market Square.

The server looked surprised but nodded as he did a quick headcount of their party as everyone crammed themselves inside the booth. Rahelu found herself squashed in, shoulder to shoulder with House-born, with Lhorne to her left and another Ideth applicant to her right.

And Lhorne was looking at her again. "What?" she asked.

"Nothing," he said and gestured again before the server could walk away. "Two servings for me, then."

Rahelu narrowed her eyes at him.

He, in turn, widened his. "What?" he asked, mimicking her tone. "I'm feeling particularly hungry."

There was a sigh from the other side of the table and Cseryl said, "Only the third-best ale?"

"Third-best," Lhorne said agreeably, "because it was a draw. If only you'd managed to steal the last Isilc flag! Then we'd be having the second-best ale." He winked at Cseryl.

Cseryl gave a delicate sniff as she flicked a stray lock of blonde hair over her shoulder. "Running short on your allowance again?"

His what?

"I'm surprised your parents haven't tightened the purse strings on your spending," Cseryl said.

On some level, Rahelu knew House-born could draw on the wealth of their families as a matter of course. It was the source of the great divide between the two different classes of trainees.

But it was one thing to know that, and another to confront the concept directly. Funds flowing from the *family* to the individual?

Rahelu couldn't wrap her head around the idea. Every kez she had ever earned (there hadn't been many; the Lowdocks ran on barter) had gone straight to her parents to pay for household expenses.

"What hopeless charity cases did your bleeding heart fixate on this month?" Cseryl asked.

"Why, you lot!" Lhorne gestured around the booth, then favored Cseryl with one of his mischievous grins. "Unless you're planning on paying?"

"Let me think." Cseryl tilted her head, which caused most of her silky sun-bleached hair to cascade around her shoulders like a waterfall. "Who was soft-hearted enough to overlook history and let Issolm in? And which tactical genius decided to bet everything on a suicidal rescue that left us exposed to betrayal? I don't think it was me." Cseryl kept her tone light, and her smile held genuine affection, but the Ideth girl's eyes were hard.

Seated this close to Lhorne, Rahelu felt his resonance aura darken slightly, though he kept his grin and only shrugged. "It wouldn't have been fair to hold Elaram accountable for a wrong done before any of us were born—she wasn't Obfuscating her intentions when she asked to join us—and it wouldn't have been right to leave Rahelu to face Isonn alone."

"History is but a mirror of the future to come," Cseryl said. "And rare is the tree that bears something sweet after years of bitter fruit."

"Be fair, Cseryl, his strategies usually do work," another Ideth applicant said, the one seated to her right. He had one arm in a sling. "If we hadn't gone for that rescue, we'd have lost outright. Eh, Rahelu?"

"Um." Rahelu shifted in her seat and the padded leather cushion (*leather! cushion!*) underneath her squeaked. She had no idea how to answer that.

Also, he knew her name too? Did they all know who she was? A quick scan of the faces around the booth told her she ought to know their names, but she couldn't recall a single one.

Shit. She would have to find a way to discover and remember their names too...without giving away the fact she hadn't bothered to get to know any of her fellow trainees during the five years of their Guild training.

Cseryl's gaze slid over to Rahelu. "She has my brother's backing." Not that Keshwar's approval seemed to make a difference; the tanned girl still regarded Rahelu with the same kind of suspicion you would reserve for notorious pick-pockets.

The conversation had moved on though, and someone was recounting a story of the time Lhorne had convinced them all to take a turn serving in Ennuost Yrg's city guard during the last midsummer break.

"Gods, Lhorne, if you didn't have the Starfather's own blessing…I wouldn't go along with any of your schemes."

While House Ideth continued their good-natured teasing, the server arrived with their food and drinks. Lhorne's second platter ended up right under her nose, and the heavenly smells set her mouth to watering.

There was a whole leg of some roasted bird that she couldn't identify (it had been so long since she'd had anything other than rice and fish), next to several thick slices of fluffy white bread (she'd never eaten it; they couldn't afford flour) and a mountain of roasted vegetables (how strange! She was used to eating them boiled, in a soup). A tiny jug of dark brown liquid (what even was that? It was sludge-like, but smelled even better than the roasted bird) nestled beside a tiny plate half the size of her palm bearing a generous knob of yellow butter (sheer, utter luxury).

All around her, similar platters landed in front of the other applicants.

Individual platters of food.

She looked over at Dharyas, seated on Lhorne's other side. The Isca girl dug into her meal with relish as she chatted with a serious-looking Ideth applicant who wore his hair in a braided tail.

Rahelu's stomach growled and she prayed no one heard it. She sipped on her mug of water instead, trying to hide how overwhelmed she was by her surroundings.

Thankfully, Lhorne was too busy dissecting their group's performance like he was dissecting his roasted bird leg.

"All things considered, equal first with Isilc and Isonn isn't bad," he concluded. "It was the *expected* result, as far as the Houses are concerned."

Nods all around the booth.

"But we could have done better," he continued. "*Should* have done better. If any of the other teams had recovered their banners, they would have won outright."

He paused, looked directly at Dharyas, then Rahelu, and said, "I wasted our advantage from the first challenge." There was a longer pause as he met Cseryl's eyes. "I should have listened to your warnings." He took the time to look at each person around the table in turn before he spoke again. "I'm sorry I let you all down."

A part of Rahelu felt vindicated; she had been *right*. It was foolish to sail into a storm in hopes of a full catch if you already had enough fish for dinner.

Sling sighed and said, "At least we all got what we needed." His words were accompanied by a shimmering chime from the delicate blown glass sphere he was spinning on the fingertip of his good hand.

About half of the one hundred hopefuls had failed to earn a single sphere and had been summarily dismissed as applicants; their performance deemed inadequate and unworthy of an invitation to a private audience by the House representatives.

"A House that risks nothing is a House that will soon be surpassed," somebody else replied, and all of the Ideth applicants—even Cseryl—raised their mugs in a toast, then drank.

The challenge had been theirs to lose, but Rahelu was starting to understand why someone like Lhorne would be willing to bet all or nothing. House Ideth hadn't become a major House by acting conservatively. Failing to act boldly and decisively might actually cost them their chance to meet with their House Elders.

Still. Lhorne was so solemn sitting there, staring into his mug as if it could tell him what he could have done differently, his resonance aura a subdued deep blue like they had lost. That grin of his was nowhere in sight.

"It's not your fault," Rahelu said. "I was there; I ran the same Seeking you did—Elaram never lied. Not once. The rules never said the teams had to stay the same throughout the challenge. You couldn't have anticipated Issolm's treachery."

Lhorne stayed silent and took a large gulp of his ale. The other applicants shifted uncomfortably but didn't speak up. Silence stretched out in their booth until Rahelu could hear the barkeep's patient rejections of the server's persistent invitations to go for a walk in the orchards after they finished their shifts.

What was she missing? Besides lunch. She eyed the platter before her hungrily. The roast was cooling, but it looked as appetizing as ever.

"I don't think their betrayal was planned," Dharyas said at last, dicing up the roasted vegetables on her platter with her belt knife. "The way Issolm was running around at the end... it was more like they had discussed the possibility beforehand, so when the opportunity presented itself, they took it."

The Ideth applicant with the braided tail snorted. "Stupid. I'm glad Isonn hunted them all down and left them empty-handed."

"Calculated," Dharyas said as she speared a chunk of roasted carrot on her belt knife. "Elaram saw an opportunity to seize three banners when Lhorne sent the rest of us off to help secure the Isonn banner Rahelu discovered, so she did. There were only two hundred heartbeats or so left; if Isonn had tied us up any longer, she would have been in the clear and no one the wiser."

"We'd've been equal last with Ilyn, and my mother would have *killed* us, personally," Cseryl said, pushing her meal away half-eaten. Most of the bird was untouched—the Ideth girl had sliced off a few small bites from the thigh—so were some of the roasted vegetables and half the bread.

Would Rahelu kill someone for that half-eaten meal?

No. She wasn't that desperate.

"But we're not, so she won't!" Lhorne said, cheery mask back in place as he polished off the last bit of food on his first platter. "Ahhhh," he sighed and made a show of rubbing his belly in satisfaction. "That was delicious."

"So delicious," Dharyas agreed, as she licked her fingers. "I've never had better."

"If only I could eat another bite!" he sighed even more theatrically as he slouched back against his padded leather seat. "The food is too good to waste."

Rahelu took a long drink from her mug of water and did not glance at the untouched platter in front of her. Seated this close to him, she could feel the discordance between his tone and the flickers in his resonance aura. She looked sharply at him, just in time to see him pour the remains of the dark brown liquid in the tiny jug into his mouth.

Cseryl stood. That seemed to be some sort of signal because the other Ideth applicants also swallowed the last of their meals and rose from their seats. "Thanks for buying lunch, cousin. I'll see you later."

She blew a kiss in Lhorne's direction, then turned gracefully and sashayed off with an exaggerated sway of her hips. (Rahelu refused to believe anybody naturally walked like *that*.) The rest of Ideth applicants followed, like a long train of attendants, except for Braid, who hurried to open the door. As the tanned Ideth girl passed through the doorway, the skyarc sun gilded her backlit figure and made her sun-bleached hair glow.

It was hard to decide which was more absurd: the collective sigh from the remaining patrons (so loud it was probably audible from the street) or the eddies of desire that drifted about in the ambient resonance inside the tavern. Even the server who came to clear their table was affected.

Rahelu was suddenly very aware of how close she was sitting to Lhorne and the warmth of his knee against her left thigh.

"I've got to go too," she said and stood up. "Thank you, both of you." She took off the brooch pinned to the inside of her collar along with the pendant around her neck and set them on the table. "For...everything."

Dharyas smiled and pocketed her brooch, but Lhorne made no move to reclaim his pendant. Instead, he reached over the table and grabbed her wrist before she could slide out of their booth.

The familiar gesture was a shock; despite her resonance ward, her aura trembled a bright yellow for an instant at his touch.

He released her at once. "Don't go yet," he said. "We haven't even talked about what we're going to do with these," and he pulled out his own blown glass sphere. When he shook it gently at her, the crystal fragments inside chimed.

What was there to discuss? The House representatives had been very clear when they had handed out the spheres—audiences were granted to individuals, not teams, and they were not permitted to offer any guidance as to how applicants should prepare themselves.

Just like how Tsenjhe and Keshwar had not been permitted to speak of the challenges. Yet every single House-born applicant had shown up with prearranged alliances.

Rahelu sat back down in the newly vacant space in their booth, pulled out her own spheres, and placed them on the table.

Her first sphere was an exact match to Lhorne's—a frozen blue-tinted bubble with the sigil of House Ideth worked into its surface in an intricate mosaic of resonance crystal fragments of all different shades.

The second sphere was a hollow tangle of copper wires,

with a tiny resonance crystal at the center of each junction where one wire crossed another. The sigil of House Isca was etched into a small metal plate welded to one side, and the whole thing had no logically discernable arrangement.

But her third sphere—the one from House Issolm—*that* had been unexpected. Made from half a dozen intricately carved pieces of different woods fitted so tightly together her fingertips could not feel any seams, its polished surface shone like the glass sphere from House Ideth. The sigil of House Issolm was conspicuously absent and shaking the sphere didn't produce any sound. No matter how she fiddled with the puzzle, she could not figure out how to take it apart.

Lhorne craned his neck to look at what she was doing and his mouth flattened into a straight line. "You know these are just invitations, right? You don't have to accept the invitation if you don't want to."

She tried to imagine declining any of the invitations, and she couldn't. You didn't say *no* to somebody from the Houses, especially not an Elder.

Well, maybe someone like Lhorne could. So she ignored his question and turned to Dharyas instead.

"Are you accepting all of yours?" she asked.

Dharyas drew out her spheres: she had four. Two were identical to Rahelu's (the glass sphere from House Ideth and the wire sphere from House Isca), but she also had a gaudy resonance-crystal-studded gold sphere (gilt paint on clay, and the stones were arranged into the sigil of House Imos), and another carved from rough stone (no sigil, but it had to be from House Isonn).

"I'm not sure." The Isca girl juggled her spheres one-handed as she downed the rest of her ale. "If I do, I would need at least three Houses to support my Petition. I don't know if I have enough time for four thorough Auguries."

Everyone had been full of speculation regarding what they

were meant to do with the spheres. A few applicants had argued for Evocation, but the overwhelming majority was in favor of Augury. After all, that was the only resonance discipline that they hadn't been tested on, directly or indirectly, in either of the challenges.

"Why? You'd have to murder someone before your own House would turn you down."

And maybe not even then.

"Just because you're born of a House doesn't mean you are *of* the House. Lhorne and I are applicants, same as you. If we want to make it past the audience, we need to do the work."

"Possibly more," Lhorne said. "Aunt Mere is *very* exacting. She likes to interview every applicant personally. If there's even the slightest chance of gleaning insight into what my audience will be like, I'll take it."

"*Atriarch* Ideth is holding the Ideth audiences?" Rahelu gaped at him. Her stomach was tying itself into knots just thinking about it. "Not one of the Ideth Elders?"

"House Ideth's true strength lies not in the lands it holds nor the wealth it possesses, but in the potential of the future generations it nurtures," Lhorne quoted. "Aunt Mere likes to know what she has to work with. She won't pass anyone who doesn't meet her standards. Not like some of the other Houses," he muttered darkly. "They'll take anyone they think they can use, and they'll squeeze the life out of you."

That was certainly true of Isonn's moneylenders. Guiltily, Rahelu glanced out the window to see the sun was already well into skyarc.

Lhorne flicked Dharyas's gaudy gold sphere and sent it spinning in a wobbly arc across the table. "The more invitations you accept, the more people you have to convince to support your Petition," he said. "That's why I only accepted Ideth's; the only person I need to convince is Aunt Mere."

"I don't like having all my coins in the same purse," Dharyas said. "If the Houses didn't have such a stranglehold on the economy, I'd not be Petitioning at all. I'd take my mage license and open my own workshop in the Echo Alleys. And if I don't get any offers I like, that's what I'll do."

"You can't be serious," Rahelu said.

"If Lynath Ilyn could do it, why can't I? House Ilyn didn't even come up with any of their inventions; Atriarch Lynath merely acquired the rights from the inventors." Dharyas grinned. "That won't be a problem for me. House Idhar has a nice ring to it, don't you think?"

Nheras's grandmother was the exception, not the rule.

"How much did it cost you to make those brooches?"

Dharyas looked blank.

"You don't know?"

"I...there's a scrap bin in the Isca workshops for experiments."

"How long did it take you?"

Dharyas looked blank again, so Lhorne answered for her. "She's been working on them on and off since late harvest."

"How long would it take you to make more?"

"Um. Two weeks?"

"Six," Lhorne said. "Perhaps twelve. It always takes you at least three times as long as you say it will."

"How much coin would you need for the shop and the equipment and supplies? Where are you going to get the coin from? Who's going to go around and sell your inventions for you while you're cloistered in your workroom? How will you pay them? Where—"

Dharyas looked more and more uncertain with every question. "I don't know! Alright? But it can't be that hard. I'll figure it out."

"You'll—" Rahelu took a deep breath. "House Isonn charges my family five silver kez a week for our sloop, our market stall plus water and fish haulage—that's beside what we spend on cordage, hooks, and firewood. It takes one fisher anywhere from four to twelve spans to bring in a full catch of three baskets. If the Stormbringer is kind."

Her father spent every waking span (and many non-waking ones) out alone on the open sea. She could not remember the last time he had slept a full night.

"On a good day, we sell all three baskets; on a bad day, one—and then we have to smoke or salt the rest that same day."

Had her mother remembered to eat? Had Hzin stolen their spot yet again because she had had to help Rahelu prepare today instead of the other way around?

"In a good week, we make enough to cover our payments to Isonn, my Guild debt, and buy rice and vegetables. In a bad week..." She shook her head. "Never mind that. Do you know how long it took us to 'figure it out'?"

The other two were silent. Dharyas had hunkered down in her seat, staring at the Imos sphere in the middle of the table. Lhorne had put a hand on the Isca girl's shoulder, but he was looking at Rahelu with wide eyes.

"I was ten when we left Chanaz. By the time we arrived, I was twelve. It's been five years of scraping by and we still haven't *figured it out*."

Every coin her parents had managed to save had gone towards outfitting Rahelu: practice weapons, resonance crystals, writing supplies. Her parents had given her all they could—had sacrificed their own futures to stake everything on hers.

All in the hope that she could join one of the Houses.

That was all her parents wanted. All they had ever wanted.

And here Dharyas sat, with her Earthgiver-blessed brilliance and the Starfather's gift of Augury. No House would

ever turn her down; if Dharyas didn't have four uncondi-
tional competing offers by the end of tomorrow, Rahelu
would swallow her own spear.

She needed a House to accept her—and any House, even
Issolm, would do. If they took her as a Supplicant and
worked her like a slave for the next few years of her life, she
would take that trade. It wouldn't be enough to repay her
parents for everything they had sacrificed, but it would be a
start.

Rahelu picked up her spheres and put them in her pocket.
"I need to get back to Market."

"But what are you going to use to anchor your Augury?"
Dharyas asked, her tone subdued.

"I—" Rahelu glanced down at the burn mark on her
finger, an angry red star-burst at the center of a thin red weal
that encircled the second digit of her left hand. "Nothing,"
she said. "I'm not good enough at Augury for it to make a
difference. It's not like I have a choice anyway."

"Sure you do," Lhorne said, nodding at the pendant in
front of her.

She stared back at him, waiting for the joke. Any moment
now, he would start laughing and she could join in, before
making a quick escape. She looked over at Dharyas for confir-
mation, but the Isca applicant had stopped paying attention
to both of them, intent on fiddling around with her copper
wire sphere.

He wasn't laughing.

He was serious.

"I can't!" she said. "*You* can't!"

"Why not?"

The veins in her forehead were throbbing, she was sure.
"It's an Ideth heirloom! You can't pass it around to just
anybody."

"I'm not passing it to just anybody, I'm passing it to you.

Besides, you didn't have a problem with borrowing it for the challenge."

She most certainly had had a problem with it, but an argument along those lines wouldn't help her now.

"That was different and you know it. How do you know I won't run off, sell it to one of Imrell's fences, and disappear? The amount of coin this'd fetch on the black market would be enough to start a new life anywhere on the Ngutoccai continent six times over."

"Because we're friends," he said, and that grin of his was back.

Surely it wasn't that easy. It was probably just the elation and emotional release from surviving the brawl. If she tried to claim friendship tomorrow, would he still feel the same?

"Friends for less than a day, Lhorne."

"I'm a very good judge of character," he said.

Cseryl would have brought up the subject of Elaram's betrayal again, but the way Lhorne smiled at Rahelu made her feel all warm inside so she didn't.

"I trust that you'll keep it safe. You can return it once you find another crystal of your own."

That could take a while. Resonance crystals, even small ones, were expensive. And she was no Dedicate, to be able to stroll around openly, flaunting crystal, without repercussions.

But if the other applicants were right about the spheres and she didn't have something to help her with her Augury (and Starfather knew she would need all the help she could get with that), she would never even have a chance at Supplicant.

"If I borrow this, what will you use?"

He shrugged. "Keshwar has dozens of spares."

She had not thought of going to Keshwar.

Could she? He was her sponsor.

No. He was too far above her and had already granted her more favors than she could ever have expected.

"I will give it straight back," she said, looping the pendant around her neck and tucking it inside her tunic once more. "Luck to you both for tomorrow. I'll...I'll see you around."

"I'll count on it." Lhorne's voice drifted after her as she hurried outside. "Luck, Rahelu."

Circling around the block to make sure neither Lhorne nor Dharyas had followed, Rahelu hid in the shadows at the back of the tavern. Fifty heartbeats later, the server came outside to toss a pile of scraps into the alley.

She took the time for a Seeking to confirm nobody was watching. Nobody was, but she raised a quick Obfuscation barrier, just in case.

Despite her new alliances, she was still a fisher's brat from the Lowdocks.

And the server had thrown out at least three perfectly good meals.

11
SUBORNED

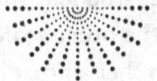

"Fish! Fresh-caught fish from the Kuath! Goldtrout, silverbream, sweetcod, and more! One from three copper kez, three from seven copper, and ten from just ten copper kez!"

"Pots! Pans! All sizes! Iron, copper, tin, clay—yours from one silver kez!"

"Carrots! Onions! Potatoes! Everything you need for a delicious stew! Buy four stoneweight, get another free! Grown right here, from the fields of Northreach, picked just this eartharc."

Rahelu kept her eyes shut, doing her best to focus on the wooden sphere inside her grasp and block out the cries of the market's vendors (her mother's the loudest of all) trying to unload the last of their wares.

She ought to be doing the same, but her mother wouldn't hear of it—Rahelu's unpleasant manners would put off customers; Rahelu would sell a single fish when the customer could be convinced to buy five; Rahelu should focus on pleasing the Houses instead of being as easily distracted as a minnow.

So Rahelu had obediently spent the rest of the skyarc attempting Augury, and two spans—*two spans!*—later, she was still failing to get even the slightest whisper of future resonance from the wooden sphere, or *any* of her three spheres for that matter.

Rahelu growled and—before she quite realized what she was doing—pegged the wooden sphere at the freshwater barrel they shared with the other seafood hawkers.

Her heart caught in her throat as the wooden sphere slammed into the side of the barrel. It bounced off, intact, and rolled back to her feet, leaving a small dent behind in the barrel and Rahelu no closer to any insight.

Her mother didn't turn from her conversation with the serving-man in lilac-and-black, didn't let any of her inner emotions escape into her resonance aura, but Rahelu knew without Seeking that she was disappointed at her daughter's appalling lapse in front of prospective customers.

"Sorry," Rahelu muttered as the Isilc serving-man left with half a basket of silverbream.

"Anger baits no lines, only wounds." Her mother stacked two empty baskets together and finally squatted down to eat the scavenged meal. "You know better than this, nela."

Rahelu wanted to scream, but she'd done a lot of that today and the day before. She stared at the three spheres sitting in the hollow she had worried into the dirt before her and voiced her fear instead.

"What if I can't do it? What if this is as far as I go? All that Guild training, all those sacrifices you and aban made, and I can't solve the first puzzle the Houses throw at me!"

Aleznuaweites liked to brag. They bragged about their wealth, their Guild, their meritocratic society, and their ideals —fairness, equality, prosperity.

She had always shared her parents' beliefs in those Aleznuaweithish ideals; that what mattered was your willingness to learn and work hard; the dream that, no matter the circumstances of your birth, it was possible to rise above the humbleness of your origins—all you had to do was prove yourself worthy.

Until now.

Now she was convinced that the dream was a lie. A very elaborate lie, composed of half-truths that embellished and emphasized certain historical facts, and glossed over others.

If it hadn't been for Onneja, chance-met on the road, Rahelu wouldn't have made it past the Guild's entrance test. If not for Tsenjhe, her Petition would have ended up in a bonfire. Without Keshwar, Lhorne, and Dharyas, she wouldn't have earned a single sphere.

She would have been right where Nheras had left her, trying to piece her future together from scattered refuse in the gutter.

"There is no point setting a course to avoid storm clouds you cannot see," her mother said, nibbling on a slice of bread.

How did her mother do that? Let every setback, every injustice, every insult float past her, like so much flotsam on the tide? She had somehow convinced Hzin, of all people, to cover the shortfall on yesterday's payment to Isonn.

While Rahelu had slept, her parents had risen with the moon, sailed out, and returned with more goldtrout. They wouldn't lose their fishing license today.

The next installment was due in a week.

How long could they keep this up?

Blood rushed to her face at the mere thought, but she had to know: could they...could they just...leave?

"Anma?" Rahelu asked. "Do you and aban ever think perhaps we should go back to Chanaz?"

"Back?" Her mother spoke around a mouthful of cold,

roasted bird. "What for? We sold everything; there is nothing left in Chanaz."

"We have family there," Rahelu said. "Don't we?"

Her mother didn't answer the question; she nodded to the dent Rahelu had made in the freshwater barrel instead. "Patience and time, nela; those two together will untangle any knot. You will go tomorrow, before the Elders of these Houses, and you will answer their questions to the best of your abilities. Where those currents will take you, only the Starfather knows. But you will catch nothing if you do not cast your net."

With that, her mother stood, hefted the third half-empty basket onto one shoulder, and made her way towards the Highdocks, calling out as she went: "Fish! Fresh-caught fish from the Kuath! Goldtrout, silverbream, sweetcod, and more! One from two copper kez, three from five copper, ten from just eight copper kez!"

Meaning that Rahelu should try again, but with a different tactic. And that she should carry the empty baskets home when she had finished.

Rahelu sighed and picked up the wooden sphere. But no matter what she tried, she couldn't move past the present. Her mind kept slipping into Evocation, picking up fleeting impressions of the sphere's previous handlers:

—mild interest, as it tumbles from long, elegant fingers. A thumb-sized resonance crystal, set in a white-gold band, gleams on the second digit—

From earlier in the skyarc.

—serene patience, as it waits in the dark—

A pocket? A silk bag?

*—a different pair of hands (larger, more masculine, wearing...
gloves?) clicking its wooden parts into place—*

Not enough detail for her to figure out how to take the
Issolm sphere apart and get to the resonance crystal inside.
There *had* to be one—it didn't make sense that the Issolm
sphere had none when the Ideth and Isca spheres had so
many—but she couldn't sense it at all. It must be hidden by
an Obfuscation barrier far beyond her ability to breach.

There weren't any more resonance echoes either, even as
she strained to reach further back in time. No hidden
message, buried as a Projection within the object's history, to
speak to her across time.

At least, not in that direction.

She blinked rapidly and shook her head as she jerked her
mind back to the present. It was much quieter now, with the
other vendors packing up their stalls for the day. She would—

"Can I ask you a question?"

Rahelu started at the sound of Dharyas's voice. The Isca
girl sat on the dirt beside Rahelu, knees hugged to her chest,
her resonance aura a thrumming pale green. The self-assured
confidence Rahelu associated with all House-born was
nowhere in sight. How long had the Isca girl been sitting
there?

"Why do you want to join one of the Houses so much?"
Dharyas's hurried words tumbled over each other, leaving no
opening for a reply. "And I don't mean the obvious reasons.
What do you strive for?"

What a useless question. The kind only House-born with
too much time on their hands would ask. She went to snap at
Dharyas, but the serious look on the Isca girl's face gave her
pause.

"I—for my parents. They gave up their lives for me. I owe
them everything."

"Why?"

"Because they're my parents."

"So? They're not you."

"No." She searched for the right words, failed to find them, and switched to Chanazian. "Their blood in my veins, their breath in my lungs." Then in Aleznuaweithish: "It roughly means 'I am of them' and also 'I am them', but it doesn't work in your language. There's too much emphasis on the 'I' when it should be the other way around."

"But it's *your* life!"

"There's no distinction in Chanazian."

"What does that matter? You live in Aleznuaweite now."

"So do you." Rahelu looked pointedly at the freshly scabbed line that wound around the other girl's left forearm. "But you still add to your scars."

Dharyas fell silent, leaving Rahelu free to glare at her wooden sphere as if she could intimidate it into revealing its secrets. She tried imposing her will upon it with Projection—mentally commanding it to show her its future, the way songhouses liked to dramatize the resonance disciplines—but all she ended up doing was slamming her mind into the barrier between now and tomorrow repeatedly.

She had to stop when the muted ache in her temples turned into a steady throbbing. "I fucking hate Augury."

"It's not so hard as everybody thinks," Dharyas said. "You just can't work an Augury the same way you run an Evocation."

"Why not? It's the same principle of reaching through time—it's just going forward instead of backward."

"Yes. Evocation's opposite." Dharyas straightened out of her slump. "Stop trying to see a specific moment—no one can know the whole of the Starfather's grand design or how it will unfold. If you want to catch glimpses, you need to be open to the possibilities."

"It can't be that simple," Rahelu said. "If it were, the Houses wouldn't guard their Augurs so jealously."

"I assure you it is. There is no such thing as an inborn gift for Augury. That's just an excuse House-born like to use, so they don't have to think beyond their narrow lives."

Rahelu looked—really looked—at Dharyas for the first time.

"Of course, I have the opposite problem," the Isca girl said with a wry smile. "Sometimes all I can see are the possibilities." She got to her feet without bothering to brush off the dirt clinging to the seat of her trousers. "And I still don't see enough. Thank you for your earlier honesty," she added, almost as an afterthought.

"Luck, Dharyas," Rahelu said.

"I'd wish you luck too, but I don't believe in that superstition. See you on the other side." Dharyas grinned and waved as she walked off towards Blackforge. "And if you're still struggling, practice by looking into someone else's future first so your emotions don't get in the way."

The three spheres in front of Rahelu glinted in the fading light. She closed her eyes to them and cast her resonance senses out into the market.

Emptying her mind of thoughts, Rahelu breathed in the Guild's slow seven-count for Seeking and allowed herself to drift upon the ebb and flow of the ambient resonance—aimless—the way she used to let the gentle currents of the Elumaje guide her raft as she stretched out to bask in the sun. Instead of honing in on a specific resonance, she tasted lightly of each one, like letting her fingers and toes trail through cool waters instead of submerging herself entirely.

Here, in the corner dedicated to seafood stalls and butchered meat, there was a strong sense of contentment. Satisfaction, coupled with an eagerness to be gone, over a mild undercurrent of longing for home.

Good trading for the day, then.

Hzin was feeling particularly self-satisfied, his every motion fueled with extra nervous energy. Rahelu sifted through his resonance aura with care, only drawing on the emanations from his body, staying away from a direct Seeking.

Seeking wasn't mind-reading—nobody, not even the arch-mages of legend, could do *that*. Seeking was all about making guesses: educated guesses, sure, but guesses nonetheless.

Most people performed some variation of a basic Seeking without ever recognizing it as such. Sensing the emotional resonance of a crowd, a group, an individual in the moment as they experienced it was as natural as breathing; something every child learned to do, even while they were within the womb. Everyone was born understanding how the people closest to them felt and what event had caused the feeling, just as a child instinctively understood how to cry aloud and Project their sense of hunger long before they could speak.

A Guild-trained mage, however, learned to do more with their resonance sense than simply sensing the most domi-nant emotion in a crowd. They learned how to Seek out the truth of an event by discerning resonance patterns. Seeking was a discipline that required both attention to detail and abstract thinking: you had to sort through all those different resonances, isolate the relevant ones, reconstruct the physio-logical responses that would have caused those resonances, and then work backward to determine the physical actions that had taken place.

So when Rahelu concluded that a large part of Hzin's satisfaction stemmed from beating her mother to Market Square to secure the best spot—on the very edge of the unmarked border dividing the fruit and vegetable sellers from the seafood hawkers, close enough that his stall was in direct line of sight of the well, yet remained shaded from the direct sun by the shadow of the central pavilion that held the live meat stalls—she had guessed.

She had based her guess on small, mundane details observed in the moment (as he folded his mat and stacked his baskets, Hzin kept patting the coins in his heavy purse like he couldn't believe his good fortune) and over time (he and her mother had fought over that spot for years; not a single day had gone by where one didn't curse the other when they were forced to set up in a lesser location).

It *was* a guess, but a reliable enough guess that it could be taken with reasonable certainty. The only way she would get a more reliable answer would be to perform a direct Seeking, and that wasn't allowed without consent (or an investigative warrant).

She shifted her breathing pattern into the even slower five-count the Guild taught for Augury and kept her focus on Hzin, suppressing her instinctive urge to seize upon the sense of his satisfaction. Instead, she tried to heed Dharyas's advice by questing gently after that resonance, to follow those echoes forward moment by moment, along Hzin's impending departure from Market Square:

Wary caution as he walks through a dimly lit alleyway, one hand on his coin pouch, another ready to draw his belt knife in an instant. Relief as he arrives without incident in front of an unmarked door with a worn bronze handle, unevenly polished over the years by the many hands that have grasped it. He hesitates, then turns the handle to enter. Nervousness, as he descends a set of rickety stairs, leaving a trail of clammy sweat on the railing, then approaches—

A man? A woman? Rahelu couldn't make out their features clearly in her Augury.

—with a handful of coins. He is shaking again—this time from antici-pation, which grows stronger and stronger as he follows the blurred figure through a maze of claustrophobic corridors to a squalid room with a thin gray curtain, like a fish thrashing on the line, gasping. A stab of guilt as he steps through the curtain. Inside is a slave who wears a band forged from linked resonance crystals worth a House-born's ransom. Hzin unbuckles his trousers and holds out his left wrist to receive a smaller, matching band. It floods him with sensa-tion: the rough texture of coarse bed linens against naked flesh, the scent of dreamleaf and stale flesh, the doubled vision of himself standing at the doorway, stroking his cock. He can do anything, anything he wants, and what he wants most is—

Rahelu was retching her guts out before she had even opened her eyes.

Every inch of her trembled, almost as badly as she'd been shaking after surviving the second challenge.

Suborned. He was going to a Suborned den.

Rahelu spat, wiped her mouth on her father's tunic, then spat again before she forced herself to scoop up all three of her spheres, the remains of the salvaged meal her mother had left uneaten, and the two empty baskets.

Hzin called to her as she passed by his stall on her way out of Market Square.

"Luck, Rahelu, for your audiences with the Elders tomor-row," he said. "May the Starfather smile upon you!"

Gods, she couldn't look at him.

"Thank you," she managed to ground out. She nearly wished him a calm stormarc out of habit, and her stomach almost revolted again at the thought of what she'd seen in her Augury.

She hurried home, feeling like a failure and in desperate need of a bath. She would make sure her father ate *all* of the food she had scavenged, go down to the Kuath at low tide, and scrub herself with ash and sand until her skin was red and raw.

And then she would attempt another Augury with these stupid spheres until the moon set and the sun rose again, in someplace far, far away from other people.

12

AUDIENCE

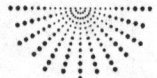

THE 24TH DAY OF EARLY SUMMER, 530 A.E./A.F.

HOUSE ISSOLM WAS HEADQUARTERED ON THE south side of Westgate, an easy quarter-span's walk from the palace, and its architecture was a scrupulous imitation of the palace writ small: a sprawling, blocky two-story affair done in white marble, with a central scrying tower that spiraled up to touch the clouds. Its granite wall was twice her height, and the solid bronze gate in its center was at least fifteen strides wide.

Today, that gate was barred. Rahelu was only permitted to enter through the smaller side gate after presenting her wooden sphere, whereupon she was escorted through a series of spacious stone hallways and deposited at the lower entrance to the scrying tower.

"Wait here," said her escort, a Harbinger who had outlined the black flame emblazoned on his white leather armband with gold resonance paint. "Elder Anathwan will see you shortly." He took her wooden sphere and strode up the steps without a backward glance.

Alone, with no one else in mundane or resonance sight,

Rahelu succumbed to exhaustion: she propped herself up against the stone wall and let her heavy eyelids shut, praying that she wouldn't fall asleep and make a complete fool of herself.

She'd already done that in her audience with House Isca. After a full night of attempting Augury, she had failed to sense anything other than a vague confusion from the wire sphere. She had duly presented herself at the Isca headquarters in the Blackforge district at the second span after dawn anyway, thinking there might be some way to bluff her way through the audience.

But the Isca Elder had simply led her to a workshop filled with wire contraptions like her sphere and asked her a single question: "Well?"

What, exactly, was she supposed to do? Rahelu had had no idea. The wire sphere was evidently a key of some sort, but she couldn't make heads or tails of it. She had frozen, afraid to touch any of the delicate assemblies, getting nothing but jumbled resonance in her Seeking, though the meaning of her Augury was now clear: the confusion she had sensed was her own.

Not even a third of her allotted quarter-span had lapsed before she had admitted defeat and returned her wire sphere to the Isca Elder. He had stowed it away in his pouch with a sniff and a shake of his head, then turned his attention back to a different, even more complicated assembly on his workbench. She'd stood there awkwardly for another hundred heartbeats, waiting for him to dismiss her, before she realized he no longer registered her presence.

Gods. She hoped Dharyas was having better luck.

A growing beacon of curiosity jolted her out of her thoughts, and she Projected a quick pulse of acceptance in return.

Applicant Rahelu. Elder Anathwan's Projection was full of warm welcome. *Please come upstairs.*

Rahelu took the stairs two at a time. About a quarter of the way up, she switched to jogging, one stair at a time. By the time she was three-quarters of the way through her ascent, she had to rest a hand on each knee as she climbed.

When she arrived at the top, where Anathwan of Issolm waited, Rahelu was embarrassed to realize she was actually panting.

The white-robed Elder—who was *very* young for an Elder; she couldn't have been more than a decade older than Rahelu herself—sat cross-legged on a silk cushion upon the bare stone floor, her golden curls a loose tumble around her shoulders. A lacquered wooden tray rested on the stone next to her, holding a steaming cup of tea and Rahelu's wooden sphere.

The Harbinger who had escorted Rahelu to the scrying tower was nowhere in sight.

Anathwan of Issolm's smile was every bit as warm as her Projection. "It's quite a hike, isn't it? I climb this tower every day, and I still find it strenuous. Come," the Issolm Elder said and patted the bare stone on her other side. "Let me get to know you. Your performance in yesterday's challenges was wonderful!"

Rahelu crept forward and sat. "I am honored by your esteem, Elder. But truly, it was possible only due to the efforts of my teammates and the Starfather's blessing."

"Forging an alliance with House Ideth, however temporary, is impressive nonetheless. How do you judge their recent move? I would hear your thoughts."

What move?

Rahelu tried to keep her face impassive, but she didn't manage to stop her eyes from widening slightly, nor could she suppress the flicker of yellow-green in her resonance aura.

Her eyes darted to the wooden sphere on the tray. If only she had managed to glean *something* from the sphere; then, perhaps, she would know what the Issolm Elder meant.

But Rahelu had tried and tried all stararc without success: as far as she could tell, the wooden sphere was just a wooden sphere.

There was no way that the Issolm Elder could have missed her confusion. Still, Anathwan looked at her expectantly, like Rahelu was another Elder, full of wisdom and insight, someone of equal status.

She desperately wanted to be worthy of that regard, but she had no idea what the question meant, let alone what her answer should be.

"It is difficult," Rahelu said, "to judge such a move in isolation from other factors. House Ideth is an ancient House, one of the foundational pillars of old Aleznua before it became Aleznuaweite. Many of its Atriarches have held the honor of Exaltation, and many believe an Ideth Atriarch will be Exalted once more, possibly soon. The current Atriarch can trace her lineage back to the archmage Dethiram, who once shifted the winds of Fortune and held the balance of fate in her hand. Ideth never plays a single hand at once—and never for short-term stakes."

None of what she had said contained any substance whatsoever. Mere generalities, drawing from hearsay and public record, rather than verified resonances. But it sounded weighty and serious (she hoped), like the kind of thing another Elder who knew exactly what Elder Anathwan was talking about would say.

"Should House Issolm oppose Ideth?"

Rahelu paled. How was she supposed to answer that?

"House Ideth's economic stability is second to none: they control four-fifths of the arable farmland in Aleznuaweite, a third of the resonance crystal market, nine-tenths of the grain trade, and virtually all of the textile trade, other than silk and leather. Even House Isilc, with its mines and unrivaled wealth, cannot compare, and the only House that controls more land is House Isonn."

She could have gone on. No other House could hope to stand alone against House Ideth; they had mages, food, and resonance crystals in abundant supply. At the first sign of open hostilities, House Ideth could cut off their supply chains to the entire continent and outlast any other House for years.

But talking up one House's strengths while you were in a private audience with another seemed unwise.

"However, there is also the Ideth reputation to consider. Their Atriarches are famed for their fairness and exact dealing—the current Atriarch is no different. Before she became Atriarch, she was a Seeker of great renown, and when she was betrayed by another Seeker on a joint assignment, she did not demand her betrayer's life or estates as she could have by right—she only took his resonance crystal."

And then, Rahelu thought of the attempted coup by the Issolm applicants yesterday. It had almost worked. It should have worked; it *would* have worked, except for a shift in the Stormbringer's whims.

If it *had* worked, it would have been an astonishing win— to the detriment of all other applicants. But then again, that wasn't so different from Lhorne and Dharyas convincing her to secure all ten tokens in the first challenge.

"House Ideth is not invulnerable, and what is good for House Ideth does not necessarily benefit us all. But their farmlands, resonance crystals, and textiles are vital to the Dominion, so any threat to House Ideth would also threaten the stability of Aleznuaweite."

She hoped that was good enough.

Anathwan sipped from her teacup as she studied Rahelu with intent blue eyes. "Is that a 'no'?"

Shit. The Elder was going to force her to answer one way or the other. Saying 'no' would be an insult to House Issolm; saying 'yes' would be a violation of Aleznuaweite ideals.

"The first duty of any House is to the Dominance of Aleznuaweite," Rahelu said, hedging behind the platitude. "No House should oppose another lightly, and no House should become so powerful that it threatens the Dominance. But the winds of Fortune are fickle as the winds of the Aleituan Sea. A wise House prepares for fair sun or foul storm alike so they may steer a safe course to prosperous shores, no matter what."

The Elder said nothing and took another sip of tea as her blue eyes continued searching Rahelu's face. And although the Elder said nothing, Projected nothing, and her resonance aura revealed nothing, Rahelu felt that something had changed between them.

Please, Rahelu thought. *Please, please, please let that be good enough.* She didn't think she could come up with any more not-answers.

She needed to find another six, before her allotted quarter-span was up.

Anathwan of Issolm released her from the scrying tower with warm assurances that a House representative would be in touch to advise the result of her Petition in due course.

———

THE IDETH HEADQUARTERS were a stark contrast to the palatial splendor of House Issolm's; it boasted no soaring scrying tower or marblework, not even a central building. Instead, it was a simple warehouse in the Temple district, not far from the Highdocks. Rahelu had nearly left, certain she'd taken a wrong turn, but when she turned away from the utterly ordinary building, the resonance signal of the glass sphere in her hand went from an insistent pulsing to almost nothing in two-and-a-half strides.

No one greeted her as she entered, even though it was still high sun. At this span, a warehouse should be a hive of activity: there ought to be workers rushing to load and unload supply wagons, trade factors haggling with clerks, and the constant movement of goods and people—yet the entire place had the creeping feel of a Lowdocks back alley after dark.

"Hello?"

Her voice echoed in the cavernous space. No one answered, but the glass sphere in her hand pulsed frantically, the tiny resonance crystal fragments inside jangling.

Rahelu's skin prickled. To her left, not far from the entrance, was an iron ladder that led up to a loft above the warehouse floor, that she definitely did *not* want to climb. It was half-rusted and looked like it might fall apart if she tried to set foot on it. But she didn't want to stay down here, exposed. Anything could be hiding behind one of those shelves or abandoned pieces of old plows.

"Is anyone here?" she called again, closing her eyes. She centered her Seeking on herself and tried to follow her emotions forward in time. "Applicant Rahelu, here to see—"

Her Augury came back with a clear sense of pain, radiating from her right side.

Rahelu dropped flat to the floor, avoiding the sweeping blow meant for her ribs. She cradled the glass sphere to her chest and rolled, just in time to avoid the iron-shod butt of a mirror-bright length of polished oak. It slammed into the wooden floor, right where her heart had been. She scrambled to her feet, sphere in one hand and fumbling for her belt knife with the other, as she turned to face her attacker.

At first glance, Rahelu mistook the older woman for another applicant—perhaps Nheras or one of the many others who had many reasons to hate her after yesterday. The older woman wore a roughspun cotton tunic (of a slightly finer quality than the one Rahelu had borrowed, once again, from her father) over undyed linen trousers, but she carried a mage-staff topped with a resonance crystal the size of a small melon, the largest one Rahelu had ever seen.

"Slow off the mark," the woman said, shaking her head. "Whatever my son saw in you, it didn't include quick thinking."

"Atriarch Ideth!" she said, dropping her knife and going to her knees at once. She kept her head bowed as she offered up the glass sphere in both hands. "Please, I beg your forgiveness."

The Atriarch plucked the sphere from her hand and pocketed it without comment. "Stop cringing and get up so I can look at you properly."

Rahelu obeyed, standing still and straight, fighting the urge to dust off her borrowed tunic and pick up her knife.

Atriarch Mere Ideth circled her like a shark.

"What do you make of House Imos's recent move?"

Fuck.

"It is difficult," Rahelu said, "to judge such a move in isolation from other factors. House Imos is—"

"Bah! Spare me the platitudes. If I wanted Issolm wishy-washiness I'd grant audiences to their applicants. I need Supplicants, not sheep—I have plenty of those already." The Atriarch rapped her mage-staff on the stone floor of the warehouse. "Speak up, Rahelu. I'm a busy woman with a House to run. I want to hear your thoughts, not a summary of the idle chatter that passes for conversation in this city."

Oh, *fuck*.

"House Imos," Rahelu began, then hesitated. Was it even safe to voice her suspicions?

If anywhere was safe, it would be here, in audience with Atriarch Ideth. Rahelu doubted anyone, short of another Atriarch or a Conclave archmage, could spy on them through an indirect Seeking without Atriarch Ideth's knowledge.

"House Imos is the weakest of the major Houses," she said slowly. "They control virtually no land within the Dominion of Aleznuaweite itself, other than their family estate. Their wealth is built on trade deals, founded primarily on the strength of the connections between their vassal, House Imrell, and a number of prominent...mercenary companies in the Free Territories."

"Don't dance around the facts. House Imos are in bed with conscienceless thieves and pirates," the Atriarch said. "Stop talking like you're some Chronicler's record; this isn't a Guild examination. I don't care how clever or talented my son thinks you are—that does no good if you're not willing to use those brains to speak up and act."

"Atriarch Imos is planning a coup!" Rahelu blurted out, then gulped.

She shouldn't have said that, even if she thought it was true. Accusations were serious things. Anyone who wanted to bring a formal accusation against another citizen had to submit to a direct Seeking so the basis for their accusations could be independently verified by a Guild-accredited Seeker.

And that was just when the accused was an ordinary citizen, without the standing of House or Guild. The procedures for accusations brought by one rival guild member against another, by one member of a House against another, grew increasingly complex with the station of the accused and the severity of the accusation.

A mere common-born applicant accusing the Atriarch of a major House—a member of the Royal Council—of treason?

Rahelu wasn't sure of the exact protocol because there was no historical precedent.

It simply wasn't done.

But instead of rebuking her, Atriarch Ideth merely nodded. "Do you understand why?"

Two reasons came to mind.

In principle, the Exalted Dominance was first among equals. When an Atriarch became Exalted, they gained no new lands or industries for their House; in fact, they *lost* their seat on the Royal Council. The Exalted Dominance could make no laws on their own prerogative; the Royal Council had to vote to pass the law by a simple majority, and some laws (such as those affecting national defense and monetary policy) had to pass unanimously.

In many respects, it could be argued that an Atriarch lost more power in becoming Exalted than they gained.

In two respects, however, the Atriarch gained a lot.

The first was pure prestige. On the scale of nations, the Exalted Dominance *was* Aleznuaweite; they stood on equal footing with any Archmage of the Chanazian Conclave or the Divine Holiness of Belruonia.

And the second was the power to levy and enforce the collection of all manner of taxes.

Which was it? Prestige or power? Which would Rahelu crave the most, if she could have either?

She ventured a guess. "Atriarch Imos's treasury is low because he can't recruit enough Supplicants from the Imos and Imrell families alone to sustain the Imos operations. He has spent the last five seasons burning through his reserves by hiring companies from the Free Territories.

"If an applicant like me can divine his intentions, then all of the Elders and Atriarchs must know, including His Exalted

Dominance. He can't recruit from the other major Houses because he can't risk his actual plans becoming known. He needs to move soon, or he'll run out of kez to pay his mercenaries. He needs the tax revenue to make up his shortfall."

Atriarch Ideth nodded again. "True, but wrong."

Rahelu opened her mouth to argue the point, then closed it. Atriarch Ideth had demanded her to be frank with her answers, but she was pretty sure that wasn't an open invitation to speak her mind.

After another sharp glance from the Atriarch, Rahelu spoke her mind in a hurry. "Pardon the disrespect, Atriarch Ideth, but how can the truth be wrong?"

"What births a storm?" the Atriarch asked. "Is it the winds, the clouds, or the rain?"

Finally! A question she could answer with confidence.

"The Stormbringer pulls the winds," Rahelu said. "The winds bring the clouds, and with the clouds come the rain, which births the storm."

"True," said the Atriarch, "but wrong. It is the sun."

The sun? Rahelu hated pointless riddles and was about to say so before the Atriarch cut her off.

"Don't talk back."

What?

Atriarch Mere Ideth was the most confusing person Rahelu had ever met.

And, as if she wanted to prove the point, the Atriarch changed the subject without warning. "Who is Lhorne to you?"

Rahelu's hand flew to the resonance crystal pendant that still hung around her neck. "A friend." She felt herself flushing.

The Atriarch didn't remark on the color in her cheeks. "And who are you to him?"

"A friend," she repeated. "He…"

He chose to be on a team with me, because he thought I was smart. He saw that I was hungry and tried to buy me food, without making me feel like a beggar.

He treats me as his equal, despite the disparity in our stations.

"Keshwar recommended me to him," she said instead. "He thinks—he thought we made a good team."

She held still under the Atriarch's keen regard, steeled her nerves, then met the older woman's eyes without flinching.

"Rahelu," the Atriarch said. "I ask your consent to perform a direct Seeking."

This time, Rahelu did flinch. A direct Seeking wasn't mind-reading, but it came awfully close. It would allow the Atriarch to sense all of her emotions, including her deepest desires; desires that she did not dare to acknowledge to herself.

"And if I refuse?"

The Atriarch held up one hand. "This forms no part of your audience. Whether you choose to give your consent or not will have no bearing on how I judge your Petition. I ask this as a personal favor."

A personal favor.

Could she really say no to an Atriarch?

Even if she could, would her refusal really play no part in the Atriarch's consideration of her Petition? Could she even risk that it would?

Her disastrous audience with Isca meant there would be no support for her Petition from that House. And over the course of her audience with Issolm, Elder Anathwan had gone from sisterly warmth to cool formality.

Rahelu had to agree. She couldn't jeopardize her only remaining chance at an offer to join a House.

Not just any House—House Ideth!

Yesterday, she had counted a few years of slavery as a Supplicant to House Issolm a good trade.

It's not the same, a part of her mind insisted. *You'd be baring your soul to this woman. It's one short step away from being Suborned.*

But Supplicant to House Ideth! And Atriarch Ideth would owe her a personal favor.

Rahelu took a deep breath. "I consent."

13
AUGURY

THE GRAND HALL INSIDE THE GUILD DID NOT LIVE up to its name. Its ceiling was so low even Rahelu felt the looming weight of the second floor above as a gigantic foot that would come down any moment. The hall's few windows faced northwest, mere arrow slits that were overshadowed by the teaching halls. Wrought-iron lamps lined the walls—one every two strides—but did very little to dispel the gloom, and being on the first floor, there was no skylight.

Rahelu edged her way around the room, scanning the crowd for Dharyas and Lhorne. The assembled applicants were mostly from Houses Isilc, Isonn and Ideth, though the other Houses weren't without representation. They milled around before the raised dais, discussing their audiences in hushed tones as they awaited the Houses' verdict on their Petitions, and their collective resonance aura was the pale gray gloom of a distant harvest storm, like her own.

Ghardon was at the back next to Elaram, who had her right arm in a sling. He held himself stiffly—arms crossed, eyes narrowed—as he watched his sister smile up at an Imos boy who had cut off the sleeves of his shirt to better flaunt his scars.

Elaram reached out to caress the Imos applicant's bare arm, tracing her fingertips over the raised edges of the intricate scars from toned bicep to shoulder.

Ghardon rolled his eyes, and a faint green-brown sheen appeared in his resonance aura.

Rahelu agreed wholeheartedly.

Down at the front of the hall was Nheras. Alone, without Bhemol and Kiran tagging along at her sides. She hovered around the Ideth applicants gathered before a large resonance board. At their center, were Lhorne and Cseryl, engaged in animated debate. He was tracing lines in the air to illustrate a point. (What it was, exactly, Rahelu couldn't make out from this distance.) Cseryl only paid him partial attention: she had her head tilted, sun-bleached hair falling to her waist, and seemed more preoccupied with angling her body so that her back was always firmly to the Ilyn applicant.

It was the kind of well-timed, subtle, indirect exclusion Rahelu herself had never been subjected to. House-born trainees rarely mixed with those who weren't. Every common-born trainee balanced their Guild studies with a full day's labor in their family's trade. None of them had had the luxury of so much as a quarter-span of idle time to themselves, let alone the energy for frivolous socializing.

Rahelu actually felt a little sorry for Nheras.

Undeterred, Nheras circled around to try and catch Lhorne's eye, but Cseryl had distracted him with an Augury. The Ideth circle closed in, heads together, to examine the ghostly fragments of the possible future the tanned girl had summoned in her hand.

Well, that was a very clear signal: anybody who was not of the Ideth family was not welcome.

Dharyas was still nowhere to be seen, so Rahelu stepped

inside a shadowed niche where she could wait in peace, away from the petty House-born games.

Conversation in the hall died as the Imos representative who had supervised the first challenge strode out onto the dais. Lamplight glinted off the large resonance crystal pendant on his chest, its golden chain and the gold-and-resonance-crystal inlays in his Guardian armband.

"If I call your name, step to this side of the hall." He pointed to the side with the windows. "Kyrosh of Isilc. Jhobon of Imrell. Enith of Isonn…"

One by one, the successful applicants left their huddles to stand by the windows. The names didn't *seem* to be in any obvious order: Elaram was called long before Ghardon but shortly after Ylaen of Imos (the boy she'd been flirting with), while Lhorne and Cseryl were called one after another.

Nheras's face and resonance aura grew paler and paler with each name.

"Dharyas of Isca."

The scarred Isca girl did not appear.

"Dharyas of Isca," the Guardian repeated, louder this time, over the murmuring of the assembled crowd. He waited for a full count of twenty, and when Dharyas did not step forward, he continued down his list. "Rualk of Isonn…"

Where *was* Dharyas?

"…Nheras of Ilyn."

Nheras visibly relaxed as she walked over to claim her place with the twenty-eight other House-born by the windowed wall.

"The Houses officially recognize you as Petitioners. You may stay to receive your armbands and assignments," the Guardian said. "The rest of you are dismissed. Your Petition is at an end."

Rahelu couldn't move her feet.

She…she had failed after all.

Nheras had succeeded, and she had failed.

She saw Lhorne frowning, his eyes scanning the hall, and was glad she had hidden herself away at the back of the crowd; gladder still of her resonance ward muffling the ache in her heart and that every other dejected hopeful felt the exact same way, and gladdest of all that she had returned Lhorne's pendant to Atriarch Ideth at the end of her last audience.

She dragged herself out after the others, allowing years of muscle memory to retrace her steps through the hallways, into the sweltering courtyard underneath the full might of the high sun, past the Guild gates, and onto the Northroad.

Days.

Weeks.

Years.

Of rising before dawn, reciting resonance theorems to herself as she went about her chores—catching fish, mending nets, cleaning fish, patching sails, salting fish, hauling water, selling fish, smoking fish, eating fish—only setting down tools to pick up borrowed weapons and resonance crystal at the last possible heartbeat.

Of paying fierce attention to every moment of instruction, arriving early to each class and staying behind to grill her instructors on further details that hadn't been covered, foregoing scheduled breaks (meals at the Guild's dining hall cost extra) in favor of working on her assignments because, Starfather knew, as soon as the last class concluded, she would make her way home to help with whatever work was still left undone into the early spans of stormarc.

All for naught.

In two more blocks, she would have to decide: Lowdocks or Market Square? And then…and then…

A voice in her head.

One she had not expected to hear, ever again.

Nela, Onneja sent.

Rahelu missed her next step and ran into a potter with her handcart. Glazed porcelain swayed precariously—Rahelu steadied it with one hand as the potter shouted in alarm. The delicate cups and plates fell back into position with a clatter as the potter scolded her, nearly jabbing Rahelu in the eye with one furious finger.

She barely registered the reprimand.

You're in a fine tempest today. As agitated as the Tsojo in full flood.

Onneja! Rahelu sent back. The Conclave journeymage did not hold with formalities. *You're here? I thought...I thought you had returned to Anazvela.*

I am but passing through, Onneja sent, along with an image of roughly carved stairs in an enormous rock above the harbor.

Stormbane's Rest, Lhorne had called it.

Come and meditate with me, nela. There is still another span or two before I must leave.

A dutiful daughter would not go.

A daughter worthy of her parents' sacrifices would not wallow in self-pity; she would sail out into the Kuath Bay with her father or sell fish with her mother to atone for her failure.

I am coming, Rahelu sent.

———

SHE FOUND Onneja at the very top of the seacliff overlooking the Eastward, seated cross-legged upon the bare rock: eyes closed, back against the sun, facing west into the future. The Conclave journeymage looked unspeakably wise, radiant with power, like the legendary archmages of old. Skyarc rays glinted off her cropped, silvered hair and filled in all the shadows in her lined face, making her look ageless.

Stepping into her presence was like sinking into the still fathoms of the Elumaje—Onneja's resonance aura was a bubble three strides wide and all relaxed control; a uniform shade of cool, gray-blue without the slightest ebb and flow. As soon as Rahelu crossed over the boundary into Onneja's sphere of influence, soothing calm settled over her, swallowing up the dark cracks and throbbing crimson in her aura.

Rahelu greeted the Conclave journeymage by pressing the middle three fingers of her right hand to her heart, even though she was no true apprentice of Onneja's or the Conclave. "Anaz."

"Sit," Onneja said, indicating the space in front of her without opening her eyes.

An invitation—one supported by the Conclave journeymage's tone and resonance aura—but Rahelu still felt it as a command. She folded her legs and sat, facing Onneja and east, into the past. Unprompted, she settled into the familiar rhythms of the basic four-count pattern universal to both Guild and Conclave.

The first meditation she had ever learned.

The one Onneja had taught her six years ago (by a burbling river, sat upon a rock very like this one), along with other tidbits of wisdom. Insights from a master of the resonance disciplines, gathered over decades of practice, freely shared with a little girl who constantly hovered around and didn't have enough training to appreciate the priceless value of that knowledge until years later.

The Conclave journeymage was not a woman of many words. Rahelu didn't truly know her, having only seen her thrice before. But if her past two visits had been anything to go by, Onneja ought to have inquired after Rahelu's studies by now.

"Is something wrong?" Rahelu asked.

There was a long pause. "I do not know. The winds of Fortune feel strange lately." Onneja opened her eyes and focused her gaze on Rahelu. "I would ask of you a favor."

"How may I serve?"

"You consent so easily." The Conclave journeymage raised her eyebrows. "You have no other questions?"

Rahelu shook her head. Onneja was the only reason her family had been able to cross the border into Aleznuaweite without trouble; the only reason she had managed to graduate with a half-decent Guild rating. Whatever favor she could give, it would never be enough to repay Onneja.

"Very well," Onneja said. "I must perform an Augury. One that spans the next decade. Perhaps longer."

"I—" Rahelu had to drop her gaze to the bare rock before she managed to swallow her shame and force the words out. "I doubt I'll be much help."

"Do not fret, nela," Onneja said. "I only require you to be my focus."

Rahelu looked up so fast that her vision blurred for a moment. "Could you…" The words she wanted to use were *'foretell my future'*, but she knew better than that so she asked, "Would I see the Augury too?"

"I look not into your future, but the future of Ennuost Yrg." Onneja smiled at the regret that tinged Rahelu's aura, then closed her eyes to sink into a meditative trance once more. "Relax. And simply *be*."

Rahelu breathed in the tang of the sea air and felt the cool, rough texture of the granite boulder through her thin cotton trousers. Closing her own eyes, she tried to calm the thudding of her heart, the rasping of her breath, still the trembling of her limbs, and just *listen*.

She heard the crashing of breakers upon the shore, their ponderous drumming against the seacliffs slowly easing the anxious rhythm of her heart. Somewhere, high above and to the right, were the eager-shrieks of two mated gulls hunting, as they wheeled and circled in the updraft. Further to the right, hidden below the clifftop, were the softer hunger-chirps of their nestlings.

The restless sea breeze tugged at her hair, lifted sweat-dampened locks off her neck and blew stray wisps across her eyelids and nose and lips, tempering the light of the high sun coating her skin like hot mud.

What should she do, now that the Houses had rejected her?

What were Bhemol and Kiran doing with their time? Were they back at the Guild, honing their resonance skills in private, until they could Petition again?

No. Bhemol and Kiran would have shrugged off failure as a minor setback. They would while away the next year with dinner parties and other idle amusements until they could skip the preliminaries to the challenges once more, thanks to their sponsors; *their* families weren't waiting on them to earn enough coin to survive.

If it had been difficult to find a sponsor as an unproven graduate, it would be impossible now. She could not hope for Keshwar's sponsorship again, not when she had failed him so. Perhaps Tsenjhe...but no, she had let Tsenjhe down too.

The Guild Registrar had been right. What would be the point of asking her parents to invest further in her future as a mage, fruitlessly Petitioning the Houses year after year? How could the selfish thought even cross her mind?

It was time to admit the truth: she was not good enough —would never be good enough—for the Houses. The quick path to security, the prosperous life her parents had dreamed of, was beyond her reach. Pretending otherwise was foolish.

Rahelu scrubbed furiously at her eyes, feeling black threads of despair webbing their way through her resonance aura, twining around yellow lightning. She tried to settle herself into the six-count meditation for Augury; tried to refocus on the feel of the wind, the song of the waves; tried to remain seated, cross-legged and still, up there atop the boulder at the highest, easternmost point of Ennuost Yrg.

What options did she have left?

Rahelu cast her mind forward in time, down towards Market Square and then the sea:

Four thousand suns carve the sky in two as they rise and set. The deck beneath her bare feet is rough, empty; so are her nets and baskets. Back to the horizon, she brings the sloop into the harbor and ties the vessel up at the twelfth berth of the fourth pier. No sign of Bzel or Hzin's boat—or any others.

She finds her father at the Nightmarket, sitting upon a dirty mat, bent and blind with age. He has no tunic, no basket beside him, no coins on the cloth in front of him, and only one white-knuckled fist; its fingers curled tight around a small resonance crystal.

'Avela?' he asks. His voice shivers as badly as he does. 'Is that you, my love?'

'No, aban,' she answers. She clasps her warm hands over his chilled fingers, her swollen fingertips brushing against the crystal's dull, uncut surface. 'She sails with the Stormbringer now.' She lifts him easily—he is so frail, she can hardly feel the weight of his head upon her shoulder—carries him back to the pier so they can lie down beneath the sloop's waxed canvas sail.

Her throat tightened, tension spreading through the back of her neck and up the bridge of her nose. What if...?

For weeks, she walks the length and breadth of the Echo Alleys— listening to door after door slam in her face. Next, the circuit of common-born operated establishments: she begins in Northpoint at summer's end and works her way through to Southwatch. They all turn her away—every entry-level job for a newly graduated mage is already taken, and every remaining opening requires two additional Guild licenses she can't afford, years of experience she doesn't have, or both.

Sunset is out of the question…and so is the Blackforge (for the opposite reasons). Tlareth, too, turns her away: there have been few guests at the Sable Gull all harvest. At deepnight on the winter solstice, Rahelu leaves the meager shelter of her family's hovel to kneel in the Seaspire's moonshadow, letting blood drip freely from her wrists onto the newest heap of pebbles until she can no longer hold out her arms.

Gods. Was there no way out?

She is five years older—with a faded knife scar down the left side of her neck, wearing sturdy linen and a white-and-black cord knotted about her upper arm—and looms over a bruised and battered man in an alleyway.

'Please. Give me one more day,' says the chandler, backing away from her. 'I can pay then. I promise, I—'

She lunges at him; slams her elbow into his face. Though his screams are shrill as he crumples to the ground with his hands covering his broken nose, they are an improvement on his pathetic pleas. She takes another stride forward, lands a savage kick against his ribs, lifts her booted foot again. Someone yanks her backward by her collar. Like a kit flailing its paws at being scruffed by its mother, she dangles at the end of her partner's hamfisted grip, legs kicking, choked by her own shirt until the older, heavyset woman drops her with a glare.

'Damaged goods pay no debts.'

Never. She would see herself Suborned first.

An unmarked door. Worn bronze handle. The bite of crystal around her neck, the only anchor in a sea of gray curtains and dreamleaf haze

that blurs heartbeats into decades and an endless parade of tormentors
into a single, constant, twisted presence in her mind—

Her wet eyelashes clung together, and Rahelu had to force
her eyes open, her breath shuddering in her lungs. Only
Onneja's cocoon of calm kept her centered; only the sound of
Onneja's quiet breathing (in a five-count, not six) kept her
from outright sobs.

Then she saw the workings of Onneja's Augury:

A tall woman in white robes steps out of a moonbeam, a rippled blade
in her fractured hands—

Large, pallid hands open a wooden, velvet-lined case; they lift out a
gold-flecked obsidian crown to place it upon a head of dark curls—

Forked lightning plays around a storm-tossed ship as it leans heavily
to starboard—

Thousands upon thousands of futures spun around them,
a vortex of pearlescent light. The summoned visions clouded
about the apex of Stormbane's Rest, crowding the ambient
resonance, filling her eyes—so vivid they overwhelmed her
mundane sight; so thick they blotted out the sky, the ground
and the sea, leaving her reeling, unanchored, suspended in
their midst.

Possibilities flashed in and out of existence—far quicker
than she could follow. She reached out with her resonance
senses anyway and was pummeled ferociously. Foreign
emotions crashed into her like breakers upon the shore:

—unrelenting determination and dark avarice meet in a blaze of
power before a towering golden throne—

Gouged deep furrows into her resonance aura, flaying her mind.

—bleak desperation grapples against bitter regret as sharpened steel shatters glowing crystal then slices through dark fluttering robes, severing—

Like receding waves dug sand out from underneath her feet.

—four gargantuan ebon obelisks sunk deep into a circular abyss beneath strange stars—

Her heart hammered. Eyes shut.

—rage flares in the winter night, burning brighter and hotter than the flames consuming the tall vine-and-iceflower-wreathed bier—

Lungs gasped.

—stark terror as a serpentine knife descends in a relentless black arc to carve open her mother's chest—

Screamed—

Fierce joy.

Insidious pride.

Poisonous envy.

—until Onneja released her Augury, and Rahelu found herself whimpering soundlessly against her fists, the backs of her hands bleeding from being gnawed by her own teeth.

"Nela?" Cool fingers brushed sweaty locks off her brow.

She peeled her eyes open; tried to speak but found herself voiceless so she reached for Projection instead.

What…what did I…what did you see? she asked. *What does it mean?*

"Trouble." Pale gray shivered through the Conclave journeymage's resonance aura. "Worse than I feared."

How certain is it?—then, before she could stop the foolish words—*Can it be averted?*

"I do not know," Onneja said. "I must go." She leapt up with a spry motion that would have been more natural on a woman half her age.

Onneja, wait! Rahelu scrambled to follow the Conclave journeymage as she descended from the boulder with the swift surety of a mountain goat. *Please, my mother*—

Bone-white cracks splintered her resonance aura, now that she was no longer cradled inside Onneja's sphere of influence.

—*I saw my mother die. What should I do? How can I save her?*

The only response she got was from the gull nestlings, shrieking in hunger as their parents returned from the sea. Her mother's sandals slipped, and Rahelu slid down the rest of the irregular steps cut into the rock to land at the bottom in an ungraceful heap.

Onneja was already three-quarters of the way to the other side of the plateau.

Please, she begged shamelessly. *Help me!*

The Conclave journeymage disappeared from view, down the Eastcliffs, even as Rahelu picked herself up and kept running, ignoring the scrapes on her right side.

I cannot, Onneja sent. *I am sorry.*

No! She cursed inwardly as she had to slow down to make out the twisting steps through blurry eyes.

You must Seek the answers for yourself—the key to your desires lies in your Guild and your family's salvation with your House.

What?

And let no one discover what you have seen.

I don't understand! I—

She reached out ahead with her resonance senses, hurled Projection after Projection, but try as she might, her Seeking came back with nothing.

Onneja was gone.

14
ANSWERS

Rahelu burst through the Guild gates.

She had given up all hope before, but if Onneja had Augured a future where her mother was alive, where she had sworn to one of the Houses—that meant there was a path forward.

Her Isca audience had been a disaster, but that didn't matter so long as both Ideth and Issolm supported her Petition.

Who had she failed to convince before? Just one or both of those Houses? How could she change their minds?

Approaching Elder Anathwan was out of the question; normally, only Dedicates or somebody of an equivalent rank would be granted an audience with an Elder. No Supplicant, even one sworn to House Issolm, would be admitted to see her, let alone a failed applicant who hadn't even been recognized as a Petitioner.

This went doubly so for Atriarch Ideth. As a member of the Royal Council, she no doubt spent most of her time deliberating issues that affected the Dominion at large with the other Royal Councillors or the minor Atriarches, or clos-

eted with her Elders on matters affecting House Ideth—
though Rahelu *could* get around that if she really wanted to.

Was that the key?

But a personal favor from an Atriarch was not lightly
given, and Rahelu had spent too long hoarding copper coins
like gold kez to be tempted. She would only call in that favor
when she truly had no other means of resolving things
herself.

Guardian Maketh was the next House member in line. As
the Dedicate in charge of the Petitioners and their assignments, he would have the answers and she had every right to
approach him despite his prohibition on questions—and she
was ninety-percent confident that prohibition only applied in
the context of the first challenge.

No, the real problem was Rahelu couldn't find the man.

He wasn't in the grand hall; it was empty when she poked
her head inside, except for five Isilc Petitioners who were
arguing in front of the resonance board.

He wasn't in the training yards—those were filled with
second-years in sparring circles, practicing basic combinations of weapon and Projection drills—or the classrooms in
the upper levels of the central building.

He wasn't at work in any of the administrative offices in
the Guild's southwest wing. Every Guild official who had
answered her knock gave the same spiel: the Guild had
nothing to do with the Petitioning process; they merely hired
out the Guild facilities for the Houses' use; all queries
relating to Petitioning should be directed to the Houses; no
they could not provide her with the names of the House
representatives, she ought to make her inquiries with each
House at their headquarters; and was that all because they
were very busy at this time of the year so if she had no
further questions then they would bid her a good day and
could she kindly shut the door.

Rahelu did as they asked, then departed, regretting her decision to leave a grimy sandal print on the stone wall next to the Guild Placements Officer's door.

Kicking something that didn't break or give in the slightest only made the yellow-green in her resonance aura and clouded wake in the hallway's ambient resonance roil more violently. It also left her gingerly favoring her right foot and exceedingly disinclined to the idea of trekking all the way to the opposite side of the city, assuming Maketh had even returned to the Imos headquarters in Southwatch.

Why did Maketh have to be a Guardian? If he had specialized in any other discipline, she'd put her odds of tracking him down through Seeking as one in five—many a mage graduated only having mastered elementary Obfuscation.

But no. He was a Guardian. If she wanted to find him, she would have to do it the hard way, and Rahelu was so very sick of doing things the hard way.

She wandered the Guild's deserted hallways, until she could walk normally again, and found herself back at the grand hall.

It was dark and empty at this span—the wrought-iron lamps had burned themselves out. The only source of light in the hall (not even true light, since it could only be perceived with resonance senses) was the resonance board: instead of a pale, unattuned gray, it now shimmered in varicolored sections.

She ran her hands over the crystalline surface, feeling the slight ridges and gaps where thin crystal plates (so small that they would have qualified as fragments, save for the uniformity of their shape) butted up against each other.

Memories unfolded in her mind as she delved into a light Seeking:

...a vicious bharost raiding Ideth herds, somewhere in the Northreach, dragging its most recent kill across a forest floor...

...a consortium of wool merchants gather a mountain of forensic evidence for their litigation against one of their trade factors ...

...discrepancies in cargo shipments, where the amount of spoilage was unusually high for the season...

On and on the list went, a litany of all the mundane but important business that was the task of administrating the Dominion. Each memory came from a Dedicate, imprinted with their resonance signature as proof of authenticity, and was accompanied by a clear Projection with the assignment's objective, parameters of operation, and the criteria for successful completion. Some memories glowed an anticipatory yellow; they had other resonance signatures appended to them. From teams of Petitioners, she realized, signifying those who had committed to the assignment.

As she sifted through her Seeking, another memory changed. A new resonance was added, its signature vibrating in sympathy with a linked crystal somewhere else in the city.

First, a Projected memory:

A ledger of grain shipments, next to a sheaf of parchments. Each record appears for a handful of heartbeats as the index fingers of two separate hands compare figures.

Then, a clear Projected note:

No discrepancies between the dockmaster's ledger and the bills of lading held by the ship's officer.

Followed by a vivid Evocation that threatened to overwhelm the grand hall:

She is aboard a ship, bailing out water with several other crew members inside the cargo hold half-filled with seawater. The Summer's Wish *has been caught unprepared by an early squall—they ought to have consulted an Augur at Peshwan Yrg but the captain had been in a hurry to make port before spring's end—and the hull had sprung a cursed inconvenient leak. By the time the squall had passed, the water that had seeped in was a good three or four hands deep, and it would take spans to bail it all out.*

The Evocation blurred, moving two weeks forward to when the *Summer's Wish* anchored at the third pier of the Highdocks and unloaded its cargo:

The first mate descends the ladder into the hold, pries open several barrels to gauge the condition of the wheat: all are damp and every handful of grain the first mate pulls out is slimed with rot.

Two familiar resonance signatures, then the resonance transfer ended, causing that section of the resonance board to pulse a brilliant green.

She glanced out of one of the window slits to gauge the sun's arc, but couldn't see it clearly. Perhaps two or three spans had passed? Ghardon and Elaram moved *quickly* to get from here to the Highdocks and locate both the records and the crew member. Would they need to return to the Guild to select their next assignment?

No. Whatever relay node they had been given contained a key permitting them to modify the resonances in the board, so they should be able to sign out another assignment without delay.

Sure enough, a second crystal square changed from blue

to yellow. The first pulsing green glow steadied, then faded entirely, and two more squares in a blank section of the resonance board lit up with the same green. Running her fingers over those triggered another Projection:

> *Petitioner/s: Elaram of Issolm; Ghardon of Issolm.*
> *Task: Investigate the variance between the expected and actual tonnages of grain shipments on the* Summer's Wish.
> *Expected level of difficulty: Easy*
> *Evaluation: Completed satisfactorily and within acceptable timeframes.*
> *Evaluated by: Dherghann of Isonn, 22nd day of early summer, 530 A.F.*
> *Compensation awarded: 20 silver kez*

Rahelu drew in a sharp breath.

This was it.

This was the key to her desires, the means to bring about her family's salvation.

If she could find a way in.

While she might not be as brilliant as Dharyas, she had done a little independent study on the construction of message relays to see whether she could create one for her parents. Nothing elaborate (her parents didn't have the training to Project clear thoughts); just a simple stud to pick up strong emotions, so she would know the instant her father ran into trouble on the sea or if her mother was about to be robbed.

She could have saved herself the effort. Relays were complicated things, and their range depended on the size of the crystal. To span a distance as far as the Kuath Bay, you needed a second-class crystal or better. (Which meant her idea, however well-intentioned, was a non-starter: she could only afford fragments, not whole stones.)

Rahelu sat down cross-legged in front of the resonance board. Physical contact was ideal for mapping the relay's structure, but the constant flux of resonance transfers would be a distraction.

Every message relay had a control point that was also the weak point in the system: the crystal's heart—the part that remained after cutting away each piece of the relay. This would be where the artificer (or, more likely, an entire team of artificers working in Concordance) had Imbued self-sustaining Seeking, Projection, and Evocation spells, keying each crystal plate to the heart. Encrypted relays had an additional layer of Obfuscation spells that wrapped the whole construction, preventing anyone without a physical key from listening in.

Destroy the heart, destroy the relay.

Or—if all you wanted to do was to get in—simply override the heart's existing Imbuement to recognize your personal resonance signature. Then, as long as you were within Seeking range, it would treat you like any other relay point.

Easy as spearing a bluegill in the shallows.

Rahelu breathed in the slow eight-count for Seeking, focusing on the beating of her own heart and ignoring the noise of the constant resonance flux from incoming transfers.

There. A coded pattern that started from the top left-hand corner of the resonance board and ghosted diagonally through to the opposite corner like the ripples from a pebble thrown into still water.

She kept her eyes closed—this visualization was complicated enough that she didn't want to try overlaying it on top of her physical sight—and touched the corner. A tingling sensation spread from her fingertips, up through her arm and throughout her body, until it felt like her heart was beating in sync with the coded pattern of the relay's crystal heart.

Her fingers found a smooth, many-faceted crystalline surface, hidden behind a false panel of the wall.

Golden elation ran through her in an electric thrill, and she had to clamp down on it immediately—she could not risk even the faintest trace of uncontrolled emotion slipping into the relay's heart, especially not one as complicated as this.

She sorted through the overlapping resonances stored inside the crystal's matrix until she found a recent addition. Of the thirty new signatures, she recognized three. The matrix had enough room for five more. She withdrew her senses just a little—enough for her heart to beat its own rhythm again—placed her left hand over her heart, and pushed her own resonance signature into the matrix.

Somebody, somebody with the strength of a bharost, tore her away from the wall. Her head cracked against the polished stone floor, and she opened her eyes, dazed.

The Guardian from House Imos loomed over her, extreme displeasure written across his face. "You have some explaining to do."

He waved a hand and blasted her with gray-blue calm.

The panicked words that were bubbling up froze on her lips as he hauled her to her feet by her arm and dragged her out of the grand hall.

Everything was going to be fine.

RAHELU HAD NEVER BEEN inside the northeast wing of the Guild before. This section was restricted to full members, and the Guardian had to present his armband before the two of them could pass through the doors.

Instead of bare stone, the walls were draped with embroidered hangings, and there was carpet underfoot. Large ceramic pots that stood eight-and-a-half hands high dotted the hallway at regular intervals. Their decorative designs were done in resonance paint and reminded Rahelu of ancestral urns—except, instead of containing ashes, they held plants.

What a bizarre thing to have—to do! Who would think to dig up a plant by its roots and stick it in a pot? They passed a worker pushing a water cart, who stopped by every single plant to ladle some water into its pot. What purpose did these pots serve, other than to create a whole lot of work?

A part of her thought that perhaps she would be better served if she focused on preparing her excuses or pleas for mercy, but it was a very small part, largely overruled by the sustained Projection of calm flowing from the Guardian.

There was no reason to fear. None at all.

Not even when he took her inside a small room with a single table and two chairs—and locked her wrists inside the crystalline shackles embedded in the center of the table.

He shoved one of the chairs into the back of her knees with a practiced kick—the *clatter-scrape-screech* of its legs across the rough stone floor made her wince—and she sat. Sitting allowed her to rest her arms flat along the tabletop, which was more comfortable than standing on her feet, hunched over to keep her arms from bending at an awkward angle.

The table was a curiosity: its top was glossy black marble with white-gray veins resting on a smaller square block of plain sandstone—a perfect, even plane marred only by a circular depression on one side and the shackles embedded in its center. Her shackles, too, were curious: they ought to have felt cool and smooth on her wrists, like the table, but they itched with a faint discordant hum that prickled against her resonance aura, even though it was blanketed with gray-blue calm.

She glanced over at the other chair—it was identical to

hers, roughly glued together from unfinished planks of rough pine—but the Guardian ignored it, choosing to glower at her from the opposite side of the table. He pulled out a resonance crystal the size of an egg from his pouch and set it inside the circular depression. Drawing on its power, he sent three separate Projections through it—each a focused bolt of alarm—and was answered in turn by three Projections in rapid succession.

The Guardian dropped his Projection of calm and Rahelu's terror emerged with full force. Those answering Projections...she recognized two of those resonance signatures.

Elder Anathwan Issolm.

And Atriarch Mere Ideth.

She yanked her arms in a desperate attempt to free herself, and it was about as effective as a gasping redfin's attempt to leap back from the deck into the water. The edges of the solid crystal cuffs were sharper than she thought, and they cut into her skin, leaving stinging pink lines that were spotted red.

Gods. *Gods*.

What had she done? Stupid, stupid, *stupid* to think she could find the heart of the resonance board without being detected. She hadn't sensed any Obfuscation barriers, hadn't seen any resonance wards, but that meant nothing: her skill in Obfuscation was passable at best.

What did she think was going to happen? That she could just...add herself to an authenticated list of Petitioners, go around completing House assignments of her own accord, and be *accepted* without anyone questioning how her name got onto the list? Or why she didn't have a Petitioner's armband?

How utterly, utterly *stupid*.

A House-sanctioned intelligence mission was one thing; a

common-born tampering with Guild records was an entirely different matter.

No, not Guild records. House records. *Gods*. Was that better or worse? And...four heavens. A thin golden line sparkled through the stark white of her jagged resonance aura despite herself.

She'd been *successful*.

If the charges were proven, Maketh could obliterate her mind with a thought, Obfuscate all memory until she had no recollection of who she was, until she *had* no thoughts.

The discordant hum from her cuffs grew stronger—vibrating in a pattern that was close to (but not quite) the pattern for direct Seeking Atriarch Ideth had used on Rahelu —until it overwhelmed everything else in her resonance senses.

What? The terse sending had the gruff, abrupt manner of the Isca Elder she had disappointed earlier in the day.

Peace, Elder Nhirom, Elder Anathwan sent, her tone as warm and friendly as ever. *I trust Guardian Maketh would not call for such a conference without good reason.*

Let us skip the idle pleasantries, Atriarch Ideth sent. *Why've you hauled this Petitioner into one of the Guild's interrogation chambers? This seems an excessive measure for a slip of a girl.*

At that, Rahelu's terror abated just the tiniest bit, but not enough to stop her frantic tugging at her resonance crystal shackles—they were cinched as tight as they would go, but there was still a slight gap between her thin wrists and the cuffs. Dozens of cuts had opened up all over the base of her hands now, and her attempts to escape had left a faint smear of blood around the insides of the shackles.

Someone tripped my Obfuscation alarm barrier around the Petitioners' assignment board, Maketh sent. *I discovered her in the grand hall, with her hand to the relay's heart, digging through its matrix.*

It would not be the first time that some ambitious hothead with more talent than sense or integrity tried to tip the scales in their favor by sabotaging the records, Atriarch Ideth sent. *The standard punishment is a fine of twelve gold kez, dismissal, suspension from the Guild, and a prohibition against re-Petitioning for five years. This does not explain the need for an interrogation chamber.*

That is precisely the issue, Maketh sent. *She is not a Petitioner. Or she should not be, according to the reported outcomes of your respective audiences with her—unless I have erred and referred to an outdated list of records. That is possible, as I began my preparations a quarter-span ahead of when the final audiences concluded. Thus, Honored Elders, Atriarch, I wish to confirm whether you have changed your evaluations since your initial submission?*

No, Elder Nhirom sent.

I have not, Atriarch Ideth sent.

There was a pause before Elder Anathwan's next sending. *Guardian, what were the reported outcomes per the records you referred to?*

A 'no' from Isca, a 'yes' from Ideth, and an abstention from Issolm, Maketh sent. *Thus, in accordance with section eight of the Houses' joint recruitment and admissions policy, I did not include her amongst those who were inducted as full Petitioners.*

It was stupid, at this point, to feel a little swell of warmth. What did it matter that Atriarch Ideth approved of her? Rahelu had still been caught. Even calling upon Atriarch Mere Ideth's favor would not save her now. She breathed deeply, trying to wrestle her terror under control, falling back on the two-count Onneja had taught her for focusing. She stopped struggling wildly with her shackles and started twisting only her right arm instead. If there was more blood, if she could squeeze the bones of her hand together tightly enough, she could pull free and...

And what? She would barely make it three strides before

Maketh caught her, only she couldn't imagine that he'd be anywhere as gentle a second time.

She kept trying anyway. She had to do something—anything! On the scale of possible offenses, surely this barely qualified as a misdemeanor. A Dedicate had to have other priorities. If she could get away and hide for long enough, surely his attention would be called to some more important task.

Did the girl alter any assignments? Elder Nhirom sent. *Or did she just look?*

No assignments were altered, Maketh sent, with some reluctance.

Then send the girl on her way with a warning, Elder Nhirom sent. *And next time, set up the assignment board in a restricted area of the Guild rather than the grand hall, even if the specifics of the assignments are of a public nature.*

Access to that information is not my concern, Maketh sent. *My concern is that our security has been breached. The authenticated list of Petitioner identities includes the girl's resonance signature. This may be the work of Chanazian operatives, or perhaps the girl is a Chanazian operative herself, in an attempt to infiltrate our ranks.*

Fuck. He wasn't going to let this go. The Guardian's resonance aura was locked tight behind an Obfuscation barrier as solid as the city walls, but she could imagine the unrelenting steel-gray determination behind it. Even if she ran and somehow managed to hide from him, he would track her until he found her.

She is not, Atriarch Ideth sent. *I will vouch for this personally.*

Never had Rahelu been so glad to have let another person see into her soul. All the discomfort of feeling another person's consciousness dig through her innermost emotions, like eels burrowing through sand flats, had been worth it.

Guardian Maketh, your vigilance in your duty does you credit,

Elder Anathwan sent. *I agree with Atriarch Ideth, however. I do not think this girl is an intelligence threat to the Dominion.*

Then how am I to account for the discrepancy in the records? Someone must have altered them, and she was in the position to do it. Logic dictates that the simplest explanation must be the truth. I request authorization for a direct Seeking to verify this.

Rahelu was tempted to agree of her own volition. She had nothing to hide—at least, not in respect of her loyalties to Aleznuaweite.

Onneja's warning rang in her mind.

She concentrated on working her left wrist instead.

You are absolutely correct, Guardian. The simplest explanations are the likeliest to be the truth, Elder Anathwan sent.

Rahelu had expected it—had braced herself for the inevitability—but she felt her heart sink anyway.

Had she been wrong? Had *Onneja* been wrong?

No Augury was certain.

However, there is an even simpler explanation than the one you proposed, Elder Anathwan sent, still all warmth and friendliness. *As you surmised at the beginning of this conference, there was always the possibility that one of us had changed our vote, and there was a delay in the resonance transfer. Let it be clear that the final vote from Issolm was 'yes'.*

Issolm had voted 'yes'.

She hadn't failed.

She *had* made it. She had done enough to impress Elder Anathwan during her short audience in the scrying tower.

Hadn't she?

Then I apologize for the disruption to your day, Maketh sent.

Unnecessary, Elder Nhirom sent. *You rightly feared the worst and acted swiftly to bring this to our attention. A prudent response, even if it is inefficient. It would have been better to prevent the possibility of tampering in the first place.*

Indeed. Atriarch Ideth's reply was tart. *You'd best see to her induction without delay, Guardian. It would not do for her to be disadvantaged due to an administrative bungle.*

The discordant hum of Rahelu's shackles quieted as Atriarch Ideth's presence withdrew, as did Elder Nhirom's, though Elder Anathwan took a moment to prolong the impromptu conference.

You did well to bring this to my attention, Guardian Maketh, Elder Anathwan sent, the sense of her presence fading. *I will give my personal regards to your Atriarch the next time I have the privilege of attending him.* Her awareness lingered on Rahelu, who felt it through her restraints as a light scratching over her resonance aura, and then that sensation dissipated— leaving only the stinging self-inflicted cuts on her hands and wrists, and the faint itch of a prickling blanket as her crystalline shackles became quiescent once more.

The Guardian regarded Rahelu with a hard stare as he unlocked her cuffs; they were slippery with blood. She immediately prostrated herself at his feet.

"Forgiveness, Guardian, for having caused you trouble," she said, making no attempt at Obfuscation, letting waves of pale blue relief wash over the bone-white terror that still dominated her resonance aura.

She did not move until he tossed two items onto the stone floor in front of her.

One was a clean rag for her wrists.

The other was the armband of a Petitioner of the Houses.

RAHELU JOGGED after the Guardian as he strode out of the interrogation chamber, moving so swiftly that his white-and-yellow robes flapped like the wings of a shearwater as it emerged from a successful dive. She felt like a shearwater herself, with the way her feet skimmed the sandstone floor; her resonance aura brimmed with so much elation it looked like golden sunlight.

Her mother would be safe. Onneja's secrets were safe. *She* was safe.

And her parents need never know how close she had been to the brink of failure. As long as she didn't do anything else stupid—her family's future was all but guaranteed. Thirty-one Petitioners and twenty places for Supplicants? The odds of success had never been so favorable.

Truly, the Starfather had blessed her.

It was impossible not to touch her new armband, with its embossed sigil of a circle surrounding the Guild's seven flames—her fingers kept tracing the circle over and over again.

Ridiculous to be so emotional about it. Her old armband (the one that had marked her as a graduated mage) had been identical in every respect—except for that circle.

They exited the restricted northeast wing and passed through the many hallways of the Guild's administrative building until they reached the main corridor. But the Guardian did not turn left into the grand hall as she expected; he went outside and started crossing the courtyard towards the Guild gates.

"Guardian?" she asked.

He kept walking.

"Guardian...I...who should I report to? What are my instructions?"

His glance held the same irritated expression he had worn two days ago in the training yard, recalling to mind his exact words then: *you miss something, you figure it out, either with your brains or with Evocation.*

It didn't faze her. What could he do to her now, even if he still suspected she had tampered with the resonance board? An Atriarch and two Elders had spoken, and their word was as good as law.

"I understood there was to be some sort of induction?"

"I have issued you your armband," he said. "And since you have already…familiarized yourself with the assignment board, I see no need to belabor the obvious."

"But—"

"I will make this very simple…Petitioner." Maketh stopped and turned to face her so abruptly she nearly ran into him. "For the next three weeks, the Houses officially recognize you as a member whose specific allegiance is yet to be determined. But do not mistake your new status for anything other than what it is: an acknowledgment that you were able to demonstrate the basic skills required of a Supplicant under controlled conditions."

He made the ordeal of the past two days sound no more difficult than breathing. The sharp rebuke stung, shattering the radiance in her resonance aura as it negated her sense of accomplishment.

"If you desire to make your membership permanent, perform the same feat, consistently, under real conditions."

Behind. She was behind *again*. It was like cresting the summit of one mountain, only to discover it was but the foothill of the next.

"And if you do not intend to be at the bottom of the rankings in one week when the first round of eliminations takes place, I suggest you spend less time waiting for someone to lead you by the hand and more time demonstrating the House votes in favor of your Petition were not misplaced."

He left through the gates without waiting for her to finish bowing.

As she straightened, she skimmed through the open assignments via the relay in her armband, appended her resonance signature to the nearest assignment with a difficulty rating of 'easy', and sprinted through the gates herself.

She had to make up for lost time.

INTERLUDE: STARBOUND

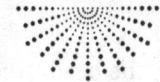

AZOSH-EK LOVED THE STARRISE.

He loved the slow way the Starfather's blade cut the land, how suddenly the quiet hush would bloom at the inescapable edge of night, until all the world lay as still as death in contemplation.

But in this cursed city of unbelievers, they defied the darkness. Bonfires and torches and lanterns and lamps and candles polluted the night, blazing in every courtyard and every window on every street. Their impure light blinded him —blinded the stars.

Sacrilege.

His compulsions were getting stronger. They warred with each other for control in Iweth-na's absence; urged him to extinguish the unholy blazes with the blood of every heathen; to flee, screaming, into the wilderness, before he himself burned.

Even as he wraps his left arm around the throat of the kneeling sacrifice, his right hand spasms. The sacred blade slides in at the wrong angle; misses the opening between the ribs. Its edges scrape against bone as he forcibly corrects its trajectory with a twist.

Why, Iweth-na?

Flames.

Why did you forsake me?

Tremors.

I was not made for this.

Finally, a clean slice.

First, the heart. Next, the head. And last, the limbs.

Power lanced through the air from behind. The ghostly bone-white bolt slammed into his heart, arresting him mid-step—

A silver-robed figure sits on an ebon throne, choking on the veil of blood that pours from the obsidian crown on its head...

—and the black links around his neck immediately flared up in response. No more than a hundredth of a heartbeat later, he was free. He whirled around, whipped his right hand up high, sacred blade poised to strike at the heathen guard who had stumbled upon him.

He saw nothing. Just a patchwork of shadows that rippled as the deepnight breeze pulled a curtain of clouds over the moon.

"Interesting."

Hope blazed up within him at the sound of the low-pitched, feminine voice, only to die almost immediately. Its timbre was right, but the tone and the speech were wrong. The voice lacked Iweth-na's pure depth, and they would never have spoken to him in that corrupted dialect.

"Anyone other than an archmage ought to have succumbed to me." The voice circled him. "Yet I sense no resonance from you."

The street in front of him was a blur of silver and black.

He kept his silence and his eyes on the ground, matching the shape and motions of each flickering shadow to the physical object of its origins until he found the odd one out: a rounded blob ten strides away whose outline flowed like water.

"What do you do here in my city, starbound? Where is your keeper?"

Not a guard. One of those heathen adepts, then? The separation between the temples and resonance adepts was another thing he could not understand, but his place was not to understand. Azosh-ek stretched his eyes, held them open to stare unblinking at the spot above that odd shadow, even though all he wanted to do was to look anywhere else.

Three breaths later, the compulsion melted away, and one of the moonbeams in his watering vision resolved into a tall, white-robed woman. She wore a tiny smile on her lips and a large crystal pendant around her neck on a chain not dissimilar to his own, and the intricate scars that decorated her hands glowed with the color of sunset.

He exploded into motion, sailing over his meticulously arranged sacrifice in a single leap. They had never expected to be able to remain undiscovered, but it would not do to be unmasked so soon. The woman's death was a necessary waste he regretted, but he had committed far greater sins.

And for this particular sin, he needed no guidance.

Azosh-ek slashed down with the sacred blade, ready for its serpentine edges to sink deep into the woman's throat. This time, he would be strong. He would not let her death echoes make him question their cause. But he would grant her the respect of meeting her eyes as he bled her dry.

Even a heretic deserved that much.

The amber eyes that met his gaze were not the terrified eyes of someone about to die. They gleamed with the amusement of a predator discovering its prey had claws. Her scarred hand moved more swiftly than he could track and there was a bright *clang* as she met the ebon blade in his hand with a knife of her own.

It was a copy.

A shining steel copy with distorted proportions—waved edges frozen in the wrong frequencies—and a leather-wrapped hilt studded with crystal. The sight of the profanity sent him into a righteous rage.

Azosh-ek snarled, ignoring the growing warmth of his anchor and the way its links hummed against his skin. He could not decide which cleansing ought to come first: this city or the Divine Kingdom. The whole world was corrupt—was it any wonder that the Starfather had turned from them?

He disengaged with a quick twist and pulled back for a flurry of strikes, this time aiming for those laughing eyes. The woman deflected each blow easily, her smile broadening into a wide grin.

"I should execute you," she said, her tone not strained in the slightest. "Not only have you murdered one of my citizens, but you also dared attack me. But this…"

Her free hand snaked out and grabbed him by his throat, pressing the hot black links into his windpipe. A strong grip, one that caused the edges of his vision to darken.

"This is worthy of study."

A new sensation slithered its way up through the veins in his neck and inside his brain. It urged him to fall to his knees; to kiss the bloodstained dirt beneath her feet; to let go of his misplaced desire to command his own destiny.

OBEY ME.

The imperative sizzled like the smoldering point of a hot iron brand—his hand faltered, lowering the sacred blade—and found no purchase on the scarred layers of his mind. In the same heartbeat, he drove the sacred blade towards her side, aiming for the gap between two of her lower ribs.

Kill me, and you lose the earth and sea.

No. Azosh-ek froze as ruby blossomed from the tip of the black blade, where it pierced her pristine robe. She had to be lying; it had to be the empty threat of a doomed soul. But her face was serene, the pressure of her thumb on his windpipe didn't vary in the slightest, and her eyes were alight with the triumph of one who has lost the battle but won the war.

So many of their plans had ended in failure; they could not afford another. Azosh-ek licked dry lips and spoke. "How?" The word came out as a croak that did not befit him.

"You hide so poorly a child could Seek your secrets out." She tilted her head slightly as she considered him, paying no mind to the sharp knife that still dug into her side; the red bloom he had put there was starting to grow roots. "A trade," she announced and abruptly released her stranglehold. "You will allow me to examine your bond."

Her fingers boldly caressed the links of his anchor—a violation of his soul so great that, despite what was at stake, his urge to run her through redoubled.

"In return, I will help you open the Endless Gate."

15

ASSIGNMENT

THE 25TH DAY OF EARLY SUMMER,
530 A.E./A.F.

"HOW MANY MORE TO GO?" RAHELU ASKED AS SHE stopped channeling ambient resonance into the tiny resonance crystal fragment in front of her.

She squinted—there was only one magnifying lens, and Tsenjhe was using it—picked up the fragment with a pair of delicate cotton-tipped copper tweezers, and dropped it into one of the thirty different glass jars in front of her. Each jar was the size of a large mug and ranged from near-empty to over three-quarters full of crystal fragments, all sorted according to size, shape, clarity, and hue.

It was her second day on this assignment and she already hated it.

"Well there are fifteen or so sacks in here," the Dedicate said from the adjoining workbench. She tapped the back of an awl the length of her finger with an equally tiny mallet, punching a pinprick-sized hole through a sheet of copper beaten so thin it was a half-step removed from foil. "They're about two stoneweight each."

It was not a difficult assignment, just one that required

care, attention to detail, and constant vigilance: take a dulled crystal fragment, put it into the corundite crucible in front of her, and concentrate resonance around it. There were plenty of sources around in the Blackforge, and the fragments had been well-cared-for—their charge was only substantially depleted, not dangerously low and one fish scale away from dissolving. The hardest part was finding a source with a similar resonance to the fragment's natural attunement—and that wasn't even strictly necessary; just more efficient and, therefore, slightly faster.

Not fast enough though.

Tsenjhe's expected timeframe for completion was one week. Rahelu was almost two days in and had hardly made a dent in the first sack. It sat atop the workbench, mouth gaping open in a mocking grin.

"There's another thirty in the storeroom."

Rahelu groaned and put her head down on top of her folded arms. At this rate, she wouldn't finish before the summer solstice, let alone week's end.

She tried to summon some sense of urgency, a measure of the desperation that had fuelled her for the last three days. The emotions came at once, but—like a sustained Projection whose intensity never varied—her mind had grown accustomed to their weight.

Rahelu remained slumped over the workbench, unable to stir herself into action.

This was supposed to be an easy assignment. A simple task that Tsenjhe expected any Supplicant of House Isca to be able to complete within a week.

An expectation Rahelu had no hope of living up to.

Unless…

Had she been doing this the incredibly stupid way?

Rahelu grabbed a whole handful of fragments, poured

them into a wooden tray, and shook the tray until the fragments were spread out in a thin layer.

She closed her eyes. Listened to the *clip-clop* and *crunch* of shod horses pulling carts over the graveled road outside; the *snip clink-tap snip-snip* of Tsenjhe's pliers on copper wire and resonance crystal. Breathed in the scent of charcoal, hot metal, and acid in a slow eight-count.

Her tray was a varicolored glow of clashing resonances; the depleted fragments came from different crystals. Discards from an artificer's workshop. Some had been salvaged from larger resonance crystals that had exploded from resonance overload.

Rahelu touched one fragment that glowed a dim sky-blue. Its faint resonance pulsed against her fingertip in relaxed, roughly equal beats. She carefully combined its residual power with the same contentment wafting from the gray-and-white striped cat lazing in the shaft of late skyarc sun by Tsenjhe's feet. Next, she held out her other hand above the tray and then gently pushed the resonance she had gathered through her left palm in a weak Projection.

A third of the fragments hummed in sympathetic resonation.

Rahelu grabbed her tweezers, hunting down the fragments that jumped like fleas.

Once she got every last resonating fragment into the crucible, she covered it with her left hand and squeezed her Projection into a tight beam the width of its diameter. A dull ache started to build inside her skull, right behind her eyeballs. She held the effort for a hundred count, then a thousand, and another thousand until the ache behind her eyes turned into stabbing needles and she released her Projection with a whimper, both hands flying to massage her eyelids.

"Not bad," Tsenjhe said as she peered over Rahelu's shoulder. The Dedicate poked at the humming pile of contentment inside the crucible with her awl. "Another hundred count and you'd've fully charged them. Of course, if you had agitated the crucible as you went, you could've doubled the absorption rate and cut the recharge time in half. And if you had filled the crucible to the brim, you could've cut it in half again."

Rahelu stopped rubbing her eyes long enough to stare at the Dedicate through her fingers. "You could have told me!"

"I wanted to see whether you could figure it out," Tsenjhe said. "Isca needs Supplicants who are inventive, and it's getting harder and harder to find them with the Guild's insistence on teaching practical application of the resonance skills. It wouldn't kill them to ground their graduates in a little theory as well. There's still so much we don't understand about the resonance disciplines."

Rahelu looked at her crucible, the tray, the glass jars, the open sack and its fourteen duplicates stacked along the far wall of the workshop, and wanted to toss it all into the air and smash it to bits.

"Don't be like that," Tsenjhe said, patting her on the arm. "If it makes you feel better, most Dedicates wouldn't know either. The Guild method works just fine if you're only charging a few crystals."

"You wouldn't really have let me sit there for weeks, charging these one by one, would you?" Rahelu asked. "At some point, you would have had mercy upon me, right?"

Tsenjhe laughed.

For a moment, there in the warm workshop with the air tinted a gold-red by the rays of the setting sun, it felt like the two of them stood once more in the shallows of the Elumaje when Tsenjhe had laughed after a seven-year-old Rahelu had

finally speared her first fish after a whole day of futile efforts.
She had flipped her spear around, the bluegill still flopping
desperately on the barbed point, and knocked Tsenjhe's legs
out from under her, dumping the older girl into the shallows.
After a brief tussle where the fish nearly escaped and that
ended with both of them half-drowned, they had crawled
ashore, grilled the bluegill over a bed of warm coals for
dinner, and gobbled its tender white flesh beneath the Starfather's benevolent gaze.

Rahelu forgot herself—forgot that Tsenjhe was a Dedicate
and she a mere Petitioner—and, having no spear at hand,
swept her right foot around one of Tsenjhe's ankles and
yanked.

But they were no longer thirteen and seven, and this
was Ennuost Yrg, not Chanaz; so when Rahelu moved,
Tsenjhe was ready—legs planted wide and firmly braced;
immovable as the earth—and then it was her turn to fall as
Tsenjhe shifted to one side and helped her down with a
light shove.

Rahelu lay on her back in the packed dirt of the workshop
floor, winded yet again.

Gods. What was *wrong* with her? When would she finally
learn her place? The stabbing sensation returned to her eyes,
though this time, it wasn't resonance backlash.

Roll over and apologize, she ordered herself. *And stop screwing
things up!*

Her muscles protested as she got on her knees to place
both hands and her forehead on the floor. "Forgiveness,
Dedicate, for my insult. How may I make amends?"

She did not want to look up—could not bear to confront
the anger that must be written all over the Dedicate's face—
and so she kept her head on the ground and blinked her eyes
furiously. The tears dripped out anyway, making tiny little
mud puddles on the floor, and there was a horrible, deep,

gasping noise coming from her throat, even as she tried to clamp her jaws shut.

There was a rustle of cloth as Tsenjhe knelt beside her and pulled Rahelu's head into her lap.

"Nelan," she said as she stroked Rahelu's hair, finger-combing out the tangled locks as she had done when they were very young, and the Chanazian term Rahelu had not heard for nine years was an ache all on its own. "Of course I would have shown you, if you had not figured it out by day's end. Did I not show you how to cast your spear properly in the end?"

So Tsenjhe had. After Rahelu had struggled to do it on her own all day.

"Why could you not have shown me earlier?" Rahelu whispered into Tsenjhe's lap. "Why did you leave me to struggle alone, venaz?" she asked.

"While you can learn from the experience of others, learning from your own experience is better, and failure is the best teacher of all."

"Will it ever get easier?"

"No, nelan," Tsenjhe said. "But you will grow stronger."

Rahelu didn't want to get up; she wanted to stay here, on the floor, pretending she was seven years old again when all she had had to worry about was whether it would rain or not.

But she had embarrassed herself enough for the day, so she straightened up, wiped her face with the bloodstained rag Maketh had given her earlier, and faced Tsenjhe.

"Sorry," she said. "I won't do that again."

"It's alright," Tsenjhe said with a smile. "I have missed you too." The Dedicate reached out and hugged her close. "I am not angry, though you have cost me," she added as she released Rahelu. "Now I will have to buy Keshwar dinner. He will be insufferable."

"You..." Rahelu paused in the middle of blowing her

nose. "You two made a bet?" she asked. "And you bet against me?" She narrowed her eyes at Tsenjhe. "I take it back. You don't have a size advantage anymore."

With that, she lunged at Tsenjhe, and when Rahelu was victorious at last, their laughter rang throughout the building so loudly it made Elder Nhirom thump on the door and holler at them both to be quiet.

NOW THAT RAHELU knew the trick of it, Tsenjhe's assignment became easier.

On her third day, she borrowed a few resonance instruments and a small wax tablet from Tsenjhe to experiment with different combinations of resonances, volumes, and agitation methods—plotting Projection intensities against absorption rates and crystal volume (Tsenjhe had had to help her with those equations) according to recharge times until her eyes crossed in an attempt to figure out the most optimal method of recharging the contents of all forty-five sacks.

She chafed at the delay—every instinct screamed that she was losing time, and she ought to stop messing around and get things done—but forcibly restrained her impatience. Keshwar had been right: ability and the willingness to dive into a task weren't enough. She needed to start thinking strategically.

By the fourth day, she had refined her process down to something suitable for a production line of one, and—to Tsenjhe's amusement—had taken over three-quarters of the workshop. One quarter had all forty-five sacks (some still full and stitched shut) stacked against the wall; Rahelu had transformed another quarter into a dedicated sorting area filled with barrels, crates, and trays so she could separate the crystal fragments according to resonance type—size and shape didn't seem to significantly affect the recharge rate, but similarity of resonance frequencies did.

Next to the sorting area was a recharging station: she had abandoned her crucible for a large corundite cauldron so she could stir the fragments like a kettle of soup. (The material and shape of the container seemed to affect recharging efficiency; she guessed it had something to do with how reflective the material was with respect to resonance and specific pathways taken by the resonance reflections.)

The cauldron wasn't completely optimal—she could only fill it four-fifths of the way full before she ran into spillage issues—but the larger container meant she didn't have to focus her Projection as tightly. That decreased the absorption rate, but it was a trade-off she was willing to make. Without a focus stone, intense Projections gave her constant resonance backlash and the recovery time she required nullified the benefit of a higher absorption rate.

She should have honed her Projection skills regardless—it'd make her a better mage—but it would do her no good to sacrifice short-term results for long-term gain. The other Petitioners were working in teams, and the steady stream of their resonance transfers to sign off assignments as completed and sign out new ones was a constant reminder of how far behind she was. Rahelu had started taking off her Petitioner armband as soon as she entered the Isca workshop so she wouldn't be tempted to consult the assignment board every quarter-span.

Finally, on the fifth day, she had all of the fragments sorted into batches of similar resonance frequencies. The assignment became surprisingly mechanical. Once she had locked on to the appropriate resonance frequency, all she had to do was to find a similar source in the ambient resonance, then act as a conduit. So long as she kept a handful of partially charged crystal fragments in her cauldron as seeds, she didn't have to expend as much effort to sustain the Projection across batches—the seeds kept the sympathetic resonation going.

She could even stop relying on visualizations to an extent and hold a conversation.

"I think I'm actually going to miss this," she said to Tsenjhe on the sixth day as they worked on their respective projects in companionable ease. "It's almost as peaceful as mending nets...only I don't end up with blistered fingers."

"Gods," Tsenjhe said. "That's one thing I don't miss. Fanuen never had a kind word to say about my nets." The Dedicate gave a mock shudder.

Tsenjhe had said very little about her own journey from Chanaz to Ennuost Yrg—from Rahelu's experience, she gathered it had not been pleasant—but the Dedicate had talked a little about her time as a trainee and a Petitioner.

It was eerily similar to Rahelu's story.

"Do you ever wonder..." Rahelu lowered her voice to a whisper. "...if we should have tried to apprentice to the Conclave instead?"

For a long time, there was only the sound of passing traffic, Tsenjhe's pliers, and Rahelu's crystal fragments.

"Keshwar performed that Augury for me once," Tsenjhe said at last.

Rahelu almost lost her grip on the current resonance frequency she was working on—this batch had been attuned to regret, a complex emotion that had been difficult to locate in the ambient resonance.

Atriarch Ideth was famous for her Auguries—it was how House Ideth had accumulated such strength and stability. No matter what Dharyas had said, more often than not, you could trace the ability for true Augury down generational lines. Keshwar likely had the latent potential and access to the training to develop that potential into something more.

"Some things in those futures were not so different. Other things…" Heartbeat after heartbeat stretched out as Tsenjhe calibrated a particularly intricate assembly. "…had unexpected ramifications. Far-reaching impacts that I would not have thought possible."

Not just latent potential then.

An Augur's time was precious beyond any other resource —a priceless tool that should always be employed for the benefit of their House rather than wasted on satisfying idle curiosity.

Keshwar must love Tsenjhe beyond sensible reason to perform such an Augury for her.

"Were you…happier?" Rahelu asked.

"In some ways, yes." Tsenjhe picked up another recharged fragment and wired it into her construct. "My life would have been simpler," she said. "The Conclave is the pinnacle of magical research on this continent. Even the newest of their researchers are given budgets that dwarf what Elder Nhirom receives for his efforts—and House Isca is the most inclined towards innovation of all the Houses."

Tsenjhe waved her pliers around at her workshop and the half-abandoned constructs crammed into every shelf Rahelu had not borrowed for her production line.

"The experiments I could have conducted…the discoveries I could have made…" Tsenjhe's eyes grew pensive, and a pale violet-blue longing flickered through her resonance aura. "I would have changed the world."

"You still can," Rahelu pointed out. "Can't you? Especially if you saw what you would have done. You could find different ways of doing the same here."

"I wish it were so simple. Augury is not like Evocation— Keshwar could only show me brief glimpses of my greatest triumphs and regrets. If my life was the ocean, then I only saw the peaks and troughs of the largest waves, not the great expanse of water that makes the ocean what it is. And," Tsenjhe added, "I did not say that I changed the world for the better, only that the world changed because of me."

Tsenjhe was the kindest person Rahelu knew. How could anything that Tsenjhe accomplished not end up changing the world for the better?

"Maybe there was a mistake?" Rahelu asked, then felt compelled to add: "Not that I'm questioning his ability. Something could have interfered with his Augury."

Tsenjhe gave her a sidelong glance. "He does have faults, you know. Ideth heir or not, he's still only human."

"To you, perhaps," Rahelu said. "Are you..." she trailed off, unsure of whether she should ask the question—whether she could ask the question. Her mother would have, but Rahelu wasn't her mother (a fact her mother reminded her of on a daily basis).

"No," Tsenjhe answered the question anyway, even though Rahelu had not asked it. "He will consort for the good of his House, as he must." There was a trace of bitterness in her voice. "Until then—" she shook her head and changed the subject. "There is no sense in getting lost in Augury. Things are what they are, and some things cannot—or should not—be changed."

Rahelu shivered at those words, one hand going to her pocket. The glittering black gem inside was warm.

"I need no consortship as proof or to complete my life. It is better this way."

Tsenjhe seemed convinced but Rahelu wanted to ask the next question: *better for whom?*

She left that question alone though, unwilling to push the conversation further. If Tsenjhe was content, then that was all that mattered.

Their conversation drifted towards lighter topics: they swapped anecdotes about Guild instructors, hotly debated the best street stall for fried dumplings, and laughed at Tsen-jhe's stories from her days as a Supplicant. All too soon, Rahelu finished charging the last batch of crystal fragments, donned her Petitioner's armband, and signed off the assignment as completed.

She lingered in the workshop, hovering close to the half-completed construct on Tsenjhe's workbench while the Dedicate countersigned the assignment as satisfactorily completed within an acceptable time frame and fetched her compensation. The construct resembled a skeletal hand; assembled from hundreds of copper wires in twisted strands. Resonance crystal fragments glinted through the gaps in the strands—like bone, Rahelu thought, or perhaps blood.

"Thank you," she said as Tsenjhe handed her a small pouch of silver coins. "Later, after I've completed my Peti-tion...you might be able to spare some time to have dinner with my family?"

"I would like that very much. Until then, give my regards to your parents." Tsenjhe smiled and embraced her. "Do not be a stranger, nelan. You can always find me here."

Rahelu hugged her back. "I will not forget."

Her new coin pouch clinked softly in a happy little ditty; a perfect accompaniment to the tune she hummed from Enjela's ballad. She left Tsenjhe and the warm Isca workshop behind with a spring in her step to answer Maketh's summons, walking through the streets of the Blackforge unimpeded, thanks to her Petitioner's armband.

Tsenjhe approved of her work and still considered Rahelu her heart's sister. She had enough coin to repay the shortfall her mother had borrowed from Hzin *and* the next two weekly instalments on her family's Isonn debt *and* some left over to put towards her Guild debt.

Let the Houses and the other Petitioners judge her as they

will; Rahelu had judged herself, and she was pleased with what she had accomplished.

She did not know what challenges the Houses would set before her next, but that did not matter.

She was ready.

16
TEAM

THE 30TH DAY OF EARLY SUMMER, 530 A.E./A.F.

THIS TIME, WHEN RAHELU STRODE INTO THE GUILD, she held her head high, shoulders back, and marched straight through the middle of the grand hall towards the assignment board.

I belong here, she told herself. *I have every right to be here.*

It was easier to believe that when she was one of the first Petitioners to arrive.

The section tallying results by Petitioner consumed two-thirds of the board's right-hand side. There were two enormous wedges of green on yellow: thirty-one rows of glowing squares arrayed in descending order. The top two rows boasted ten green squares each; Rahelu's row was five from the bottom, ahead of three that only had a single yellow square each and one that was blank.

Reluctantly, she touched one finger to the last row, triggering the Projection:

Petitioner: Dharyas of Isca

Just her name and nothing else. Where was she?

Tsenjhe had not seemed overly concerned when Rahelu brought up Dharyas's absence. The Isca girl had stopped by Tsenjhe's workshop after her audience with Elder Nhirom in a flurry of excitement, made some cryptic remarks about working on something big, something world-changing, then left for her audience with Ideth.

No one in House Isca had seen her since.

Apparently, that was normal. Tsenjhe assumed Dharyas had gotten some new idea from Elder Nhirom and had disappeared off to some hidden bolthole in the city after the rest of her audiences.

So Rahelu tried to put all thoughts of Dharyas aside and scanned the rows at the top of the list instead: Ghardon of Issolm and Elaram of Issolm were still in equal first position.

They had focused exclusively on easy, bureaucratic investigations clustered in a specific area of the city. Each one was a day's effort for a single person, but working as a pair meant they could complete each task faster.

And they had signed out multiple, similar assignments at the same time.

Smart.

With that strategy, they had completed ten assignments within a week. No other Petitioner came close—the next few rows were dominated by Isonn Petitioners, each with five or so completed assignments. All were hunts, like the one for the bharost she had seen, and required them to travel outside of the city, to outlying hamlets to the north and west. They, too, seemed to be working as a group: four was not truly big enough to qualify as a hunt-circle, but their approach made sense.

Everybody else lagged behind with only two or three completed assignments. Nheras, to Rahelu's relief, was not doing much better than she was—the Ilyn Petitioner had also completed only one assignment, though the note from the supervising Dedicate indicated it had been completed 'with exemplary success' and qualified for a performance bonus. Further examination of the attached Evocation showed Nheras defending a caravan against a small, ragged band of outlaws.

Fuck. Rahelu had been going about this all wrong.

She should have looked for something that played to her strengths. Rahelu turned her attention to the left third of the board. Most of the squares were blank. The few remaining open assignments were rated moderately difficult and none looked like tasks she could attempt on her own.

She needed a team.

She turned away from the assignment board and—despite her earlier resolution—tucked herself into a recess close to the wooden dais where she could see most of the room and the entrance.

It didn't take long before the Guardian arrived and started calling out names.

"Ralosh of Isilc, Tsimol of Isonn, Hnith of Ideth, and Dharyas of Isca."

Three Petitioners stepped forward with stiff backs, stiff gaits, and crimson-tinged auras.

The Guardian did not bother glancing around for Dharyas.

"Unfortunately, you have not met the standards required for a Supplicant to the Houses. Your Petition is at an end."

The entire room watched in hushed relief as the three former Petitioners made their reluctant way up to the dais and relinquished their armbands into the Guardian's hands before they slunk out of the hall.

"The rest of you are to be congratulated." Maketh's gaze roamed over the remaining Petitioners standing before him. "You have proven yourselves capable of carrying out the most basic aspects of a Supplicant's duties. That alone, however, will not be sufficient. His Exalted Dominance intends to spread the wealth and prosperity we enjoy here in Aleznu-aweite to the entire Ngutoccai continent. As such, the Dominion has greater need of the Houses than ever before. In the coming years, we will be sorely stretched, with our Dedicates and Elders preoccupied with matters of great strategic importance."

The pale squares on the left side of the resonance board flickered out. Then, one by one, new assignments flared to life, white lights piercing the dimness of the grand hall like a tiny starrise.

Rahelu tapped into the board through her armband and saw overflow cases from the Healers' Guild, temple commissions for advanced Imbuements, delicate maintenance work on critical Chronicler installations and relay networks—all duties that would traditionally be the remit of Dedicates.

"We tell you this so you may understand why you are being held to a higher standard than any other previous intake of Supplicants—the very stability of Aleznuaweite depends on it."

One last square lit up, blazing more brightly than the rest. A request for aid—marked urgent—from the city guard, with three Evocations attached.

...three murders reported in the last two weeks across multiple districts. Preliminary investigations yielded no suspects and no commonalities between the victims other than the unusual manner of death...

Her throat seized up at the sight of the meticulously arranged dead bodies with their mutilated chests.

"Soon, our Dedicates and Elders will be unable to spare any attention for matters not directly related to His Exalted

Dominance's expansion initiatives. And so, gods help us, the Houses will need to rely on you to hold the Dominion together."

The Guardian gestured at the tallied results on the right-hand side of the assignment board and reset every square to a blank, light-gray.

"From now on, you will be judged according to how your actions impact this city and its inhabitants. There are no restrictions on the methods you may use—so long as you uphold all the laws of Aleznuaweite and act in accordance with the Guild's code. Act honorably and with wisdom for the good of Aleznuaweite."

And with that, Maketh strode out of the hall, leaving the Petitioners to their speculation.

RAHELU DID her best to avoid notice as she rushed for the exit, but Lhorne must have been searching for her.

"Rahelu!" he called, raising his voice over the clamoring of the other Petitioners. "Over here!"

She waved but continued pushing past House-born towards the doors. "I'll be right back!" she yelled as she skirted around a clump of Isonn Petitioners, chasing a glimpse of two chestnut heads slipping through the throng. Someone from House Isilc bumped into her, causing her to collide with someone else wearing jeweled armbands and too many earrings.

"Watch it!" Nheras shoved her with one jangling arm, then her eyes slitted as she recognized Rahelu. "Fish guts," she said flatly. "I thought something stank."

"I don't have time for this," Rahelu said and shoved back, sending Nheras into another Imos Petitioner. "Excuse me."

She shut out Nheras's voice, squeezed past two more

groups of Imrell and Isilc Petitioners, and burst through to the fringes of the crowd to see the two Issolm siblings leave the hall.

"Wait!" She jogged after them. "Ghardon, Elaram, wait!"

Ghardon didn't break his stride, but Elaram glanced back. When she saw Rahelu, she tugged at her brother's elbow to stop.

Rahelu halted before Elaram's beaming smile and Ghardon's scowl. The two were otherwise perfectly matched —from their impeccably groomed hair and immaculately pressed tunics to the spotless gleam of their leather boots.

And except for the sling and bandage Elaram wore around her right arm and shoulder.

"I'm sorry about your collarbone," Rahelu said.

"Oh, that!" Elaram waved her left hand airily. "Don't worry about it. You did what you had to do."

That threw Rahelu off. She had expected demands for reparation (monetary or the right to strike back), demands for her to grovel, or demands of a favor owed. But the other girl's tone was genuinely unbothered, and so was her resonance aura.

"I...really?"

"Yes, of course! I was lucky that you were the only one who came after me," she said. "And you stuck to using the blunt end, even in all that madness. It was pretty impressive, actually!"

"Uh, thanks," she said. Elaram's smile unnerved her—it was wide and open with no edge behind it.

At least Ghardon still regarded her with suspicion. "Come on," he said to Elaram, ignoring Rahelu completely.

That was normal and Rahelu could deal with that. She seized on the opening he gave her.

"Where are you going?" she asked and immediately regretted it because that was not only presumptuous but also intrusive, so she followed up with: "I mean, which assignment are you doing?" which was also stupid because she could have looked that up by using the relay in her armband.

To the eight hells with it.

"Because if it's not the one with the weird knifings, then I think you're wasting your time," she blurted out.

"Really?" Ghardon snorted. "I didn't notice your name at the top of the rankings. I don't think we need advice on what assignments to take from you."

"Your previous strategy won't work anymore," Rahelu said. "The new assignments don't even have timeframes or tasks listed; only objectives."

"So?" he said. "What difference does that make? An assignment is an assignment."

"Were you not listening to the same speech from Maketh?" she asked. "Everything just got harder! Much harder. Do you really think you can outmaneuver Isilc or Isonn with no allies? After the stunt you pulled during the challenges? The rest of your House didn't make it past their audiences."

The Issolm Petitioners exchanged a look.

"We didn't do anything that wasn't allowed under the rules," Elaram said. "I don't understand why everyone can't be more mature about this. It wasn't personal."

Rahelu wanted to roll her eyes—it didn't matter if the reasons behind Issolm's betrayal hadn't been personal; betrayal was betrayal, which meant, by definition, it *was* personal.

"The lead you had this week is gone." She gestured at the grand hall; inside, the other Petitioners had formed into small huddles. "If you want to stay at the top of the rankings, you need to make a difference in this city. And I don't care how good you are on your own; you'll still be more effective if you join with me."

There. She'd said it—more assertively than she had intended.

('*If I join you*' would have been more politic; '*if you join with me*' implied she wanted to lead their hypothetical team which...well, she supposed she needed to.)

"Give us a moment," Elaram said.

One moment stretched into two, then became several as the Issolm Petitioners conferred in a silent Projected conversation. Tiny expressions flickered over their faces; the changes were too quick for her to decipher, but she had already waited long enough.

"Look, if you want to try and successfully mediate the trade dispute between the shipwrights and the carpenters, or put an end to the dreamleaf smuggling with just the two of you, then I wish you the Starfather's luck," Rahelu said. "I'm going to find a way to get that assignment before Imos or Imrell or some other team do. Maybe Ideth will listen to me."

She turned back towards the grand hall, trying to keep her disappointment under control so it wouldn't flare up past her resonance ward.

It hadn't worked.

Worse, she shouldn't have let Lhorne and Dharyas fool her into thinking it might have worked. She should have just gone to Lhorne in the first place since he had been willing to follow her lead before, and since Ideth willingly followed him...

Rahelu laughed at her own folly.

Forget Lhorne and Ideth and Issolm. No Augury was certain, but a possibility was a possibility. She could stop the killer on her own.

And then, two pairs of jogging footsteps followed her inside the grand hall. She looked over her shoulder to see Elaram, pulling Ghardon along with her.

"Do you think you could talk Ideth into working with us too?" Elaram asked.

RAHELU WAS NOT REMOTELY successful at convincing House Ideth.

When she approached Lhorne with Issolm in tow, the rest of the Ideth Petitioners stepped between them, all previous friendliness gone.

Cseryl looked past Rahelu at Elaram and Ghardon. "Issolm." Her tone had the exact chill of ice in a truewinter blizzard.

"Ideth," Ghardon said, mimicking her inflection.

"Please excuse my brother's manners, Petitioner Cseryl," Elaram said. "And let us all be civil with each other."

"Civility is for friends, allies, and worthy opponents," Cseryl said. "Not traitors."

"Fortunately, there are no traitors present." Elaram smiled. "Just Petitioners doing their best to achieve the objectives set by the Houses."

"Very true," Rahelu said before Cseryl could say anything else. "And on that topic, I propose an alliance between the seven of us for the purposes of investigating the strange knifings."

All four Ideth Petitioners stared at her.

Lhorne found his voice first. "You *want* to take the assignment on the *knifings*?"

"You want us to *ally* with these two?" asked the Petitioner with the braided tail. He jerked one thumb at Elaram. "After she left one of us for dead?"

"I did not," Elaram said. "I miscalculated the amount of force I should have used but honestly"—she gestured at Lhorne, who stood head and shoulders taller than her, and then at her own, more diminutive frame—"who can blame me?"

"We can," muttered the fourth Ideth Petitioner, the one who had his arm in a sling just like hers.

"It's better to use one attempt to disable an opponent than two," Elaram continued as if he hadn't said anything. "You would have done the same in my position. No hard feelings, right?" and the Issolm girl flashed a dimpled smile at Lhorne.

Rahelu wanted to punch the Issolm girl in the sternum with excessive force to see how she would like it.

But the reason Elaram had her arm in a sling was because of Rahelu—Elaram had even complimented her on her emotional control—so she decided she wasn't going to give the Issolm Petitioner the satisfaction.

"Everyone should want the assignment on the knifings," Rahelu said. "It's got the highest value to the Houses. It's the obvious choice; the only option that makes sense."

Her only choice.

Lhorne scratched his head. "I've said this before, and I'll say it again: I'm not following. Why would you *want* the most difficult assignment that involves going after an insane killer? The amount of compensation on offer doesn't even enter into the equation."

"Which of these assignments would make a real impact?" Rahelu asked. "Which of these issues are causing real problems for the citizens of this city and would normally require the attention of Dedicates to resolve?"

This *had* to be one of the primary divergence points.

"I see where you're going with this, but I won't do it," Cseryl said. "Not for love or friendship; nothing short of the Skymother coming down from the heavens will make me work with traitors. And neither should any of you," she added as she stared each Ideth Petitioner in the eye—saving a particularly firm glare for Lhorne. "I'd rather spend three insect-bitten weeks hunting nheshwyr in the Westwoods with Isonn," she said with a toss of her sun-bleached hair. "At least they're honest."

Cseryl sashayed away towards the Isonn Petitioners in the other corner without a backward glance. Not that she needed one, because Braid and Sling peeled off to follow her wordlessly.

Fuck. Was that another divergence?

Elaram looked a little hurt. "We're honest too," she called after Cseryl's receding figure. "You just didn't ask the right questions!" Then she beamed that dimpled smile at Lhorne again—this time, accompanied with a hefty batting of long eyelashes.

Lhorne wasn't looking at the Issolm girl though. "Rahelu," he said, and she felt his tentative Seeking at the edges of her resonance aura. "You're going to take this assignment no matter what I say, aren't you? With or without me?"

"You say that as if she would be alone," Ghardon said. "She will not; Elaram and I have both given our word."

"Forgive me if I don't trust in your word or your sister's," Lhorne said. "The last time I did, I ended up with a mild concussion."

"I'll be more careful next time," Elaram said, "now I know how fragile you can be."

Rahelu glared at the other girl. "Will you cut it out? You're not helping!"

"It's fine," Lhorne said. "She has a point; I should have known better. As Cseryl said, Issolm can't be trusted." At that, Ghardon's face darkened, and even Elaram lost her smile.

More House-born politics she wasn't privy to. Rahelu had had enough.

"You too," she said as she turned her glare on Lhorne. "I don't know what happened between Ideth and Issolm, but none of this is helping. Grow up and put your feuds to one side, or we won't have a hope of succeeding. You can get back to it after we catch the killer."

Ghardon went to speak and Rahelu rounded on him. "*What?*"

"Nothing!" The Issolm youth held up both hands defensively. "I was only going to agree with you." He grinned at her. "It will be a nice change to have someone else yell at my sister for me."

The sigh of relief whooshed out of her lungs like wind leaving the mainsail. "Thank you."

"Well, Ideth?" Ghardon held out his arm.

Lhorne said nothing as he considered the three of them in turn.

"Please, Lhorne," Rahelu said. "I followed your crazy plan, didn't I?"

"I asked you to run around a training yard under the controlled conditions of a mock battle. You're asking me to track down an unhinged murderer loose in the city. I don't think those two things are anywhere near equivalent."

"I know," she said. "But I also know that we can pull this off so long as we do this together."

Say yes, she begged him silently, wishing they still had Dharyas's brooches. *Please say yes. I don't want to do this without you.* She stared into his green eyes as if she could Project those words at him with her gaze alone.

"And I promise to not hit you in a way that would cause you to experience another mild concussion or to intentionally cause you any physical harm for the duration of this joint assignment, except in the event that such an action on my behalf would prevent you from coming to greater physical harm, for example, in the possible event that I have to push you off the roof of a building in order to save you from being stabbed by an insane killer," Elaram said without pause.

All three of them turned to look at the Issolm girl.

"Repeat that?" Rahelu asked. "I want to know how you managed to say all of that in a single breath."

"Practice!" Elaram beamed, and this time, the wink and the dimples were aimed at her. "Here, watch. I promise to—"

"Don't encourage her," Ghardon said, clapping one hand over his sister's mouth. "Please."

The closed expression on Lhorne's face cleared. He grinned and clasped Ghardon's arm. "With assurances like those, how could I say no?"

WALKING out of the Guild's grand hall at the head of a team was a decidedly odd experience. They loped through the hallways and the grounds, in synchronous strides with one another, and their Petitioner armbands drew stares from the trainees who scurried past on their way to the final classes of the week. Rahelu caught the eye of one trainee who had stared a little longer than the others—he wore a heavily patched tunic over fraying trousers and had a Chanazian cast to his features. Before she could even smile, the trainee bowed three times and remained bent at the waist, shoulders hunched over as if he expected a blow from her just for looking.

Stand up, she wanted to tell him, but he'd fixed his stare to the ground so he wouldn't meet her gaze again. *I'm the same as you.* She should stop and talk to him—Tsenjhe would —but the three House-born at her back hadn't noticed a thing, and so she was swept along like a lost redfin in a school of silverbream. Their pace quickly carried her past the trainee into the courtyard, and when she looked back, he was gone.

Rahelu was still thinking about the trainee as they exited the front gate. One spot looked strange; fresh gravel had been piled on top of a familiar dusty little depression in the road. From this angle, the bits of shattered rock seemed trivial; tens upon tens of them were displaced with every step she took, and it was impossible to track how each bit had been affected by her passage.

She had taken four strides southwest towards Market Square before she realized their group had split off in different directions.

"Um, the Eastward is this way," Elaram said. She had turned southeast at the Guild gate. "I want to interview the victims' next of kin before we do anything else. There might be a pattern to who the victims are that the city guard missed. That should save us from looking in the wrong places."

Ghardon shook his head. "We can interview those people at any time. We should hurry to the murder sites before the resonance fades beyond our ability to Evoke the events—the city guard Evokers aren't particularly thorough, and it might already be too late for the first site."

"That's the least of our problems," Lhorne said. "The killer has struck once every five days without exception, each time between moonrise and deepnight. It's almost been two full days since the third victim died, so we only have two more to figure out who's next. Since Cseryl won't help us, we need to find someone else to perform an Augury, or we'll have another dead citizen in three days."

Fuck. They needed to do *all* of those things. Damn Cseryl and her stubborn Ideth pride. If the other three Ideth Petitioners had joined them, they could have split up. As things were...

"Let's split up then," Elaram said.

"No," Rahelu said. "That would defeat the purpose of teaming up."

"I thought the point of teaming up was so we could do things four times as fast," Ghardon said. "Not do everything with four times the people."

"Faster isn't always more effective, Issolm," Lhorne said.

"Oh, I think Elaram and I have proven that it is. Might I remind you that we have completed more assignments than all of Ideth combined?"

Gods. Rahelu's head began to ache as Lhorne and Ghardon faced off right there in the street, and she wanted to belt both of them over their heads. If those two were going to clash over every decision like bharost fighting over hunting territory, the four of them would never get anything done.

She looked over at Elaram. The other girl hadn't moved. Her face seemed a little paler than it had been before and she kept making slight adjustments to her sling. There were dark shadows under the Issolm girl's eyes, which had a glazed look to them, and when Rahelu examined Ghardon's face, she found a set of matching shadows under his eyes too.

How hard had the two Issolm Petitioners been pushing themselves? She consulted the assignment board through the relay in her armband and scanned the timestamps of their sign-offs.

Eight hells. A sign-off every nine spans? They must have been working through the nights.

While Rahelu's week with Tsenjhe had been demanding, the Dedicate had insisted she pace herself—refusing to admit her to the Isca workshop building before the second span after dawn and sending her away early so she could help her mother pack up at the market and meet her father's boat. Even so, it had been difficult: her constant heavy use of Projection made her feel as if she had been lifting stones with her mind—if she had to, she could probably force an Evocation for the most recent murder, but she would pay for it in resonance backlash.

Lhorne *seemed* to be in better condition. But there was a slight shakiness to his motions as he gestured, a faintly perceptible unsteadiness to his stance, and tiny furrows in his forehead that hadn't been there last week.

The moment Ghardon drew his arm back, Rahelu lunged forward and yanked, toppling him backward to the ground.

"That's enough," she said. "I thought you two agreed to be good." She ignored the scowls both boys directed at each other to offer Ghardon a hand up from the ground.

He turned his scowl on her and slapped her hand away, muttering curses at her under his breath.

Rahelu clenched her right hand—the one Ghardon had rejected—into a fist but refrained from decking him in the nose since that would have been somewhat hypocritical of her.

"This *isn't* a normal assignment, so we are not going to rush into doing things as if it is." She had to raise her voice to be heard over the protests of the other three Petitioners. "We're not going to be able to help anybody if we keel over the moment we use any resonance skills. Also, none of us have our primary weapons with us, which seems like a colossally stupid lack when we're chasing a deranged killer. And if Lhorne's right, then we have another two days before the killer strikes again. I'd rather have more time, same as any of you, but that's what we have. Even supposing that we know exactly who the killer is and who they're targeting next, answer me honestly: are we in any condition to take them on?"

All of them fell silent so she took that as agreement and plowed on.

"No interviews. No Evocations. No Auguries. We spend

the remainder of the day making preparations, and then we're all going home to *rest*. For a full night, at least. We regroup at first light tomorrow at the residential district west of the north stair to the Lowdocks," she named the oldest of the three murder sites, "and Ghardon and I will attempt an Evocation while Elaram and Lhorne conduct interviews. After we do that, we can try to find someone who might help us out with an Augury. Are we all agreed?"

"Yes, oh wise leader of ours," Lhorne said, with a grin. "We hear, and we obey."

"I'm not—"

"You can stop lying to yourself because you aren't fooling any of us," Elaram said.

"This was your idea, and we agreed to follow your lead when we decided to join you," Ghardon added.

"You didn't—"

"We did, but don't let it go to your head," he said. "Now, if we're going to spend a day on preparations, then I think we should do something else besides fetching weapons and resting." His eyes roved over her father's oversized borrowed tunic that she had belted with spare cord and her mother's fraying rope sandals. "No one will take you seriously when you're dressed like that."

Suddenly, she had a very, very bad feeling about this.

"Oh no." She backed away from the group, edging towards the alleyway.

"Oh yes!" Elaram clapped her hands and then winced. "I love shopping!"

"I really don't think that's necessary. The murder sites are in Temple and Southwatch—"

"And Northpoint," Lhorne said.

Barely. One block west and the third murder would have taken place in the Guild district.

"—I'll blend in better than any of you."

Ghardon rolled his eyes. "The point isn't to blend in; it's to get answers."

"Which is going to be quite difficult when you don't have a focus stone anymore," Lhorne said, in a tone that was ever so slightly accusatory.

He'd noticed.

But of course he'd noticed. Atriarch Ideth would have returned his pendant to him a week ago—it was back around his neck right now. She was the one who had been avoiding him.

She grimaced. "I've been doing fine without one."

"Well, you were the one who just lectured us all on the importance of being properly prepared. You going without a focus stone makes our whole team weaker."

Damn.

Worse, Ghardon was nodding in agreement. "We're handicapped enough as it is," he said, pointing at his sister's sling. "Let's not saddle ourselves with another completely avoidable liability."

Before she could think of any more arguments, Elaram draped her left arm around Rahelu's shoulders and dragged her down the road to Westgate.

Away from the cheaper clothing stalls in Market Square.

"Come on," the Issolm girl said. "I know the perfect place."

"Alironn's?" Ghardon asked.

"Of course not," she said. "Shuath's."

"Neither of those places sell focus stones," Lhorne said. "We should go to Hnuare's."

Rahelu had lost the first battle, but that didn't mean she had to lose the war. "Why don't we go to Nolm's?" she asked. "Market Square is closer."

The wave of disbelief rushing out from all three of the House-born Petitioners into the ambient resonance was nearly enough to bowl her over, and then they overruled her in unison.

"No," Lhorne said. "The moment you try drawing on one of those fifth-class crystals, you'll explode it."

"Not a chance," Ghardon added. "At best, you'll look like a pizuar; at worst, they'll sell you hemp at silk prices."

Elaram didn't say anything at all; she just looked horrified and then redoubled her efforts to drag Rahelu away.

17
DEBTS

RAHELU STOOD AWKWARDLY IN THE MIDDLE OF THE Impeccable Mage—her arms full of fine wool tunics, tightly woven trousers, three sets of leather boots (all in slightly different shades of tan, with varying heel heights and length), and half a dozen leather belts with their assorted pouches and buckles—doing her best to not sneeze all over the very expensive merchandise that Ghardon and the shopkeeper had shoved at her. The two of them were rummaging through yet another corner, pulling out…colorful pairs of silk socks?

What would she even need those for? A plain cotton bandage wrapped around her feet was more economical, just as effective, and much easier to launder.

Meanwhile, Lhorne leaned over one of the glass counters to inspect the array of resonance pendants and rings. None as impressive as the heirloom he had tried to loan her, but all had stones sized for working mages—the smallest was twice as big as her training crystal had been.

Which reminded her that she had yet to report its destruction to the Guild. Rahelu resisted the urge to feel at the coin pouch that hung at her waist—not only would that make her drop something and subject her to further looks of despair from the shopkeeper, but it wouldn't miraculously turn the twenty silver kez she'd earned from Tsenjhe into gold.

"Bring everything and come with me," Elaram ordered as she held up a linen shirt. This one was dyed a rich wine-red, trimmed with pale yellow silk, and had a pattern of vines embroidered at the collar and cuffs. "I want to see how this would look on you."

"Is that really necessary?" Rahelu asked. She eyed the shirt Elaram held out in front of her. The two of them were of the same height, but the Issolm girl had a slimmer build and narrower shoulders. "It'll fit fine. All of these too," and Rahelu hefted her bundle. "Let's just pick something and get out of here." She wrinkled her nose and wished her hands were free so she could pinch it; the smell of sandalwood and jasmine itched in her nostrils.

"No," Elaram said and dragged her off to the back of the shop, through a set of velvet curtains, and into another room with four empty alcoves—each hung with even more velvet curtains—and an enormous mirror of polished bronze on one wall. She threw the shirt at Rahelu (it landed on her head; she shook it off onto the pile in her arms) and pointed at the first alcove. "In."

Rahelu opened her mouth to protest but Elaram cut her off.

"The sooner you try these on, the sooner we can leave. If you need help, I'll go and get Hnuare."

Hnuare had given a muffled little shriek at the sight of Rahelu, requested she stay put in the entryway until two shop assistants had lit several more sticks of incense and fetched a warm bowl of scented water and a delicate wash-cloth, and made her wash her feet while one assistant went to dispose of her mother's worn sandals. Rahelu had had to snatch the sandals back, which caused the shopkeeper to give another little yelp of despair and summon more bowls of scented water and washcloths.

All while Lhorne, Ghardon, and Elaram looked on.

It was the most mortifying experience of her life—and that included Nheras's humiliation in front of everyone on Petition Day. But humiliation was a small price to pay to keep her mother's sandals, which were now wrapped in the first washcloth and banished to a corner of the entryway.

The mere thought of Elaram calling in the stern shopkeeper to help her was frightening—Rahelu wasn't sure who would be more horrified by the experience—so she went inside the alcove, drew the curtain, and undressed.

"Try the wine-red linen shirt with the black linen trousers first."

Rahelu tried the wine-red linen shirt. And the silk shirt in pale violet. And the other silk shirt in forest-green. A quarter-span later, Elaram decided that she needed to try everything on again, but this time with the tan trousers in heavy cotton instead of the black linen ones. Sometime between the light-orange tunic with carved wooden buttons and the ivory tunic with gold laces, Hnuare wandered in with four pairs of socks that must have met with Ghardon's approval, and Rahelu was subjected to another half-span of torture as Elaram and the shopkeeper alternately tugged and pinched at whatever new combination of tunic or shirt over trousers they had made her put on while debating the minutiae of cloth, cut, texture, and something about whether Rahelu's Chanazian complexion meant she was more of a truewinter night than a late spring day.

"And her hair!" Hnuare wailed. "We must do something about her hair. It is ruining the entire effect."

Rahelu looked at her image in the giant polished mirror and a stranger clad in the rich clothing of a House-born Petitioner looked back. She glanced around the disarray of dyed linen, embroidered cotton, and swathes of silk discarded all over the fitting rooms—every single item worth more than all her parents' worldly possessions—and wanted to bolt.

"Excuse me," she said, but neither Elaram nor the shopkeeper noticed; they were too busy debating what she assumed had to be potential hairstyles, even if the terms they were using sounded like plants to her.

She went back into the alcove to don her father's tunic and her own trousers, picked the plainest tunic out of the nine she had tried on and the least expensive-looking pair of boots, then snuck out while Elaram and Hnuare were preoccupied with choosing yet another combination of outfit for her.

If her budget wouldn't stretch to cover both items, Rahelu would give up the boots. Her mother could get by without her sandals for a little longer but her father needed his tunic: aloe and fish oil only went so far to prevent blistered skin.

She had hoped that Lhorne and Ghardon would have gotten bored and left, but when she emerged from the back room they were both still there, ensconced in two of the plush velvet armchairs. Ghardon had actually given in to his exhaustion and fallen asleep while the assistants had made themselves scarce, so it was only Lhorne who looked up as she walked over to the counter.

"How much for these?" she asked as she handed her choice of tunic and boots to the assistant.

"Fifteen silver and seventy-two copper kez."

That would leave her with just enough coin to cover the next installment due to Isonn, with a handful of coppers left over for the smallest pot of burn salve from Gherorg's Elixirs. Her family could still scrape together the coppers for the repayment on her Guild debt if they went without rice next week. She ought to haggle—but unlike the going rate for a third-hand cotton tunic at Nolm's stall, she had no idea how much these things ought to cost, and the expectant way the assistant looked at her suggested haggling wasn't something that House-born did.

She reluctantly handed over the coin pouch Tsenjhe had given her.

The assistant said nothing, but his surprise at her use of kez was plain in his resonance aura. He waved at another assistant to take over wrapping up the garments in a thin square of plain cotton so he could retrieve her change from the safe.

She felt, rather than saw, Lhorne move to join her at the counter. He tapped the glass above one of the rings and said, "This too."

The second assistant bowed and retrieved the ring from the glass cabinet, placing it inside its own velvet-lined box and wrapping it with her new clothes.

"Wait," Rahelu said. "I don't need the boots."

She truly didn't. Her mother's sandals would be fine.

"And"—she scanned the display, then hastily pointed at a different ring, with a resonance crystal half the size of Lhorne's pick—"I'd rather have that ring." She kept her eyes fixed on the second assistant and tried to hold her hands still instead of drumming her fingers on the glass.

The assistant paused and looked from Rahelu to Lhorne, then back again. "Are you certain?" she asked. "While that ring is one of our more popular items, it is truly only suitable for trainees. This one"—she tapped the ring Lhorne had selected—"would be more appropriate for a Petitioner like yourself. It will last you through your years as a Supplicant, until you are ready to swear your oaths of Dedication and choose a pendant, or perhaps a mage-staff."

"I'm certain," Rahelu said.

"Very well," the assistant said. "The total will be nineteen gold, eighty-six silver, and sixty-one copper kez," a sum that was greater than all of her family's debts combined.

"I…" Rahelu's eyes darted to the tunic, then to the boots, neither of which was worth a fraction of the ring. "I'm sorry," she said, and the words came out at a higher pitch than usual. "I don't have the coin now. Perhaps—"

"Perhaps you could charge the first ring to my account and include the boots after all," Lhorne said smoothly as the first assistant returned with her change. Both assistants smiled, bowed again, and did as he said.

Rahelu whipped her head around to look at him. "I can't afford this," she hissed. "Not if I completed every single open assignment by myself!"

He shrugged, unmoved by her protest. "Maketh told us to use any means at our disposal. This counts as one of them." Then he rested one elbow on the counter and grinned as he leaned in towards her. "If you feel bad about this, then by all means, you can pay me back by buying me dinner tomorrow night."

Rahelu dipped her head to count her change, resisting the urge to look at him again as she waited for the punchline. She lost that battle; her eyes seemed to dart a glance at him through the curtain of her hair of their own will.

Twinkling green eyes waited for her reply.

Skymother's harp.

While he hadn't been serious about wanting repayment, he was serious about wanting to have dinner with her—there were faint eddies of purple and yellow in his resonance aura.

Four silver and twenty-eight copper kez.

Enough for a decent meal for one or a scanty meal for two at a tavern in Northpoint or a Sunset songhouse.

Or two weeks of reprieve from Isonn's moneylenders.

The debt to Lhorne was a new one, and it had been incurred in order to buy equipment for her. As a Petitioner, she was not sworn to a particular House, but perhaps any House making her an offer could be persuaded to foot the bill; whichever House she swore her oaths of Supplication to would have to outfit her properly anyway.

And if not, well, her share of this assignment would see all her parents' debts repaid with some left over.

Salvation.

As Onneja promised.

Rahelu rolled the coins in her hand. Could they afford her frittering away four silver kez on one dinner with another Petitioner? Or would her mother be disappointed that she hadn't seized the chance to bait a hook for a son of Ideth?

If her mother had those specific kinds of hopes, Rahelu should invite Tsenjhe for a meal much sooner than the summer solstice.

What did she want?

Rahelu didn't know.

She only knew that two weeks of reprieve from Isonn's moneylenders would go a long way to easing her parents' burdens. (Her father might even get a full night's sleep.)

So she closed her fingers over the coins in the palm of her hand, met those clear green eyes, and tried to think of some polite way to tell Lhorne no.

His grin faded when he saw how tightly she clutched her coins. "That was thoughtless of me. I'm sorry." He cleared his throat and straightened. "Don't worry about paying me back. When we complete this assignment, I'm sure Aunt Mere will make you an offer. I'll see that she includes the cost of the ring in your contract. Just think of it as an advance on your wages as a Supplicant."

"Thank you," she said quietly.

He nodded as if that had been exactly what he expected to hear, then gestured towards the velvet curtain separating the front of the shop from the back. "You'd better go fetch

Elaram while I wake Issolm if we're starting before dawn."
His voice was light and untroubled despite the sharp blue-
black sting that spiked briefly through his resonance aura. He
smoothed it over with a blurry gray that wasn't quite a fully
formed Obfuscation barrier but still distorted her ability to
sense his emotions.

To her surprise, Rahelu found an echo of the same blue-
black in her own resonance aura.

"Lhorne, wait," she said before he had taken more than a
few steps towards the armchair where Ghardon still snored.

He turned to look at her with eyes the exact color of the
lakegrass that grew at the bottom of the Elumaje. "Yes?"

She forced the words out before she could change her
mind again. "About tomorrow night..." Unlike him, she
couldn't hide the faint catch in her voice. "Do you like fish?"

18

BET

THE 1ST DAY OF TRUESUMMER, 530 A.E./A.F.

THE FIRST OF THE MURDER VICTIMS WAS WELM, A grain trade factor in his fifth decade.

Rahelu stepped around the dark patch of packed earth where his body had been found, in a quiet residential area on the northeast edge of Temple. Squared-off wooden houses stood in neat gabled rows, presenting a united front of shuttered windows and barred doors to the common courtyard.

(It was the kind of very nearly respectable neighborhood that her parents sometimes aspired to, when they'd had a particularly good catch and paying off their debts didn't seem like the task of a lifetime.)

Elaram took four heartbeats to begin a Seeking and methodically worked her way through the houses, pointing out the occupied residences with her unbound hand. Lhorne followed in her wake, pounding his fist on the first door, then the second, without success.

That was no surprise. Rahelu wouldn't have opened up either.

He moved on to the third door. At this rate, the interviews would take all day.

"Are you just going to stand there ogling Ideth, or are you going to help?" Ghardon asked, from where he crouched next to the bloodstained patch of dirt.

Rahelu ignored the jibe. She was *not* ogling. "I was just thinking this is a very odd place."

"Oh? Are there less odd places for an insane killer to murder someone?"

"Think about it. Why would you murder someone in the middle of a residential street?"

"I don't know; I'm not an insane killer. Maybe it was convenient. The killer simply wandered around and killed the first person they ran across after moonrise instead of picking a location."

"And proceeded to hack the body apart with a bladed weapon in the middle of the street like they were butchering a hog?"

"That sounds about right for insanity."

"Ghardon, I live in the Lowdocks where an average of five people are stabbed each night. Most of it is over sex, blood, or kez—sometimes all three—though I once heard of a man who was killed for his eyelids."

Ghardon stared at her. "His eyelids."

"Apparently his killer thought they were very nice and was unhappy when the man didn't want to give them up." She shrugged. "We may not understand it, but killers always have their own reasons for what they do."

"So what's your theory?" Ghardon delivered his challenge with the academically detached tone of their fifth-year instructor for Evocation, the one laced with a subtle undercurrent of amusement at his less adept students about to pursue a flawed line of reasoning during a practice investigation.

Fine. Two could play at that game.

"Welm was killed at moonrise." Rahelu spoke slowly, the

way Ghardon did whenever he had been asked, as the first-ranked student, to explain the obvious. "The corpse lay here for at least eight spans—look how deeply the blood has soaked into the earth; we can still see it even though more than two weeks have passed since his body was first discovered." Rahelu spun her spear around and used its point to sketch out lines in the air over the bloodstains. "This is not a well-trafficked road, and the people who live here are rich enough to have their own residence but not wealthy enough to hire servants or keep palanquins. They walk, and they've been avoiding this spot—"

"Quite understandably."

"—so it was left untouched, except for vermin. The Stormbringer has been distant; we've not had any rainstorms since spring's end."

"And?"

"You don't think it's odd that the killer didn't try to be a little more careful with the blood? If we'd taken this assignment a few days after the murder instead of a few weeks, we wouldn't have issues with an Evocation." She dug the point of her spear into the darkest part of the patch. "As things stand, I doubt we'll get a glimpse of anything."

"Less talking, more doing," Ghardon said. He grabbed the clump of bloodstained dirt Rahelu had dug out and began a Seeking, trying to sense any residual resonance from the dried blood.

He was treating the clump of dirt as if it were an object, but it was too contaminated. Even if they dug up the entire bloodstained patch of road, whatever trace of resonance it might have carried would be too diffuse for them to detect. A true Evoker, someone who had spent their years of Dedication honing their skill in Evocation, might be able to do it (and anyone on the level of an archmage certainly wouldn't have that limitation), but then again, this assignment was supposed to be a test to see if they could perform beyond the level of ability expected of a Supplicant.

To her surprise, Ghardon managed *something*.

Not the full ghostly vision of a successful Evocation. Mere flickering shadows, tinged the dark gray of mild unease, that lacked the usual substance of his Evocations.

The effort strained him though; his fist gripped the clump of dirt so tightly that bloody grains crumbled off the edges through his whitened knuckles. She could feel him fighting to anchor the faint thread connecting past and present to the focus stone he wore on his right hand. He drew on the crystal's stored resonance, wrapped it around that temporal thread, and pulled.

Flickering shadows deepened, became a hazy fog instead of fragmentary candle flames, and then the thread snapped.

Ghardon grunted in pain as resonance backlash set in. "Skymother," he swore. "I was sure I had it."

"You almost did." Rahelu tapped the point of her spear on the ground, then tucked it under her arm. She carefully positioned herself at the very edge of the bloodstain, faced away from it towards the end of the street, and took a half-stride forward.

This would be easier if the street had gravel instead of packed earth, but her resonance ward should still work. She turned until she stood perpendicular to the bloodstain, then paced out a circle, using the point of her spear to etch a thin line in the dirt.

"Get inside," she said when she reached Ghardon, nudging him with the toe of her new boot. "Right on top of the spot."

He eyed her with trepidation but did as she asked so she could finish her circuit. The completed circle was perhaps four or five strides wide. Once she had closed the basic ward, she laid her spear on the ground and drew her belt knife instead, scratching deep, thin lines that curved towards the center. She made sure to anchor each line so that one end touched the edge of the circle and the other touched blood-stained earth, stopping periodically to wipe her blade on the rag Maketh had given her.

"Ghardon, would you mind lying down?" she asked. "I suggest on your back because that's how Welm was found. Do you recall whether the city guard's notes specified which way his head was facing?"

"You're not serious."

She looked up from the fifth set of interlocking triangles she was scratching out to see that he was locked in a staring contest with the bloodied dirt—jaw clenched, eyes narrowed, lips pressed tightly together—and the corners of his mouth turned so far down they practically reached his shoulders. "Why are you standing on your toes?"

He immediately lowered himself a few finger-widths, but his heels still weren't touching the ground.

"I can see that, you know, so my question remains."

"So does mine. Why do you want me to lie down? Standard Guild methods don't require any such thing."

"This will work better if you do."

Assuming it even worked. Trying an Evocation on a place instead of a person was not generally done. But Ghardon's earlier glimmer of success suggested it might be possible.

Like objects, places could absorb ambient resonance. It could happen over time—like how Tsenjhe's workshop had accumulated a steady pale blue luster of patience over the years as inventor after inventor persisted in their experiments—or as a result of a particularly resonant event. The Exaltation of a Dominance, for example, would resonate throughout the streets of the capital for days afterward due to the sheer number of people in attendance, and it was said that travelers to Kuast Yrg in old Aleznua could still feel the after-echoes of Tsilm's death, even centuries later.

And there were certain places in the Lowdocks that everyone knew to avoid. You had to be blind drunk, unconscious, or a murderer yourself, to go willingly into the Raven's Roost or the Red Passage.

She finished etching the resonance ward, wiped her blade down, put away her knife, and then blinked.

Ghardon still stood on his toes. It was an impressive feat of balance that wasn't helpful in the slightest.

"You're not lying down," she said. "Not only that, you're..." She blinked again. "Are you afraid of a little dirt?"

"It's not just dirt. How would you like to have some murdered soul's blood smeared all over your clothes?" he asked, as if the answer were obvious.

Maybe it was.

"It wasn't my favorite experience, but since I got away in one piece, I honestly didn't mind the two days I spent soaking and scrubbing my tunic and trousers with ash and piss," she said. "The stains eventually faded."

This time, it was Ghardon's turn to look horrified, like he'd never seen someone murdered before. But his eyes were staring at her tunic, so maybe he was just horrified at the thought of having to wear the same clothes again. Now that she was paying attention, she noticed his tunic and trousers weren't the ones he had worn yesterday.

He swallowed a couple of times. "How about you try it without me lying down first? Or we could swap?" he asked.

"You couldn't Evoke your own memory of breakfast right now, let alone attempt this," she said. "Stop mincing around like an ishtrel that's about to lose its breeding plumage; this is going to be hard enough as it is."

"This better work," he said as he reluctantly arranged himself into the strangest imitation of a corpse Rahelu had ever seen: he had his arms lifted slightly off the ground and knees in the air, trying to keep as much of his clothing from touching the dirt as possible.

She stifled a snicker and thought about pointing out that Welm had had his arms sprawled out in opposite directions and lined up with his shoulders instead of close by his sides, and his legs spread wide so that they marked four equidistant segments of a half-circle if you drew a line connecting fingertips to kneecaps from the left hand to the right.

But Ghardon's face was the perfect picture of misery so she behaved herself and sat cross-legged on the ground by the western point of the circle, facing east into the past.

She closed her eyes, breathed in the steady three-count for Evocation, and listened to the street.

Five houses down, towards the end of the street, there was the clatter of a deadbolt being drawn as Lhorne and Elaram were finally admitted inside one of the houses. Further away: the telltale *thump-clatter thump-clatter* of someone pushing an empty handcart down the north stair towards the Lowdocks instead of taking the twisting ramp. But this street itself was as still as truewinter ice and quiet as the third span after deepnight.

It took Rahelu more than four heartbeats to locate fourteen bone-white resonance auras inside the houses. (One— the one with Lhorne and Elaram—pulsed a little more frantically.) That resonance carried a jumpy sense of being watched by something in the shadows; a resonance that was heightened whenever they had to walk through the street, past a certain point in the middle, where someone they had known —had loved—had been brutally slaughtered.

The spot of heightened resonance aligned almost perfectly with her ward: it wasn't centered on the largest part of the bloodstain as she had thought but slightly off to the side, so one edge overlapped her shins.

Good enough.

Rahelu gathered up that shared terror, filtered it through her new resonance crystal, and sent it into the ward. She tethered her consciousness to the faint boundary between the general wash of the ambient resonance and the pale white that marked where Welm had died, then drew more power from her crystal to fuel her Evocation:

A shadow—two shadows?—moved in the dying light, their outlines indistinct and faded.

Which was which? One looked to be pursuing the other, but their positions were reversed: the shadow in front was headed away from the street, towards the courtyard, and the one following behind had come from—well, she had no idea because it was outside of the range of her Evocation, but it had to have been somewhere in the street.

A gloved hand—robed arm?—with a blurry knife whose blade was the length of her forearm.

Useless. They already knew it was some sort of bladed weapon. The crystal on her finger grew warmer as she bore down on the Evocation, straining to make the details of the knife clearer, but they eluded her so she allowed the vision to continue, slowly slipping forward in time.

Night falls. The two shadows merge; blend with darker shadows on the ground. A sense of...anticipation? Like lust, but not for flesh or blood. And yet, there is also ecstasy mixed with...disgust? No, not disgust. Regret, perhaps, or despair.

Eight hells. This was the problem with anchoring an Evocation on a place instead of a person: you got a blended mess of emotions from everyone there at the time, instead of one set of emotions filtered through a single perspective. She assumed the anticipation and ecstasy had been the killer's and the regret or despair the victim's, yet the resonance traces were so muddled it could well have been the other way around or some other combination.

Rahelu held on to the Evocation, hoping to see something other than rippling shadows. The pain behind her eyes was still manageable, and while her crystal was warmer than usual, it wasn't hot. If she skimmed through the past faster, at least until she got to the part where the body had been discovered...

"Can I get up now?" Ghardon asked. "We learned nothing and my clothes are ruined."

She let the Evocation go and waved at him, then rested her head in her hands, massaging her scalp.

"Not nothing. We know that this wasn't a revenge killing now. There was no jealousy or anger involved." The ache in the base of her skull reminded her of something else. "There was no pain either. Odd."

"Not necessarily," he said, and she heard the light, repeated brushing of his fingers over his silk-embroidered tunic. "Welm could have taken numbweed, or willowbark, or even dreamleaf; any apothecary would have those for sale."

A stupid thing to overlook. She was kezless again (not that she had been kezful for long) so the thought that people might buy powders, possets, or pills for pain relief hadn't crossed her mind.

"I'm not ruling it out," she said as if it *had* crossed her mind, "but my understanding was that those don't take pain entirely away. And the ones that do, such as the ones used by the Healers' guild, are restricted substances. Even then, Welm would have had to take it within a span of when he was killed for it to still be in effect."

More bits of crumbled dirt and dried blood fell in front of her. Ghardon had gotten up, moved to an unstained patch of dirt, and started stamping around in an attempt to dislodge the bits that had stuck to the soles of his boots. "Perhaps somebody put it in his food then."

"Now you're just making wild guesses," she said, still massaging the back of her neck. "And if you're going to be walking around like that, could you kick some dirt over the ward? We should take it down before we leave."

"I've already ruined my tunic for this; I'm not adding my boots to the list of casualties. You're welcome to do whatever you please to yours while you wait for my sister and Ideth." He glanced down the street, trying to gauge Elaram and Lhorne's progress. "They're not even halfway done, so I'm going to a bathhouse. I'll meet you three at the Golden Crust."

"A bathhouse," Rahelu repeated, just to be sure she had heard correctly.

"I'd prefer the comfort of my own bath, but since we are on a schedule and on the wrong side of the city, I can't exactly spare the time."

"But you can spare the time to go to a public bathhouse?" she asked, incredulous. "The closest one is the Tidepool," Rahelu named the only bathhouse in the Lowdocks that didn't double as a pleasure den, "over by the south stair."

"Gods, no. I'm going to hire one of the rooms at the Seven Springs"—of *course* he would choose the most expensive inn in the Highdocks—"so I can have a private soak while one of the launderers on staff tries to save my tunic."

She continued staring at him without saying a word. After twenty or so heartbeats, he finally stopped picking away at the finer grains stuck in the weave on his shoulder.

"Would you like to come?" he asked, with a suggestive lift of his eyebrows and a glint in his eyes. "I promise it'll be more to your liking than the bath Hnuare made you take last night."

"That's not hard; washing in the Suusradi would be more enjoyable," she said. "I've got a better idea: how about you come with me instead so we can get these interviews done faster?"

"If my sister and Ideth aren't getting far, then I doubt we will either. We're a team, Rahelu, so we should stick to what we're good at."

"We're a team so we should be helping them, not slacking off!"

"The best way we can help them, right now, is by staying out of the way."

Rahelu glowered at him.

Ghardon laughed. "Let's make a bet. You win if you can convince even one of these people to open their door in your current state. If you do, I'll buy you a new belt."

Her hand went to the spare cord around her tunic. "This one is fine," she snapped. "It ties things to my waist; what more does a belt need to do?"

"Please, it's a travesty. You'd actually be doing me a favor because then I don't have to look at that eyesore and wonder if you'll slice yourself every time you draw your knife."

She sucked in a breath, held it for a count of three, and then let it out again slowly. "That's not how a bet works, Issolm. If I win, you do the next thing I ask of you for this assignment without any objection or complaint. Even if it's to go and crawl through the sewer in your favorite outfit, sifting through the muck for the murder weapon with your bare hands."

"And if you lose? Do you do the next thing I ask of you without any objection or complaint?"

She sighed. "Within the bounds of this assignment, yes."

He smirked and she hurried to add, "As long as it has a *direct* connection to catching the killer."

There was no way she was going to let herself be dragged back inside the Impeccable Mage to look at belts.

Ghardon laughed again and extended his arm. "Deal. But I don't think I'm the one who's going to regret this."

Rahelu sealed the terms of their bet with a firm clasp of his arm, then watched him saunter away and summon a public palanquin.

A palanquin. To convey him *three* city blocks to the next district over.

When she won their bet, she was going to find it difficult to decide on what she ought to make him do.

Rahelu snorted at her foolishness and walked towards the next door Elaram had marked out.

There was no contest.

Ghardon's complaints could be ignored with determination (and by stuffing her ears with cloth or wax), but there was only one way to compel him to do something like a normal person instead of a spoiled House-born.

THE GOLDEN CRUST was nowhere near as nice as the Atriarch's Cup, but it wasn't crowded and had a menu listing the day's specials. Which, thankfully, only cost between fifteen and twenty copper kez—an amount that Rahelu was still reluctant to part with. While Lhorne and Elaram paid for full meals, she haggled with the server and eventually settled on paying three copper kez for half a loaf of yesterday's bread.

The three of them sat around a rough wooden table in the farthest corner, drinking their ale and waiting for their food (and Ghardon) to arrive. Rahelu had already filled the other

two in on their limited success with Evocation and specu-
lations.

"The pair of us are done for the day," she concluded. "If
Ghardon doesn't show up in the next span, we should leave
him to rest. I'm surprised either of us managed to Evoke
anything at all. Trying to sense resonance from so long ago
without a clear target…in a spot that isn't even considered to
be a distinct place in its own right…" She rubbed her eyes.
"We won't be able to do that again for another day, at least. It
might actually be harder with the next two sites."

"How?" Lhorne asked. "The second and third murders are
more recent; that should make things easier, if anything."

"Recency is only one component," Rahelu said. "Sapience,
complexity, and intensity are the others. Someone murdering
a former lover in a jealous rage or one gang member stabbing
another to death as part of a blood feud—these kinds of
events normally resonate through time like a shout.

"The more bitterly the lovers parted, or the longer the
blood feud, the louder the echoes. The act of killing is like a
release for the killer's emotions, see? The more strongly they
feel, the easier it is for echoes to transfer from their aura to
the ambient resonance.

"I only managed to Evoke something from the street
because the first killing happened long ago enough that the
residents began to think of the murder site as a place of its
own."

"Alright, I see what you're saying." Lhorne frowned. "That
probably won't be the case with the other two sites. Not
enough time has passed, and instead of a quiet street, we
have the public relay station in Southwatch and the alleyway
behind the fountain in Northpoint. Too many events happen
at the Southwatch relay station, and while the fountain is a
common meeting place, the alleyway behind it isn't a place of
significance to anyone."

"Did any of the people you interviewed see anything?" Rahelu asked. "If we had eyewitnesses, we could Evoke the killer's resonance signal from their memories and use it to track the murderer down."

Maybe. If the killer was trained in the resonance disciplines, then they might be skilled enough at Obfuscation to mask their resonance signature.

Elaram shook her head. "Only five of the fourteen residents were willing to talk to us, and most didn't even see Welm's body. The only one who did was so traumatized by the sight that he went straight from reporting the discovery to the city guard to a healer to have the details Obfuscated."

Rahelu swore. "Why didn't the watch officer take a record of the memory before letting him go to a healer?"

"City guard procedures don't require it," Lhorne said, and Rahelu wished every horror from each of the eight hells upon the fish-brained simpleton who designed the city guard's pathetic investigation protocols. "The man isn't resonance trained. Elaram couldn't pull the memory out because the whole Obfuscation barrier was constructed to draw on his resonance, and the moment I tried to look at the thing, he started having convulsions."

"We could try finding the healer he went to and see if they'd be willing to talk, but it would be a waste of time," Elaram said. "I already looked into the possibility; healer/patient confidentiality is one of the two prime mandates enshrined in Healers' code. The only exception is if they suspect their patients are likely to cause harm to themselves or others and this man wouldn't fall into that category."

"What about any objects of significance?" Rahelu asked. "We can't track the killer with one, but we could at least try Evoking the victim's memory of their death, depending on where the victim was carrying that object at the time. We might be able to get some clues about who the killer is, or the specific details of the murder weapon…"

Lhorne and Elaram shook their heads.

"All of the victims were stripped naked and the killer harvested whatever resonance crystals had formed. The man remembered that much, just not the exact details of how the killer had done that," Elaram said, fiddling with her sling on the opposite side of the table. "And it's been long enough that their families have burned the bodies."

"Could you try an Evocation on their ashes?" Lhorne asked. "I'm guessing that's not as good as having the actual corpse but it would be better than nothing, right?"

It was Rahelu's turn to shake her head. "If we had the corpse we might be able to Evoke something similar to the resonance from an object of significance. Not likely, since most of the victim's resonance would have either drained away with their blood or crystallized upon death, but not impossible. With only the ashes though, whatever trace resonances that had remained in the body would have been destroyed by the fire. Ghardon shouldn't even have been able to do what he did with the dried blood—it's not even really an object in its own right so the fact he was able to Evoke a hint of anything at all is impressive. I couldn't have done the same."

"Don't let him hear you say that," Elaram said. "He gets enough praise from our parents as it is for bringing home those Guild medals every year."

"Too late!" Ghardon said cheerfully as he sat in the last remaining chair at their table, between Elaram and Rahelu. His hair was still wet but had been neatly combed and styled, and his tunic was indeed freshly pressed and…

Rahelu sniffed, then let herself sneeze since she wasn't holding any expensive merchandise.

"Hey, watch it! I just had this laundered."

"In what? Perfume?" she asked. "There are certain plea-sure dens in the Lowdocks—ones that you can smell from ten strides away—that don't reek half as bad as you do right now."

Lhorne choked on his mouthful of ale, spraying most of it back into his mug. The rest splattered all over the table, some of it on the front of Ghardon's tunic.

"Sorry," Lhorne gasped, masking his laughter with a fit of coughing.

"I swear to the Stormbringer, Ideth, you did that on purpose." Ghardon scowled as Elaram snickered.

Rahelu pulled out the rag she had been using. "Here."

Ghardon couldn't scramble away from the small cloth she was waving at him fast enough, and the way his eyes bulged as he leapt up and knocked his chair over sent Lhorne and Elaram into fresh peals of laughter.

To be fair, the blood-and-soil-encrusted rag no longer bore any resemblance to the tidy white square Maketh had dropped in front of her the week before.

On the other hand, while she hadn't had the time to wash it properly, it was still dry enough to soak up the spill.

"I hate you all," Ghardon said as he untangled himself from the wreckage of the chair (which had not been well crafted enough to survive the encounter) but he said it without rancor. "Give me that," he said and snatched Rahelu's dripping rag by pinching it between two fingers, then stalked off towards the hearth at the other end of the tavern's common room.

"Hey!" Rahelu called after him. "I wasn't done with that."

He made a rude gesture at her and threw the rag in the fire. "You offered it to me and *I am* done with it," he said, snapping his fingers at one of the servers as he walked back to their table. The server hurried over at once and began mopping up the remainder of the spill as Ghardon pulled over a new, sturdier chair.

"You should join us for dinner tonight," Elaram said to her. "Mother and Father dote on him so much that he's completely spoiled; it would be so nice to have one dinner where the conversation doesn't revolve around my brother."

"There are plenty of those!" he said.

"Uh," Rahelu said, trying to think of some way to wiggle out of this one without inadvertently revealing more than she ought to. "Some other time. I already have plans tonight. And"—she tapped her armband—"we still haven't sent our updates through the relay."

Elaram waved her objections away. "We've all got reports to transfer; that won't take more than a quarter-span. You said yourself that you can't do any more Evocations. Poring over the details of the assignment with resonance backlash won't do you any good."

"It's not that," she said. "My parents will be expecting me. They'll worry if I don't show up before moonrise."

That was true. *Please, Elaram, please leave it at that.*

"Oh, that's easy," Elaram said. "Your mother has a stall in Market Square, yes? We can stop by to let her know on our way to see if any Augurs are available. If they're worried about you traveling back alone after dark, well, you won't need to—you can stay over in one of the guest suites."

"I...that's very generous of you," she said. "But—"

The other girl snapped to attention and Rahelu sensed her Seeking straight away. "You really do have plans," she stated.

Oh eight hells.

"I said that, didn't I?"

"Yes, but I thought they were plans, you know, not...*plans.*" Elaram dragged out the word with an exaggerated up-and-down singsong inflection. The Issolm girl looked left and right, but they were sitting at a corner table and there was no room for her to squeeze past either of the boys —Earthgiver be thanked—so she remained firmly trapped on the other side of the table.

This didn't dissuade Elaram from leaning forward as far as the table would allow. "Well?" she demanded. "Do tell!"

Now Rahelu was in for it. Various options sprang to mind: *'it's none of your business'* being the first one (too abrasive; Elaram was just being friendly, and she wasn't so flush with friends that she could afford to turn down any offers), then *'I'm meeting a friend'* which was true (but Elaram would demand to know who and Rahelu wouldn't need to say anything before the other girl worked it out from the changes in the ambient resonance), so that left *'I don't want to tell you'* (also true, but it would raise even more questions).

She desperately wanted to look to Lhorne for help, but that was as good as giving an answer, so she looked right.

Ghardon seemed to be equally intrigued by her dinner plans.

"Why do you want to know?" she asked.

The two Issolm Petitioners exchanged looks and then Elaram shrugged and settled back in her chair. "Just making conversation," she said. "All these years at the Guild together and we don't really know you. We never saw you at any of the parties, not even at graduation."

"Well of course not. None of the common-born were ever invited."

This time, Lhorne joined the other two Petitioners in staring at her.

"I'll admit that's true for most of the parties," he said, "but the Houses take turns hosting the graduation party—and every graduate is invited. It was House Ilyn's turn this year. Do you not remember Nheras giving you the invitation?"

"What invitation?"

Elaram conjured a very small Evocation:

Nheras walks over, with Bhemol and Kiran at her heels. They carry large satchels bursting with cream-and-gold envelopes. Nheras offers up two: they are addressed to 'Elaram of Issolm' and 'Ghardon of Issolm' and stamped with the glittering red-and-cream resonance seal of House Ilyn.

"Never got anything like that," Rahelu said.

The three House-born exchanged another look, then Lhorne cleared his throat and said, "The graduation party wasn't very interesting anyway. That's why Cseryl and I are having another celebration for anyone who successfully completes Petitioning. You're all invited, as I've no doubt that all four of us will succeed in getting offers." The tight smile he directed at Ghardon bore little resemblance to his usual generous grin—though it *was* genuine nonetheless. "Yes, even you, Issolm."

Ghardon's answering smile was also tight. "Very kind of you, Ideth."

The banter continued as the server finally brought over their meals and Rahelu was saved from having to participate in further conversation about attending dinner parties by virtue of being able to gnaw on her end of stale bread. Parties sounded incredibly boring; she couldn't imagine many things that she wanted to do less of.

Scraping barnacles off the hull of her father's boat with her bare hands; hauling water from the well in Market Square with a leaking bucket and only one hand; rethatching the roof of their hovel in a thunderstorm—she'd rather do any of those things than go to a dinner party.

Regardless of whether she had received and forgotten her invitation to the graduation party (possible) or if Nheras had deliberately excluded her from the guest list (more probable),

Rahelu decided she was grateful for the result. From the sounds of the current discussion, once she had accepted the invitation, it would be a grave insult to not attend; and once she was there, she wouldn't be able to leave prematurely without giving great offense to the host, which meant she would be forced to stand around making idle conversation with people she didn't know until the host decided the party was over—and still the torture wouldn't be done, because then there would be an endless round of subtle negotiations over who would be holding the next party and she would have to accept that invitation as well, or risk giving further offense.

"This is all so ridiculous," she said, interrupting a debate about whether or not House Isilc's decision to have a veritable army of servers offer bite-sized portions of food to their guests at the last affair was: an act of hubris designed to shame all the other Houses with a crude display of wealth, a brilliant innovation that made the night more enjoyable as one needn't retire from conversation and socializing to eat at the buffet, or a calculated move to reduce House expenditure by only serving as much food as the guests ate instead of over-catering and then having to dispose of the excess. "Why do you have to go to these absurd lengths of posturing to prove who's better? Just have regular contests of ability and be done with it."

Elaram blinked. "What fun is that?"

"What *isn't* fun about the right to challenge anyone I disagree with and prove the point experimentally?" Rahelu countered. "You can't argue with facts and results. If they're right, they win. If I'm right, I win. Either way, the job gets done and nobody wastes any time arguing about which way to do it."

Ghardon cleared his throat. "On the subject of winning..."

Fuck. She'd forgotten about their bet.

"How many people did you convince to open their door and let you inside to interview them?"

Rahelu made a show of leaning back to look outside the tavern. "Oh, would you look at the time?" she said as she hastily got to her feet. "It's almost high sun; I'd best get started on seeing if we can find anybody to run that Augury." She waved Lhorne away as he made to get up as well. "No, no, you three aren't finished with your meals yet. You can come find me later at Northpoint."

"I'll take that as 'none'," Ghardon said, with a smug grin. He rubbed his hands together and cackled.

She fled.

19

PLANS

✦

UNLIKE THE OTHER RESONANCE DISCIPLINES, there weren't any shops in the Echo Alleys that offered Augury services. If the four of them were properly sworn Supplicants, they could have tried consulting their House's Augurs during one of the weekly slots kept open for unscheduled Auguries.

Alas, they were only Petitioners. None of the Houses would admit them—not even Ideth or Issolm—so perhaps Dharyas had been right in asserting that being House-born didn't guarantee success or favor.

Rahelu was surprised to find herself feeling discouraged; the fact that the other three couldn't leverage their birth and familial connections should have restored her faith in Aleznuaweithish ideals.

But—principles be damned—she would gladly consign the ideals to the fifth hell and never complain about inequality ever again if it meant that her mother would be safe.

They trudged out past the sumptuous golden gates of the Imos headquarters. Even Ghardon dragged his feet, heedless of what the paved tiles were doing to the soles of his second-favorite pair of boots.

"Still nothing from Cseryl?" Rahelu asked Lhorne.

Lhorne shook his head. "She's ignoring me because I didn't listen to her. Nobody holds a grudge quite like Cseryl."

"You don't need to tell me that," Ghardon said.

"Alright, but she's not the only one with a talent in Augury around. What about Keshwar?" Rahelu asked.

Lhorne quashed that hope too. "We can't go to a Dedicate for help, and especially not Keshwar. He can turn a blind eye to me borrowing supplies and equipment but if I were to ask him for help directly, he would have to turn me down. Otherwise, what's to stop anybody from getting into the Houses without proving themselves? It would undermine the whole system."

The two Issolm Petitioners nodded along with that so Rahelu wasn't about to start an argument over all the obvious flaws in his logic.

The sentiment was nice. Maybe it was uncharitable of her to judge all House-born by Nheras's example. While Ghardon would probably never stop challenging her, his reasons generally made sense.

Except for the wardrobe-related ones. She doubted that she'd ever be able to understand those.

Rahelu sighed. "Does anybody have any other ideas?"

Glum silence. They turned left at the next road and headed north as the bottom of the sun crossed the horizon. In the fading orange-red light, the long shadows thrown by the scrying towers of the palace stretched out over the heart of the city, like black, skeletal fingers.

One more day before the killer would strike again.

"Alright then," Rahelu said when no one volunteered further suggestions after another quarter-span of walking.

"Nobody use any more resonance skills tonight; let's get some rest so we can investigate the other two sites first thing tomorrow."

She looked over at Ghardon, trying to gauge whether he would still be at risk of running into resonance backlash then.

Ghardon gave her an irritated glance but didn't snap at her. "Judging by today's results, we'll be better off using your method at the last two sites." He said that through gritted teeth, like the admission pained him. "With both of us trying, we might have the strength to Evoke something."

Skymother willing. It was the only lead they had left.

"We can help," Elaram said as she exchanged looks with Lhorne. "It sounds like Evocation is working better than our interviews anyway. Maybe if we run Rahelu's method through a Concordance we'll find something?"

Ghardon nodded. "But I'm not playing dead again. Ideth can do that this time."

"Hey now," Lhorne said. "I—"

"No counting our profits until we've realized them," Rahelu said. "I'll see you guys at the first span after dawn, by the Southwatch relay. I've got to go check in with my mother."

Just a brief Augury while they packed up the baskets, to make sure none of the immediate probabilities had changed since eartharc.

"I'll walk with you to Market," Lhorne said. "It's on my way back to Northpoint."

Elaram gave both of them a sharp look.

"Sure," Rahelu said, trying to not notice the way her heart thundered in her chest. She glanced up at the sun. "If you don't mind hurrying. She might already be half-packed, depending on how well today has gone," her mouth babbled.

Gods, why couldn't she stop talking? Elaram's eyes gleamed in the shadows and Rahelu didn't need an Augur to tell her that if she didn't escape *right now* that she would regret it.

"So I'm sorry to rush off but I really have to go, good work today everybody, see you tomorrow." She tripped up at least three times trying to get the words out, all while struggling to control her surging resonance aura so it would stay within the bounds of her resonance ward.

Very subtle of her. Time to cut her losses. Rahelu walked away as fast as she could without breaking into an outright jog.

She didn't wait for Lhorne. He could catch up.

"See you tomorrow," he said, echoing her words in farewell.

Unfair. How did he sound so calm, as if nothing were out of the ordinary?

"Enjoy your dinner." Ghardon didn't bother to keep the smirk out of his voice. "Have pity on Ideth and don't run so fast, Rahelu. He might not be able to keep up."

Neither did Elaram. "I look forward to hearing all the details tomorrow."

Cheeks burning, Rahelu gave up on her dignity and launched into a sprint, ignoring Elaram and Ghardon's chortling.

Lhorne easily caught up to her with his long-legged stride, well before they were out of sight.

He reached out to take her hand.

She let him.

EVEN AT DEEPNIGHT, the Highdocks were bright and beautiful.

Instead of a cluttered, slime-covered wharf, it boasted a wide, elegant boardwalk of thick cedar that wound along the shoreline. Small benches were scattered along its length— one every fifty strides or so—placed to offer an unobstructed view of graceful merchant cargo ships and fast courier vessels that were docked, and the open expanse of the Kuath Bay. A sturdy guardrail lined the seaward edge of the boardwalk, each post adorned with a twelve-sided lantern of carved wood and crystal.

Rahelu and Lhorne meandered along that winding path, following another promenading couple some two hundred strides ahead.

She felt as though she dreamed. Span by span, sunset, starrise, and moonrise had come and gone, each moment winging past as swiftly as a questryl. Their impressions lingered as shivers in her resonance aura that were a breath away from partial Evocations.

The tranquil peace of gentle waves lapping against the pier, echoed by the soft rustle of the sea breeze through the trees of the lush parkland to the west; the glimmer of moon-light on open water blending with lantern flame—these things were the stuff of songhouse tales.

She kept wondering when she would discover that the warm clasp of Lhorne's hand about hers was an illusion; that she'd flung her own hand into the cooling ashes of the fire in her sleep. Any moment now, she was certain, she would wake: either due to the shouts of mercenaries brawling when they'd more than drunk their fill and were thrown out into the street, or the screams and the smell of burning cloth and wood as yet another fisher's pitiful personal possessions were destroyed due to their failure to make timely repay-ments on their debts.

But there were no shouts or screams; only a companion-able silence as she and Lhorne walked the entire length of the boardwalk from south to north, then turned back the way they came.

If this was what Keshwar normally meant by a lovely stroll by the pier, then Rahelu thought she finally understood why Tsenjhe might consider it romantic.

They passed a walkway that branched off west, towards Market. It was long past when they should have parted, yet Lhorne did not say anything so neither did she as they passed another walkway and another again.

Perhaps he, like her, felt that if neither of them spoke then time might stand still and they could keep walking along the shore like this. All too soon, they approached the point between the Saltcliffs and the north stair, where Lhorne would turn back towards Eastward while Rahelu would continue a little further, until she could slip through the Oldgate to the Lowdocks and head back to the ramshackle hut she shared with her parents.

Their footsteps slowed and then stopped altogether when they reached the next walkway. Rahelu readied herself to let go of his hand and bid him a good night. She looked up, already braced against those clear green eyes, and found that she was not so well-prepared as she thought.

"Rahelu," he said very softly. "Thank you for dinner."

It had not been much of a dinner. Her mother had sold out of goldtrout, silverbream, and sweetfish too. All that had been left were several runty redfins that had probably gotten caught in her father's net by mistake, and Rahelu had had to trade most of them to the woodcutter for half a bundle of firewood while her mother held Lhorne captive with blunt queries in broken Aleznuaweithish.

The stars were bright by the time they escaped to the stretch of lush parkland in the Highdocks, where lovingly tended willows and winterbirch and starblooms had been planted in carefully cultivated groupings on the gentle hill that rose behind the boardwalk. Lhorne had picked a secluded spot overlooking the harbor: a private bower with silver-white pillars of smooth tree trunks that held up the sky, branches and leafy crowns intertwining in a delicate lace ceiling that tempered the brilliant yellow-blue light of the waxing moon into a softer glow more akin to candle flame.

She had expected him to chatter—had hoped he would shoulder the burden of making conversation (with or without her participation) as he was usually wont to do; as he had done from Market Square to the Highdocks—but he had been content to watch her build their small, illegal fire. Even the loud rumblings of their stomachs hadn't been enough to get more than a brief chuckle out of him. She had had no idea what to say to break the silence, and so she'd concentrated on salting and grilling the remaining redfin instead, but the feel of his gaze upon her (and her growing sense of hunger) during the half-span it took for the fire to burn down made her so nervous that she'd rushed and botched the cooking. The outside of the redfin was scorched to charcoal while the inside was still half raw.

Yet all Lhorne had done was smile and help her peel away the ruined bits, pick out the bones, and slice up the remaining flesh into tiny morsels.

(Apparently, platters of thinly sliced raw fish were a dinner party delicacy. Lhorne genuinely seemed to savor his share of the scanty meal; she had choked down the slimy pieces with sheer force of will.)

Then the redfin was gone, her whole world narrowed to the two of them alone, surrounded by the sweet scent of star-blooms and a rustling silver-green veil of willow leaves. His green eyes had been bright as he went from lounging on the other side of the embers to leaning in across them and she'd panicked at the sudden rush of warmth through her body.

That was when she'd gotten up to stomp out the remains

of the fire and asked about his offer to take her for a stroll along the pier, so she could look at the ships, the bay, the lanterns—anything other than his eyes.

Now that she was looking, she found it difficult to look away. And he seemed to be waiting for something, so she said, "I'm glad you enjoyed it."

There was so much more that he did not say, that she wanted to say, standing there beneath the lantern, the moon, and the stars, but then she heard the distant sounds of hollow footsteps approaching.

"See you tomorrow," she said as she stepped back and released her hold on his hand.

"See you tomorrow," he echoed, but he did not let go of her fingers. He stepped forward, cupped her cheek, and tilted her face up so he could keep looking into her eyes.

Rahelu trembled, wavering between holding still as stone, backing up another step, or rising on her toes to close the remaining distance between them.

She should turn away and go, right now, before the faint wisps of rose-pink drifting through their auras blossomed in the ambient resonance and made it harder to leave.

She found that she didn't want to though. A part of her— a larger part than she had thought possible—yearned to stay. The more rational side of her screamed in protest, dredging up all the reasons why staying was a terrible idea, that no ephemeral moment of joy was worth the horrible complications it would cause tomorrow and in the days to come, that nothing good could come of aiming so far above herself, as Tsenjhe's example had proven.

But in that fraction of a heartbeat, she didn't care about any of those things. So she ignored the noise of the footsteps that intruded on their moment, took a tiny step forward and rose to meet him on her tiptoes, and—

"I don't believe it," Nheras said.

RAHELU COULDN'T COPE with looking anyone in the eye.

So she rose while it was still stararc, before her parents stirred (thus avoiding a barrage of questions from her mother about the nice Petitioner who had stopped by the market with her), and ate a breakfast of cold rice and stewed fish. She poked at the embers, added a handful of tinder and several new sticks of firewood, then set the pot to heat so her parents could enjoy the luxury of a hot breakfast.

When she dressed, she drew her usual resonance ward over her heart with extra care—then took the time to extend it with many more elaborate lines. The rest of her team wouldn't show up until the first span after dawn, so that gave her plenty of time to set up her resonance ward.

If all went well, she would have the Evocation ready by the time the others arrived and then they would all focus on completing their assignment and she could avoid the subject of last night's dinner plans entirely.

Her booted footsteps were loud in the empty streets—all around her, the city slumbered soundly beneath the Skymother's cloak. The quiet gave her time to be alone with thoughts that she did not want to think.

What *had* she been thinking?

Answer: she hadn't been thinking. Stupid. Not thinking was something she'd been doing a rather lot of lately. At a time when she could least afford it.

How had Nheras found them?

Answer: unknown.

Elaram and Ghardon had guessed she and Lhorne had plans, but they wouldn't have known where they intended to go. *She* hadn't known where they intended to go; she'd been entirely focused on the problem of acquiring sufficient food for a meal, and then scrambling for a suitable location to cook said meal. They had only wound up at the Highdocks because she'd told Lhorne of how Keshwar and Tsenjhe had insisted on escorting her home; he'd laughed then asked if she wanted a fairer comparison of a stroll by the pier. But for that story, they might have gone elsewhere: to the Sunset gardens or perhaps the orchards.

Nheras could have happened upon them by random chance. But the Ilyn Petitioner had not been surprised to see them.

She had been *angry*. And then, as quickly as she had intruded, Nheras had turned on her heel and stalked off.

And that made no sense at all.

How did Lhorne feel about it?

Answer: unknown. The very moment Nheras had interrupted them, Rahelu had jerked away from him and he'd thrown up an Obfuscation barrier around them. When Nheras left, he had dropped the part of the barrier surrounding Rahelu but kept his in place.

How did Rahelu feel about it?

It took the half-span for her to walk the long way from the Lowdocks to Southwatch before she found the courage to admit the answer to herself.

She was *glad*.

Glad that Nheras had saved her from making a stupid, short-sighted mistake.

Glad that she wouldn't have to deal with sorting out the implications of how such a distraction would impact their ability to complete the assignment.

Glad that Lhorne wouldn't be caught between the demands of his House and family, and a possibility that couldn't be.

This was one failure Rahelu didn't intend to experience personally.

Learning from Tsenjhe's experience was educational enough.

Kneeling by the faint reddish-brown stains in front of the public relay station, Rahelu took out her vials of salt and ash and got to work.

20
DHARYAS

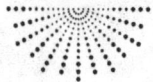

THE 2ND DAY OF TRUESUMMER, 530 A.E./A.F.

Two shadows: one, a figure wearing dark, cowled robes; the other, a woman in a rough linen shirt and cotton breeches. She rushes through the street, knocking on door after door, only to find them all shut to her. She sinks to her knees, exhausted, as the cowled figure approaches her from behind. Then...

SHE'D SEEN THIS BEFORE—THE WOMAN; THE streets; the doors. But the woman's face...was it the same? Her Evocation blurred; Rahelu growled, remained kneeling, and yanked more power through her resonance crystal, ignoring its growing heat against her finger:

...the robed figure pulls a long knife from its sleeve with a gloved hand. The knife's serpentine edges reflect the last ray of daylight—

That knife.

—and plunges into the kneeling woman's back—

Something struck her between the shoulder blades and Rahelu toppled over onto the cobblestones, face down:

—then another robed arm turns the woman's limp body over. The blade slices her open from collar to navel; its sharp tip pierces through worn linen and skin to reveal the rib cage, glistening red in the—

A rough hand grabbed her by the shoulder and rolled her over onto her back, and before she could even open her eyes, she sat up, screamed herself hoarse, then fell over again to retch up her breakfast.

"Eight hells!" someone swore and then, "Rahelu!" another voice said, a voice she should know, but there was somebody shoving a canteen at her even though she had no hands free to take it because she was too busy trying to claw the serpentine knife out of her ribs and pull her bisected flesh back together, yet there were robed arms everywhere, everywhere, pinning her wrists to the ground in the same cold, viselike grip of the crystalline cuffs in the Guild interrogation chamber; her legs were free though, so she kicked and she felt one of her boots clip the killer's jaw before someone else, someone *heavy*, sat on top of her thighs and pinned her throat to the ground with their forearm as the entire canteen of water was dumped out upon her head.

Rahelu, that voice again, as a reverberation through the cool resonance crystal pendant resting against her heart, on the chain that dangled from the killer's neck. *Come back.*

She was lost in the shadows, in the dark span of her Evocation and she could not find her way back to the present, until someone tore a hole in the cowl of the robed killer and let in the sunlight and she could stop struggling and breathe again, in huge, gut-wrenching gasps.

For a moment, there was blessed silence.

Rahelu opened her eyes to cool blue-green relief. And

then, screams filled the air again—this time, from her teammates.

"Idiot!" Ghardon roared. His shirt was covered with half-digested rice and stewed fish. "Who draws a circle this large for an Evocation on a place? Yesterday's effort on a circle a quarter this size was already bad enough! Of all the reckless, insane, arrogant—"

"Half a span!" Elaram shrieked, her words slurring as she held her left hand against a bruise on her jaw. "You couldn't wait half a span? If we'd gotten here a heartbeat later, your mind would have snapped! The best healer in the Dominion wouldn't be able to piece it back together, even if—"

"We're a team, remember?" Lhorne yelled, his green eyes livid and uncaring of the fact that he was crushing her legs. "We're supposed to do this together! How dare you risk your life like this? It is irresponsible beyond belief! Did you ever stop to consider—"

Rahelu let her head fall back against the ground and breathed, trying to force her hammering heart to settle back into a normal rhythm as she waited for them to finish.

When the torrent of condemnations finally ceased a quarter-span later, she said: "I'm sorry," only to have Elaram glare at her anew.

"You are not sorry," the Issolm girl said. "You're only sorry it didn't work."

Rahelu thought about denying that but it would be pointless. And insulting. They'd just saved her life; it would add both 'rude' and 'ungrateful' to her list of sins.

"You're right," she said. "All of you. I was wrong to start without you and I won't do that again. We'll do the next one together, as planned."

"No," Ghardon said. "The three of us will do the next one. *You* will sit in the corner and keep watch, like a good little kit, because you've made yourself completely useless for the next two days."

She opened her mouth to protest but he cut her off.

"You will *shut up and do as I say* without any objection or complaint," he snapped. "We made a bet and you lost. Now, are you going to keep your word?"

Rahelu shut up.

"Alright then," Ghardon said. "I'm going to buy a new shirt." He stomped off towards the clothier a stone's throw away from the relay station, leaving Elaram and Lhorne to continue glaring at her.

It was probably better to not say anything, but Lhorne was cutting off the circulation to her legs.

One look at his angry eyes convinced her that asking him to move was a bad idea. She didn't really need her legs right now.

"I'm sorry about your jaw," she said to Elaram instead, hoping the other girl would forgive the bruise as easily as she had forgiven the broken collarbone.

That hope flailed around helplessly and died like a fish pinned on her spear.

"And so you should be," Elaram said. "At least you're telling the truth this time. You knew it was a stupid thing to do; you knew there was no chance you would pull it off, yet you went ahead and did it anyway. Why, in the Starfather's name, would you do such a thing? This isn't even about the assignment, is it?"

No.

"No," Rahelu said.

I was afraid.

"I was afraid," she continued.

I needed to do something so spectacular none of you would even think to ask any questions about last night.

"I keep thinking you three will wake up one of these days

and realize you made a mistake in deciding to join me," she finished.

That was true too.

Lhorne rubbed his head as if it ached. "You idiot," he said, but he finally got off her and helped her sit up.

Elaram was a little more contrite. "I can't honestly blame you for thinking that, given our track record in the challenges. That was a game. This, though"—the Issolm Petitioner gestured to the bloodstain from where she sat, right next to it, inside Rahelu's ward of salt and ash—"this is not a game. Lives are at stake."

"Did you guys see it then?" Rahelu asked. "The killer? And their weapon?"

Both of them nodded.

"Still not much to go on though," Elaram said as Ghardon rejoined them, wearing an orange wool tunic trimmed with silk and embroidered at its cuffs that even Rahelu could tell didn't match his green trousers. "I couldn't sense any resonance signals. Either the Evocation wasn't strong enough or the killer was using an Obfuscation barrier."

"It wasn't an issue with the Evocation," Ghardon said grudgingly. "Even if we had used a Concordance, we couldn't have Evoked something that wasn't there in the first place. I'm putting my coin on a barrier."

Lhorne's eyebrows rose. "You can't just buy that kind of Obfuscation barrier. It's highly specialized work; I doubt any of the independent mage shops could do it."

He let that sink in.

"Well, that complicates things," Elaram said. "What about the weapon? Do any of you recognize it?"

Lhorne and Ghardon both shook their heads while Rahelu hesitated. She wasn't completely certain, but...

"It looked an awful lot like the kind of knife used in a Free Territories scarring ritual," she said at last. "A lot of their ships are anchored in the Lowdocks, a few for quite some time. Weeks. Seasons. Long enough that some of their crews felt the need to add to their scars."

"We could ask Ylaen," Elaram said.

"Who?" Rahelu asked.

"You know," Elaram said. "The Imos Petitioner with those beautifully sculpted biceps and the gorgeous mane of wavy black hair?"

Rahelu must have looked blank but something had clicked for both Ghardon and Lhorne.

"No," Ghardon said. "I don't trust him."

"I agree," Lhorne said. "I don't trust him either."

Elaram sniffed. "Both of you are just jealous that you aren't half so good-looking. Come on, Rahelu, surely you've noticed him?"

Rahelu tried to dredge up the faces of the various Imos Petitioners and found that they were all fairly fuzzy and unremarkable in her memory, except for one, who stood out purely because he wore his uniform differently.

"No-sleeves?" she asked, startling a laugh out of Lhorne. "The one who oozes around, flirting with anything that moves?"

"No-sleeves?!" Elaram smacked her forehead with one palm. "That's what you noticed about him?"

"I take it back," Ghardon said with a snicker. "Your fashion sense is not a lost cause after all. There is hope for you."

"Yeah, I vote 'no' to him as well," Rahelu said.

"Fine." Elaram pouted. "Who would you ask then?"

"Dharyas of Isca," Rahelu said. "If it's a Free Territories ritual knife, she would know. And she's an Augur."

"She's not a Petitioner anymore," Ghardon said as if that were the end of it.

"And that doesn't seem weird to you?" she asked. "She

was right there with me and Lhorne through all the challenges. She had *four* audiences."

That had to have been more invitations than any other Petitioner had received. Most Petitioners received just one or two; either from their own House or from an allied House.

When neither Elaram nor Ghardon responded, she turned to Lhorne. "You aren't even the least bit worried? Nobody's seen her since the audiences."

"That's Isca for you. I've known Dharyas half my life; she always disappears when she's not supposed to. Like before our Guild entrance tests. Tsenjhe spent all day scouring the city, and then Dharyas just turned up at dinner with a partially working construct. Tsenjhe forgot the whole ordeal as soon as Dharyas started asking questions." Lhorne shook his head. "Like as not, she changed her mind about Petitioning. Again."

Rahelu frowned. "Well, if that is the case, surely we wouldn't be circumventing the system if we asked her?"

The boys shrugged. Elaram didn't look convinced, but neither did she look like she had any other ideas.

"Fine," Elaram said. "Let's go check out the last murder site and confirm that really is the murder weapon, and then we'll go ask Dharyas of Isca."

———

AFTER SHE HAD DRAWN the resonance ward, Rahelu sat quietly at the mouth of the alleyway behind the fountain in Northpoint and kept watch as the other three worked. When they broke Concordance a quarter-span later, pale-faced and trembling, she passed out full canteens without a word.

"It has to be a cult or something," Lhorne said.

Elaram nodded as she ticked off each of their discoveries on her fingers. "The precisely timed killings. The deliberate arrangement of each body, the alignment of the limbs along cardinal points, with the head pointing west. The ecstasy—no, the religious fervor at every site. The dark cowled robes. The ritualistic weapon. Nothing else fits the pattern."

"What kind of cult would still be actively practicing? The temples stamped all that nonsense out," Ghardon said.

Rahelu shook her head. "The bigger question is, how do they have enough funding to cover their resonance tracks?"

The biggest question of all, though, was who was backing the killer and why? Was it one of the Houses? Or the meddling of some power outside of Aleznuaweite, as Maketh had suspected?

And if it was one of the Houses, how had this assignment even ended up on the Petitioners' board for them to solve?

The whole thing stank of suspicion and she could see her teammates thought so too.

It was Elaram who broke the silence in the end. "Let's not worry about who is backing the killer. It's beyond the scope of the assignment. So long as we stop them from killing more people, we'll have fulfilled the objective."

Rahelu wanted to argue. This was all part of a bigger conspiracy. Even if they caught this killer, who was to say another wouldn't keep killing?

"Fine. But we'll aim to keep them alive," she said. "Dead bodies answer questions poorly."

That got her more stares. Were they going to keep doing that all day whenever she said the obvious thing? She ignored them and moved on to their next priority: finding Dharyas when the Isca girl didn't want to be found.

"Tsenjhe last saw Dharyas after her audience with Elder Nhirom. She had three more audiences scheduled: Ideth, Imos, and Isonn."

"Her audience with Ideth was during eartharc too, after

mine," Lhorne said. "I saw her name on the list of expected visitors, but I didn't see her."

Elaram frowned. "She had to have won support from at least one more House, otherwise her name wouldn't even have made it on the list of Petitioners."

"Does Dharyas have a workshop at Isca?" Ghardon asked.

Rahelu shook her head. "Only Dedicates are allocated workshops. Tsenjhe let her borrow equipment and space whenever she had something complex to fabricate, but otherwise, she worked on her projects elsewhere. Tsenjhe wasn't sure where." He opened his mouth to ask a different question and she preemptively shook her head before he could speak. "No objects. Even if we did have one, it probably won't work. She's carrying at least three miniature Obfuscation barriers."

Elaram's eyebrows shot up to her hairline. "That little brooch you had? That was her invention?"

Rahelu nodded.

Ghardon sighed. "Relying on mundane senses. My favorite thing to do."

"Skymother forbid you might have to exert yourself," Lhorne said. "In case you've forgotten, Issolm, there's a citizen's life at stake here."

"I forget nothing, Ideth. Including that—"

"Including that we're wasting time. Let's split up," Rahelu said. "Lhorne starts from Ideth, you two check with the guards at Imos and Isonn, and I'll go ask some more questions at Isca." She tapped her armband. "Log your findings via resonance transfer and check in every quarter-span for updates. Meet back up at the Guild in two spans; maybe someone there might know something."

If her teammates thought there was anything suspicious about her sudden willingness to split up, they kept it to themselves as they helped her sweep up the scattered salt and ash on the ground. While she got quite a few worried looks at how often she stumbled, nobody hovered over her solicitously, or referenced last night's dinner plans.

It was exactly what she wanted, so she should be content. Glad, even, that everybody was so focused on the assignment. Resonance ward dismantled, the four of them left the alleyway and then went their separate ways with only a brief nod to the others.

No personal questions.

No irrelevant banter.

Just pure professionalism.

She went back to the Isca workshop in the Blackforge to make a nuisance of herself by asking questions the Dedicates and Elders had already answered last week:

No, they had not seen Dharyas since the day of her audiences, but they had heard that she'd struck some sort of deal with Elder Nhirom.

No, they didn't know where Dharyas might have gone.

No, it was not unusual for her to disappear for weeks at a time.

No, she didn't leave anything behind in the workshop.

No, they had no idea what agreement she had struck with the Elder; Dharyas had insisted with an air of grand mystery that it was commercial in confidence.

Rahelu walked out of the Isca workshop, pleading the urgent need to file her assignment updates to avoid Tsenjhe's attempts to draw her into conversation and invite her to lunch. Instead, she wandered over to the fishpond in the Sunset gardens and sat underneath the willow tree by the footbridge, watching the colorful carp swim.

Nine days ago, Dharyas had asked her a question: *why do you want to join one of the Houses so much? What do you strive for?*

Rahelu couldn't remember how she had answered. Something about her family. Her parents. A promise of a better life, as tantalizing and distant as the horizon.

Had their life in Chanaz really been so bad? She knew her parents hadn't made the decision to embark on the overland journey to Ennuost Yrg lightly, but she couldn't help contrasting long days spent on the water as a family, together, to the long days they now spent apart: her father on the sea, her mother in the market, and she at her studies— excepting the rushed moments before dawn or after dark spent going over the next day's budget and which of the debt payments they might be able to defer.

What was it all for?

Hadn't there been a time when her father had sung her songs about Enjela, and her mother made shadow puppets of her hands and scraps of twine? There was an entire guild devoted to the art of storytelling here in Ennuost Yrg, and the shows they put on in songhouses were a flashy, useless application of the resonance disciplines—not that she'd ever seen one, because the price of admission was more than a month of her Guild tuition fees.

She tallied her physical injuries: the bruises on her stomach from Nheras were nearly faded, there were at least two dozen half-healed slices in her wrists from her short visit to the Guild's interrogation room (several had reopened and were bleeding afresh), and lingering resonance backlash that made her head ache as if someone had hammered a hundred nails into her skull. Those were just the injuries worth noting —there were numerous other aches and pains, each too insignificant to count individually, but taken together, they contributed to an overall fatigue that she struggled to ignore.

Rahelu got up. Forced herself into a jog to atone for her disgusting display of self-pity.

Why did she keep pushing herself so hard?

Because there was nothing else for her to do.

RAHELU ANNOUNCED herself with a knock on the inside of the entryway to the Guild's grand hall. "Apologies for disturbing you, Guardian. Have you seen Dharyas of Isca?"

Maketh looked up from his contemplation of the assignment board. "Not recently. She came to collect her armband at the end of Firstday last week and she is yet to return it."

Rahelu quickly consulted her team's records via the relay:

House Isca: last seen on the twenty-fourth day of early summer, one-and-a-half spans after dawn at the end of her audience with Elder Nhirom.
House Ideth: last seen on the twenty-fourth day of early summer, at the third span after dawn, after her audience with Atriarch Ideth.
House Isonn: last seen on the twenty-fourth day of early summer, at the last span before high sun, after her audience with Elder Jhei.
House Imos: did not arrive for her audience with Elder Nhorwen on the twenty-fourth day of early summer, which was scheduled for the second span after high sun.

She added:

Guardian Maketh Imos: last seen on the twenty-fifth day of early summer, at the last span before dusk, when collecting her Petitioner's armband.

"Guardian," Rahelu said slowly, "is it permitted for you to share the reported outcomes of her audiences?"

He regarded her with the same suspicious stare he had worn back in the interrogation chamber when he thought her a Chanazian spy.

"She's my friend," Rahelu added hastily, "and I'm worried something might have happened to her."

He glanced back at the assignment board, which was now divided into six sections—one for each team of Petitioners, detailing their progress on their assignment. Cseryl's name was listed with two other Ideth Petitioners and all four remaining Isonn Petitioners, making theirs the largest team. They were camped somewhere in the Westwoods, having killed twenty of the nheshwyr infesting the area, and were making their way towards the nest.

Nheras was working with a mixed group of Imos and Imrell Petitioners to catch the smugglers. They had located nine hideouts so far, including the smugglers' main base of operations, and planned to strike next week.

Every team's section was full of respectable progress towards their objectives, except for hers. Their section was a dismal wash of gray dotted with a handful of red squares indicating the options they had explored and dismissed as dead ends.

"And we need her help," she admitted.

The Guardian said, "I cannot share the specifics of how each House voted," and turned his attention back towards the board.

You shared the specifics of mine, she wanted to say, but reminding him of that incident seemed like a bad idea. She tried a different question: "Did any Houses abstain?"

He tilted his head slightly as he considered, then answered, "Yes."

"Was it House Imos?" she asked, all too conscious that the two of them were alone, in the gloom of the Guild's grand hall.

The Guardian looked at her, standing there in her new (if somewhat rumpled) clothes and boots, and she wondered whether he found the contrast as unconvincing as she did.

"Under the recruitment and admissions policy, in the event that an invitee does not attend their audience, the outcome is reported as a null result, with the vote held in abeyance."

"Thank you," she said and bowed.

She waited until he nodded permission to withdraw, and then made her way outside to the courtyard where she stood in front of the large firepit to fiddle with the strange gem in her pocket and review her earlier Evocation:

...a woman flees through the streets of Southwatch...

The face *was* different but the murder was the same. Relief and guilt flooded through her in equal measures.

What had she done?

...Xyuth rushes to the portmaster's office, a heavy sack of coin in his arms; Xyuth leaves the Highdocks, downcast; the Tattered Quill's doorbell chimes merrily as early summer warmth yields to truesummer heat; gold and silver coins spill across his ink-stained counter from a pair of scarred hands...

Pain exploded behind her eyes and she stumbled, though this time, someone caught her before she fell face down into the firepit.

"You just don't learn, do you?" Lhorne murmured against her ear as he cradled her. His words were exasperated but his arms were gentle and she really didn't want to be reminded of what could have been last night.

"I'm fine," she croaked, wobbling on her feet. "Thank you. You can let go of me now."

I don't want to let you go, he sent, and she immediately jerked away, breaking their skin contact.

"I'm fine, thank you for your concern," she repeated, all while staring at the flagstones. "Please let me go."

He released her and she felt a sudden pang of loss, though whether it had been from him or her she wasn't sure, but if it had been her then she was extra glad of her resonance ward. She chose to look up at the sky, to gauge the sun in its arc, and then at the gate, and then she was saved from having to look back at him when Elaram and Ghardon walked into the courtyard. "You're here! Great, let's go."

Elaram's eyes widened. "You found her?"

"No," Rahelu said. "But I know where to look."

21

BROKEN

Rahelu squeezed her way through a gap between two of the sturdier structures that lined the shabby street to the alley on the other side.

"I don't like the look of this," Ghardon said from where he stood in the unnamed laneway between the Smoking Phial and Gherorg's Elixirs. "Why can't you ever take us to places to do things that don't involve me ruining my clothes?"

"Be realistic, Issolm," Lhorne said, trying to wedge himself through the gap next. "You knew what you were signing up for." Part of his tunic caught on the point of a half-rusted nail. There was an audible rip as he forced his way through. "Shit."

"Not so funny when it's your tunic, is it?"

"What I want to know is why someone would choose a place of business that's so hard for customers to get to." Elaram slipped through the gap effortlessly, even with her sling. "The rent might be cheap but it's cheap for a reason."

Ghardon still eyed the gap with distaste.

"Would you hurry up?" Rahelu asked. "The sooner we find Dharyas, the better. We don't know how long she might need for an Augury, and if the killer sticks to the same timetable, we only have thirty spans—maybe less—before they'll strike again."

"Fine," he said. He started unbuttoning his tunic.

Rahelu stared at him. "You're not serious."

"I *like* this tunic."

"You're ridiculous," Lhorne said. "Come on, Rahelu, let's go."

"Jealous, Ideth?"

Elaram laughed. "Come, brother. Mother might have convinced you that you're the Skymother's gift to the world but Ylaen's got twice the physique you do and all Rahelu noticed was that he had no sleeves."

"Yes, well, she's still looking." Ghardon smirked. "Aren't you?" He tossed his discarded tunic through the gap at her.

Rahelu caught it one-handed and shrugged. "You're a little too slender for my tastes. I am, however, wondering if you're going to stop at the tunic, or whether you're desperate enough to keep going."

When Ghardon's hand went to his belt, Lhorne strode forward and snatched the tunic out of Rahelu's hand, blocking her view of Ghardon and the laneway completely. "We're on a schedule," he said, glaring at the Issolm Petitioner. "Practice your routine for the Wanton Warrior in your own time."

"On that note, we'll leave you boys to finish your juvenile posturing contest and you can find us inside when you're done pretending to be men." Elaram waved her left hand airily in the direction of the gap and sauntered off down towards the end of the alley.

Rahelu gave her own snort of amusement and followed.

The entrance to the Tattered Quill looked even shabbier than Rahelu remembered. Had its windows been broken before? Shards of shattered glass still ringed the frame so it yawned like a razorfang gulper.

"You're sure this is the place?" Elaram asked.

"Yes," Rahelu said. She gripped her spear tightly.

"I don't like the look of this."

"Xyuth is not a bad sort, even if he is a smuggler who sells secrets to the highest bidder." The door swung open at a light push of her hand, and the creak of its rusty hinges nearly drowned out the muffled chime of the doorbell.

The greeting of 'hello, hello!' that she had expected did not materialize.

Rahelu gagged on the smell of clotted blood that had pooled on the splintered floor underneath the scrivener's bloated corpse. Behind her, she heard the sounds of Elaram's retching.

"Stormbringer!" Rahelu ran forward to squat beside the body, only to discover the scrivener hadn't died alone, and then she knelt and began swearing in an unintelligible mix of Aleznuaweithish, Chanazian, and Free Territories speech for a very long time.

They had found Dharyas of Isca at last.

———

Xyuth looks up at the muted chime of the doorbell. 'Hello, hello!' he says to the three robed figures entering. Their cowls are drawn and he cannot make out their faces. 'Come in, come in. How may this humble scrivener assist you?'

Two of the robed figures stride over to his shelves, rummaging through the contents carelessly. He scurries out from behind his counter; hovers in the middle of the shop floor.

'Ah, ah, please, allow me to assist. Those inkstones are delicate, delicate, carved from the foot of the Cloudspire peak—'

One of the figures loses patience. Cases of ink sticks and polished inkstones fly from the shelves, in a rain of lacquered bamboo and porcelain, falling in neat little arcs to smash into pieces upon the splintered floor. Deep orange panic floods through Xyuth's resonance aura and makes his decision for him: he darts left towards the second set of shelves.

He has forgotten the third robed figure who whips a black chain of jagged resonance crystal over his head.

A dozen jagged crystal teeth bite into his throat; their sharp points puncture the skin all around his neck, drink his blood, and with his blood, his swelling panic too, until all in the room is as it was.

'Where is the stargem?' The Free Territories speech is twisted, oddly stilted and sepulchral in intonation, without the unfettered expression of a practiced speaker.

'I do not know of any stargem,' he says. His voice is flat; expressionless.

'Search this place,' says the one who has chained him. 'Iwethna...' It shudders. 'I can smell the scent of you...'

Xyuth leads them to the back. They gouge up his worktable with his penknives; break open the floors and the walls and his safe; dismantle every part of his workshop with surgical precision.

The choked song of the doorbell is inaudible over the noise of the destruction to them, but not to him—he knows the hundred variations of its three-note tune better than his consort's moods. This one, with its jaunty wild ring, means it is the little inventor girl.

He wishes to turn, hurry out, send her away—but the chain compels him to stay and dissect every square finger-width of his workbench in search of the stargem.

'I've got it; I've got the rest of your fare!' she calls. 'Just leave me your keys and...' The light skip of her footsteps ceases abruptly. 'Xyuth?'

A metallic whisper as her steel shortsword clears its leather scabbard; a creak as she treads on the fifth plank of the floorboard in the spot beside his counter.

Go and send the girl away.

The new compulsion propels him through the partition between his workshop and the shop floor.

'Go away,' he says.

'Xyuth, what happened here?' she asks.

She does not sheathe her weapon.

SHE SHOULD NOT BE HERE.

'You should not be here.'

The ambient aura stirs around her in a bloody haze. A crimson bolt lashes out from her hand to strike his heart—

This girl. She is precious to him.

'Xyuth, what is that chain you wear around your neck?'

SAY NOTHING.

'It is...it is...'

The chain is warm; it is hot; it is searing pain. It sizzles upon his flesh and he cannot scream because the chain forbids it.

KILL HER.

His hand reaches for the crossbow he keeps armed and ready beneath the counter and he aims it at her face; a face dearer to him than that of his own daughter.

And her other hand, her other hand has lifted her blade high above her head and she brings it down in a sweeping blow against his neck.

The ring of steel on chain. He falls, like a tree felled by an ax. The chain does not break but her blow shatters one of the crystals and he can scream and scream and scream as dark-robed figures leap over him to strike at her with their serpentine knives.

She lands a powerful blow on the first; partially severs a gloved hand at the wrist. Blood gushes out from the wound. She parries a stab from the second, but the third knife takes her in her back...

BE SILENT.

...but he does not stop screaming as he watches them carve open her chest listens to the grinding of the black knife on bone as it saws through her ribs the squelching noises as a gloved hand tears away one of her lungs to pluck out her heart the faint blubbering of her blood pumping through her dangling arteries and he continues to scream

because she the brightest and best thing in this world is not screaming and he should save her he should kill her he should save her by killing her so he picks up the crossbow and he shoots her straight and true—

The bolt caves in the left side of her skull.

The crimson haze fades.

And the arteries holding her beating heart shatter into crystal dust, leaving the trembling gloved hand grasping an uneven chunk of crimson-hued resonance crystal that drips with warm blood.

'It is not here…' says the one who has chained him, in a voice that shakes as violently as its gloved fist. 'Where? Where is it? Where are you? Why did you leave? Starfather…'

'Another false trail,' says the one she maimed. It saws at its own wrist with its black knife until the dangling hand falls to the floor and binds the oozing stump with the edge of its sleeve. 'The stargem's loss is a deep wound, but one of many we have already borne. It is time you accepted this.'

The one who has chained him does not seem to hear the words. It leaves the new crystal as an offering before the bronze likeness of the Earthgiver and wanders his shop erratically: picking up and putting down objects with jerky, barely controlled movements that alternate with sweeping grace.

It is the third robed figure's turn to speak. 'Control yourself.'

'The Endless Gate…' the one who chained him moans. 'We need to open the Gate. She will help us…' It screams; smashes his windows. Throws itself upon the broken glass and embraces the shards as a lover.

'Your heathen adept cannot be trusted.' The third robed figure moves to strike flint and steel against the shredded pages of the illuminated volume on anchor formations in the time of Tsilm.

The handless one holds up its stump. 'Let us not hasten to draw attention by lighting a funeral pyre.'

'Very well,' the third figure says. 'Starbound, come put down your dog and let us begone.'

Xyuth cringes as he stares up at the one who has chained him. The

*cowl is pulled far forward and though its opening is within arm's
reach; he cannot see the face. He feels as if he should be screaming, he
is still screaming, he should not be screaming as the black blade cuts
his throat.*

RAHELU SAT to one side in the wreckage of Xyuth's shop,
watching workers from the scriveners' guild and House Isca
with slitted eyes.

They were quick and practiced as they went about the
grisly task of preparing the butchered bodies for the Earthgiver's death rites: they had brought buckets of water and
stiff-bristled brushes and sponges to scrub congealed blood
off the faces; rinses and combs and brushes for the hair; rags
and polishing cloth for the cracked resonance crystal lens
that had fallen out of Xyuth's pocket, oil and whetstone for
Dharyas's shortsword; two large sheets to wrap the dead
(plain canvas for the scrivener; embroidered silk for
Dharyas); smaller sheets for their personal effects. The crumpled corpses had been straightened out and attired in fresh
clothes: Xyuth in simple robes; Dharyas in copper-stitched
navy formal robes over dress tunic and trousers. There was
very little that Isca could do about Dharyas's caved-in skull,
save dig out the crossbow bolt and turn her face to one side.
They didn't bother with needle and thread to sew up the
gaping cavity in her chest, though they had replaced her lung
and her sawn ribs before they covered up the ruins with a
square of waxed linen and dressed her in the tunic.

While they worked, a small army of clerks from the
scriveners' guild and the Isca landlord moved throughout the
ruins of the shop, cataloging what remained of Xyuth's
inventory, sorting through the ransacked shelves to divvy up
what was left between goods that were still in saleable condi-

tion and those that were usable for training purposes, and discarding the rest.

All throughout the shop, there was chatter. Chatter that drove a thousand tiny noises into her ears, worming inside her throbbing eyes through her brain, no matter how hard she tried to muffle the sounds by putting her head between her hands or her arms or her knees.

Not just the idle chatter—of weather and food and mutual acquaintances and families—that Rahelu detested even at the best of times. There was speculative chatter too. Chatter about the strange manner of the deaths (cut short by Lhorne as he loomed over the talkative workers with a grave expression, reddened eyes, and thickened voice to impress upon them that the deaths were under an active investigation by the Houses, and they were not to go spreading panic around the city by engaging in harmful, uninformed, wild gossip); argumentative chatter about the best way to arrange Dharyas's hair (Rahelu had balled up her fists; got up despite her resonance backlash—Dharyas was *dead*, so what did her hair matter? The Isca girl had worn it pulled back in a single tail—but before she'd taken more than a single stride, Ghardon had bumped into her, and by the time she'd gotten around *him* Elaram had finished strongly suggesting a simpler hairstyle to the workers); callous chatter of clerks from the scriveners' guild and the landlord tallying and debating the liquidation value of Xyuth's few remaining assets, as if the only thing of significance was whose priorities ranked ahead of whom's when it came to using the proceeds to settle the unpaid balances of his numerous liabilities.

He had had a consort. And a daughter. A little girl who liked ragdolls.

Rahelu felt at the glittering black gem in her pocket, fingertips itching at the tiny rough bumps of its gold-flecked surface.

She should have let him go, instead of meddling. She should have listened to him and thrown the cursed thing into the Aleituan Sea.

The sun was low in its arc by the time the clerks and the wagon of salvaged goods and the workers and the very nearly presentable bodies of Xyuth and Dharyas were gone, leaving the four Petitioners alone with the pools of congealed blood.

Lhorne was slumped over against the wall, fingers pressed against his temples.

Elaram's face was nearly as pale as Dharyas's had been, and the shadows under her eyes stood out like someone had rubbed a thumbful of ash under each socket.

Most alarming of all, Ghardon was still half-naked—he lay perfectly flat and still on the bloodied, splintered floor in a macabre imitation of Xyuth that was far superior to his attempt at imitating Welm yesterday, and he was using his tunic as a cold compress over his eyes.

"Ready?" Rahelu asked Elaram.

"Does it matter?" The Issolm girl's smile was wan. Brittle. She dipped her fingers into the smallest pool of blood, the one that had held a severed hand. "Even if I'm not, do we have any other choice?"

Not if they wanted to find the killers before they completed their ritual to open the Endless Gate.

Whatever that was.

"I'll help," Rahelu said. "Give me a moment." She stifled a grimace as she shifted into a cross-legged position, tried to settle into the seven-count for a Seeking, tried to dredge up the barest of resonance visualizations. Her breath responded sluggishly; her eyes crossed. Instead of the usual pearlescent overlay of ambient resonance over mundane vision, she saw double, then triple, and fell over for the third time that day. "I might need another moment," she said, her breath heaving in and out of her lungs.

"Stop, Rahelu," Lhorne said, and his voice was bleak. "You need another week. I'll do it." Floorboards creaked as he shifted.

She half-expected Ghardon to chime in with agreement, but he said nothing. If not for the rise and fall of his chest, she would have thought he looked as dead as Dharyas had.

She probably looked about the same. So she didn't argue with Lhorne; she just lay there in a sprawled tangle of trembling limbs, and thought about taking off her own tunic and soaking it with the contents of the only canteen of water they had left, so she could copy Ghardon and put it over her eyes. That required more movement than she felt capable of, so resting her eyes would have to suffice.

"I can't find them," Elaram said. "Either the blood is too old or—"

"Or you need more of us in the Concordance," Rahelu said.

"Or it's that cursed Obfuscation barrier," Lhorne said.

"You can't get anything? Not even the slightest of echoes?" Rahelu asked.

"Not from the city. There are no resonance signals within three kual of here that match the trace resonance in the blood."

"Just a blank? Like a Seeking over empty ocean? Can you sense anything odd?"

"Yes." A pause. "No." Another pause. "Maybe? If I push..." Elaram's voice became strained, "there's a...background hum, somewhere near Market Square. Like the whine of a discordant tuner. It's not the same signal as the one from the blood."

Rahelu forced her eyelids open and jerked upright.

The room spun.

"Eight hells," she said, trying not to throw up again.

Should have kept her eyes shut. "Does it feel like a shattered resonance link?"

"That's it! It's that Suborned chain." Elaram's eyes snapped open as she dissolved the Concordance, but her pupils were dilated and unfocused.

While the four of them had waited for the scriveners' guild and House Isca to arrive, they had searched for the black chain of jagged crystal without success. They hadn't even found the fragments of the crystal Dharyas had shattered.

Not that they had really expected the cultists to leave something so valuable behind.

"If you can sense that through the barrier, then either the broken link's resonance signal is interfering with the barrier itself or they haven't set up the barrier properly." Lhorne rubbed his forehead. "We won't know which it is, unless I can get close enough to try and figure out how they've anchored it."

"How long would that take?" Rahelu asked. "Can we find them tonight?"

He shook his head.

"But—"

"We're done, Rahelu. All of us." Lhorne pointed at Ghardon, who still hadn't moved. "Issolm's half-killed himself with the last Evocation; you're near half-dead your-self thanks to all the reckless stunts you've pulled today; Elaram can't see straight, and even if she could, she still can't fight with her arm in that sling; Dharyas—" His voice cracked. "Dharyas was in twice the condition I am right now and she didn't last more than fifty heartbeats, and they're using the kind of Obfuscation barrier that even a Guardian like Maketh would have trouble breaking on his own."

Rahelu couldn't argue with any of that and she hated it. She hated being so weak; hated falling short and failing when they were so close to the goal; hated that she couldn't do the impossible with sheer force of will.

But, above all, she hated the possibility of the killers getting away with their crimes.

"We should go to the Houses," she said. "The scope of this assignment has escalated beyond what Petitioners ought to deal with. I don't care what Maketh said; not even the most experienced Supplicants on the cusp of swearing their oaths of Dedication would be expected to handle this. We investigated the murders, we discovered the killers and their plans, and we have enough information for the Houses to plan a coordinated raid. We should file our reports right now and sign off the assignment as completed."

"That won't work," Elaram said. "The objective was to apprehend the killer. If we do as you suggest, then in the eyes of the Houses, we will have failed and don't deserve to be Supplicants."

"That's horseshit!" Rahelu snarled. "If this gods-cursed system was so fair, it would recognize that we, as Petitioners, have done a *fucking impossible job* with not even a hundredth of the fraction of the resources a real team of Dedicates would have been given for this assignment."

"Gods." Lhorne laughed. "The system isn't designed to ensure fairness; it's designed to ensure the exact opposite, from the way Petitions are selected down to the kind of assignments given. The Houses aren't interested in fairness —they thrive on exploiting uneven advantages."

"And here I thought that the purpose of the Houses was to safeguard the stability and security of the Dominion, so that all who live within its borders may flourish in peace and prosperity."

"That's the most naive, Chanazian thing I've ever heard you say."

Naive? *Naive?*

"It's called integrity," Rahelu said, making a deliberate effort to keep her voice as firm and cold as truewinter ice. "How did the Houses stray so far from their duty?"

"The Houses have not," he said. "If they had, all Aleznu-aweite would live in the anarchy of the Free Territories, where there is no rule of law, or as mindless thralls of the priest-mages in the Divine Kingdom in Belruonia. For all that the Conclave likes to boast, I don't see Chanaz being a marvelous, shining beacon of equality.

"There is *nothing* fair about this entire plane of existence but the closest approximation of it is *here*, imperfect as it is. The system is not fair. What of it, Rahelu? What the Houses want to know is: how are you going to deal with it? Are you going to give up at the first sign of unfairness or are you able to turn a disadvantage into a strength?"

She glared at him. "Do I look like a quitter to you?"

"Those were quitting words before," Elaram said.

"Knowing when to retreat is *not* the same as quitting. I may have done a lot of stupid things but, believe it or not, I am not suicidal."

"You could have fooled me," Lhorne said.

"Well if you don't like my plan, what do you three propose we do instead?"

They watched the last rays of the sun crawl over the floorboards in silence.

When only a single, faded ray of orange-red remained, Ghardon finally stirred. He sat up, took his damp, folded tunic off his face, and said:

"I propose that we call some palanquins to take us to the nearest bathhouse, get ourselves into clean clothes and some food into our bellies—in that order—and then, and only then, will we allow ourselves to contemplate what we are going to do about the killers for no more than five spans.

"Whatever we come up with, so long as it has an acceptably low likelihood of death or permanent injury, that is what we're going to do, no matter how stupid the idea. And I swear by the Skymother's harp, if even one of you makes a single joke about my dire, immediate need for a bath and new clothes, I will personally tie you up in chains in the middle of Market Square underneath a large sign that reads 'DEAR EVIL CULTISTS: FREE VICTIM FOR RITUAL SACRIFICE' and help them carve out your heart with the dullest knife I can find. Are we clear?"

And nobody, not even Rahelu, made fun of Ghardon for proposing the bathhouse first.

SIX SPANS LATER, a freshly scrubbed, freshly robed Rahelu tore into a fluffy steamed bun, heedless of how it burned her fingers and the insides of her mouth and the water dripping from her hair onto the woven rush mats.

For once in her life, she paid no mind to how much everything in sight cost. She was too hungry, too heartsick, too exhausted to care, and besides, she'd used the last of her copper kez to send a runner with a message for her parents.

"For the last time, 'wander around Market Square until we spot something that could be a physical anchor and then try to break it' is *not* a plan." Ghardon flourished his ivory comb like a dagger at his reflection, though from his perspective, he'd have aimed it at Lhorne. Molten sparks swirled out into the ambient resonance from his aura. "It's a wild stab in the dark; the very thing we're supposed to stop."

Lhorne stalked past the dining table, clutching the ends of a small bath towel around his waist, and dragging a similar resonance haze of fiery orange in his wake. "Neither is 'follow random people around Market Square and hope they'll either turn out to be the killers or that they'll run into the killers.' At least my suggestion has the potential to work." He threw open one of the sliding partitions separating the dining room from the sleeping rooms and it partially rebounded with a loud clatter as he walked through.

"Both of those are terrible ideas because they rely on *us* locating something or someone the killers don't want us to find," Elaram said, around a mouthful of braised duck. She had awkwardly draped a towel on her head and wrapped another around herself, to avoid the need to wrestle her right arm and sling through the sleeve of a robe, and struggled to eat one-handed while keeping her towel in place by tightly pressing it between her ribs and elbow. "There are too many variables that can go wrong. We know they need one more sacrifice and we *also* know their rough whereabouts and *when* they need to make the sacrifice. Therefore, we should set a trap"—she looked meaningfully at the glittering black gem that sat in the middle of the table—"and make the killers come to us."

Lhorne and Ghardon broke off from yelling at each other across the room to turn on Elaram.

"No!"

"Absolutely not!"

Elaram rolled her eyes as she pushed the dangling edge of the towel on her head out of her face with the back of her left wrist. "If neither of you are going to be reasonable, then I'm going to go meditate and then sleep." She grabbed a lacquered wooden box as she rose, then disappeared into the second of the sleeping areas and slid the door shut.

The boys continued arguing. The orange-red sparks in the ambient resonance began coalescing into slow-moving eddies that seeped into the corners of the room.

Rahelu quietly polished off the pickled carrots, the boiled dumplings, and the stewed pig trotters as the subject of their disagreement shifted into the technicalities of why none of the four standard methods of bypassing an Obfuscation barrier would be useful since the killers weren't relying on any of the basic constructions but a proprietary construction similar to one of the more advanced formations, such as Mrellos's Gambit or Dethiram's Shield.

"They are *not* using Tsilm's Defense!" Lhorne said as he finally emerged from the first sleeping room clad in the largest robe he could find—it was still too short by a good hand-and-a-half so he wore it over another, larger towel. "Not only is it the most inefficient configuration for a barrier of that size, the design is fundamentally flawed because of its reliance on sympathetic resonance for stability."

"Your insistence that the killers must be using some secret method nobody knows isn't founded on reality."

She tried the braised duck, made a face at the taste of mashed purple yam coating the meat but ate all of it anyway, then began working her way through the rest of the dishes laid out on the low dining table. Lhorne and Ghardon's mutual irritation grated on her own aura, and the thought of flinging the dishes at them was becoming increasingly tempting.

"Uh, guys? Can you please try to calm down?" she asked. "I don't really want to risk resonance backlash in order to put up a barrier right now."

Neither of them registered her request.

Inconsiderate pigs. Just for that, she was going to eat all of the best dishes first, starting with the fried squid.

"Did you somehow miss their use of ritual knives forged out of a mysterious resonance-sucking substance to murder people? These cultists are full of secrets."

She did not touch the roasted pheasant.

It had been carved down the middle from throat to tail with an arrangement of beaconflame flowers poking out of its chest cavity.

She stacked empty plates; built towers of them to entomb the pheasant so she would not have to look at it.

"Secret weapons, yes. Secret creepy cultist rites, sure. Secret Obfuscation barrier construction methods superior to every known configuration? Unlikely. Every large-scale barrier has taken years of research to develop. The most likely explanation is a modified version of a known formation and my coin is on Tsilm's Defense."

"And I've already explained why that's not possible seven times! Just how dense are you?"

This time, Rahelu raised her voice. "Can both of you please shut up? We don't know what the killers are using and we won't know until we can get a closer look tomorrow. Further speculation is pointless."

"Yes, thank you!" Lhorne said. "You're outvoted, Issolm."

"She didn't actually agree with your stupid not-plan," Ghardon said. "Because it is stupid. And not a plan."

She should have saved her breath.

By the time Rahelu had to admit that she could not eat another bite, the argument had devolved from a rigorous debate grounded in resonance principles and sound theories into something vastly more mature.

"Just because you can't create an effective barrier with sympathetic resonance doesn't mean it's useless. When an anchored resonance comes into opposition with an unanchored one, the anchored resonance always prevails."

"Very good, Issolm. You could drill the first- and second-year trainees in their recitations. And then you could move on to repeating the fourth-year subjects on barrier design and anchor alignment except that—oh wait, that's right, you *didn't* complete those because you failed the third-year prerequisites!"

Ghardon flushed. "Nobody needs those; they're mostly theoretical subjects without relevance to practical application. If you're so confident that Tsilm's Defense is flawed, then you can prove it."

"There's nothing to prove. A novice could overwhelm Tsilm's Defense by sneezing on it. I'm done trying to enlighten your uninformed mind; clearly, it's a hopeless cause."

"Oh, that's right." Ghardon cupped his chin as he looked into the mirror, carefully parting his damp curls with his comb. "Sorry, Ideth, I forgot myself. I thought I was talking to someone with a spine."

A muscle in Lhorne's throat jumped but he turned his back on Ghardon and directed his attention to the food, which had grown cold. He frowned at the empty dish that had previously held fried squid. "You couldn't have left me one bite?" He picked up a piece of duck instead.

"That's your own fault," she said. "If you had wanted some, then you should have said something. How else was I to know? That, or come to get some yourself before it was all gone."

"One bite. *One*."

"Neither of you seemed to want any so I wasn't going to let it go to waste."

"You didn't even ask!"

"Why should she have to? If you were half the man you pretended to be, you would have acted and then you would have exactly what you wanted right now. Instead, here you sit, whining like a babe who's lost his mother's teat."

Lhorne continued eating as if Ghardon hadn't just gravely insulted him, red spikes of anger crackling through his resonance aura.

"That is out of line, Ghardon," Rahelu said. "Apologize to Lhorne and let it go."

"It's fine," Lhorne said. "Words from House Issolm are

like the wind: they change as the wind changes direction and count for nothing."

"Just like a well-trained monkey!" Ghardon paused to slow-clap three times before he continued fussing with his hair. "Life in House Ideth must be so dull. It's a wonder that any of you remember how to breathe without being told to by your Atriarch."

Lhorne didn't rise to the bait. "It's a wonder that House Issolm remains even a minor House, without the discipline to act for the common good."

Ghardon shrugged. "What good is a martyr to a House? Issolm understands that when you serve the needs of the individual, it is in the interest of the individual to serve the House. We look after our own."

"What a glorious reputation to have for a House: the fact that you can only be trusted to look out for yourselves and no one else."

"If a House can't be trusted to look after its own, how can it be trusted to look after others?" Ghardon waved dismissively. "By all means, continue to pretend that I'm wrong. I know how much you love to mask your cowardice under that pretense of moral superiority."

"Issolm." Lhorne's voice was low and deadly calm, but his resonance aura was anything but: it had gone from a lethargic rumbling to churning chaos. "I'm warning you. Go no further."

"Or what?" Ghardon asked, turning away from the mirror at last. "Don't threaten me, Ideth, you'll just embarrass yourself. We all know you won't do a thing. All these years"—he laughed as he set aside his comb—"and you are still no closer to getting what you want, even when it's right there in front of you. It's pitiful."

"Both of you, stop this idiocy," Rahelu said. "*Before* you kill yourselves with resonance backlash."

"Stay out of this, Rahelu," Lhorne said. He got up from the table without even looking at her.

"Oh no, don't. I think it would be better if you were involved, Rahelu," Ghardon said, stepping towards Lhorne. "Maybe you could finally make a man out of him."

Lhorne's mouth flattened as he faced off against the Issolm Petitioner in the cramped area between the dining table and the room's entrance. "Don't bring her into this."

"Why not?" Ghardon folded his arms. "Let her be the judge. I think that would be rather fitting, all things considered."

"Are we really doing this now?" she asked. "When we have an evil cult to stop tomorrow and no plan on how we're going to stop them?"

"Yes!" they both snapped.

"Fine!" She shoved the dining table into one corner, grabbed the ceramic urn of tea-infused sea salt flakes (twenty copper kez a pinch!), and paced out a circle. The line of green crystals was uneven and broken in at least four different places, but she wasn't constructing a ward, just a shitty circle for this senseless duel over—fuck if she knew. "Resonance skills only. No focus stones, no hand-to-hand combat. Ruleset?"

"Standard," Ghardon said. "Ideth gets a quarter-span and three attempts to break my barrier."

Lhorne shook his head. "Quick spar: I have unlimited attempts and Issolm has to outlast my attacks for twenty heartbeats."

"In that case, I'll raise the stakes. Winner picks the sleeping arrangements." Ghardon's smile had a predatory cast to it. "I hope you enjoy my sister's sonorous snores."

"Quick spar, five attempts and five heartbeats," Rahelu said, eyeing them both. "This is not a ritual duel over House honor."

"No, it's not," Ghardon said. His resonance aura shifted into a steady gold, a bulwark of pride as solid as plates of overlapping steel. "It's a test to see if there's a man beneath all that Ideth pretension, instead of a scared little boy who waits for his Atriarch to tell him when he may piss and who he can fuck."

Lhorne's resonance aura flared like a bonfire doused with oil and Rahelu called out: "Begin!"

Lhorne's first Projection was a bludgeon, an outpouring of the hot anger he had kept under firm control. Ghardon hissed; the Projection consumed a chunk of his defenses but his barrier remained intact.

"One."

The molten haze in the room rushed towards Lhorne. He gathered it into a second Projection: a cloud of stinging needles that pierced Ghardon's barrier in a thousand places. The Issolm Petitioner gasped and put his fingers to his temples—Lhorne had left him with very little ambient resonance to draw on.

"Two."

Lhorne drew on the glowing red spikes in his resonance aura, packing all of his anger into a crackling beam, then he cast it like a spear at one of the weakened spots in Ghardon's barrier. The concentrated Projection drilled through the pitted surface of the Obfuscation and the Issolm Petitioner's barrier shattered; the resultant resonance backlash drove Ghardon to his knees.

"Three," Lhorne said, breathing heavily as he looked down at his defeated opponent. "I win."

Ghardon's only answer was a groan.

Lhorne turned to Rahelu, green eyes ablaze. He stepped deliberately in the direction of the first sleeping area and did not take his gaze off her for a moment.

"Are the two of you satisfied now?" she asked.

"I am," he said. He paused within arm's reach, his hand resting on the edge of the half-opened partition: the silk cloth was painted with a landscape of willows and starblooms beneath the moon. "And I am going to bed. Are you coming?"

"Yes," she said and she turned to walk the other way—to the closed partition of the second sleeping area, the one Elaram had chosen.

WHEN RAHELU CAME in from the dining room, Elaram was curled up on her left side on top of her blanket, still half-wrapped in towels, with her back to the entrance. Her lacquered meal box sat squarely in the middle of the room between the two sleeping pads. Beside the box was a finger-sized bottle and its cork.

Rahelu eyed the empty bottle but left it alone as she shut the partition, leaving Ghardon and Lhorne to figure out their own sleeping arrangements. She shed her robe and towel, burrowing into her bedding like a clam digging into the lakebed, shrouding herself with layers, and pressing her hands to her ears.

And still, she could not block out the low keening from the next room, thanks to the floor's diligent efforts to repro-duce every muffled note. Each reverberation became flatter and flatter until the dirge broke down into choked sobs that were accompanied by a heavy black mist indistinguishable from the shadows.

Anger, that familiar companion, she knew how to channel.

Denial, too, could be used to reinforce the partial Obfus-cation barrier she had carefully (unwisely) erected around her memories of Dharyas.

But Lhorne's grief seeped through the gaps between the

bamboo wall partitions and her barrier, its leaden weight dragging on her resonance aura as inexorably as the undertow, until she struggled for breath, face pressed against her sodden pillow, wishing for someone, something, to save her from drowning.

Even then, it was not too late. She could go to him, they could find comfort together...but Ghardon was outside, his blackened aura warping the ambient resonance with knotted chains of mottled crimson, green, and brown.

So she remained as she was, utterly lost, until the dark tide abruptly ceased.

22

DARKNESS

THE 3RD DAY OF TRUESUMMER,
530 A.E./A.F.

RAHELU WAS THE FIRST TO WAKE, AT HER HABITUAL span before dawn. She lay still, listening to Elaram's snores with her eyes gummed slightly shut, and debated whether she ought to rise or whether she should force herself to sleep some more. Sleep would be the wiser option—the others would not wake for spans yet and her head still felt as if someone had hollowed out the insides and filled it with broken glass—but try as she might, she could not sink back down into blissful oblivion.

It was too warm underneath the feather blanket and the way its silk cover glided over her bare skin whenever she moved felt strange. After a quarter-span of tossing and turn-ing, she felt warmer than ever so she threw her blanket to one side. But the air was also warm and still—there were no windows in here—another, larger blanket that lay heavy on her; one she couldn't kick away. The cotton sleeping pad, though, was a different story; so she rolled off it and used one foot to shove it against the wall with her blanket.

And then, for a whole blessed count of a hundred, she felt the cool relief of woven rush mats against her hot skin...until she realized the room was getting hotter. Sweat beaded and pooled in the small of her back, in the crease of skin between forearm and bicep and the back of her knees and thighs and underneath her breasts, turning the floor mats sticky.

Earthgiver's embrace! Rahelu reached for one of the large towels she had discarded on the floor last night and lay on that instead. She closed her eyes, counted to a hundred, and then—twice as slowly—counted to a hundred again as Elaram snored on, oblivious. The sound of each inhalation of air making its tortured way through the other girl's blocked nasal passages into her lungs was as loud as the rattling of cart wheels over cobblestones and the throaty *aaaaah* of every exhalation through Elaram's open mouth bordered on outright moaning.

Most irritating of all, there was no regularity to the snoring—though it *was* periodically interrupted by an interval of snorting so violent that the first time Rahelu heard it she'd thrown off her covers and leapt to her feet with her knife in hand. It had taken her exhaustion-addled brain a long count of fifty heartbeats to realize the dark line across Elaram's throat was only a lock of hair and the twitching of Elaram's arms was just the normal movements of someone dreaming.

Exhaustion had allowed Rahelu to go back to sleep last night but it eluded her now as she lay on her towel, drenched in her own sweat, forced to listen to Elaram's choking gasp-moans.

Ghardon had *not* been joking.

This had to qualify as some kind of torture.

On the other side of the thin wall that divided the two sleeping rooms, in the stretches of silence, she heard the quiet, even breathing of someone else in deep sleep.

And then, for a moment—just a moment, in the darkness before dawn, as she lay there with her skin bared to warm air

—she let her thoughts wander and her hands wander with them:

> She stands poised between three futures, beneath lantern, moon and stars; chooses a different path. It leads her to a bower of silver-white pillars crowned with a lacework ceiling beneath the Skymother's infinite star-studded cloak, awash in the soft, yellow-blue moonglow and a rising mist of rose-pink and deep red in the ambient resonance and the sighs of the sea.

There, Rahelu abandoned all thoughts of the distant future and its complications, the near future and her responsibilities, the imminent future and its dangers—embracing only the urgent heat of the present, the sensation of her fingers sliding over and against her slick, slippery flesh and the promise of temporary pleasure.

She felt her own breathing become faster and grow erratic...and she allowed it; she heard her voice join Elaram's throaty *aaaaahs* in its own low moan on each exhalation...and she allowed that chorus too—though she was careful to time each one and keep it subdued so that no one might hear her over the other girl's snoring.

But when she felt herself at the very crest of her pleasure, discovered that her lips were in the process of shaping a specific name instead of a wordless cry, she bit down hard on her tongue and let the wave break and rush through her body in shuddering silence.

That was too much, too tempting, too dangerous, to allow.

Even this one ephemeral moment of joy—even this shadow of what could have been—might have been too much. Already, she was drawn to the other room, toying with the idea of a casual dalliance, methodically working through the possibilities of an arrangement that involved simple physical pleasure, and nothing more.

Of course, that was a line of thinking doomed to failure. This one moment of weakness was proof of that. If she continued indulging herself in impossible fantasies, she would inevitably find ways to rationalize their existence and then feel compelled to turn those fantasies into reality.

It had only been one dinner. Even if that dinner had hinted at something more, it was foolish to think it might eventuate into an offer of consortship. If someone like Tsenjhe wasn't good enough for House Ideth, Rahelu stood no chance.

And even if consortship was a possibility...it felt like cheating. Like selling herself to buy the life her parents dreamed of—and that was the one thing her parents had never contemplated, no matter how badly they needed kez.

That was why they had had only Rahelu and no other children.

No more, she decided and swore an oath to herself. *This much, this one moment of distraction, I will forgive and allow myself, but nothing more.*

She got up, wiped her fingers on the towel and used the towel to wipe off the wetness between her legs and on her thighs, then threw on a robe and went to look for her laundered clothes and spear.

THE SUN WAS ALREADY WELL into late eartharc when the others woke at last and forced themselves to rise.

By that time, Rahelu had gone for a run around the ornamental garden of the Four Blossoms (one hundred circuits, the garden being fairly small), completed four sets of stretches and spear exercises, all twenty variations of the

Guild meditations for the four basic resonance disciplines as well as the handful of Conclave meditations Onneja had taught her (meditations *only*), eaten the food that Ghardon and Lhorne had left untouched last night for breakfast (outside, away from Elaram's snores), and then took a second bath for good measure. (Who knew when she would ever set foot inside such an expensive establishment again?)

She made sure to use the common bath instead of the private one attached to the suite Ghardon had hired so she wouldn't risk being there, alone, when either of the boys woke up. (The private bath was also full of cold, bloody water. Stains had begun to soak into the wood—pity the poor servant who would have to scrub it out.)

The common bath was large enough for *swimming* but it was the worst swim she'd ever had. There was no current so the water felt dead and it was uncomfortably hot. The swim made her feel like a fish in a stew pot, even if it did loosen up all of her cramping muscles.

Finally, she could delay her return no longer. If she was not there—inside their rooms, within heartbeats of the others waking up—they would no doubt come looking for her, thinking she had gone to chase the killers herself.

Rahelu didn't know which offended her more: the fact that they believed she would do something so stupid, or the fact that they were sort of right—the thought of going out to scout Market Square alone *had* crossed her mind. She knew everyone who ought to be there by heart; it would have been much easier to spot who belonged and who didn't in the early spans when everyone was still setting up their stalls.

It also wouldn't have helped. If the killers were going to strike, she couldn't take them alone, and if they weren't, she still would have had to come back.

But at least she wouldn't have had to listen to the other three repeat the *exact same conversation* they had had last night as they went over their weapons, though Lhorne and Ghardon had finally found the sense to keep their verbal sparring somewhat civil.

Rahelu did her best not to look at either of them. Not that it mattered. Ghardon was too busy casting dark glares at Lhorne as he checked over each arrow in his quiver and strung his bow, while Lhorne's gaze remained fixed on her, even as he oiled and sharpened his longsword.

In the end, it was Elaram's plan that prevailed, for lack of any better alternatives.

"We're going with Elaram's plan because it's the only one that has even a chance of success!" Rahelu said, cutting off any further protests. "Besides"—she eyed Ghardon as they made their way south—"using one of us as bait was your idea. Why do you have a problem with it now?"

"Gods, Rahelu, it was a joke."

She shrugged. "You were also the one who said we were going to go with whatever we came up with, no matter how stupid the idea. This qualifies."

"We still need a way to deal with those Obfuscation barriers," Lhorne said.

"No, we don't. Whatever Obfuscation barrier they are using is irrelevant. It stops us from finding them, but we already know roughly where they are and that they plan to strike at day's end."

"It also protects them from Projection and Seeking," Lhorne said. "We'll be limited to physical combat techniques."

"Does that matter?" she asked. "When none of us can Project or Seek worth a damn right now?" *No thanks to you idiots and your ridiculous duel last night,* but she left that part unsaid.

She hadn't been a paragon of wise decision-making either.

"No," Lhorne admitted. "I still don't like it though."

"By all means, you two can go around and break anything you think might be an anchor," she said.

After all, they could afford to replace it.

One night in the Four Blossoms had cost twelve gold kez and Ghardon hadn't even blinked.

Trading was in full swing when they got to Market Square. Lhorne and Ghardon peeled off in opposite directions—Lhorne working his way around through the crowds, charming city guards, street urchins, gawking travelers, and belligerent hawkers alike; Ghardon to browse the more expensive stalls and listen for any talk of strangers in dark, cowled robes.

Meanwhile, Rahelu and Elaram took up their perches on the wide, gently sloping stone roof of the central pavilion that divided the foodstuffs and livestock trade on the eastern side (under Isonn administration) from general wares on the west (under Ilyn management). The other girl's face still looked wan and shadowed—the longer they could put off a Concordance, the better. So the two of them lay flat on their stomachs, setting their weapons down to one side, and peeked over the eastern edge of the tiled roof—scanning the crowds for suspicious figures with their eyes rather than resonance senses.

She spotted her mother right away: at the center, in prime position, where it was well shaded by the overhanging roof of the central pavilion. Her father's catch looked lively in their tank, scales catching the sunlight reflecting off the money-changer's whitewashed shop walls.

Yet the tank and the baskets of salted fish were still two-thirds full.

A slow day? Had the crowds been smaller than usual? Or was Hzin undercutting their prices again?

Rahelu found the rotund bearded man six stalls down, on the edge of the seafood hawkers' section: an awkward space between the southern entry to the pavilion and the east-west thoroughfare, with no tank, no shade, and a longer walk from the well. He'd left his barrel of live fish to stand in the sun; his rickety handcart was empty but his mat and baskets were nowhere in sight.

He wasn't selling fish.

He was *cooking* fish, in a medium-sized iron pot and on a metal grate that he'd placed over a hot coal fire built on top of a stack of clay bricks. Beside his makeshift stove, he had several bundles of trimmed bamboo (two handspans long; cut into three equal parts lengthways so that they resembled hollowed-out bones), a pile of rectangular packages wrapped in bamboo leaves, and a shallow wood basin made from fitted pieces of bamboo with its own lid.

He also had a line, twenty customers deep, that stretched all the way to the vegetable sellers' section.

As she watched, Hzin pulled out a piece of—was that fish skin?—from the bamboo basin and dropped it into his iron pot to fry. After a hundred-count, he lifted a rigid golden-brown curl out of the hot oil using a pair of long wooden sticks, placed it on one of the long bamboo pieces next to one of the wrapped packages, added a pinch of something from a small clay jar, and then handed it to the woman at the front of the line.

What? What had happened? When had this happened? Rahelu had been gone for barely two weeks and Hzin seem to have changed his business model entirely.

Around the third span after high sun, when his last customer walked away with four bamboo platters, Hzin switched to skinning, gutting, and fileting more fish. The skin (scales and all) went into the bamboo basin, the filets were chopped into little cubes and wrapped inside bamboo leaves after being sprinkled with the juice of some small yellow fruit, and the guts went on the ground, where it was immediately set upon by a bunch of stray cats that had been lounging around in the sun.

She smelled the food long before Lhorne's head popped up over the edge of the tiled roof.

"I must have talked to at least a hundred people," he said. "And not a single one of them has noticed anything or anyone unusual, except for the new fish stall." He set down three platters—Rahelu spied the fourth platter on the ground next to her mother. "Not even the Riverrats."

"How much is Hzin selling these for?" she asked.

"Twenty copper kez," he said, around the palmful of crispy fish skin he had jammed into his mouth. "I've got to tell Cseryl," he said, licking the crumbs from his hand.

"He could charge twice this and I'd still line up for it," Elaram said, licking her own fingers. "It's genius."

Rahelu sniffed suspiciously at the platter Lhorne had pushed in her direction, picked up one of the golden curls, and tentatively touched the tip of her tongue to it.

She wanted to hate it on principle but the tantalizing aroma and the smoky, salty, sweet combination of spices she couldn't name had her salivating. Before she knew it, she, too, had wet her fingertip, was swiping it over her empty bamboo platter in methodical lines so she could pick up every remaining speck of spices and fried fish skin and lick it off her skin. She peeled open the rectangular package next, eyeing the gray-white cubes of raw sweetcod and the wedge of yellow fruit inside with extreme doubt.

"Try it," Elaram urged her. "It's better than anything House Isilc has ever served."

Rahelu gingerly took a cube and chewed. Expected to have to choke it down like the slices of raw redfin two nights ago. But the tangy bit of sweetcod melted in her mouth, leaving her tongue refreshed and craving another bite.

She swallowed every last cube inside the bamboo packet

and tipped the remaining juices down her throat for good measure.

"Starfather," she swore. "This will put my parents and every other hawker out of business. Who's going to want to buy and cook their own fish?"

If Lhorne and Cseryl served Hzin's food at their celebration, Rahelu might actually accept the invitation.

She glared over at Hzin's stall and tried to figure out how much capital he must have invested in this new venture. The jar of blended spices alone had to have cost two gold kez—the cheapest sale she'd ever heard the spice merchant make was fifteen silver kez for a pinch of cinnamon—not to mention the oil and the equipment: the pot, the grate, the clay bricks for the stove, the sheer cost of the coal, the bamboo.

Had he sold his boat?

No, he wouldn't do something so risky.

She looked around again then realized there was no sign of Bzel. And come to think of it, she had not seen Bzel for quite some time. Not since...

...not since Petition Day. Hzin had been so pleased about his purse the day after. She remembered the unmarked door with its worn bronze handle, the brief stab of purplish-blue guilt in the maze-like corridors, the smothering crimson rush of arousal...

And Rahelu felt as if she had swallowed a stone sinker instead of food. She rushed over to the western edge of the roof in hopes of descending to the ground below, so she could retch her meal back up in private without being asked why, except she nearly knocked Ghardon off the stack of hay bales.

"Sorry," she said as she grabbed him by the front of his shirt before he fell. She waited for some sort of jibe or admonition but Ghardon just looked preoccupied as he joined them. "Did you find something?"

"I'm not sure," he said. "The merchants I talked to have seen nothing unusual. No disruptions to the resonance crystal trade. No rumors of other butchered corpses. No sightings of dark-robed figures. It's almost as if these murders have occurred in a void."

Ghardon glanced down at the remains of their lunch and didn't even remark on the fact there were only three platters, not four.

"The last two murders weren't planned though," Elaram said. "They weren't there to kill the scrivener but to look for something." She glanced at Rahelu's pocket but left it at that. "And Dharyas just happened to be in the wrong place at the wrong time. If we hadn't come looking for her, their bodies might not have been discovered for a few more days."

"We also quashed all speculation around the last two deaths," Lhorne said. Only the reddened corners of his eyes and the slight hoarseness to his voice betrayed him.

"There should still be rumors," Ghardon insisted. "People talk. Even if you make them swear an oath, they will take someone into their confidence, asking *them* to swear an oath as well. That's not even accounting for the impact of the message relays. You only need to look at how word spreads in even a small group like our—"

Elaram gave him an abrupt look of warning and Ghardon changed what he was about to say.

"—like our House," he said. "One small thing gets discussed, interpreted, embellished, combined with other details, and before you know it, conclusions are drawn and accepted as truth."

Rahelu frowned. "But the House Seekers…"

"Don't have time to chase down and sort through every rumor," Elaram said. "Alright, brother, you've convinced me.

This is odd. The merchants aren't talking and the crowds aren't talking but *somebody* should be talking."

"The potential witnesses weren't talking either," Lhorne said slowly. He overturned and rearranged the empty platters into a rough square, then used his belt knife to scratch a crude map of the city on the bamboo. "The first three victims were found at the northeast edge of Temple, the public relay station in Southwatch, and the alleyway behind the fountain in Northpoint. The Tattered Quill is over here by the north-west quarter of the Blackforge and we know that they're planning something at Market Square."

All four of them bent their heads over Lhorne's map and studied the points he had marked out. The northern end of the city looked stretched out while the southern end was too cramped, which placed the Lowdocks at the same distance from Market Square as the Highdocks when the actual distance was more like two-and-a-half kual to one kual.

Rahelu tried to make the mental adjustments in her head of how the map should actually be laid out and visualize some lines connecting the murder sites. "It looks like a misshapen crystal?"

"No, it's more like a rod," Elaram said. "See how far apart the first and last points are?"

"It could be one of the variants on the foundation anchors in the fourth construction of an intermediate Obfuscation barrier," Lhorne said. "Except that—"

"Except that your map drawing skills are utter shit," Ghardon said. "The proportional distances between the city gates and Market are completely off. We can't work like this." He stood up and dusted off his trousers. "I'm going to go buy a proper map," he said and disappeared down the stack of hay bales.

Three sets of clothes in as many days. Hired palanquins to convey them to the Four Blossoms. Twelve gold kez for a night in an entire suite of rooms with a private bath and a full banquet, in addition to his earlier visit to the Seven Springs. A map.

Surely Ghardon's allowance wasn't so generous that what amounted to five years of household expenses for Rahelu's family was only a minor inconvenience?

She twisted the ring on her left hand and rubbed its resonance crystal as she snuck a glance at Lhorne, who was scowling and carving more landmarks on his makeshift map.

"This is the eighth time your brother has pulled out his coin purse in three days," she said to Elaram, who had resumed her watch. "Is there some sort of reimbursement policy I'm not aware of?"

"No?" Elaram didn't look up from her observation of the square below. "Why?"

Why? *Why?*

Rahelu wanted to haul the pair of them over to the Lowdocks—minus their fat purses and personal relay crystals with all memories of being House-born Obfuscated—just to see how long they'd survive.

When Ghardon returned with a proper map, marked with the location of every known murder site, the pattern became more obvious.

"It's a half-circle centered on Market Square," he said. "Or it would be a half-circle, if you ignore the Tattered Quill and added another point here." He tapped a spot near Stormbane's Rest. "The first three sites are all points located along the Old Wall. They're almost equidistant from each other."

Rahelu stared at the map, her eyes traveling from one bold cross in red ink to another, along the thin hatched line that marked the inner wall. There was something familiar about the shape of the pattern that itched at her memory.

Elaram unhooked the crossbow at her belt and set it down on the roof. "I don't see how that helps us," she said, flopping over onto her back to gaze up at the sky, left arm and both legs splayed out like a seastar. "It doesn't explain why there aren't any rumors and it doesn't help us pinpoint the killers' current location. We've only two spans until sunset. Let's just try a Concordance now and see if we can pin down that Suborned chain. Waiting another span won't make enough of a difference to matter."

The Concordance they formed was their most pathetic effort yet. It spoke volumes that Rahelu could feel that she was the stablest one in the link: Elaram's mind was brittle, like frost; there was a wobbly feel to the way Lhorne anchored their working to his pendant; the vividness that was Ghardon's usual hallmark entirely absent.

She took the lead and centered their combined Seeking on the well at the heart of Market Square, then directed their focus outwards in wide, radial sweeps, looking for a discordant whine in the sea of pulsing resonance signatures from all the people of Ennuost Yrg.

Each person resonated with their own unique rhythm as they went about their immediate business:

—*a ragged, barefooted child chasing a pigeon by the fountain in Northpoint, haloed in golden joy; steady pale blue focus emanating from a white-haired tailor, bent with age, bent even further over the intricate embroidery on a hem inside his Westgate shop; jagged, black-red spikes from a woman hammering her fists against a locked door; rose-red blazing from the lovers who couple in a secluded corner of the orchards on the edge of Sunset—*

The city was a living patchwork of every emotion on the spectrum. There were so many signals it was like hunting one particular striped minnow in a shoal of thousands. Drawing more power and pushing out the range of their Seeking didn't help; it amplified the tumult tenfold.

Rahelu felt her control slipping. The moment they broke this Concordance, she would help Ghardon paint the letters on his 'DEAR EVIL CULTISTS' sign and sit underneath it herself. It was a stupid idea, but no stupider than any of the other ideas really, and *this* had been useless, *useless—*

She sent their Seeking arcing over Stormbane's Rest in the final part of the Seeking pattern. Resonance signatures winked in and out of focus, registering as individual blips of anger, love, joy, pain, fear, lust, regret, ecstasy, despair, and—

Wait.

Rahelu jerked their Seeking back, honed in on the faint traces of lust/ecstasy and regret/despair leaking out into the ambient resonance at Stormbane's Rest. That specific area was devoid of people, a dark fuzzy gap in the city's glowing rainbow haze, yet there were wisps of the resonance she detected, swirling around an empty spot.

"What is that?" she asked. "It's not a resonance signature. It looks like..."

"Like the echoes in our Evocations, but much fainter," Ghardon said.

Rahelu frowned. "Elaram, can you take over? Get us a clearer sense?"

Their Concordance wavered as Rahelu relinquished control—her skill in Seeking wasn't refined enough to make out further details without more power and Lhorne was already pulling in as much as he dared through his pendant. When Elaram took the lead though, she *compressed* their combined Seeking, packing the same amount of power into a focus that was a quarter of its previous size under Rahelu's direction. And when Elaram trained the heightened focus of their Seeking on that blank spot, the swirling wisps of twinned brilliant yellow and blood-red upon coal-black solidified into a thin liquid border that seeped out of a blank circle, as if someone had punched a hole in the middle of a spill.

"Fuck," Lhorne swore.

"That's the Obfuscation barrier," Ghardon said. "I told you, Ideth, I fucking told you it was a—"

"Not the time, Issolm! I'll write you a formal apology later. Elaram, if I take control, can you still hold this focus together? We might be able to pierce through with a Projection and…"

Elaram didn't answer and Lhorne didn't finish his sentence.

They'd fucked up.

Whoever the latest victim was, it was already too late to save them.

Fuck!

How had they gotten the location wrong? Rahelu should have scouted out the market at first light on her own; she would have known immediately that there was nothing unusual. They could have spent the day searching the city instead of wasting time staking out an irrelevant location. If they had started sooner, if they had tried plotting the murder locations on a map first—

"I don't sense that chain here," Rahelu said. "Pull back along the bay so we can see if—"

Their already shaky Concordance trembled and Lhorne grunted as he strained to keep it anchored. But between last night's duel and the Concordance, he had pushed himself too far. The foundation of their working snapped and Rahelu found herself gasping for breath and curled up on her side on the roof of the pavilion.

Tears streamed down her face from the feel of a thousand tiny knives sawing at the base of her eyeballs. She scrubbed them away furiously with the back of her hands, forced herself into a sitting position, then looked to the west. Her eyes managed to register a blur of purple-red sky and a multitude of dim orange orbs drifting in an inevitable descent towards the horizon before the tears welled up again and she had to close them against the dying sunlight and the pain of resonance backlash.

No!

She scrambled onto her knees and blindly swept her hands around the roof for a sheet of heavy parchment, weighted down with copper coins. Made contact with an outstretched arm (silken skin, thin wrist, palm facing up; Elaram's), someone's shirt (soft thick wool, neatly tucked at the sides; that was Ghardon) and the muscled contours of someone's thigh (*oh gods*, she thought and hastily moved her hands away from Lhorne).

Where was that *fucking map*?!

It had been right here, at the center of their cramped circle. She ought to have felt it the moment she reached out since she had been practically sitting on top of it—*eight hells*, she *had* been sitting on top of it. She grabbed one side and yanked, forgetting to move, and it tore in two with a loud rip.

"Fuck!"

She rolled off the other half of the map as she wiped her eyes with her left sleeve, forced her eyes open again, willed them to stay that way, and shoved the two pieces of parchment back together.

It had grown dark enough that the few remaining vendors in Market Square were beginning to light torches as they finished packing up their stalls. Rahelu squinted, trying to make out the lines of bold ink Ghardon had drawn earlier.

"Light!" she cried. "Can one of you get a light?"

Match head scraped against rough stone then light blossomed overhead as Ghardon handed her a lit candle. He looked like he'd been through the seventh hell, but at least he was up; Lhorne clutched his head, moaning, while Elaram hadn't moved—she was still splayed out on the roof like a seastar, unconscious.

"It *is* a half-circle," she said, tracing her fingers over the line that connected Temple, Southwatch, Northpoint and now Stormbane's Rest.

"Too late," Ghardon said, abandoning his bow and quiver to drag himself over to Elaram's side. "We failed. They succeeded."

"No," Lhorne said. He sat up with a groan, the heels of his palms pressed against his eyes. "Not yet. They'll be carving up the body and"—he suppressed a dry heave as he waved one hand—"and doing whatever other steps their ritual demands."

The body. The bodies. She banished the memory of Dharyas's butchered corpse and the scrivener's slit throat for now—the two of them were anomalies that didn't fit the pattern. The rest...

"We could still catch the killer," Lhorne said.

"You can't even stand. And I'm not leaving my sister here alone."

Rahelu looked over to Elaram. The way the other girl lay on the rooftop was eerily familiar—if her right arm wasn't strapped to her chest in a sling and her left arm was a little higher; if she'd sprawled out a little more so her legs formed a right angle—you could draw an almost perfect half-circle centered on her ribcage if you connected the arc of fingertips to knee to knee and then fingertips again.

"You think I like the idea? I don't!" Lhorne didn't look like he was in any condition to get up, but he tried anyway; his legs shook and refused to take his weight. "But if we don't go *right now*, we fail. Put aside your *Issolm* self-centeredness for once and do what's right for everyone. We have a duty to the Houses, to the people of this city—"

"Fuck you, Ideth. *I'm not leaving my sister*." And Ghardon curled up next to Elaram, both hands gripping her free left hand tightly, his forehead to hers, as if he could reel her back to consciousness with a direct Projection.

Rahelu's eyes darted back from Elaram to the map. If she imagined the city of Ennuost Yrg as a person, with the shoreline of the Kuath Bay as two splayed legs and its knees where the arc of the inner wall met the sea walls, the spot behind the fountain as the tip of its left hand and Stormbane's Rest as its right, then the heart of the city wouldn't be just west of Market.

It would be Market Square.

Right at the southern point of the triangle formed by the well, the statue of the Earthgiver, and the seafood hawker stalls.

"This isn't over," she said. "We weren't wrong about where they were, we just didn't anticipate that they would split up. Whatever ritual they're planning, it's still unfinished. They need one more sacrifice here." Bright golden sparks of hope flared in her aura, past the bounds of her resonance ward. "We can still stop them!"

Rahelu crawled past Elaram's prone body and peered over the edge of the rooftop. Long shadows stretched out over Market Square—they grew from the base of the crowded buildings on the western side of the market, the base of the statue of the Earthgiver, and the well itself—rapidly encroaching upon the small band of fading daylight that bisected the market from north to south as they hungrily swallowed the rest of the square.

She saw only two figures out in the open below.

Hzin.

And her mother.

Her mother was *still there*, halfway through her meticulous redistribution and consolidation of the third basket's contents into the other two.

Then, as Hzin dismantled the last of the hot clay bricks in

his portable stove and stowed them in his cart, two of the shadows moved.

One slipped out from behind the Earthgiver's statue and glided towards Hzin's cart.

The other materialized from the mouth of an alleyway by the southern exit of the market. Fifty strides away from her mother, who had sorted the last of the fish from the third basket into the other two and stacked the empty basket underneath one of the others.

"Sunfire, starbolts, and stormwinds!" Rahelu swore, heart thudding in her chest as she watched her mother stoop down to pick up her baskets. "They're here. We've got to get down there, now!"

She pushed herself away from the edge of the roof and looked at her teammates—and the bright golden sparks in her resonance aura were extinguished as if they had never been: Elaram was flat on her back (still unconscious); Ghardon collapsed over her limp body, shaking (that was resonance backlash; he'd pushed himself too far); Lhorne, finally up, but on his hands and knees instead of his feet (and he looked like he might fall back down any moment).

The silence in the square was broken by the groan and squeak of Hzin's handcart as he lifted the handles. His cart trundled its way east, the clatter of its rickety wheels on cobblestone drowning out the pounding of her heart, leaving her mother to plod in its wake. Stooped forward as she was, with one hand stabilizing the full basket on her back and another steadying the stack balanced on top of her head, there was no way her mother could see the two cowled figures stealing out from behind Hzin's cart and the alleyway, their paths set to converge with hers at the exact moment she crossed over the heart of the half-circle of the four murder sites ten strides away.

No!

No, no, no, no, NO!

Run, anma! Rahelu thought as she gathered up the swell of chalk-white panic in the ambient resonance around her, whimpering at the sensation of a thousand red-hot needles stabbing into the back of her eyes.

She prayed to the Stormbringer as she shaped it into a lance, eyes watering. *Grant me this one desire and I will make a full blood offering at the Seaspire this very night and give a fifth of all I earn for the rest of my days to your temple.*

Rahelu thrust her right hand out and hurled the lance of panic at her mother.

And she fucking *missed*. Her Projection crashed into Hzin's cart, shattered and flooded the ambient resonance with unrestrained panic.

Hzin stumbled, his cart coming to an abrupt halt, and her mother jerked—the resonance was too diffuse to make them do anything more than startle. The stacked baskets on her mother's head teetered, fell; the basket on her mother's back, too, swung wildly as she overbalanced and landed on her side. Sweetfish, silverbream, redfin, and goldtrout spilled all over the cobblestones, half their shimmering scales tinted orange-yellow in the flickering light of Hzin's torch and the other half burnished a red-gold from the last rays of the sun.

The two cowled figures were unaffected—too far away, protected by an Obfuscation barrier beyond Rahelu's ability to sense.

They drew their serpentine knives.

She wept as she scrabbled around the rooftop for her spear. It had been *right here*—she had propped it, point-up, on the edge of the roof so she could snatch it at a moment's notice. Her fingers closed on the smooth haft, the comforting weight of solid ash settling into her palm.

Breathe in.

Rapid blink away the tears.

Find the target: a flapping shadow moving four strides to a heartbeat.

Judge the distance between where she balanced on the edge of the rooftop, and the shrinking gap between her mother and the swift, descending shadow.

Steady breath out.

Back one step, and another, as the left hand rises to aim and the right arm draws the spear point level with her eyes.

Inhale.

Arch the spine, pull the shoulder back for power, then:

One.

Two, and—

Her spear hurtled forward, propelled by all the strength she could muster and a desperate shout that reverberated around the empty square.

It struck the cultist straight through the shoulder blades; impaled the dark-robed figure to the ground five strides away from her mother's terror-stricken face. Rahelu's shout trailed off as the gold-flecked black blade clattered onto the cobblestones from the cultist's limp hand, leaving only the irregular gurgling of blood in the cultist's lungs to echo through the empty square.

Stormbringer be praised.

Rahelu sank to her knees on the rooftop, a finger's width from the edge; watched her mother heave herself to her feet and flee, leaving the fish and the baskets behind. She had no weapons left, no resonance ability left, and barely any strength in her limbs, but it didn't matter because her mother was safe.

Her mother was safe. Her mother—

A scream tore through the air and shook her out of her daze.

Fuck.

Hzin!

The rotund little man had eluded the last cultist's death-stroke by sheer luck—in his panic to get away, he had tripped and fallen over the cart's handles so the downward slash aimed at his heart had merely sliced away his ear instead.

She needed to get up, needed to find a way to stop the cultist from killing again—though how, exactly, she was going to do that from this distance with no weapons and no resonance attacks, she had no idea.

A small, traitorous part of her disagreed. *You've done what you can*, it said. *More than anyone had any right to expect. And if someone has to die, it might as well be him.*

There was nothing she could do to stop it. She was so tired. So weary, from the relentless grind of rising before dawn to eke out a miserable existence that never seemed to improve. She wouldn't even need to present the body of the cultist to mark their assignment as complete—the scope of the assignment had specified that there was a single killer who was to be apprehended and a dead killer who was no longer able to kill more people qualified—all she needed to do was include her memory as part of her report during the resonance transfer.

And Hzin's death would make things so much easier for her family. It would end the threat of his new scheme and restore the balance of competition in the market.

"Please, have mercy!" Hzin begged in a quavering voice, as he ducked away from the cultist and huddled beneath his cart. "I have a consort—"

A consort he regularly abandoned, spending kez that he didn't have so he could indulge in his twisted depravities in Suborned dens.

"—and thr—two children."

Two children.

Not three.

Because he had sold Bzel. *He'd sold his own fucking son.*

Let the cultists have Hzin for their stupid ritual to open the Endless Gate, whatever that was.

"Please, I beg you!"

Hzin deserved to die.

She owed him nothing.

Lhorne's voice sounded from behind her, strained and low. "Rahelu."

She turned around to see that he had managed to crawl forward, dragging Ghardon's bow and quiver with him.

And those clear green eyes of his stared into her soul—full of unshakeable belief in her integrity; her unwavering belief in the ideals Aleznuaweite represented despite the imperfections of its reality; her adherence to the duty of the Houses, even though they were Petitioners still, with their oaths of Supplication and Dedication unsworn.

Rahelu took the bow and plucked an arrow from the quiver.

Hzin's pleading dissolved into another scream as the cultist dragged him out into the open by his hair; she ignored it as she raised the unfamiliar weapon.

An arrow was just like her spear, except smaller.

An arrow flew, propelled by the tension on the bowstring—like a stone by its sling—but an arrow spun in the air during its flight, just like her spear.

And then it was as simple as turning to one side, drawing the bow as you drew your breath, remembering to aim a little higher than your target to account for its parabolic arc, just like her spear.

Rahelu breathed.

Felt the oaken arrow shaft glide over the first joint of her thumb.

Bird feather whispered against her cheek.

But the taut bowstring did not kiss her lips: her arms were buckling under the strain of trying to draw Ghardon's bow—a weapon much too big for her—and the arrow shook, its shaft rattling against the grip of the tensioned bow.

And down below—a hundred strides away, at the exact center of the city—the cultist raised their black serpentine blade above Hzin's bowed figure. Black links of resonance crystal glittered around Hzin's neck as they drank in the very last ray of the dying sun.

"Lhorne!" she cried. "I can't!"

Then she felt his arms around her as he braced her from behind; his hands wrapping around hers to lend her the additional strength she needed to stabilize the draw and guide the string to her lips, lifting the bow higher to correct her aim.

They let go.

The arrow streaked towards its target—but the cultist's knife found its target first.

The black blade sank deep into Hzin's ribs and he slumped over. Out came the knife and Hzin's lifeblood spurted from his side, spilling onto the ground, before the arrow slammed into the cultist's left eye.

23
SLOOP

IT TOOK A QUARTER-SPAN TO CLIMB DOWN FROM the roof, hobble over to the cart, and gather the two sacrificial knives and the black chain for safekeeping.

They needed to get moving. Go and track down the third cultist who must still be up at Stormbane's Rest, butchering the corpse of another person they had failed.

Rahelu looked over at Lhorne and didn't open her mouth. He sat with his knees up on the cobblestones, vertical only thanks to Hzin's cart, head lolled to one side, eyes squeezed shut in pain. His resonance aura was an exact match to hers: a storm of tiny dull red ripples shot through with dark, knotted threads.

Even relaying a simple message had been too much.

They should have been bubbling over with golden elation at stopping the cultists before the ritual could be completed —or at least the steady pulsing of satisfaction and quiet pride at pulling off a near-impossible assignment.

Yet all she felt was self-loathing.

They had made one mistake, when they could not afford any mistakes, and another person had died. *And you don't even*

know who it is, because you're too busy sitting here wallowing in your
self-absorbed misery instead of hauling your ass over to Stormbane's
Rest.

No. Not just another person.

Two.

Except that wasn't fair, was it? Hzin's death was entirely on her account. She had been willing to let him die. Would have let him die without feeling the slightest remorse. Would have gladly let him die and rejoiced in the excuse that she couldn't have prevented it—if it had not been for Lhorne.

Rahelu tried to summon up the will to tear apart the tangle of black threads but it was like trying to harvest lakegrass with her bare hands and only one lungful of air. Futile.

So while they waited for House Isonn workers to arrive and take care of the bodies, she set about doing something that was marginally more productive—picking up the scattered fish.

If she managed to gather a whole basket's worth before the wagons and palanquins arrived, she would permit herself to rise a quarter-span later than usual tomorrow.

If she managed to gather all the fish, she might even let herself sleep an entire span longer and only rise at dawn.

Here was a silverbream that had landed too close to the cart. They rarely got to eat any silverbream since those usually fetched such good prices, but this one wouldn't. While its body was still intact, if somewhat grubby, its head had been crushed beneath the cart's wheels.

Rahelu put the silverbream in her pocket to take home for dinner.

Here was a redfin the size of her forearm, twice as big as the runty one she'd shared with Lhorne. She would not have spotted it save for its long trailing belly fin and tail—those stuck out of the pool of Hzin's blood which was much too small for the fish even if it did provide camouflage that was far superior to seagrass: the fish's brilliant red scales made it blend into the tiny scarlet pond almost perfectly.

Rahelu looked at the well, forty strides away, then at the redfin lying in its scarlet pond.

She left the redfin alone.

Here was a goldtrout that had gotten mixed in with a pile of sweetfish, right by the basket her mother had been wearing on her back. Its scales shone in the torchlight and it looked like a much larger version of the tiny gold charm Hzin's consort wore on her wrist (a betrothal gift of gilt paint on lead and the loveliest thing Rahelu had seen anybody wear in the Lowdocks).

Rahelu put the goldtrout in her other pocket, then scooped the sweetfish back into the basket. A gift of goldtrout was traditional for auspicious occasions; they were supposed to bring good fortune to new beginnings.

She mentally rehearsed her speech: *Tseiran, Hzin is dead.* Because she had failed to act. *Here, have a goldtrout.* As if a fish could replace a dead consort who had sold her firstborn into slavery. *I am sorry for your loss.*

Was she actually sorry? She prodded at her conscience; found that she couldn't—didn't want to—tell. It was easier to haul the basket over to the next bit of ground and make a few half-hearted attempts to chase off the stray cats dragging off the unexpected bounty.

Best to keep it simple. Just the goldtrout and nothing else.

The basket was nowhere close to full by the time the workers and two palanquins arrived: one to convey Elaram and Ghardon to the Issolm family estate, and another for Lhorne. All three were loaded inside their palanquins in short order and the Issolm palanquin departed immediately.

She ought to keep going—there were still so many fish strewn all over the cobblestones—but Lhorne had summoned not just Houses Ideth and Issolm, but also House Isonn and the city guard. With so many people flooding into the square, the cats quickly scattered, scampering off with the fish they could carry, leaving the rest to be trampled underfoot.

Another failure then. She had quite the collection now.

"Petitioner Rahelu?" someone asked.

She tossed the redfin she held into her basket and turned to see a woman dressed in the pale-green-and-sky-blue livery of an Ideth servant, hovering nearby.

"Yes, that's me."

"Petitioner Lhorne invites you to join him in his palanquin and offers to convey you home."

She thought of the long trek ahead of her, through the Highdocks, around the Saltcliffs, past the Oldgate, down the north stair, through the Lowdocks proper past the seedy inns and bawdy taverns then three hundred strides up the rocky hill, and every fiber of her being yearned to accept. It would be so nice to let someone else carry her for a little while, so she could rest. Let someone else do the work for a change.

What was she even thinking?

Rahelu shook her head. "Please thank Petitioner Lhorne for his kind offer but I must decline. Tell him that—"

That what? She'd been about to say '*I'll see him tomorrow*' but that was no longer true, was it? Their assignment was complete; all that remained was to file their final reports, wait for their evaluations and compensation, and hope the Houses would make them offers.

In the meantime, he would go back to his House-born life, planning elaborate parties with Cseryl, and she would go back to the Lowdocks.

"—that I enjoyed our time working together."

The woman bowed and retreated to the front of the Ideth palanquin. At her signal, the palanquin's four bearers hoisted its elaborately carved frame into the air and carried Lhorne off into the night, leaving Rahelu alone with a half-empty basket of fish.

She tipped its contents into the empty basket her mother had stacked on top of the third basket—that way, she could stack all three baskets together and carry everything using the back strap. She patted her pockets for her rag before she remembered Ghardon had burned it in a fit of disgust, then reluctantly picked up her spear barehanded. The workers had removed it by pushing its length through the dead cultist's corpse so the haft was gummed up with bits of lung and partially dried blood. She doubted that even two spans of scrubbing with saltwater and a stiff-bristled brush would rinse it clean.

Tomorrow she would join her father on their sloop, she decided as she hefted the baskets up onto her shoulder and plodded towards the southeast exit of Market Square. Her mother too.

The three of them would sit in peace, floating in the little rented sloop upon the open waters of the Kuath Bay, beneath the cloudless sky. Perhaps he would even sing her the ballad of Enjela to pass the time as they waited for the fish to come —away from palanquins and House-born and the city itself. Far beyond the Seeking range of anyone who wasn't on the level of at least an Elder with a mage-staff.

Tomorrow, and every single day after that, until she could recall the simple conviction that anything she did for the sake of her first oath—the one her parents had not asked for but which she had sworn on her training crystal all the same— was the *right* thing, no matter the cost.

RAHELU ARRIVED home two full spans after dark, leaning heavily on her spear and staggering under the slight weight of the baskets on her back.

Her mother was inside.

The lamp had been filled to the brim with fish oil and lit (with two cotton wicks so the light it gave was twice as bright as usual); the water in the trough full of red swirls. Yet her mother continued scrubbing with ash and sand, fresh pink rivulets sluicing off her arms with each jerky, mechanical motion.

She didn't register her daughter's arrival.

But when Rahelu unthinkingly dropped the baskets by the entrance, her mother jerked, knocking into the trough. Stark white terror flooded the ambient resonance along with pink trough water, and her mother picked up a knife—*a knife!*— and pointed the weapon at the sight of Rahelu in the doorway, one hand still gripping the bloodstained spear.

She had to leave it outside before she could join her mother in scrubbing her own hands wordlessly. They ate half of the salvaged silverbream—boiled, with a handful of leaves —in quick, efficient silence.

Like many other things, Rahelu and her mother did not speak of what had happened in Market Square. The two of them simply left the issue untouched and buried in the past. After dinner, Rahelu drained the trough so her mother could refill it with clean water to rinse the clay pot and their wooden bowls while she cared for her spear.

Her father returned sometime after deepnight, hauling a half-empty basket of his own. By that time, Rahelu and her mother were sitting around the fire, salting and smoking what she'd salvaged. He raised an eyebrow at the unusual sight; listened to her terse account of the night's events (so brief that it hardly qualified as a summary with the amount of detail she had omitted) and agreed to her proposal immediately. Silverbream devoured, he kissed his consort and daughter then retired, leaving them to smoke the rest of his catch.

They left with the dawn tide and sailed far out beyond her father's usual fishing grounds, following the coastline north and east.

Rahelu did not bring her spear because her mother could not look at the weapon without shuddering so it remained behind in their hovel, hidden in one of the ceiling beams so no one would steal it while they were gone.

She half-hoped that someone would, the amount she'd have to repay to the Guild for its loss be damned.

The armband...

She could have left it behind. She had finished filing her report just as the fish oil lamp guttered out in the pre-dawn light.

...the armband came with them.

The first day was the worst. They dropped anchor inside a sheltered cove shortly before sunset, far too late to go ashore. That night, her father slept in the middle, though 'slept' was putting a generous spin on things. Both Rahelu and her mother tossed restlessly in the dark, plagued by nightmares that surrounded their little sloop with a thick purple-black fog.

The second day was better. They spotted a pod of dolphins frolicking in the distant waves—a sign of good fortune from the Stormbringer that had put a brief blue sparkle of wonder in their resonance auras.

By the third day, her mother was smiling again, at the sound of her father's strong baritone singing the ballad of how Enjela stole the stars from the Skymother's cloak and Rahelu's far more tentative attempts at harmony.

The little sloop barely had room for the three of them and their supplies, let alone a decent catch, but that didn't matter. For a whole blessed week, they did nothing except explore the coastline—diving for scallops; sculpting misshapen animals on small, unnamed beaches; watching gulls and shearwaters hunt—all the way beyond the Kuath Bay, to the edge of the Aleituan Sea.

Rahelu couldn't remember a time since they'd arrived in Ennuost Yrg when the three of them had been together as a family for more than ten spans—even their sleep schedules didn't align enough for that. Every restful moment was a balm to her soul: there was no House politics, no fighting, and no pointless chatter. Just the wind in her hair, the song of the waves, and the open horizon with its promise of uninterrupted serenity stretching out into infinity.

She would have been content to sail like that forever, to the other side of the world.

After a week on the open water—when Rahelu felt a little more like her old self and her mother no longer reached for a knife at every flap of the sail when the wind changed direction—they reluctantly turned south and west again, towards their debts and obligations.

The moment their little sloop sailed into Ennuost Yrg's harbor, their usual routine claimed them. She and her mother raced the sun, hauling heavy baskets up the north stair and as far as the Oldgate, before she tugged at her mother's elbow to slow down.

There was no need to hurry any longer.

———

DESPITE RAHELU'S FINE TUNIC, her Petitioner's armband, sturdy boots, and newfound patience, the Guild Registrar was no less dismissive of her when she finally showed up in his office to report the destruction of her training crystal.

He sniffed as he consulted her Guild record by touching one of the thin crystal plates that had been affixed as inlays on the marble counter.

"You were issued with a fourth-class crystal. White, with eleven minor flaws in the central lattice and not attuned to any specific discipline."

"Yes."

"Cause of destruction?"

"Resonance overload."

During her reconstruction of a destroyed Guild seal.

She eyed the Registrar balefully as he made the note on her record. Nheras might have been the one who tore up her Petition but the Guild wasn't entirely blameless. The one silver kez charged as a processing fee (for simple copywork any half-trained scribe could do) was thievery—the additional five silver kez for expedited processing was pure extortion. If not for those policies, she wouldn't have had to attempt the reconstruction in the first place—she could have just gotten another Petition.

"That will be six gold and eighty silver kez."

Rahelu winced. That was almost a third of the coin purse Maketh had handed over when she went to collect her share of the compensation for completing the assignment, and there was still her Guild debt and the Isonn debt besides.

"Nearly seven gold kez? That crystal was over ten years old!"

"That is the replacement cost for a like crystal." The Registrar folded his hands and shrugged. "The terms of your training were clear. You are responsible for the care of any Guild property issued to you during the course of your traineeship, including proper maintenance and the cost of replacement in the event of its destruction."

She had been twelve when she signed that agreement and

hadn't been able to speak more than a few words of Aleznu-aweithish, let alone read any of it.

But she had spent a great deal of her return voyage contemplating every little intricacy in that agreement.

"*If* the destruction was due to inappropriate use or a lack of care, not equipment failure due to normal wear and tear," she said, folding her own arms. "The thing was on the verge of dissolution when I first got it five years ago. If you look up the annual condition reports, you'll see that I've taken good care of it, beyond any reasonable expectation of its useful life."

The Registrar palmed his relay node again and frowned. "It says here that you recharged it yourself, instead of using the Guild's artificers' services."

Well of course she had. The Guild's artificers' prices were ten times what an independent mage shop in the Echo Alleys charged—and she hadn't even had the kez for that.

"Yes. You'll see my Guild rating for Projection is adequate for such an undertaking."

"I don't see a record of your artificer's license."

Rahelu's impatience flared past her resonance ward and orange-red spikes sprouted out of her aura. She tore off her Petitioner's armband and threw it on the marble, not feeling the slightest bit of remorse (and in fact, quite a bit of satisfaction) at his yelp when the thick studded leather landed on his fingers.

"Consult the House records then, and note that a Dedicate of Isca, a known artificer of considerable talent, personally approved of my work—which involved recharging ninety stoneweight of assorted resonance crystal fragments of all grades, attunements, and condition in a week."

She tapped her foot impatiently as he pored over the record.

He pushed her armband back over the counter. "Unfortunately, the Guild policy is specific. Unless the crystal was serviced by a properly licensed artificer, I cannot rule out the possibility that improper maintenance was a contributory factor to its destruction."

Rahelu resisted the urge to grab the Registrar by the front of his robes and shake the smug, protocol-bound bastard until all his teeth fell out of his head. She tried a different tack instead: she pulled a crumpled bit of torn parchment out of her pocket and smoothed out the creases on top of the counter, turning it so that the tiny Guild seal in purple resonance ink faced the Registrar.

"Is this appraisal still valid?" she asked.

The Registrar tapped the seal, which shimmered briefly, and gave her a quizzical look. "Yes. It is valid as of the sixteenth day of early summer."

"Fine then." She grabbed the parchment and the quill from the inkstand sitting on one side of the counter, scrawled her signature in the corner beneath the Guild seal and dated it: sixteenth day of early summer, 530 A.F. "I'm purchasing the damned training crystal." She counted out one gold, ninety-five silver, and twelve copper kez from her coin purse onto the piece of parchment—still more than what she wanted to pay (because she would rather pay nothing at all) —and shoved the whole lot at the Registrar.

"You can't buy an asset that doesn't exist!"

"It existed. I was late with the paperwork and the payment."

The Registrar scowled. "In that case, interest applies at the standard Guild rate of four percent per annum, compounded daily."

The clacking of the crystal beads on the abacus as the Registrar computed the exact amount of interest was enough to make her lose the last vestiges of control over her temper.

"For the love of—" Rahelu bit off the end of the curse and

tossed another handful of copper kez onto the counter. "Will that do?"

"That's too much," the Registrar said as he began picking up the coins. "The interest is only—"

"You know what, I don't care," she said, regretting the words as soon as they left her mouth, but she *had* said them and so she wasn't about to embarrass herself and take them back immediately. "Keep the change and use it to buy yourself a set of pliers to remove that rod of iron rammed up your ass."

She stalked out of the Registrar's office, leaving a trail of red-and-orange spikes swirling in the ambient resonance behind her.

And it was a credit to her Earthgiver-like patience that she didn't go back and punch him in the face when she heard his muttered remarks about rude Chanazian gheliks throwing their pathetic weight around as soon as they found a little success that didn't involve grubbing around in the gutters.

RAHELU SETTLED her Guild debt with the Guild's Exchequer in a much more seemly fashion. She had every intention of putting every last kez towards the outstanding balance of her parents' Isonn debt in a like manner but the Starfather had other plans.

"I'm sorry, could you repeat that?" she asked.

The Isonn clerk sighed and obliged her for the third time. "That debt is no longer held by House Isonn. It has been discharged from our ledger."

Discharged? How was that even possible? Who would go to the trouble of buying up a thirty-year loan on a third-rate fishing sloop?

It couldn't have been Lhorne.

Could it?

She twisted the ring around and around on her left hand —the one which had cost him more than all her family's combined debts and that he had bought without even blinking an eye—worrying at the resonance crystal with her thumb.

"Could I see the loan discharge documents?" she asked.

The clerk sighed again, then grabbed a small crystal node and slid it across the wooden desk to her. Rahelu dove in with a light Seeking, skimming through the Projected memories stored inside until she found the one she sought:

Lender: House Isonn
Borrower/s: Jenura and Hemoru of Aleznuaweite, formerly of
the Anuvelomaz region, Chanaz
Loan term: 30 years
Principal: 19 gold, 37 silver, and 27 copper kez
Interest: Four percent per annum, compounded quarterly.
Current balance owing: Nil
Last repayment: 17 gold, 50 silver, and 31 copper kez
Date of last repayment: 2nd day of truesummer, 530 A.F.

The second day of truesummer?

That had been a week and a day ago, the same day that they had discovered Dharyas and Xyuth, murdered in the Tattered Quill. No resonance signatures were attached, other than her parents' and that of the Isonn representative who had witnessed the original agreement.

It couldn't have been Lhorne—he had been with her for practically every waking moment, from the time they'd taken the assignment right up until they'd completed it—he simply wouldn't have had the time.

Wait. That wasn't true, was it? There had been that stretch of time during eartharc after the disastrous end to their dinner—between her foolhardy Evocation at the South-watch public relay station and regrouping at the Guild—when the four of them had split up.

Rahelu looked through the loan records again, more out of disbelief than anything.

It *couldn't* have been Lhorne—he'd gone to retrace Dharyas's steps from the Ideth headquarters, on the other side of the city—but she couldn't think of anybody else who might have had the funds to pay off her family's debt *and* the inclination to do so.

"Thank you," she said as she returned the node to the clerk, who sniffed and wiped down the cylindrical crystal with a small cloth before putting it away.

Rahelu walked out of the Isonn headquarters, perturbed. Twice? *Twice?* While the streets down by the south end of the Highdocks were mostly empty, she still felt compelled to disguise her own surreptitious sniff as wiping her nose on the sleeve of her tunic.

Salt, charcoal, and dried sweat. There wasn't the faintest whiff of fish; she had taken extra care while gutting their latest catch.

She was halfway down the street when she realized something else. The debt was no longer in House Isonn's books, but the clerk had not given her the title deed to the sloop.

Someone, somewhere, still held her family's debt.

24

MESSAGE

THE 9TH DAY OF TRUESUMMER, 530 A.E./A.F.

THE FIRST MESSENGER FOUND HER WHEN SHE WAS passing by the wool storehouses in the Highdocks, on her way back to Market Square. The messenger in pale green and sky-blue gave a shallow bow, handed over a sealed scroll, and then left without waiting for a response.

She broke the seal and unfurled the parchment. It was addressed to 'Rahelu of Elumaje' (*not* Aleznuaweite, not even Chanaz). The words were written in a plain hand and there was nothing else below her name, other than a large resonance seal in green-and-blue ink:

This agreement is made on the ninth day of truesummer in the year 530 A.F. between House Ideth ('the House') and Rahelu of Elumaje ('the Supplicant'), whereby the Supplicant shall provide the House with ten years of guaranteed service in exchange for training in all of the resonance disciplines, with further specialist training to be provided if and when the Supplicant demonstrates particular aptitude or inclination towards one of the disciplines.

Rahelu blinked. Ten years was a long time to be contracted. Significantly longer than what she had expected—just from listening to Elaram and Ghardon, the standard term of service was somewhere between three to five years.

1. During the Supplicant's term of service, the House shall:

i. Remunerate the Supplicant at the rate of forty-five gold kez per annum, with further performance bonuses to be awarded at the House's discretion.

ii. Pay all costs of outfitting the Supplicant with equipment, including but not limited to the provision of suitable clothes, weaponry, resonance crystals and other supplies and consumables as the House deems necessary for the Supplicant to carry out their assigned duties. All amounts paid shall accumulate as the Supplicant's training debt to the House.

iii. Provide food and board to the Supplicant for assignments based in the locale of Ennuost Yrg, and a daily allowance of fifteen silver kez for remote assignments.

Fairly standard terms that were more or less consistent across the Houses, but forty-five gold kez per year was…low.

Then again, they could afford to be less generous. The draw of training with some of the Dominion's best Seekers and Evokers was compelling all on its own.

iv. Pay a death benefit to the Supplicant's next of kin in the event of the Supplicant's untimely demise during the course of performing assigned duties.

Two columns of figures followed: one listing increasing lengths of service periods and the other listing the corresponding amount of the defined death benefit, starting at ten gold kez during the first six months of service.

The amount made Rahelu raise an eyebrow. That was— she wasn't sure considerate was the right term. Seeing the value of her own life reduced down to a number was simultaneously illuminating and sobering.

2. All wages, performance bonuses and other forms of remuneration will be applied first against the Supplicant's accumulated training debt.

3. The House shall provide the Supplicant with a copy of the ledger of the Supplicant's account on a quarterly basis. Where the Supplicant's accrued wages exceed the Supplicant's training debt, the Supplicant may apply to the House for an amount no greater than the surplus balance to be paid out to the Supplicant.

She scanned back through the earlier portions of the resonance transfer for any mention of a signing bonus or an allowance or any other form of upfront payment in coin, that might let her pay off her family's debt to House Isonn entirely.

There was none.

Fuck.

4. The Supplicant's performance will be evaluated at the conclusion of each assignment, with an overall evaluation performed on a quarterly basis.

5. The House may dismiss the Supplicant from service at any time for unsatisfactory performance.

6. In the event the Supplicant fails to demonstrate sufficient

proficiency in the resonance disciplines within three years of the
Supplicant's oaths of Supplication, this contract and all oblig-
ations thereunder will automatically terminate.

7. The net balance of the Supplicant's account with the House
will become immediately due and payable and shall be settled
within one week of the termination of this contract. Any
amount owed to the House that remains unpaid after one week
will accrue interest at ten percent per annum, compounded
daily.

The last thing was a basic ledger, showing a single debit of one hundred gold kez for one resonance crystal ring, dated the thirtieth day of early summer, before the resonance transfer ended with Atriarch Ideth's personal resonance signature. There was a short pale orange pulse of mild curiosity from the Ideth network followed by a blank silence, where she was meant to countersign the offer with her own resonance signature.

Lhorne had kept his word.

How could she be so grateful and still feel despair at the same time?

Unless she earned some sizable performance bonuses, it would take at least two years to pay off the resonance crystal —and that was before accounting for any other expenses. She tried to estimate the cost of her future training, then glared down at the parchment when she realized she had no point of reference.

The House could name any amount it cared to and she would have no basis to argue otherwise.

Rahelu scowled, taking her finger away from the seal without countersigning, then shoved the scroll inside her tunic.

All these years, all the sacrifices her family had made for

the sake of the offer she held in her hand, only to discover that these terms were *worse* than the Guild debt and the Isonn sloop debt which had governed their lives. They were as good as a Suborned chain around her neck—once she accepted, she wouldn't be able to leave House Ideth.

Her parents would point out that it didn't matter. Acceptance into House Ideth was a promise of future security. It guaranteed upward mobility into the influential circles of Aleznuaweithish society. A better future for her children.

(That itself was an idea that Rahelu was not ready to contemplate, and was not sure that she ever would be ready to contemplate.)

As long as she didn't do anything that displeased the House.

The second messenger found her not long afterward, at the bend in the East Road that led towards Market. The messenger bowed, proffering a scroll tied with a large white-and-black tasseled cord, then waited patiently as Rahelu digested the scroll's beautifully scribed contents:

Rahelu of Aleznuaweite,

> *My sincere congratulations on the successful completion of your assignment, above and beyond the original parameters of the set task. House Issolm has great need of resourceful and talented mages in the challenging times ahead.*

> *I am assembling a team for a mission of the utmost strategic importance to the Dominion. Ordinarily, such a mission would be entrusted to Dedicates; however, the Exalted Dominance's expansion initiatives have stretched our House to its limits and our Dedicates cannot be spared.*

But the Starfather always provides. It is my hope that you will agree to lend your skills to this critical mission.

Regards,
Elder Anathwan of Issolm.

The bottom of the scroll, in the space above the ornate brushstrokes of the Issolm Elder's signature, was stamped with the Elder's personal seal in white-and-black resonance ink. Touching one fingertip to the seal rewarded her with Elder Anathwan's warm Projection:

Petitioner Rahelu, you have exceeded all my expectations. I wish I could give you more details on the nature of this mission; however, I cannot trust that the information will not fall into the wrong hands, though I have taken all precautions.

I can tell you this much: I, and the team I have chosen, will board the Winged Arrow *at the Highdocks and depart tomorrow.*

I will be frank with you. It will be dangerous. In consideration of this factor, House Issolm will pay a base compensation of five hundred gold kez—

The eye-watering amount made Rahelu fumble and nearly drop the scroll, waves of yellow-shock radiating through her resonance aura.

"Is everything alright, Petitioner?" the messenger asked.

Rahelu shook herself. "Yes," she said, tamping down her aura so it wouldn't interfere with the sealed Projection.

—with one-quarter to be paid upon your acceptance of this offer and another quarter to be paid into an account in your

*name with House Issolm at the moment of departure. Those
funds will be yours, with no conditions attached, regardless of
the outcome of the mission. Should you fail to return from the
mission, the account will be paid out to your next of kin.*

*The remaining half of your base compensation will be paid into
the same account once the mission is complete, after which time
neither you nor House Issolm will have any further obligation
to one another.*

*To accept this offer, present yourself at our headquarters to
swear your initial oath of Supplication, which will be considered fulfilled in full upon our return to the city. If you perform
commendably during the course of the mission, I will make you
a more permanent offer and you may swear your final oath of
Supplication to House Issolm upon our return.*

*I, unfortunately, will not be at liberty to personally receive
your oath but I hope to see you aboard the* Winged Arrow *at
dawn.*

That was all.

Stunned, Rahelu rolled up the Issolm scroll mechanically
and put it inside her tunic with the scroll from House Ideth,
then resumed her walk along the East Road towards Market
Square.

"Petitioner Rahelu?"

She hadn't even registered the Issolm messenger keeping
pace alongside her.

"I have been instructed by the Elder to ask whether you
wish to respond," the messenger said as they passed by a
leatherworker's shop. "And that I am to provide you with
immediate escort to the Issolm headquarters, should you
wish it."

Rahelu shook her head. "I have other business to attend to first. Please let the Elder know that I am very honored by her esteem and that I will consider her offer."

The Issolm messenger bowed again. "The Elder has left instructions that you may present yourself at the gates of our headquarters at any time—even to the last span before dawn —though the *Winged Arrow* will depart the Highdocks at first light."

Duty done, the Issolm messenger disappeared into the crowd. Rahelu walked on towards Market Square, feeling a profound sense of disconnection. She kept to one side of the street out of habit so that she would not be in the way of the passing palanquins—which meant that she ought to be weaving her way around the traders with their loaded wagons, dodging apprentices and servants.

But she was able to walk from one block to the next in a straight line. More than once, she felt eyes upon her; though when she glanced around, everyone was preoccupied with their own business, yellow-green resonance auras hissing.

She knew that resonance well—it had been a constant in her aura for too many years. But there were no Dedicates or Supplicants within line of sight. The crowd's odd reaction had her scanning her surroundings, scrutinizing every passerby, all while the hissing built up to become a steady drone, until she realized that *she*—strolling down the street in her fine tunic and leather boots with only the edge of her armband peeking out from its sleeve so the sigil denoting her status as a Petitioner was hidden—was the cause.

The third messenger had left her an envelope—a thick square of cream-and-gold paper with her name written on the front in Lhorne's hand—that her mother had propped up on the wooden divider at the back of their stall, well out of splatter range.

Rahelu ignored it and went to sit by the tank, knife out and ready to work.

Her mother halted her with a firm rebuke. "Don't," her mother said, inspecting Rahelu from head to toe. "You will dirty your clothes."

"I will not," she said.

"Better to not risk it."

"You didn't care earlier." Rahelu eyed the envelope with suspicion. "Why do you care now?"

"Open it," her mother commanded.

"I already know what it is, anma," Rahelu said. "I am not going."

"A House has requested your presence. You must go."

"The invitation is from Lhorne, *not* House Ideth. I can decline and not give offense."

"That nice Petitioner?" Her mother's eyes sharpened. "You *will* go."

"I will not," she said.

"Don't be foolish. It is not the fish that comes to the fisher, but the fisher who goes to catch the fish."

"He's a person, not a fish."

"People and fish are not so different as you think," her mother said. "Use the right kind of lure and you will catch them all the same."

"*I* am a *person*," Rahelu fired back. "*Not* bait."

Her mother snorted. "What you are is childish, if you believe that the world cares what you think."

Just two weeks ago, she would have agreed with her mother. But that had been before Keshwar and Tsenjhe; before her audiences with Elder Anathwan and Atriarch Ideth; before four House-born Petitioners agreed to follow her lead based on the merits of her arguments.

The world *did* care what Rahelu thought. She had proof in the form of the two scrolls tucked inside her tunic.

So instead of meekly bowing her head to her mother, eyes lowered in submission, she raised her gaze to meet her mother's stare. "And *you* are dreaming if you think a son of Ideth would have any serious intentions towards me."

Then, of course, she went and undermined herself by twisting the resonance crystal ring he had bought her around her finger.

Her mother let her disrespectful retort pass as if it were no more than a wavelet. "No goldtrout is easy to catch. But you will catch nothing if you do not cast your net."

The feelings Rahelu had suppressed all eartharc bubbled out, spilling past her resonance ward, into her aura and the ambient resonance beyond.

"A wise person places no speculative bets before they have secured a stable foundation," Rahelu said, flinging each word of the Aleznuaweithish proverb at her mother like pebbles. "Tsenjhe has held the affections of Atriarch Ideth's son for years now—he has eyes for no one else—yet Keshwar will not choose her as his consort. I will not waste the best years of my life chasing uncertain gain."

Her eyes burned from meeting her mother's gaze so Rahelu glanced away, fixing upon the stalls in the next row over.

"We are only friends," Rahelu said. "Nothing more." She sat, planting herself unrepentantly on the cobblestones, which were damp with muddy seawater and fish blood, and grabbed the first fish she could lay hands on from the tank—a redfin that flopped piteously in her grip until she pierced its brain with her knife. She bled it, went to gut it, and misjudged the cut; instead of a neat slice along the belly which would have let her rip out all of the internal organs cleanly, the point of her knife punctured the stomach, spilling dark liquid all over the insides, coating her hands.

Fuck!

Throwing her knife down in disgust, Rahelu crammed her fingers into the fish—yanking out bits of liver and spleen, the guts and the swim bladder, digging out the chunks of blood that had congealed inside the tiny cavities along the spine with her fingernails—making a mess of her hands and the redfin's delicate flesh.

She swore quietly, under her breath, for all the good that did. Her mother would have to be at least five more strides away to not hear her, even with the din of Market Square.

A pair of callused hands (smaller than her own, the sun-wrinkled skin beginning to show spots with age) gently pried the fish away from her with strong fingers that were so thin that they gave the impression of being almost skeletal, replacing the redfin with a small wooden basin half-filled with faintly pinkish water.

"Where did my nela learn to value herself so cheaply?" her mother asked. "It is not a lesson that I taught you."

Rahelu wanted to laugh but her mother's resonance aura was equal parts exasperated love and puzzlement, through and through.

"This Lhorne is not Keshwar and you are not Tsenjhe. Why should you try to live your life as if you were?"

Her mother reached out for Rahelu's hands and rinsed them in the basin (as she had not done since Rahelu was four years old) then wiped their hands dry with a clean corner of her tunic.

"Go," her mother said as she pressed the cream-and-gold envelope into Rahelu's hands, "and live the life you have earned."

"Look at me, anma," Rahelu said, gesturing wildly. Her tunic and boots were at complete odds with her stained and patched trousers and—she was forced to admit—her hair, which was an unkempt mane of tangled locks. "How can I go, like this? I don't belong."

"Oh, is that all?" Her mother looked unimpressed. "The repayment on our Isonn debt was only five silver kez, even accounting for the late fees. Was there no coin left over after repaying the Guild?"

"Yes, but—"

"Well I don't see the problem then," her mother said. "Except for the fact that you're still here instead of at the Tidepool, getting ready."

And that was how Rahelu found herself standing before the imposing wrought-iron gates of the Ideth estate in North-point—freshly scrubbed with her hair combed, clad in a new pair of trousers from the Impeccable Mage that matched her tunic which had been cinched tight with a leather belt Hnuare had chosen to complement her boots—handing the cream-and-gold envelope with her name over to the guards.

25

IDETH

THE PARTY WAS NOT WHAT RAHELU HAD EXPECTED.

Instead of showing her inside the elegant building on the gentle hill, the servant in pale green and sky-blue livery directed her to a path that wound around the enormous dwelling to the rear of the estate. The path was wide enough for four, paved with fine gravel that crunched like sand underneath her boots, and bordered with smooth river stones taken from the northern banks of the Suusradi. Strings of colorful paper lanterns lined the way through the clustered trees, whose sweeping branches were hung with long strands of tiny leaves and delicate white flowers.

Rahelu stepped towards the living curtains of silver-green and white, heady with the flowers' sweet perfume. She paused, half-hidden, on the very fringes of the trees, to look out at the intimate gathering.

There was no sign of the usual attire of cotton and linen tunics or shirts over trousers; everyone was dressed in formal robes. Some wore their armbands openly—flaunting their new status as Supplicants sworn to Houses.

Over by the rippling waters of the small, artificial pond, a woman held court: Cseryl, by the glowing white-blond hair done up in an elaborate crown of braids and the small crowd lounging at her feet on the soft, velvety grass.

Ideth and Isonn.

Lhorne wasn't among them.

The only other person she could pick out immediately was Ylaen of Imos. He had, of course, no sleeves because he'd decided to forgo clothing for his upper body altogether (unless you counted his gold torc and bracelets), in order to better show off his Imos armband and scars. The petite, slender figure beside him had their right arm in a sling: Elaram, resplendent in pale yellow silk robes that were trimmed in gold. It took longer to place the other two without their usual garb: Csinyrg and Jhobon of Imrell.

She had expected that Ghardon would keep close to his sister, but he was off mingling with the other large contingent in the garden: Isilc, by the haughty way they held themselves and their crystal-dusted golden robes actually eclipsed Ghardon's silk brocade finery.

Rahelu counted heads. There were three orbiting Ylaen and six paying court to Cseryl which made eleven; Ghardon and the five in the Isilc contingent made seventeen.

That left Lhorne and Nheras (neither of whom were in sight) and Rahelu herself, the only one wearing a belted tunic over trousers and boots.

She looked at the garden full of House-born, arrayed in silks and adorned with crystal and jewelry, and the small amount of courage she had gathered dissipated, like smoke before a strong breeze.

Footsteps crunched behind her, each one accompanied by a lighter, metallic jingle.

Rahelu wheeled around, every muscle tensed, to face Nheras of Ilyn.

Instead of her usual halo of tight brown curls, Nheras had

pulled them back from her face and arranged them into a formidable pile of hair on top of her head—extending her height by a good two-and-a-half hands—with jeweled pins that caught the light of the skyarc sun. Her form-fitting robes —actually two sets of robes: a sheer outer robe made from cloth-of-gold (so sheer that the gold hue was barely visible, other than as a delicate shimmer) worn over a sleeveless inner robe of cream over a pale blue silk shift, stitched with a thousand tiny sigils of Fortune in silver thread that formed a greater symbol of Prosperity—were cut high at the front with a short train at the back, framing her ankles, which were adorned with thin gold bangles that matched the jeweled ones on her arms.

Dazzling.

Nheras was the very embodiment of the Skymother, descended from the heavens, clad in living light. She even wore tiny rings studded with small resonance crystals on her painted toes—an extravagance that was only practical for a House-born who was ferried from one immaculately maintained estate to another in a palanquin. There was not a speck of dust or dirt or grime on her lofty, sandaled feet. Though Rahelu ought to have had the advantage of the high ground, standing at the crest of the path's gentle incline, Nheras's kohl-lined eyes were level with hers.

Rahelu held her defensive stance, turning warily to keep Nheras in view as the Ilyn girl climbed the last few strides to the top.

It was unnecessary. Nheras wouldn't attack her here, in the heart of the Ideth estate. And even if she did, one good shove was all it would take to topple her over in a flurry of gold robes and jeweled bangles.

Rahelu looked at the other girl, mincing her way up the gravel path with severely shortened strides thanks to those comically high-heeled sandals.

Wondered if that delicate, sheer, cloth-of-gold outer robe would tear as easily as parchment.

Imagined the humiliation Nheras would feel if her arrival was announced by a shrieking, maladroit tumble down the hill; the rage when her long-planned grand entrance was spoiled by the ruinous disarray of robes and hair and makeup.

An intoxicating blend of emotions that was all the more tempting for its familiarity. Sweet and thick and strange, when you weren't the one caught in its maelstrom.

Rahelu shifted half her weight forward.

But Nheras had reached the top now...and Rahelu was forced to look up.

"Nheras."

The Ilyn girl sniffed. "Rosewater?" She wrinkled her nose and then pulled out an intricately carved wood fan from the silk sash at her waist. "What did you do, borrow a pleasure den worker's perfumes? I think your usual odor of fish guts suits you better."

Rahelu concentrated on *not* leaping forward and lashing out with a fist.

Factually speaking, that wasn't too far from the truth. She wasn't going to waste kez buying scent of her own for one party and the Tidepool, the only legitimate bathhouse in the Lowdocks, had wanted an additional silver kez for lotions and creams on top of the eighteen copper kez for entry. So she'd gone to Tlareth, the only person she could think of, for help. And sometimes, during the low season, when there weren't many travelers staying at the Sable Gull, Tlareth made up the shortfall by offering companionship by the quarter-span.

She still didn't like what Nheras implied. There was nothing wrong with what Tlareth did—it was honest, resourceful, and profitable, without exploiting anyone in the process. What more could you ask for?

"But it *is* endearing of you to try," Nheras said. "And while it isn't your fault that you've gotten it so terribly wrong, you should turn around and go back to the Traveler's Bliss. That way, you won't put the rest of us off our dinners and you might earn a few kez for your troubles."

Calm. She was all unruffled blue-gray calm, the exact color of the Elumaje on a cloudy day when neither sun nor rain nor wind disturbed the water's tranquil surface. Rahelu had learned better; she was *not* going to ruin her clothes by brawling again, no matter how satisfying it would be to bring Ilyn down to her level.

"On second thought," Nheras added, "the Lowdock streets might be better. Even the bed warmers at the Seafarer's Comfort would rather cut off all their hair than be caught smelling like a quarter-span alleyway rut."

The breeze carried the sounds of laughter from the gathering through the trees, reminding her that there were other ways to strike a blow and that she should try some of them for a change.

"I wouldn't know," Rahelu said. "Seeing as how I spend every waking span I'm not at the Guild or on assignment hauling fish, gutting fish, and selling fish. But I'll defer to your expertise in this area and trust that you are right. I'd assume that you must have spent a great deal of time working in pleasure dens yourself, except that would require you to exert some effort, so your expertise must come from the opposite experience. How many did you need to frequent before you found someone willing to take your coin to overlook the displeasure of your company? Three? Five? Ten?"

The ambient aura around Nheras fuzzed red, but only for a moment. There were no other signs of her anger besides a slight flush of her cheeks.

Time to press the advantage, before Nheras could strike back.

"What's truly strange is that you are even here. Cseryl has worked so hard to block your every attempt at breaking into the Ideth ranks that I'm surprised your invitation didn't go... amiss on its way."

"I see the little kit grew a set of teeth and now thinks it's a bharost," Nheras said. Her jaw had become so tight that the tendons in her neck stood out against her skin, like cords. Faint jagged lines began crackling through her aura. "How adorable. It would almost be a pity to correct that misconception." Crimson rivulets spilled out from her aura as the ambient resonance went from a light reddish haze to a deep liquid ruby and the network of resonance crystals in Ilyn girl's jeweled pins, bangles, and necklace flared to life.

"Is that a formal challenge?" Rahelu smiled, drawing in power through the focus stone on her left hand, shaping its stored resonance into a barrier of blue-gray as solid and unyielding as stone. "Shall we go down there and resolve this in front of witnesses, once and for all? Bhemol and Kiran aren't here to do your dirty work, so you'll have to face me alone, mage to mage. Let's see how you fare when you can't rely on others to accomplish something for you."

Formally dueling at a dinner party probably violated at least fifty different rules of etiquette but Rahelu didn't care. Not a single person down there expected anything better from her and even if Nheras defeated her, that sting couldn't possibly compare to what she'd suffered before.

No, Rahelu had nothing to lose by dueling Nheras. But Nheras, on the other hand...

Nheras drew in a quick breath and the ruby glow in the ambient resonance died, her crystals becoming quiescent once more. "I don't see why I should bother," she said. "You didn't last more than a few heartbeats the last time we fought—what would be the point of retreading old ground?"

"Ah, yes. It was such a decisive battle that you won, with your focus-stone-fueled Projection when I was armed with no more than simple resonance wards."

"How like a whining common-born, to blame your defeat on a lack of equipment."

"And how like a spoiled House-born, to be terrified of facing a prepared opponent on equal footing," Rahelu said, holding up her left hand so her resonance crystal glittered in the sunlight.

"What a ridiculous assertion," Nheras said.

"No, what's ridiculous is this getup of yours." Rahelu gestured at the other girl's outfit. "You're wearing so much jewelry that you jangle more than a band of Chroniclers with their bells. Though at least you had enough sense to not show up wearing pale green. House Ideth could buy House Ilyn five times over and still outrank the rest of the minor Houses in terms of total net worth based on the amount of kez left in their treasury. Do you honestly think you can impress any of them with a show of wealth?" She tried forcing a laugh—to her surprise, it came out more easily than she had expected. "It must gall you so, to be unable to simply *buy* your way in."

Rahelu turned her back on Nheras and started down the other side of the path. Her earlier worries over her lack of formal attire seemed silly now, a juvenile excuse she wanted to use in order to avoid an unfamiliar situation.

She wouldn't be alone down there. She could go and greet Elaram (assuming the Issolm girl was willing to divert her attention from admiring Ylaen's biceps), endure a little ribbing from Ghardon about her belt (he'd have something to say regarding her trousers too) and, if all else failed, she could occupy herself for a good half-span or so with sampling the thirty different varieties of food laid out on the long buffet table.

"That's where you're wrong, fish guts," Nheras said. "Everyone has a price. Everyone. And in your case, I'm fairly certain I know what that price is."

There was so much triumph in Nheras's reedy voice that it lent a ringing tone to her words.

"Whatever you're offering, I'm not interested," Rahelu said, continuing down the slope. "Not at any price."

"That's a shame," Nheras said. "Though I suppose I understand—that little leaky bucket of your father's is an embarrassment to vessels everywhere. It would do so much better as firewood."

Rahelu halted in her tracks. "It's an Isonn vessel," she said. "I doubt they would agree."

"It *was* an Isonn vessel," Nheras said, strolling forward with a self-satisfied smile on her thin lips. She drew out a beribboned scroll from her voluminous robes.

Rahelu stared at the sloop's title deed. "No."

"Yes." Nheras tugged on one end of the dark green ribbon and unfurled the parchment with a flourish: and there, written in bold black ink, were the words that transferred ownership of the sloop from House Isonn to one Nheras of Ilyn, witnessed by a clerk of House Isonn and stamped with a shimmering forest-green resonance seal. "You had some nerve, stealing away my property. The terms of this lease strictly forbid you from sailing more than twenty kual beyond the Ennuost Yrg harbor."

Her parents had never mentioned restrictions like that—but then again, her parents still couldn't read more than a few simple Aleznuaweithish phrases. Rahelu hadn't ever seen the lease for herself; hadn't thought to even ask the Isonn clerk for a copy earlier, she'd been so confused.

Nheras had to be making things up. *Had to*. Even though the Ilyn girl's resonance aura was bright and clear.

"I was not pleased to have to report the theft to the city guard."

Gods. The penalty for theft was no joke. The punishment for a first offense was the thumb on the convicted thief's primary hand; the punishment for a second offense was the loss of the whole hand entirely. The punishment for a third offense, being the loss of the remaining hand, was as good as a death sentence.

"There has been no theft," Rahelu said. "The sloop is docked at the twelfth berth of the fourth pier in the Lowdocks."

"A shame that doesn't agree with over twenty eyewitness accounts, all dated from the third day of truesummer to this eartharc. Why, the watch captain sent someone to check a few spans ago and there was no sign of it."

Stormbringer.

It hadn't been there because her father had sailed out again to try for a second catch, as soon as she and her mother had unloaded the first.

"The district commander is very displeased. This kind of crime simply doesn't reflect well on him."

The district commander for the southern part of the city had a reputation for doling out punishment first and asking questions later.

"What do you want, Nheras?" Rahelu asked flatly.

The Ilyn girl rolled up the scroll and tucked it away. "Leave," she said. "Turn around and crawl back inside the gutter where you came from and I will relay a message to the district commander that the charges of theft are withdrawn."

Nheras wanted her to leave? That was all?

"Only so that you can reinstate those charges whenever you like?" Rahelu asked. "I don't think so." She drew out her coin pouch, containing everything she had left: sixteen gold, fifty-eight silver, and ninety-five copper kez. "Withdraw the charges first. And then I will leave, with that title deed transferred to my name."

"I don't think you're in any position to negotiate terms," Nheras said, ignoring the coin pouch. Her tone was dismissive but had a brittle edge to it, as if she were overcompensating for some uncertainty.

Rahelu looked at Nheras again, this time studying her carefully constructed image: how she had deliberately used her hairstyle and sandals to gain the illusion of being two hands taller than she actually was; how the tightly cinched silk sash accentuated her willowy curves; the calculated choice to omit Ilyn red and dress in Ilyn cream, liberally underscored with Ideth sky-blue.

A perfect match for any of the Ideth scions.

Or perhaps just one particular Ideth scion.

That odd memory of Nheras surfaced—how she had found Rahelu and Lhorne at the Highdocks though they had told no one where they were going, how Nheras had stood frozen on the boardwalk, her furious eyes raking Rahelu over from head to toe, the utter disbelief in Nheras's voice and resonance aura before she had stalked off into the night.

And then, the very next day, her family's debt had been discharged from Isonn's ledgers.

"Is that so?" Rahelu looked away from Nheras to the garden below and saw Lhorne's tall figure striding through the gathering at last. Her heart leapt to see him dressed in his usual wool tunic over linen trousers, though he had made one concession to the occasion in the form of an open, silver-trimmed robe in sky-blue that flapped around his frame—he had thrown it on without bothering to do up the ties.

Nheras's gaze darted unmistakably in the same direction.

Rahelu wondered if she was about to make a huge

mistake, gambling her father's hand on a hunch based on nothing more than conjecture, but all her instincts urged her forward: the conclusion felt *right*. "Then you won't mind if I refuse your offer." She nodded to the other girl. "Excuse me. It looks like someone is looking for me."

"Take one more step and not only will I press forward with the charges, but I will see that driftwood wreck burned and the ashes scattered to the four winds." All traces of uncertainty had gone out of Nheras's voice, leaving only the deadly hiss of a nheshwyr backed into a corner. "Just try me, if you dare."

Rahelu did not dare. The stakes were too high.

But she was not going to walk away with this ever-present threat hanging over her head either.

I'm sorry, Lhorne, she thought as she took off the ring he had bought her and dropped it inside her coin pouch, then held the small leather bag out to Nheras. *I will find some other way to repay my debt to you.*

Although she didn't truly owe that debt to him anymore, did she? It was now officially a debt she owed to House Ideth.

Parting with his ring—her ring—was something she had every right to do, if she had good reason for doing so. The ring was just a tool and had no significance beyond its economic value.

"Sign the title deed over to me and I will leave, right now," she said.

It was quite possibly the worst deal Rahelu had ever proposed—at least five times the sloop's initial market value if she went by the principal amount of the original Isonn loan —but she could not be sure that Nheras would agree to anything less.

Her Obfuscation barrier was an unbroken blue-gray

mirror, the perfectly smooth expanse of the Elumaje on a windless day.

It was flawless and it did nothing to mask the slight hitch in her voice.

Nheras smiled. "Done."

The Ilyn girl retrieved the title deed, unfurled its parchment, and touched a gilded fingernail to the Isonn seal. Forest-green resonance ink shimmered briefly and then Nheras presented the document, seal side out, for Rahelu to verify her addition:

> *I, Nheras of Ilyn, do transfer ownership of the Vessel free and*
> *clear of any encumbrances, liens or other liabilities, on this*
> *ninth day of truesummer to Rahelu of Chanaz.*

Even in concession, Nheras had to make a point. Rahelu bit back her resentment and nodded; released the coin pouch as Nheras relinquished her parchment.

Business concluded, Nheras floated off to join the other Supplicants-to-be without a backward glance, setting a direct course for Lhorne.

Rahelu resolutely turned away from the shining, robed figures in the garden below, lengthening her strides back along the winding path towards the wrought-iron gates until she was practically leaping from one foot to the other.

Her mother was alive.

Her father would come to no harm.

And she had just ensured that her parents would never be indebted to any House, ever again.

All things considered, it was the best outcome she could have hoped for. There was still a span or two before sunset— more than enough time to take care of a few critical errands, the first and foremost being a stop by the district commander's guardpost.

And if anyone wondered why she clung so hard to her Obfuscation barrier and ran through the city as if bharost were on her heels, well, she had just spent a week cooped up in a tiny fishing sloop on the ocean, recovering from severe resonance backlash, and there was a lot that she had to do if she wanted to have some sort of dinner (that *didn't* include fish) ready before her parents came home.

She'd also become far too reliant on her resonance wards and needed a little bit more practice with Obfuscation.

That was all.

26
BREAKERS

THE WAY THE LOWDOCKS JUTTED OUT INTO THE
Kuath Bay reminded Rahelu of a street urchin trying to
snatch discarded morsels from a House-born's table. They
had been incorporated into the city some thirty years back by
the previous Exalted Dominance, when Ennuost Yrg could
no longer ignore the growing slum that had sprung up
outside the southern walls of the city. Ships (worn ones)
crammed into the moorings, so tightly packed that she
wondered how their captains and scarred crews would disen-
tangle their patched, varicolored sails when it was time to
weigh anchor.

Rahelu hated everything about the Lowdocks.

But she was comfortable here, where the resonance aura
was full of aggression that fuelled short tempers and even
shorter, savage brawls, with her boots and the cuffs of her
trousers covered in grime. There was no pretension, no
House politicking, and survival was straightforward: be
decisive, be fast, and be willing to fight if you could not
flee.

She picked her way past the ragged row of mismatched

pier-side warehouses. Past the fisherfolk who stood on the rocks, casting lines into the ocean.

Unfortunates who had lost their boats.

A fate that, Starfather willing, her parents would never know. She rubbed at the burn scar on the forefinger of her left hand, unusually light now it was bereft of a ring again.

She felt the loss but she did not regret it: the freedom she had bought for her parents was worth the cost.

Rahelu continued along the shoreline without a backward glance.

There were no cobblestones here, just uneven bare rock, slimed with seawater, piss, and dung. Her boots squelched as she trod on one of the many piles of refuse that littered the street (unavoidable), spilling out of the gutters and into the water to clog up the harbor.

Like everyone else, she kept her purse hidden, eyes and ears alert and one hand on her belt knife.

Unlike everyone else, she also kept up her Obfuscation barrier, even though the effort was rapidly draining the mental reserves she had managed to recover. Probably stupid of her but a lesser stupidity than dropping it while she might still be in range of anybody Seeking her.

Hah.

Who was she kidding? Nobody would miss her, except her parents and Tsenjhe, and she had already said her good-byes to her parents at dinner.

Her parents' sheer relief at owning their vessel (at last!) had been so great that not only had it made up for her poor cooking, but it had also allowed Rahelu to explain away her early return with minimal evasions: yes, she had gone; yes, the Isonn debt had been repaid thanks to a gift from Lhorne; yes, of course she had thanked him profusely for the gift; yes, she had left early so she could register the change in title with the dockmaster as soon as possible; yes, she was sure to see him again, their duties as Supplicants permitting; no, she wouldn't be staying the night as Supplicants were granted lodgings by their House; and no, she wasn't certain when she could come home again, as the Houses were known to send their Supplicants on assignments across the Dominion, though she hoped it would be soon.

The storm of questions ended when her parents were forced to retire or else risk missing the dawn tide. She'd left as the first inky fingers of blue-black night reached out to cover up the blushing sky.

Rahelu took off her boots when she reached the shallows. She bent down as she waded in, rinsing off the muck by trailing her boots through the saltwater, then tied the laces together so she could sling them over one shoulder. She climbed over the slippery rocks that dotted the shore—making sure the two remaining scrolls inside her tunic were in no danger of falling out into the water—to reach the lone boulder that stuck out of the rising tide.

There, feeling full of the (absolutely terrible) meal she had attempted to cook for her parents (which they had all choked down anyway, thanks to years of ingrained habit), she lay down to watch the gulls wheeling through the clouds overhead.

It was so peaceful here, with only the rhythm of her breathing and the breakers crashing all around her, that—for just a little while—she could forget the world.

Alone, surrounded by surging seawater, Rahelu opened up her resonance senses and released her Obfuscation barrier at last.

Yellow lightning jumped out, each jagged flash a distinct worry about the days ahead. She let them crackle across her resonance aura without guidance or restraint, allowing the bolts to collide against one another. Later, she would try to make sense of it all and reassert control; force the cold logic that would serve her best to be the dominant force driving her decisions; lock away her emotions behind her resonance ward.

Later, but not now.

For now, she allowed her emotions free rein and passed no judgment on herself, because there was no one else around to pass judgment either.

She could revel in the joy of difficult goals attained at long last: her years of grueling training completed, her oath of Supplication sworn and her parents' livelihood secured.

She could shed tears—for Xyuth, for Dharyas, for Hzin—and she could be honest that she shed those tears less out of grief and more out of guilt that she did not, could not, grieve those deaths as she ought to (or as she thought she ought to, if there even was a difference between the two).

She could even acknowledge the part of her (a larger part than she liked) that envied Nheras and her extravagance deeply—a part that would have gladly spent every last kez she had earned to know what it might feel like to walk through a crowd robed in pale green and sky-blue, arm in arm with a son of Ideth, so close together that their resonance auras melded and you could not separate one from the other.

Rahelu let every one of her competing wants and desires well up and flood out of her resonance aura and into the ambient resonance around her, only to be swept away by the cleansing wind and spray of saltwater, leaving behind the stillness of gray-blue acceptance.

And then, she let go of that too, until the only thing she could feel was her heart, beating in time with the steady, inexorable rhythm of the waves.

A string of curses jolted her out of her contemplation. She bolted upright to see Lhorne, wobbling precariously, halfway down the uneven string of jagged, half-submerged rocks that stretched between the beach and the large boulder she sat on. He had rolled up his thick linen trousers to his knees, just above his polished leather boots which were now splattered with Lowdocks muck.

"Lhorne, no!" she yelled out as he sized up the gap to the next rock.

He ignored her, leapt, and teetered wildly on landing. For a breathless moment, she thought he would make it, then the next wave surged over his boots and he slipped into the water.

Rahelu took three short strides and dove off the ocean side of her boulder, feet first, into the churning surf.

Cool water surrounded her.

She plunged past the roiling surface into the stiller depths beneath, tucked her legs up before her toes could brush the tangle of seaweed that drifted past on the ocean floor, and swam in the direction of the shore.

The sun's fading light scattered apart upon the sea, unable to penetrate its surface. Only long experience in these waters and the feel of the current flowing around her limbs allowed her to distinguish where the blurry black-on-black shadows of the submerged rocks began and ended.

Ahead, she picked out the telltale thrashing of an unpracticed swimmer. Angling her body away from the seabed, she kicked out powerfully with both legs and shot through the water. One of Lhorne's windmilling arms struck her in the face. She ignored it; grabbed him from behind, hooked both of her forearms under his armpits and towed him skyward.

They surfaced loudly; Lhorne spluttered, coughing seawater out of his lungs as she drew in a deep breath and adjusted her hold on him so they both floated on their backs, facing out to sea.

"Just relax," she said, raising her voice over the crashing waves. She glanced over her shoulder at the shore and her heart sank: the undertow had dragged them out by a good ship-length or two and the current was pushing them south. "I've got you now. I won't let go."

He stopped trying to cling onto her arms like an octopus and went rigid like a log. A really heavy waterlogged log that threatened to drag them both down.

Rahelu swore and treaded water furiously with her legs *and* left arm to keep their heads above the surf.

"Not like that!" She yanked on his upper half. "Lie on top of the water, as if it's a nice feather bed. Push your head back"—she pulled on his forehead with her left hand—"and your belly up." She arched her own back to force his body into the right position. "Yes, just like that. Now, if you can manage it, kick your legs—gently! From the knees, not your hips…"

As soon as he got the hang of it, Rahelu stopped treading water and swam for the shore in earnest. She let the dusky sky guide them and—Stormbringer be praised for small miracles—it was high tide. They could ride the swell of the ocean most of the way back.

By the time they reached the shallows and it was safe for her to let go of him, the sea had swallowed the small pebbled area that was the closest thing to a beach in the Lowdocks. She gasped, every limb trembling, as they crawled out of the water onto a rock. The area was deserted; the rock fishers gone to sell their small catches at the dockside taverns.

"Never," she panted heavily, "ever do that, ever again. You idiot!" She pounded him on the back as he spat up more seawater. "What were you thinking? You could have drowned!"

"You're right," he said. "I'm sorry, I wasn't thinking of the risks." He looked up at her, with a face full of contrition and something else. "We missed you, at her funeral."

"I…"

How could she explain?

Earlier in the skyarc, she had gone to Tsenjhe's workshop and found it padlocked. While the other workshops were occupied, their heavy oak doors had been barred to visitors. No boisterous hammer falls or clanking gears disturbed the faint noises of the Blackforge streetscape that crept inside, and thick walls muted all the rest.

House Isca still mourned their daughter. Who was Rahelu to intrude upon them in their time of grief, on the basis of a single day of friendship? What comfort could a Houseless foreigner offer? Would her guilt-ridden condolences undo her Fortunement?

"I went to set a reed lantern upon the water." She had released it at the northeasternmost point of their voyage, where the waters of the Kuath Bay became the Aleituan Sea, and watched the tiny vessel sail into the dawn.

His silence lasted eight heartbeats and then he said, "Tsenjhe did the same." Seawater dripped down the sides of his face and he shivered. "The guards said that you came and went but no one else saw you. Why did you leave?"

Rahelu looked away. "We need to get off the beach and to someplace warm. It's not too far to—" She was about to say '*where I live*' but stopped.

That wasn't true. Not anymore.

And she couldn't bring Lhorne back to her parents' little doorless hut.

Maybe if they were still awake—but no. Easygoing he might be, but she didn't think he would be entirely comfortable squatting in his smallclothes by one side of the fire while her parents slept (or worse, tried to make conversation) on the other side of the fire.

Because Earthgiver knew that *she* wouldn't be comfortable with that.

"—the Sable Gull," she said. "It won't hold a candle to the

Four Blossoms, but it's as good as we'll find in the Lowdocks."

———

WHAT SHOULD HAVE BEEN a quick stroll took nearly half a span. Despite the cool stormarc sea breeze, Lhorne's skin was hot to the touch through the soaked layers of their cotton and wool tunics. He leaned heavily on her, swaying and slipping on the slimy cobblestones, and her knees shook with every step.

Night had fallen by the time they turned west, away from the bay. The rising sliver of the waning moon cast hardly any light on the streets, which were empty of wagons and carts and people but full of raucous laughter from the taverns. The sounds of merrymaking surged like waves whenever rough wooden doors vomited out stumbling, half-drunk mercenaries so they could piss on the doorstep before staggering back inside to swill more of the foulest brew on offer.

From here, the best way to get to the Sable Gull was to follow the main thoroughfare, past the taverns and gambling dens lining the waterfront, through the Nightmarket to loop around at the south stair. It would take them at least another half-span. But the fastest way was…

She swore as Lhorne's foot caught on a divot in the road and he stumbled. A nearby railing saved them from collapse.

"Sorry," he said and held onto the railing so it could take the brunt of his weight.

She gave him ten heartbeats. "We need to move."

At the next intersection, she turned them towards the Tollgate.

"Uh, Rahelu? Are you sure that's the right way?"

No.

"Yes," she said.

Lhorne eyed the alleyway with suspicion and she didn't blame him. Its darkened mouth swirled with a bone-white mist that leaked into the well-lit street.

Cutting through the Tollgate was risky, but collapsing on a Lowdocks street, no matter how well-lit, was asking for certain trouble.

"Couldn't we go to one of these places?"

He was looking at the Broken Bottle. Its owner had not bothered with the expense of a sign (a savvy decision) and so an example of the tavern's namesake had been propped upside down in the torch sconce instead.

"No." The Broken Bottle was due to erupt into its nightly brawl in a quarter-span or two. "The Sable Gull's not far. Just another fifty strides, through the other side."

The Breakers caught them twenty strides in. There were five in all: three men and two women wielding knives and cudgels, in stained, roughspun tunics with white-and-black cords knotted around their upper arms.

Their leader, a heavyset woman with arms like a black-smith, spoke. "You look like you could use some help, sweetheart."

"Thank you for your concern," Rahelu said, "but we're fine." She slowly backed them up, towards the far end of the alleyway.

"A fine catch indeed," said one of the men as he strolled forward. His nose looked like it had been broken and reset—badly—many times. "'Tis a rare honor to see a House-born, down here in the muck."

"An honor for me as well, friend," Lhorne said, sounding at perfect ease. "I've found the entire experience very educational." He even managed to affect a faint Projection of amusement.

"Fine words and fine manners from a fine catch," said the other woman, twirling her cudgel. She circled to Rahelu's right as Broken Nose drew almost level with them on her left.

Rahelu continued backing up, edging them towards the right side of the alley. Her eyes flickered to the exit.

Twenty strides away.

Too far to run.

She cursed inwardly; struggled to form the thinnest shell of blue-gray calm around them. The ambient resonance here was thick with fear; she wanted to choke on it.

"And a fine dagger too, friend." The fourth Breaker looked Lhorne up and down, taking note of the Ideth scion's well-made clothes and bedraggled appearance. "You look like you could use a drink and a hot meal. Why don't you come with us?"

"We would love to accept," Rahelu said, cutting off whatever Lhorne had been about to say, as she turned to keep all five of the Breakers in front of her. "However, we are late for another engagement. Perhaps another time. Would you excuse us?"

They laughed.

"A fine joke, my dear!" Blacksmith chuckled as she drew a dagger.

Rahelu tensed as the Breakers closed in, cutting them off from the rest of the alley.

"A fine joke between friends!" Lhorne laughed along with them. "It's been very fine meeting you, indeed. In my House, we celebrate new friendships with a trade. My dagger in exchange for another fine time with you at a later opportunity. What say you, friends?"

"I say that you're here in the Lowdocks, not in your House, friend." Blacksmith pointed her dagger at Rahelu. "In the Lowdocks, we celebrate friendship with gifts."

"I see," Lhorne said, his voice light. "I suppose the finer the friendship, the finer the gift?"

"Oh ho, a quick learner!" jeered the fifth member.

"Your dagger and your boots, my fine lad," Blacksmith said, "and your purses, the both of you."

That was it.

Lhorne might be willing to part with his possessions—House Ideth was so rich the loss wouldn't even amount to a rounding error—but Rahelu was not.

She had hoped that it wouldn't come to this, but there was no sense in hiding now. What was the point of having an advantage if you never used it?

"No," she said. "I don't think so."

And she pushed up the sleeve of her cotton tunic to reveal her new armband, with its black sigil on white leather.

The armband of a Supplicant of House Issolm.

27
GIFT

"Issolm?" Lhorne asked as he crouched barefooted before the fire, dripping seawater. All the inn rooms at the Sable Gull were tiny and this one was no exception: it was barely four strides from the door to the hole in one wall that passed for a window, and two from the small niche that counted as a fireplace to the thin pallet on the other side.

It probably didn't qualify as a closet to him, but Rahelu had been relieved the room had been available at all. She'd handed over twenty-two copper kez without attempting negotiation.

Rahelu ignored his question and went to answer the knock at the door. There was no room to open it; not until she was practically on top of Lhorne.

Tlareth stood outside with a large bundle of linen rolled up under one arm, two wooden buckets balanced on her shoulders, and a small tray of cold food and two mugs of beer in her hands. "Dinner," she announced.

"That's not—"

"No charge," Tlareth said. "Cook said it was for the pigs; I figured they wouldn't miss an end of bread or two."

"Thank you." Rahelu smiled as she took the tray from Tlareth one-handed, and left it beside the pallet.

"Your water," Tlareth said, placing one of the buckets beside the door so Rahelu could drag it into the room. Her eyes went wide as she caught a glimpse over Rahelu's shoulder.

Lhorne was in the process of taking off his sodden shirt.

Rahelu suppressed a sigh.

"Tlareth, this is Lhorne." She left his House unstated. "Lhorne, Tlareth."

"It's a pleasure to meet you," Tlareth said. She pushed the door fully open and stepped inside—into the space Rahelu had vacated—and drank in the sight of him without reservation, her eyes skipping past the resonance crystal pendant around his neck to linger appreciatively on the muscled planes of his broad chest and bare arms.

Rahelu kept a firm grip on her emotions. (Her resonance ward was gone, erased by the sea.) Tlareth preferred women, even if most of her customers were men, but she enjoyed looking at everyone—it was just how she was.

Lhorne didn't seem to mind the attention. "The pleasure is mine," he said, flashing Tlareth one of his grins as she made a show of setting down the second bucket of water.

"Now that we're all friends, how about you make yourself useful?" Rahelu nudged him with one knee and pointed to the kettle.

"I hear and obey!" He discarded his shirt and obligingly went about the task of pouring the water into the kettle and setting it on the hook above the fire.

"And here are the extra sheets and blankets." Tlareth handed over the large bundle of bed linens then lowered her voice conspiratorially. "Can't say I understand what you want 'em for. 'Tis cozy enough in here, especially with two. Jump into bed and you'll warm right up."

"Leave off, Tlar." Rahelu rolled her eyes. "We're just friends." She deliberately didn't look behind her at Lhorne; Tlareth's voice hadn't been nearly low enough and she could feel his eyes on her back.

Tlareth looked from Rahelu to Lhorne and back again. "I don't think he agrees, but if you don't want the company, you can tell him where to find me—and I won't charge for that either," she said as she departed with a wink.

Rahelu shut the door (a little too loudly) and Lhorne pounced.

"Issolm?"

She opted for the coward's path: she busied herself by shaking out the extra sheets and blankets and rearranging the bedding on the pallet. "They made a compelling offer."

"Anything they offered, Aunt Mere could beat," he said with absolute certainty.

Atriarch Ideth could probably buy half of House Issolm if she wanted to. She picked up Lhorne's discarded shirt and took her time wringing out every last bit of seawater into the bucket he had emptied earlier.

"You did ask her to match their offer, right?"

Her hands stilled. She hadn't. Hadn't even thought that might be an option. Who was she to bargain with an Atriarch?

"You didn't!" he said, aghast. "It's not too late. We can go to her, first thing tomorrow…"

"It's done," she said, dipping his shirt into the second bucket of water to rinse. "I swore my initial oath of Supplication this skyarc."

"That oath isn't irrevocable," he said. "You've still got your probationary term before you swear the final binding oath of service."

She didn't reply as she wrung his shirt out for the second time and then hung it on one of the iron hooks above the fire to dry.

He sighed. "Will you at least tell me what they offered?"

Rahelu surrendered her two battered scrolls. Resonance ink and seawater didn't go well together so he wouldn't be able to read most of it.

She hoped.

While he was occupied, she began to strip off her own soaked tunic. The cotton clung stubbornly to her heavy limbs and she struggled to get it over her shoulders, cursing as she had to give up halfway to rest.

Somewhere to her left, Lhorne started swearing again. "Those gods-cursed, arrogant, misbegotten, lucre-blinded graspers. Just because their loyalty can be bought and traded, they think they can buy anybody."

Well, shit.

She'd thought that his resonance backlash had been as bad as hers, but apparently not. He had pieced together enough of the scrolls' original contents with an Evocation.

Rahelu debated whether she should keep pretending exhaustion (it wasn't even pretense really, she *was* exhausted from having to tow his idiotic deadweight through the Kuath for two ship-lengths) so she could stay hidden behind her tunic or make some attempt at retaining her dignity.

It didn't matter. If he could Evoke her offer, then he could sense her emotions with perfect clarity. Her resonance ward was gone and she hadn't the strength to raise the most basic of Obfuscation barriers.

Dignity it was.

"Spoken just like an Ideth," she said with a wriggle of her shoulders, finally pulling the tunic off over her head.

He'd gotten up while she was struggling with her tunic,

the agitation in his resonance aura filling the room, and now he was pacing back and forth.

Which really amounted to taking two strides (though it was more like one-and-a-half strides for Lhorne, he was so tall) from the fire to the pallet and turning abruptly to take two strides back.

He kind of looked like he was just spinning around in circles and Rahelu couldn't help herself. She broke out laughing.

He scowled at her. "This isn't funny, Rahelu. Do you understand what you've traded away?" He shook the second scroll at her, the one with the Ideth sigil embossed on the reverse side of the parchment. "It's not worth the kez!" and then he threw the first scroll from Issolm into the fire, sending up a shower of sparks.

"Not to you, perhaps," she said, wringing out her own tunic.

"Not to you either," he said, stepping closer, just within arm's reach. "You sell yourself short."

Did he just equate her acceptance of one offer over another to selling herself? Red flashed through her aura before she managed to suppress it.

"Perhaps," was all she said, and he was close, so close, but she stood her ground. "But that's not the point."

"Then what is the point?" His agitation bloomed into frustration that crackled in the air between them. "I refuse to believe that the point of the past two weeks was for you to sell yourself for pocket change—"

Pocket change.

"—so Issolm can send you to die on a suicide mission at the other end of the world!"

The signing bonus from Issolm that made it possible for her family to dig their way out of a lifetime of poverty was simply *pocket change* to him?

"The point," she snapped, "was to pay off the debt my parents had incurred for the sake of my Guild training."

There was no room to take another step but she edged forward all the same.

"The point"—she balled up her tunic and threw it at his face—"was to buy myself a new tunic, so my father won't have to come home with his skin blistered and peeling from fourteen spans on the open sea every day, and new shoes"— she gestured wildly in the direction of the large rock she had had to leave her boots on when she jumped into the water after him—"so my mother doesn't have to trek barefoot carrying three baskets to market."

His expression softened as he untangled her tunic and hung it up above the fire beside his shirt. "You didn't—"

"The point," she continued, aware her voice was climbing rapidly into a shout, but she didn't care, didn't care at all, "was to buy out their fishing sloop, so they don't have to hand over three-quarters of the profits from every catch in lease payments."

It was his turn to give ground before her fury, which lashed at the resonance aura around them, a sweeping tide that intensified the dull red of his frustration into the same vibrant shade as the fire in the hearth.

"The point"—she stabbed a finger into his chest—"was so I could *buy food*"—she stabbed him again, harder—"that *isn't* day-old fish that we couldn't sell and cook it so they could eat a hot meal for once!" Her stabbing finger turned into an open-handed shove that was meant to push him back, but she had no strength left and it barely rocked him on his heels.

"Rahelu," he said softly, hands extended as if he were trying to calm a wild animal. "You didn't have to go to Issolm. Why didn't you ask me? I would have helped you."

"Why?" She pulled back, falling into a defensive spear

fighting stance by instinct, then folded her arms when she realized she wasn't armed. "Why would a son of House Ideth have helped a Lowdocks brat from Chanaz? What am I to you?"

Atriarch Ideth had not discussed what she had seen in her direct Seeking with Rahelu. Nor had she commented when Rahelu took off Lhorne's pendant and returned it at the conclusion of their audience.

"A friend," he said, meeting the challenge in her eyes cautiously. "And friends help each other."

"So they do." Behind her, the water in the kettle finally came to a boil. Steam wafted out from the fireplace to curl around the bare skin of her back. "Teaming up with me against Nheras and House Ilyn was helping. Agreeing to stop the murders with us—"

His resonance aura flared red at her use of the word 'us'; well, he had better get used to it. In the eyes of the Houses, her oath made her every bit as much Issolm as Elaram and Ghardon were.

"—was helping. The ring—"

"Which you refused," he said. "Twice!"

"—was helping! This—"

"Where is your ring?" he asked, seizing her left hand. She yanked it back but he held on firmly, refusing to let go. "*Where is it?*" Those green eyes burned into her own with accusation as he put the puzzle pieces together. "You sold it," he said, his flat tone at complete odds with the tide of crimson fury rushing through his resonance aura. "You sold it," he repeated and this time his words were a crescendo. "I bought it so it would keep you safe and you *sold* it—"

She had seen him angry before, after her Evocation in Southwatch and during his ridiculous duel with Ghardon, but he had always managed to keep a rein on his emotions.

Not this time.

Well then, neither would she.

"There's a House Ideth ledger"—she slapped the scroll he was still holding out of his hand—"that says it was *mine*." She spat the words at him, enunciating so clearly that the sound of each one cut through his tirade. "Which means *I* had every right to judge the best use for it. *And I had no other choice*."

"You had *every* choice!" His fingers crushed her hand, like a crab's pincers. "And instead of contemplating the alternatives, *you sold it* like some, some—"

She gave up trying to talk over his ranting and shifted her stance, pulled her other fist back in warning but he went on to say it anyway.

"—*Issolm* opportunist—"

She punched, aiming for his right cheek, the same place he'd struck her by accident not two spans ago when they were being tossed about by the waves, which were nothing to the waves of emotion that were crashing all around them in the ambient resonance.

He leaned to one side, letting her fist strike the empty air next to his ear, then grabbed her by both shoulders. "—when you could have come to me for help and I wouldn't have thought any worse of you for it!"

"You paid for the ring, I sold it in a time of need. Therefore, you helped." She glared up at him as she tried to wrestle herself free, daring him to deny that logic.

He didn't. Instead, he pulled her close, closer than they had been when two of them had stood beneath the lantern. "That is not what I meant *and you know it*."

His hands on her bare shoulders burned as hot as the fire behind her and their smoldering auras sparked, igniting the ambient resonance in a rose-red blaze.

Rahelu brought her arms up, slid her hands over his torso, felt Lhorne shiver at the sensation of her palms caressing his bare chest, felt her own hands trembling at the contact. His hands shook too, leaving red marks behind on her skin as he relaxed his grip fractionally and bent to kiss her.

And she wanted that kiss; wanted to know what it would feel like, to lose herself in his arms; wanted to let go and give herself over to pure abandon; wanted it more than power or prestige or security or any other thing she had ever desired.

Rahelu gathered every last scrap of willpower she had remaining and pushed him away.

"Skymother's tears, Lhorne!" she said, putting her back to him so she didn't have to deal with the shock and pain in his expression; the irregular, brilliant bursts of deep blue from his aura sweeping through the ambient resonance were bad enough. "Was the ring a gift or a chain?"

"Neither," he said. "It was an advance, as you wanted."

"Why?"

"Because I promised."

"Why?" she asked again. "Why would you go to such lengths for me? You wouldn't have even looked twice at me if it weren't for Keshwar."

She took the kettle off the fire, set it on the outer hearth, and began to pour in the rest of the water. The bucket was heavier than she thought, and it tipped over faster than she intended, sending a splash of scalding water over the kettle's rim. She jerked back immediately, hissed as some of it landed on her left arm, and dropped the bucket to cradle her arm. More water—cool water, thankfully—sloshed out, puddling onto the worn wooden floor around her feet, before Lhorne caught and righted the bucket.

"Give me your arm," he said but she didn't move. "Gods! Damn your pride to the eight hells, Rahelu, *let me help you* pour cold water on your arm before that burn gets worse, because Starfather knows you can't do this alone."

She'd always done everything alone. That was what she had to do.

That was what everyone had to do, to survive and be strong.

"Let me help you," he repeated. "Please." And a curious kind of longing seeped into his resonance aura, filling the space between them and spreading out to wash away the ambient traces of the anger, frustration, passion, and hurt from before.

That resonance made it hard to continue fighting; made it hard to remember why they were fighting in the first place.

Silently, she held out her left arm over the kettle and let her breath out as he began pouring the remaining contents of the bucket over her arm. She closed her eyes so she didn't have to look at him while he was looking at her; savored the sensation of cool water against burning skin as she sat cross-legged on the damp floor and fell into a simple meditation with a slow, even four-count.

Her heart had almost settled into the steady rhythm of her breathing when Lhorne spoke again.

"I have, you know." His voice was quiet and she only half-heard his words as they floated by, rising up to the low roof along with the steam from the kettle misting her face.

"Have what?" she asked as she combed through the tangled knots in her aura, then systematically worked on letting them go as she had done earlier, with mixed results. She rolled her head from one side to the other to ease the tightness in her neck, then rolled her shoulders for good measure, grunting in satisfaction as several vertebrae popped and realigned themselves.

The flow of cool water on her left arm ceased at last, leaving the pain of her latest injury as a low hum in her resonance aura.

"Looked," he said and she heard the soft *clack* of wooden

bucket on wooden floor as he set it down. "More than twice. It was you who never looked back."

Her mind scrambled for a memory and she came up blank. She automatically reached for Evocation and stopped as the effort sent another pulse of pain through her head.

"I'm sorry," she said. "I don't remember."

"I do," he said. There was a scraping sound as the warmth radiating from the kettle was replaced by the heat of his fevered body. It spread through her fingers as he took her hand—the one that should have been wearing the ring he had bought her—and placed it over his heart.

This is what I remember, he sent, and the tiny room on the west side of the Lowdocks dissolved around them:

He follows his cousin past the Guild gates and is left to wait in the enrolment line while Keshwar returns to his duties as a Supplicant. Other applicants arrive, each House-born trainee-to-be escorted by their sponsor—and though the common-born applicants do not have sponsors, they too arrive in the company of a guardian, a mentor or in small groups together.

In limps a girl in ragged, dirty clothing, covered in bruises, her eyes bright with unshed tears. Her gaze is fixed to the floor as she joins the line.

And she is all alone.

That doesn't seem fair so he leaves his place in line to join her.

'Hello,' he says. 'My name is Lhorne. Are you new here?'

She doesn't respond.

Maybe she is just shy? Or is it because of his Ideth dress tunic? He had wanted to wear another tunic—a plain, undyed one that didn't make the other House-born act differently around him or the common-born nervous when he tried to talk to them—but Keshwar had said he was thirteen now and should know better.

He tries again and again but she doesn't even look at him. It's not until they get to the front of the line and the Guild Registrar starts speaking to her in a strange language, rounded syllables flowing like running water over smooth river stones, that he realizes his mistake.

And though he can't understand any part of her answer, he has had enough training to Seek out her resonance aura: it is a tangled, swirling mess of red coals and yellow spikes over muted blue, and as he watches her complete the entrance test, it blazes up in shining gold until the Guild Registrar says something else, which sends hairline black cracks spidering through the golden haze.

The quick exchange that follows worsens the cracks until her entire aura is full of black despair.

'What's wrong?' he asks the Registrar. 'She passed, didn't she?'

The Registrar says, 'It's the registration fee. She doesn't have it.'

It was only a silver kez, not even the cost of half a meal. 'Does she really have to pay it now?'

'Everyone needs to pay the registration fee.'

'Keshwar says mine will get charged to the Ideth family account with the Guild. Why can't she pay later too? Aren't all trainees supposed to be treated the same?'

The Guild Registrar concedes the point.

And the smile on the girl's face as she runs out with crystal gleaming on her finger and all traces of despair banished from her aura is as wonderful as the sunrise—even if it isn't directed at him. He was the one who had put it there and that was what mattered.

Rahelu remembered that day very clearly. She remembered Nheras in the palanquin and on the Guild steps, refusing her friendship; the tall scarred mage who had thrown her to one side like trash; and Scruffy and Yellow Teeth who had stolen the coin her father had entrusted to her.

She had not remembered the red-headed boy who had tried talking to her.

Not until now.

He stands in the Guild training yards, packed full of first-year trainees arranged into sparring pairs. Like him, many are from the Houses and they carry their polished weapons with the easy confidence of someone who has been tutored in close combat from an early age. The rest of the trainees—the common-borns—shuffle nervously, gripping their Guild-loaned weapons too tightly as they study the ground, doing their best to avoid looking at their opponents. All except the girl two sparring circles down from him, struggling to wield a spear far too large for her. She faces off against Nheras of Ilyn and never ceases to get up to meet her opponent stare for stare no matter how many times the Ilyn girl knocks her down.

Memories unfolded around them, as Lhorne Evoked five. years of their shared Guild training, side by side. Each one began with him reaching out to her and each one ended with Rahelu rushing away before he could speak.

Until he caught up to her, more than halfway to the Guild gate, and she'd heard him. She relived his exultation (*at last!* he had thought, *at last*); the brief flicker of hurt at her lack of recognition; his sheer joy when she clasped his arm; then all the moments of the past two weeks flashed by in an instant until the past blurred into the present and she was back in the tiny room, his right hand pressing her left hand against his bare chest, and all she could see were his green eyes and her own reflection inside.

"Oh," she said, because what else could she say after that? She sat stiffly, afraid to move her hand—she didn't know what to do with it—afraid that if she drew back she would hurt him and afraid that if she let him continue to hold it there, against his heart, he would get the wrong idea.

He must have sensed her discomfort because he let go of her hand but he didn't stop looking at her.

"Come with me to Ideth," he said. "You are worth so

much more than what Issolm has offered. Aunt Mere would match their offer if you only asked; I know she will—"

The thought was tempting. Truly tempting.

"—and even if she won't," he said as he reached out with his right hand to turn her face towards him again, "I will." His expression was fierce, daring her to argue with him but she didn't have the heart.

Or the words.

They stared at each other in silence.

There was a loud crackle from the hearth. One of the logs collapsed into white-hot coals, its internal structure mostly devoured by flames. As the rest of the burning wood rearranged itself, the fire spat out a fragment of parchment that bore her name below the sigil of House Issolm, its blackened edges smoldering.

She picked up the fragment and doused it in the kettle until all of the cherry-red sparks around its edges had been extinguished.

"I swore an oath, Lhorne," she said. *To Issolm and to myself.* "And I will not break it."

It was his turn to look away.

Rahelu stood, leaving him to gaze into the fire, and went to the pallet where she had laid out two sets of bedding. She picked up one of the sheets and climbed on top of the pallet, drew her belt knife, then stuck it through one corner of the sheet into the wall, neatly dividing the pallet in the middle.

As she did, she heard him get up, felt the whisper of the sheet against her skin as he picked up the other end, heard the matching *thunk* of his dagger pinning a second corner to the ceiling to complete the makeshift curtain between their respective halves of the room.

They undressed without further conversation, she on her side of the curtain, he on his, each shucking wet trousers and underclothes, wringing out the remaining seawater into their separate buckets, taking turns to rinse their clothing and wash away the dried salt stuck to their skin with the luke-warm water in the kettle.

She wrapped herself in a blanket and hung up her breast-band, her loincloth, her trousers to dry, then stuck one arm out around the edge of the curtain for his things—which he passed to her without comment—and she hung them up beside hers.

The pallet gave a little rustle and bounced as she sat and tried to finger-comb the tangle of her hair. It was a snarled mess, matted with sweat and sand despite her best efforts to wash it out. She yanked at one particularly stubborn knot with both hands.

His voice drifted out from behind the curtain. "Rahelu?"

She turned to see his shadow, still sitting up. He mimed knocking on the curtain so she lifted the bottom edge to look at him across the pallet.

Blood rushed through her veins.

He was so close, just an arm's length away, but he might as well have been a continent away.

"Yes?" she asked in an unsteady voice.

"What those thugs said earlier, about friendship in the Lowdocks. Was that true?"

"It is," she said as her heart fell. "What of it?"

"Here then." He held out his hand and the crystal pendant she had returned once before glittered in his palm. "A gift."

His lips trembled, like he wanted to say more, but he pressed them together and swallowed whatever those words might have been. She stretched out her resonance senses but he had closed off his aura as well, hiding behind an Obfusca-tion barrier that she couldn't have pierced on her best day, let alone now.

This was more than a simple gift. They both knew that.

She couldn't take it.

But he'd shown her his memories and the thought of the hurt he would feel if she turned it down...

Well, that wounded her as well.

So she said, "a fine gift for a fine friendship," and before she could reach out to take the pendant, he leaned towards her—close enough for one lock of his hair to brush her forehead—and his fingers skimmed her collarbones as he hung the pendant around her neck.

He drew back as if the fleeting touch had burned, then said, "Good night, Rahelu," and turned away, the muscles in his back flexing as he lay down to face the wall.

"Good night," she said and let the curtain fall from her fingers.

And she, too, lay down to sleep, but she did not turn to face the other wall.

Instead, she watched the shadowy rise and fall of his chest with drooping eyes and listened to the sound of his breathing as the fire burned down to coals, then embers, until they both fell into the steady rhythm of deep sleep.

SPANS LATER—LONG after the embers had cooled but before the rest of the Sable Gull stirred—Rahelu woke, arms and shoulders chilled from the sea breeze blowing into the room. Bracing herself against the cold, she peeled off her blanket, eased her weight off the pallet, and padded over to the window to peer outside.

There was nothing to see. The room they'd been given was all the way at the back of the second floor, its window facing west into the twisting south stair that led up to the Temple district. The moon had set some time ago and the sun would not rise for another span. Everything outside was a coal-black smudge against the black-blue sky, the starlight far too diffuse to highlight the edges between one building and the next.

The only things that indicated she wasn't alone in a form-less void were the rough wooden floorboards under the soles of her feet, the sound of Lhorne's even breathing, and wisps of silver-violet that rose in the ambient resonance around him.

He was dreaming.

Moving slowly, so she wouldn't inadvertently knock over either of the two buckets or give the floorboards any oppor-tunity to protest her sudden weight, she blindly felt her way over to the warm, burned-out remains of the fire. Charred logs crumbled at the touch of her fingertips without a sound. She rubbed both hands in the gritty ash, doing her best to crush it into a fine even powder without the aid of a mortar and pestle and mix it into a paste with a sprinkling of water.

What she ended up with wasn't even close to adequate. The palmful of wet ash alternated between a runny mess that dribbled out between the cracks of her fingers to a clumpy mixture that flaked off at the slightest movement.

So she gave up on her current attempt at making paste and crept, cat-footed, back over to the pallet where he still slumbered, wreathed in a pale purple-blue mist. The cotton sheet that divided them sighed as she reclaimed her belt knife and she fled to the fireplace to ward her heart with thick, spiraling lines of blood-and-ash.

She pulled on her salt-stiffened, still-damp clothing; tucked away her belt knife and her purse; opened the door with every intention of walking through it without a back-ward glance.

What stopped her was the sudden surge of longing from Lhorne, the unconscious Projection far more powerful than the Evocations he had shared the previous night, stirring faint echoes of the rose-red passion in the ambient resonance.

Against her better judgment, she returned to the pallet and sat.

Stupid. This was stupid. He was asleep so what did it matter if she left without saying goodbye?

She thought of reaching out to take his hand, of answering his Projection with one of her own, of lying back down for just a few heartbeats until whatever dreamscape he wandered through dissolved and he fell back into a more restful sleep.

But the growing light inside the room reminded her that the dawn tide would not wait. So all she allowed herself to do was to gently tug the blanket she had discarded out of his grasp and drape it over his shoulders before she rose and left.

EPILOGUE: VOID

WHAT WAS THE NIGHT WITHOUT THE STARS, THE earth, the sea?

A void.

A wound in existence.

Azosh-ek's compulsions had won. He had disobeyed—had given in, delayed acting on his last instructions when he felt the Endless Gate open.

And for that transgression, the Starfather had seen fit to visit punishment upon him. Heathens had come, in their garish garb of sky-and-grass, to cage him deep within the Earthgiver's embrace.

He dashed himself against the crumbling earthen walls of his prison. The impact left him dazed, blood trickling down his face to mix with soiled sweat, his skin afire. The whole world burned beneath the pitiless sun. No matter where he moved, its baleful gaze remained fixed on him, magnified a hundredfold by the enormous crystal lens that shuttered the sky.

Behind his eyelids, his eyes rolled in their sockets in a futile attempt to escape the blinding light. Sensations assailed him. A spear impaling his chest. Searing agony in his left eye. Utter blankness in his mind.

He screamed.

Heard—

Lungs heaving.

Heart thudding.

Blood roaring.

—nothing.

Like his anchor and the sacred blade, his voice, too, had been stolen by heretics. He fell upon his knees, digging with the very last of his strength. Forsaken as he was, he would meet his end as a starbound should: with unquestioning obedience to the one who commands.

He sank, at last, into the beautiful dark, ready to give his damned soul over to oblivion...

...only to be dragged back against his will.

Primal instincts he had suppressed surged with unnatural strength; he gasped, drew new breath and tasted water: cool, poured over his head, and splashed into his mouth.

It stung.

Azosh-ek opened his eyes to behold a disheveled young man. Tall, with hair like flame and eyes of emerald—and in his right hand, he carried a glittering black gem flecked with gold.

Salvation.

Here ends Book One of the
RESONANCE CRYSTAL LEGACY

A NOTE FROM THE AUTHOR

You can follow Rahelu's journey
aboard the *Winged Arrow* in

SUPPLICANT

And if you want to find out why Rahelu didn't remember
meeting Lhorne on the day they enrolled at the Guild,
you can tap into that Evocation here:

https://www.delilahwaan.com/jointheguild

GLOSSARY

GLOSSARY

ABAN—Chanazian term of address from child to father.
  pronounced: AH-ban

ABMERDU—see Free Territories of Abmerdu.
  pronounced: ab-MER-du

A.E./A.F.—abbreviations for "After Exile/After Founding". Dominion calendars use "A.F." while Chanazian calendars use "A.E." to designate years in the present-day calendar; see also Aleznua.

ALEITUAN SEA—sea by the city of Ennuost Yrg in the Dominion of Aleznuaweite on the Ngutoccai continent.
  pronounced: ah-LEY-tu-an

ALEZNUA—a civilization that once spanned the Ngutoccai continent, and ended when it fractured into the present day Chanazian Federation and the Dominion of Aleznuaweite in an event known as "Exile" in Chanaz and "Founding" in the Dominion.
  pronounced: ah-LEZ-nu-ah

ALEZNUAWEITE, DOMINION OF—a nation on the northeastern part of the Ngutoccai continent commonly referred to as the "Dominion", governed by the Houses.
  pronounced: ah-LEZ-nu-ah-weight

ALEZNUAWEITHISH—adjective form of Aleznuaweite; also the language and culture of the Dominion of Aleznuaweite.
  pronounced: ah-LEZ-nu-ah-weith-ish

ALIRONN—a clothier in Ennuost Yrg's Westgate district.
  pronounced: ah-LEER-ron

ANATHWAN—a Harbinger and an Elder of House Issolm.
  pronounced: ah-NAHTH-wan

ANAZ—Chanazian term of address, meaning "master and teacher".
  pronounced: AH-naz

ANAZVELA—capital city of the Chanazian Federation.
  pronounced: AH-naz-VEH-lah

ANENJE—Chanazian birth name for Tsenjhe Isca.
  pronounced: ah-NEN-jeh

ANEST—a scrivener and the proprietor of the Silver Seal, a shop in Ennuost Yrg's Westgate district.
  pronounced: ah-NEST

ANMA—Chanazian term of address from child to mother.
  pronounced: AN-mah

ANUVELOMAZ—the three great lakes of Chanaz.
  pronounced: ah-nu-VE-loh-maz
ARC—unit of measurement for time. A day is divided into four arcs, with
each arc divided into six spans.
  Eartharc: dawn to high sun
  Skyarc: high sun to dusk
  Stormarc: dusk to deepnight
  Stararc: deepnight to dawn
ATRIARCH—Aleznuaweithish term meaning "ruler"; both title and rank
for the head of a House of the Dominion.
  pronounced: AY-tree-arc
AUGUR—a mage specializing in Augury and Fortunement.
AUGURY—one of the six resonance disciplines taught by the Resonance
Guild; the art of soothsaying.
AVELA—an intimate Chanazian endearment for a lover or consort.
  pronounced: ah-VEH-lah
AZOSH-EK—an exile from the Divine Kingdom.
  pronounced: ah-ZOH-sh-ek

BELRUONIA—Aleznuaweithish name for the nation on a continent to the
far east, known only as the Divine Kingdom to its inhabitants.
  pronounced: beh-LRUON-ya
BHAROST—a boar-like animal, native to the Ngutoccai continent.
  pronounced: bah-ROST
BHEMOL—an Ilyn-born applicant and cousin to Nheras Ilyn.
  pronounced: BEH-moll
BZEL—son of the fishmonger, Hzin, and Tseiran.
  pronounced: beh-ZEL

CHANAZ, FEDERATION OF—a nation on the southwestern part of the
Ngutoccai continent commonly known as "Chanaz", governed by the arch-
mages of the Conclave.
  pronounced: CHA-naz
CHANAZIAN—adjective form of Chanaz; also the language and people of
Chanaz. The Chanazian language is distinctive for its rounded syllables
and flowing sounds. The "r" sound in Chanazian is pronounced with the
tongue rolled back to the roof of the mouth. Native speakers of Aleznuaweithish typically struggle to pronounce the Chanazian "r" correctly.
  pronounced: cha-NAH-zi-an
COMMON-BORN—a child who is not House-born.
CONCLAVE—organization responsible for the training, accreditation, and
licensing of mages in the resonance disciplines, and regulation and
enforcement of laws in relation to the use of resonance in Chanaz; also the

governing body of Chanaz.

CONCORDANCE—a state of intense focus where two or more mages join minds to perform a blended working in concert.

CSERYL—an Ideth-born applicant; daughter of Atriarch Mere Ideth, younger sister to Keshwar Ideth, and cousin to Lhorne Ideth.
  pronounced: SEH-rill

CSINYRG—an Imrell-born Supplicant.
  pronounced: SIN-yirgh

CSONNYRG—Founder of House Isonn, famed for an Obfuscation barrier formation known as Csonnryg's Trap.
  pronounced: SOHN-yirgh

DEDICATE—middle rank within a House, third after Atriarch and Elder. Mages of this rank have typically developed a specialization in a particular resonance discipline.

DEEPNIGHT—time of night when the sun is at its farthest below the horizon and the sky is darkest.

DETHIRAM—a legendary archmage; Founder of House Ideth.
  pronounced: deh-THI-ram

DHARYAS—an Isca-born applicant; friend of Lhorne Ideth and protege of Tsenjhe Isca.
  pronounced: DAR-ryuss

DHERGHANN—a Dedicate of House Isonn.
  pronounced: DER-gan

DIVINE KINGDOM—see Belruonia.

DIVINE HOLINESS—ruler of the Divine Kingdom.

DOMINION, THE—see Aleznuaweite.

EARTHGIVER—deity with dominion over the earth and land-based creatures, commonly depicted as a rounded figure with horns.
  associations: darkness, harvest, protection, shield, Obfuscation

ELARAM—an Issolm-born applicant; younger sister to Ghardon Issolm.
  pronounced: eh-LAH-ram

ELDER—senior rank within a House, second only to Atriarch.

ELUMAJE—a lake in Chanaz; see also Anuvelomaz.
  pronounced: eh-lu-MAH-jeh

ENITH—an Isonn-born applicant.
  pronounced: EE-nith

ENJELA—a legendary archmage of old Aleznua.
  pronounced: en-JEH-lah

ENNUOST YRG—a city in the Dominion of Aleznuaweite.
  pronounced: EHN-nu-oh-st YIRGH

EVOCATION—one of the six resonance disciplines taught by the Resonance Guild; the art of remembrance.

EVOKER—a mage specializing in Evocation.

EXALTED DOMINANCE—the highest political office in the Dominion, chosen from amongst the Atriarchs of the Houses.

FANUEN—a net-maker from a fishing village by the shores of the Elumaje in Chanaz.
 pronounced: fa-NU-en

FORTUNEMENT—one of the six resonance disciplines taught by the Resonance Guild; the art of change.
 pronounced: for-TUNE-ment

FREE TERRITORIES OF ABMERDU—an archipelago east of the Ngutoccai continent, renowned as a lawless haven for freebooters, smugglers, and exiles, and a place where ritual scarring is widely practiced.

GHARDON—an Issolm-born applicant; elder brother to Elaram Issolm.
 pronounced: GAR-don

GHELIK—Aleznuaweithish slur meaning "foreigner".
 pronounced: GEH-lick

GHERORG—proprietor of Gherorg's Elixirs, an apothecary in Ennuost Yrg's Blackforge district.
 pronounced: geh-RORG

GUARDIAN—a mage specializing in defensive applications of the resonance disciplines, particularly Obfuscation.

GUILD, THE—see Resonance Guild.

HARBINGER—a mage specializing in offensive applications of the resonance disciplines, particularly Projection.

HEMORU—a fisher; consort to Jenura and father of Rahelu.
 pronounced: heh-MOR-ru (with Chanazian "r")

HIGH SUN—the time of day when the sun is at its apex in the sky. See also arc.

HNITH—an Imrell-born applicant.
 pronounced: hin-NITH

HNUARE—clothier and proprietor of the Impeccable Mage in Ennuost Yrg's Sunset district.
 pronounced: hu-NAH-rei

HOUSE—an Aleznuaweithish designation, given in recognition for a body of Guild-accredited mages who collectively hold sufficient wealth, power, and influence over the affairs of the Dominion of Aleznuaweite. Each House is led by an Atriarch and named after its founder, whereby an "I–"

prefix is added to the first syllable of the founder's name. The Dominion currently recognizes eight Houses.

Major Houses: Ideth, Isilc, Isonn, and Imos.

Minor Houses: Imrell, Issolm, Isca, and Ilyn.

HOUSE-BORN—a child born to (or adopted and raised by) at least one parent who has been accepted by and sworn oaths to a House.

HZIN—a fisher and seafood hawker of a stall in Market Square; consort to Tseiran and father of Bzel.

pronounced: he-ZIN (very short "he", where the "e" has an "er" sound)

IDETH—a major House in the Dominion of Aleznuaweite, founded by the legendary archmage Dethiram.

Present Atriarch: Mere Ideth

colors: pale green and sky-blue

pronounced: ih-DETH

IDHAR—a hypothetical name for a House founded by Dharyas.

pronounced: ih-DAR

ILYN—a minor House in the Dominion of Aleznuaweite founded by Lynath Ilyn; the newest and least of the eight Houses.

Present Atriarch: Lynath Ilyn

colors: red and cream

pronounced: ih-LIN

IMBUEMENT—the art of infusing objects with resonance.

pronounced: im-BUE-ment

IMOS—a major House in the Dominion of Aleznuaweite, by virtue of its vassal, House Imrell.

colors: yellow and white

pronounced: ih-MOSS

IMRELL—a minor House in the Dominion of Aleznuaweite; vassal to House Imos.

colors: orange and white

pronounced: ihm-RELL

ISHTREL—a bird with very colorful and striking breeding plumage, known for its elaborate courtship displays.

pronounced: ISH-trel

ISCA—a minor House in the Dominion of Aleznuaweite.

colors: dark blue and copper

pronounced: ih-SCA

ISILC—a major House in the Dominion of Aleznuaweite; its reigning Atriarch, Relk Isilc, is the current Exalted Dominance.

Present Atriarch: Relk Isilc

colors: purple and black

pronounced: ih-SILK

ISONN—a major House in the Dominion of Aleznuaweite.
  colors: dark green and brown
  pronounced: ih-SOHN
ISSOLM—a minor House in the Dominion of Aleznuaweite.
  colors: white and black
  pronounced: ih-SOLM
IWETH-NA—an exile from the Divine Kingdom.
  pronounced: ih-WETH-nah

JENURA—a fisher and seafood hawker; consort to Hemoru and mother of Rahelu.
  pronounced: je-NU-rah (with Chanazian "r")
JHEI—an Elder of House Isonn.
  pronounced: JHEI
JHOBON—an Imrell-born applicant.
  pronounced: JOH-bon

KESHWAR—an Augur and a Dedicate of House Ideth; son and heir of Atriarch Mere Ideth and elder brother to Cseryl Ideth.
  pronounced: KESH-waar
KEZ—Aleznuaweithish unit of currency, with denominations of copper, silver, and gold.
  pronounced: KEZ
KIRAN—an Ilyn-born applicant; cousin to Nheras Ilyn.
  pronounced: KIE-ren
KUAL—Aleznuaweithish unit of measurement for distance.
  pronounced: cue-AHL (the syllables are often rolled together)
KUAST YRG—a city in old Aleznua; the site of the legendary archmage Tsilm's death.
  pronounced: cue-AST YIRGH
KUATH BAY—small bay of the port city of Ennuost Yrg.
  pronounced: cue-ATH
KYROSH—an Isilc-born applicant, dubbed Whiplash by Rahelu for his primary weapon.
  pronounced: KIH-rosh

LHORNE—an Ideth-born applicant; nephew of Atriarch Mere Ideth and cousin to Keshwar Ideth and Cseryl Ideth.
  pronounced: LORN
LYNATH—Atriarch of House Ilyn; grandmother to Nheras Ilyn.
  pronounced: lih-NATH

MAGE—a person who primarily earns their living through the use of resonance skills. This is a regulated profession in the Dominion of Aleznu-aweite and Chanaz. Mages are required to undergo training with official bodies, complete licensing examinations, and maintain ongoing certifications in order to legally practice.

MAKETH—a Guardian and a Dedicate of House Imos.
  pronounced: ma-KETH
MERE—Atriarch of House Ideth, an archmage and a powerful Augur; mother of Keshwar Ideth and Cseryl Ideth.
  pronounced: MIR (as in "mirror")
MRELLOS—Founder of House Imrell.
  pronounced: m-RELL-os

NELA—intimate Chanazian term of address for a child, meaning "of my heart".
  pronounced: NEH-lah
NELAN—intimate Chanazian term for younger sibling/charge, meaning "of my heart".
  pronounced: NEH-lan
NGUTOCCAI—name of the continent shared by the Dominion of Aleznu-aweite and the Chanazian Federation.
  pronounced: ngu-TOH-kai
NHERAS—an Ilyn-born applicant; granddaughter of Atriarch Lynath Ilyn, cousin to Bhemol Ilyn and Kiran Ilyn.
  pronounced: NEH-ras
NHESHWYR—a deadly, venomous snake-like animal.
  pronounced: NEH-shwir
NHIROM—an Elder of House Isca.
  pronounced: NIH-rom
NHORWEN—an Elder of House Imos.
  pronounced: NOR-wen
NO-SLEEVES—see Ylaen.
NOLM—proprietor of a clothing stall in Ennuost Yrg's Market Square.
  pronounced: NOLM

OBFUSCATION—one of the six resonance disciplines taught by the Resonance Guild; the art of suppressing resonance.
ONNEJA—a journeymage of the Conclave in Chanaz.
  pronounced: oh-NEH-jah

PESHWAN YRG—a port city in the Dominion of Aleznuaweite, located on the easternmost point of the Ngutoccai continent.
  pronounced: PESH-wan YIRGH
PETITION—a formal written application for admittance to the Houses of

the Dominion. Any graduated mage in good standing is eligible to apply. Applications are accepted by the Houses once per year on Petition Day. Successful applicants become temporary members of the Houses on a trial basis, with the rank of Petitioner. Permanent membership to the Houses is subjected to the satisfactory completion of the trial period known as "Petitioning".

PROJECTION—one of the six resonance disciplines taught by the Resonance Guild; the art of amplifying resonance.

PIZUAR—Aleznuaweithish slur meaning "fake".
  pronounced: pih-ZUURE

QUESTRYL—a solitary sea bird known for its long migratory routes.
  pronounced: QUE-stryl

RAHELU—a common-born applicant of the Lowdocks, formerly of a fishing village by the Elumaje lake in the Anuvelomaz region of Chanaz; daughter of Hemoru and Jenura.
  pronounced: rah-HEE-lu (with Chanazian "r")

RALOSH—an Isilc-born applicant.
  pronounced: rah-LOSH

RESONANCE—emotional imprints left by souls upon the world which echo through time. All sapient creatures capable of experiencing emotion are born with the ability to sense and manipulate resonance.

RESONANCE CRYSTAL—a solid, crystalline substance that stores and transmits resonance.

RESONANCE DISCIPLINES—the various skills of manipulating resonance. The Resonance Guild in the Dominion teaches six resonance disciplines: Seeking, Projection, Obfuscation, Evocation, Augury, and Fortunement.

RESONANCE GUILD—the House-funded organization responsible for the training, accreditation, and licensing of mages in the resonance disciplines, and regulation and enforcement of laws in relation to the use of resonance in the Dominion of Aleznuaweite, commonly known as "the Guild".

RESONANCE WARD—a specific design constructed from physical materials used to affect the flow and transmission of resonance.

ROYAL COUNCIL—governing body comprised of the Atriarchs of the major Houses in the Dominion, excluding the Exalted Dominance.

RUALK—an Isonn-born applicant.
  pronounced: RUH-aalk

SABLE GULL—an inn in Ennuost Yrg's Lowdocks district; see also Tlareth.

SEEKER—a mage specializing in Seeking.

SEEKING—one of the six resonance disciplines taught by the Resonance Guild; also known as the art of truth-telling.

SHUATH—a clothier in Ennuost Yrg's Westgate district
  pronounced: shu-ATH

SKYMOTHER—deity with dominion over the known, commonly depicted as a feminine visage in the sky
  associations: light, day, harp, lamp, summer, skyarc, knowledge, past, present, Seeking, Evocation

STARFATHER—deity with dominion over the as-yet unknown
  associations: night, chance, stars, stararc, Augury, Fortunement

STORMBRINGER—deity with dominion over sea, lakes, rivers, and other bodies of water.
  associations: water, judgment, spring, storm, stormarc, spear, Projection

SPAN—unit of measurement for time. Each arc of the day is divided into six spans. Spans within an arc are typically numbered from the marker for that arc, e.g. the first span after sunrise.

SUBORNED—a state of being where an individual's will and consciousness is made subservient to another's through the use of an Imbued object, typically forged in the shape of a collar or a chain worn around the neck.

SUPPLICANT—a junior rank within the Houses, given to the newest recruits who have been granted permanent membership.

SUUSRADI—river located south of the city of Ennuost Yrg.
  pronounced: suu-SRAH-dee

TATTERED QUILL—a scrivener's workshop in Ennuost Yrg's Blackforge district; see also Xyuth.

TLARETH—proprietor of the Sable Gull, an inn in Ennuost Yrg's Lowdocks district.
  pronounced: teh-LAH-reth

TSEIRAN—consort to Hzin and mother of Bzel.
  pronounced: SEY-ren

TSENJHE—a common-born Dedicate of House Isca and highly reputed artificer, who hails from the same fishing village as Rahelu. See also Anenje.
  pronounced: SEN-je

TSILM—a legendary archmage who developed the advanced Obfuscation barrier formation known as Tsilm's Defence.
  pronounced: SILM

TSIMOL—an Isonn-born applicant.
  pronounced: SIH-moll

TSOJO—river located north of the city of Ennuost Yrg.

pronounced: SOH-joh

UNOMELAJE—glacier in Chanaz.
pronounced: u-NOH-meh-LAH-jeh (primary stress on "la")
UVESHT-MO—an exile from the Divine Kingdom.
pronounced: u-VESH-t-mo

VENAZ—intimate Chanazian term of address for elder sister, meaning "of my heart".
pronounced: VEH-naz

WELM—a grain factor in the city of Ennuost Yrg.
pronounced: WELM

XYUTH—a scrivener and proprietor of the Tattered Quill in Ennuost Yrg's Blackforge district.
pronounced: ZAI-youth

YLAEN—an Imos-born applicant, dubbed No-sleeves by Rahelu due to his penchant for cutting the sleeves off his shirts to display his ritual scarring.
pronounced: ye-LANE (often mispronounced IH-len by Aleznuaweites)

ACKNOWLEDGMENTS

This book would not exist without my writing group: JP Weaver, Ivy C. Kendall, Caitlin L. Strauss, and Dan Harris. Thank you for pushing me to write my own stories; if not for your encouragement (and all the memes), I never would have made the leap.

All my gratitude to my beta readers who had the courage and generosity to forge through my drafts: Rebecca Lai, Rohan Bassett, Tim T. Wong, and K. T. Lyn. I hope this final, published version lives up to your expectations.

And last, but never least, my family. You give me the strength to reach for my dreams.

ABOUT DELILAH WAAN

I am a literal bookworm who alphabetically devours my way through the shelves at my local library.

My preferred diet is epic fantasy—full of complex intrigue, morally ambiguous characters, and tragic ends—though I do enjoy the occasional quippy, fast-paced action-adventure. (Sappy romances, however, give me indigestion.)

When I'm not binge-reading the next doorstopper on my TBR list or engaging in frantic theory crafting in between Brandon Sanderson and Will Wight book releases, I like to spit bars in my best Angelica Schuyler impression and walk my cat.

bsky.app/profile/delilahwaan.bsky.social

instagram.com/delilahwaan

youtube.com/@delilahwaan

facebook.com/delilahwaan

x.com/DelilahWaan

amazon.com/author/delilahwaan

goodreads.com/delilahwaan

bookbub.com/authors/delilah-waan

www.ingramcontent.com/pod-product-compliance
Lightning Source LLC
Chambersburg PA
CBHW010254100726
47904CB00011B/2584